THE CUNNING WOMAN'S CUP

A NOVEL

SUE HEWITT

PAINTED LADY PRESS
SCOTTISH BORDERS

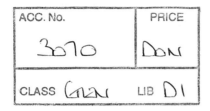
In memory of
Lewis Robert Gurr, aka 'Gramp'
(21 January 1903 – 16 June 2004)
who always felt sorry for trees because they were
stuck in one place all their lives.

Acknowledgements

Without the faith, support and encouragement of all these people, *The Cunning Woman's Cup* would still be lying beneath the compost heap:

My parents, Daphne and Harry Denton; my husband Chris; sons Timothy and Josef, and their partners Rowan and Renée; grandchildren Kiana, Beth, Ellis and Freya; Evelyn Hewitt; Sheila, Jez and Vix Walker; Maureen, Arthur, Maisie and Enid Still; Liz and Sofia Reynolds; Li Zhenyi; Rachael Guthrie; Martin and Sue Bates; Oliver, Annabel, Phoebe, Archie and William Bates; Robin, Susannah (especial thanks to you, Zanna – you really helped a huge amount) and Alec Gurdon; Clare Alexander; Veronica Litten; Shelagh Townsend-Rose; Iona McGregor and all at Kelso Writers' Workshop.

Chris Foster – without whom I could never have published – thank you for all your hard work editing, proofreading and patiently untangling my meaning and making it clear when I could not see how to form the sentence properly. Thank you.

Kit Foster – for the cover design, for help with all the technological stuff and for actually getting *The Cunning Woman's Cup* from screen to page – thank you.

CHAPTER ONE

I was Mordwand of the Brigantes. Called Dead and cast out when I was alive. People feared me. It was late in the pregnancy of the woman who bore me – too late, the old woman had said. The old woman took payment, laid her down, placed the heavy flat stone on her rounded belly, added more weight – it is but one of the ways. She died, but I survived – small, bloody, blue and broken. The old woman cringed back when I drew in breath and I cried aloud into the cold air. She left me, she said, to die. But I would not.

From the window of Alice McCleish's cottage in the hollow, the standing stone circle of Duddo bestrode the skyline. Five ancient megaliths silhouetted against an ever-changing sky. Gusty, sharp spring winds, blowing down from the north, hurled towering cloud clumps across a sky as blue as the forget-me-nots in Alice's window box. Cherry blossom petals, wrenched from the trees, were passing the window horizontally, like a blizzard of late snow. Willows and rowans by the burn, clothed in spring green, danced vigorously with the wind. Nipper, Alice's elderly Border terrier, a malodorous explosion of unplucked fur with a tail like a stiff, hairy carrot and a liquorice-black nose wet with health, woofed sharply at his lead hanging by the door. Alice wrapped up against the wind.

Today's route kept the stones in view as it gently rounded the base of the hillock on which they stood. Glancing up, Alice thought she spotted a figure. Nipper began to woof and growl, coming back unbidden to walk at Alice's side to protect her. At the field corner someone was clambering over the fence. The person was agile – young, Alice assumed – but as Alice passed, the figure disentangled itself from the barbed wire and turned around to face her. Alice was surprised to see a weather-beaten, lined female face framed beneath its hood by wispy, grey hair. They exchanged good mornings. Alice was about to continue along the lane when the woman called out.

'Excuse me!'

Alice turned.

'I don't suppose there is anywhere near here someone could get a cup of tea, is there?'

Alice laughed gently. 'No, there isn't a café or tearoom for miles. Do you have a car?'

'No,' the woman replied, exhuming a largish rucksack

from underneath the hedge. 'I'm walking.'

'Then why don't you come with me?' Alice suggested, turning prematurely for home with a disgruntled terrier reluctantly in tow.

In the small cosy kitchen, as the kettle was coming to the boil, the woman wriggled out of her hooded cagoule, revealing a fragile-looking frame. Alice wondered how on earth she managed to carry the rucksack without snapping in two, and put extra biscuits on the plate. Alice and Margaret drank deeply from big mugs of hot, steaming tea. Margaret had been on her way to the Youth Hostel at Yetholm. She had seen the stones marked on her Ordnance Survey map and decided to take a slight detour to visit them. The women chatted amiably over more tea and biscuits until Margaret rose and said she had better get on, or there would be no chance of reaching Yetholm before nightfall.

'Don't go,' said Alice, much to her own surprise. 'Stay and have lunch with me, and I'll drive you all – or part of – the way later; you could even stay here the night if you wanted. I've always a spare room made up; perhaps this wind will have dropped by tomorrow.'

Margaret hesitated, briefly. The sky was darkening; it seemed the weather was closing in. There was still a good long hike to get to Yetholm and this detour had put her much further behind schedule than she had planned.

'It'll be no trouble. Honestly,' Alice smiled.

Margaret could see the woman would be genuinely

pleased to have her company.

'Do you know, I think I just might; yes – as long as you are quite sure . . .'

Professor Margaret Allerton
2 Mistletoe Street
Durham

Dear Alice,

Just a brief note to thank you so much for your kind hospitality.

I finished my journey by following St Cuthbert's Way from Yetholm to Lindisfarne, where I arrived on Tuesday tired and hungry, and took a room at The Ship. My room was comfortable; the food satisfying – however, the company was not a patch on that of yourself and Nipper.

I am planning another jaunt following the Pilgrims' Way from London to Canterbury – and am particularly looking forward to visiting Canterbury; it is many, many years since I was last there.

Best regards,

Margaret Allerton

Alice read the letter – twice. She received few letters. Bills and useless junk mail arrived by the day, but letters were few and far between. She tucked it into the old letter rack on the wall. The letter rack had belonged to her parents – Alice remembered it from her childhood; it had always been in the family home until Mum and Dad passed on. Although worthless, it had been the one thing Alice had really wanted as a keepsake. Just a fold of cheap metal on a wooden board, embossed with the word 'Letters', it was a bygone: well used, lingering hints of red and gold enamel proclaimed its original decoration.

In the church, Alice dusted and polished. Services were now only held once a month on the second Sunday, as the minister had four churches in his parish and had to share himself about. The church was a plain building, rectangular, with a raised altar platform at one end and a simple pulpit. A local landowning family, the Wylds, had built it after the Great War as a memorial to two sons lost. Framing the altar was a window of two lights with stained glass panels depicting the Nativity and the Crucifixion. In the apex of the arch was a round tracery light with plain glass. Alice sometimes wondered if there had ever been a stained glass panel in the round window.

There was a service being held this Sunday, incorporating a christening. Alice loved a christening – a young life dedicated to our Lord, godparents and parents proclaiming their responsibility to raise the child on the right path. The couple were incomers, not regular churchgoers; that soured Alice's anticipation somewhat, but still – new life and all that, and lacy gowns, pure white innocent shawls, blessed water – and a village is not a village without children.

Orby Cottage
Henge Farm
Nr. Duddo
Northumberland

Dear Margaret,

Thank you for the postcard of Canterbury Cathedral. I have never been to Canterbury. From the picture the streets seem to be so busy, with so many people. I'm not sure I'd like it very much; Berwick on a weekday is about as busy as I like a place to be.

Yesterday, Sunday, we had a lovely service in our local church. The children from the primary school at Ford came along to sing for the harvest festival. The church was full of sheaves of wheat, baskets of apples, and eggs and cheeses from the local farmers. Trotter's bakers had donated a huge harvest loaf, a crisp golden-brown ring twist, decorated with thin white pastry ivy leaves. There were jars of jams and chutneys, some made by yours truly, and the inevitable tins of beans from those who simply do not seem to understand the idea of harvest. Harvest does not come in a tin.

Nipper has been to the vet's last week because he kept scratching and scratching; the vet injected him with an antihistamine and suggested I get him to the grooming parlour for a good wash and a haircut. He is booked in for Thursday afternoon. I don't envy the woman who is going to do it – he is not best keen on being messed about with.

   Am off now to post this on the way to get my corns done.
   Yours sincerely,
   Alice McCleish

Margaret slid the paper knife along the top of the envelope and read Alice's letter. She would never have mentioned corns in a letter to anyone – except a podiatrist.

Her ancient cottage on Mistletoe Street was an accurate reflection of her personality: spare in ornament, well organised and efficient, compartmentalised. Books never left the study, food was never consumed anywhere except in the kitchen, and the few cushions on the furniture were for comfort, not display. There were a few items with sentimental attachment. The grandmother clock, handed down from her grandmother on her mother's side. A bentwood chair with the legs amputated just below the stretcher, which had belonged to her father's great-grandfather who was reputed to have had extremely short legs in relation to the rest of his body.

Margaret Allerton's hobby and passion in retirement was walking, a contrast to her years of academic endeavour entombed within stuffy libraries and reference rooms. In her vestibule she had all the paraphernalia needed by the enthusiastic walker: a whole series of Landranger and Ordnance Survey maps, stout boots, backpack, a selection of Gore-tex clothing for all seasons, compass, GPS.

Alice McCleish's feet had improved greatly since her visit to Mrs Roberton, the podiatrist. She hoped she could now get her feet back into her very comfortable pair of Hush Puppies, which had been mouldering in the bottom of the wardrobe for some months now. They were dotted with damp spots, and a little stiff, but an hour or so in front of the range and a vigorous scrub with the suede brush and they were good as new.

'Now then, Nipper m'lad, walkies.'

Nipper woofed and wagged. He, too, was feeling good as new. His coat had been shaved close, he no longer smelt like decomposing vegetation and he had stopped scratching. The Vetzyme cream Alice habitually used for all doggy skin problems had left him with one or two pale green oily areas around the base of his tail, but his condition had improved tremendously. He was less enthusiastic when Alice picked up the bramble trug. Nipper knew there could be a lot of just standing around when bramble picking was in progress; however, if he could slink out of sight whilst Alice was busy, he could perhaps find a rabbit hole or twenty to dig and worry at.

Alice and Callum had bought Orby Cottage some forty-odd years ago from the farmer, Wyllie Turnbull, for three hundred pounds. They had won a little windfall on Little-woods Football Pools. Wyllie Turnbull had been glad to sell, really. As a tied cottage it meant nothing but endless mainte-nance bills. It was damp; the roof leaked and had slumped a little in the middle. Farming, at the time, was not in one of its profitable cycles, so he had taken the money gladly. Callum had repaired the roof and sorted out the damp, mostly: there was still the odd spot or two. The kitchen had one corner by the back door that needed a regular bleachy scrub to keep the mould marks at bay. It had been their little palace; they had planned to raise a large family there.

After several miscarriages and a stillbirth, Alice finally gave birth to a son: a big, healthy baby whom they named Michael Cameron McCleish. He was doted on by his loving parents, who nurtured their child, watched him grow, and then mourned at his move away to the city, like so many other country-raised children. They had seen him married and become a parent himself. It had been their greatest sadness that Michael and his family rarely visited. Alice understood that it was the downside of only having a son. A daughter-in-law would always depend mostly on her own mother, and London was so far away.

Alice and Callum wended their way together through life and had begun to plan for Callum's impending retirement. Unforeseen, one night, he sat up in their bed complaining of pains in his arm and chest. By the time the ambulance arrived, Alice knew he would never return home from hospital. The funeral service had been in Duddo Church. From miles around, people had come to pay their last respects and to support Alice in her grief. Michael came up from London; Penny and the grandchildren had stayed behind.

'Honestly, Mum,' Penny had explained over the telephone.

'Marsha and Dexter both have SATs tests on Tuesday. I'm sure Dad would have wanted them to concentrate on their schoolwork, aren't you?'

In truth, Alice was not so sure about that. Still, Callum would not have wanted a fuss – that much was true. If he had had his own way, he would not have even bothered with a service.

'Just pop me in a hole any old where,' Callum had often teased. 'You know fine well, woman, I've no time for any God nor Heaven.'

After the service, at which Alice's favourite hymns, 'All Things Bright and Beautiful', and 'Jerusalem' were sung with great vigour by the packed congregation, it seemed the whole rural community had come to a halt. Throughout the village, curtains were respectfully drawn. The village shop had closed for an hour, its blinds pulled down. At least a hundred people, maybe more, walked slowly from the church behind the funeral car, all dressed in dark mourning clothes. Many of them had known Callum McCleish all his life, had been to school with him, had celebrated births and marriages and birthdays with him, and now they kept him company on his last journey to the little graveyard nestled behind its stone wall. Callum had died three years ago this month. Michael never remembered the anniversary, not even on the first year.

Michael, at Penny's insistence, had advised Alice to sell Orby Cottage after Callum's death. Alice could not drive, and in Penny's opinion, at sixty-five, was too old to learn. Alice had no intention of moving; the idea never occurred to her. Callum's car was just sitting there in the lean-to, nothing wrong with it, only four years old. Lots of other women drove and seemed to manage perfectly well. Despite having heard years of Callum's comments about women drivers, Alice made a decision. She did not tell the family. She booked an introductory lesson with a local female driving instructor and although it took some time – nearly eighteen months – she finally passed her test. The lessons gave Alice something to focus on for herself. If she could just do this she could stay at Orby Cottage. She certainly did not want to move into Berwick, or even into the village. Orby Cottage was her home and she intended to finish the cycle of her life there as her husband had done. Anyway, Nipper would hate to live in the town.

Dear Margaret,

Of course you must come and stay. Etal is so close.

Your talk to the local Ramblers Group has been advertised in the Reporter. I'll air the spare room and make up your bed for you. I'm not quite sure whether I will go to the talk or not; I don't think it's really quite my sort of thing.

I shall meet you from the coach in Berwick at 3.15 p.m., Thursday the 12th. Nipper and I are both looking forward to seeing you again.

Yours sincerely,

Alice McCleish

The invitation to address the North Northumberland Ramblers' Association had come out of the blue. Margaret's first reaction had been to say no; then she recalled how beautiful the area had been last spring. The information the Association had sent about the venue interested her. The Lady Waterford Hall had been the village school until the late 1950s and was now probably the most distinctive village hall in the country, the walls being covered in Biblical murals painted by Louisa Anne, Marchioness of Waterford, between 1862 and 1883. She used local people for her models – children from the school and estate workers.

Years of foreign travel had left Margaret quite ignorant of delights such as these to be found in her own backyard. She had recalled Alice McCleish and her cosy cottage by the stones. Alice had insisted Margaret should return some day for a longer stay. It would certainly save on expenses. Margaret could stay for the weekend, then get the coach back down to Wallsend and begin a long anticipated march along Hadrian's Wall.

The talk was to be 'Walking with Pilgrims'. Margaret had sent off an unsolicited article to The Ramblers' News and it had been published some months ago. Someone must have enjoyed it and suggested to the branch secretary that she be approached. It had been a caustic article: Margaret had not enjoyed 'The Way' as much as she had anticipated. Yes, there had been areas to pass through of great beauty, rolling chalk hills, deep fertile valleys and areas of ancient oak and beech woodlands, but by and large the impression she was left with was that these gems were now surrounded and ensnared by vast road complexes, carved through by the new Eurostar track, aircraft criss-crossing back and forth across the skies . . . and the people! – so many cars, housing developments and industrial estates. Villages that had been separate satellites of towns now melded into them, becoming engulfed by their bustle and newness. Margaret's talk would certainly emphasise the threat to rural environments and the consequences for the enjoyment of the countryside by so-called progress.

CHAPTER TWO

The bitch – more wolf than hound – had lost her litter. She picked me up in her massive jaws and carried me to a scrape near the hearth and I suckled. The hound licked me clean, chewed away the cord, ate the placenta. I grew. I scavenged scraps with the hound, crawled and walked, and learnt to bare my teeth. The hound aged and died. I became the eyes and ears of the old woman. I watched, I learned; I carried water, collected faggots, gathered herbs and berries. And this, hidden deep in the forest, an arrow's cast away from the tribe of Dadda, who only came to the hovel within the circle of stones for charms and remedies.

Callum had been everything to her. In the early days of their marriage Alice had been so naive, such a child, even though she was almost nineteen when they wed. Callum had worked for Wyllie Turnbull since leaving school at fourteen.

15

Soon he learned to drive the tractors for spraying, drilling, ploughing – all the seasonal tasks. Later he learned to drive the new combine harvester, a yellow monster with rotating claws; Callum sat up high in its single eye socket.

Callum McCleish had known the intimate folds of this landscape better than anyone else. He knew where the vixen had her earth and raised her cubs, where the badger sett was hidden in the spinney, what day the swallows arrived last year and if they were late this one.

He had loved the stones. The day they moved into Orby Cottage had been one of the most memorable of Alice's life. They had moved their few sticks of begged and borrowed furniture, second-hand bed and rugs during the afternoon of the Friday before the wedding. Wyllie Turnbull had given Callum an extra half-day off, paid, to move. Callum thought his boss might be going a bit soft in the head, but he was not complaining. The wedding had been at midday, followed by a restrained reception in the village hall, then by a less re-strained party in the pub. Mr and Mrs Callum McCleish left early. There was to be no honeymoon as Callum was due back at work on the Monday morning. They left the pub to shouts of raucous encouragement from the men and whispered words of wisdom from the married women.

Callum had been kind and knowing. Still, Alice had been shocked and confused by the way this man she had married turned from a quiet, gentle soul into a sweating, grunting thing heavy above her. She had felt some discomfort – pain, even – as he entered her; yet all in all it was not as awful as she had imagined it might be from the little information she had gleaned over her nineteen years.

Afterwards, washed and dressed again, they had walked outside hand in hand to see the sunset.

'Will we walk up to the stones?' Callum suggested.

The field held sheep at that time, and they walked up through the flock as a mist congealed in the hollows below them. They reached the stones as the sun was about to set. Hanging heavy on the horizon, it reminded Alice of how Callum had hung heavy above her, afterwards – and she blushed to think of what they had done.

'See the way that sun goes down – on the solstice it rises again above this stone here, the hand stone, and in the winter it rises above this stone here, the lamp stone. See this carved-out dip out of the wind – I reckon they had an oil wick in here as a sign to light the way for the new year to begin and the days to lengthen and the sun to come back for to grow the crops.'

Alice listened in amazement. She had never heard Callum talk so much at once, and she would discover that it never happened again in his whole life. He told her that the stones showed that people had lived, and farmed, and raised their families and died on this land for thousands and thousands of years – people just like them – and how they had put up these stones as a calendar to tell them when to plant, or plough, or sow or harvest, and that over time people had forgotten these things. He told how some of the humps and mounds in the fields were not natural, but were the remains of graves and homes and walls to keep in stock. He pointed out landmarks and trees, and how, on a clear day, standing here, you could just catch a glimpse of the sea.

As he spoke, the sun slunk lower and lower and turned through a kaleidoscope of colour until the grey-blue sky above turned almost fuchsia pink, struck through with gold. In the gloaming they walked arm in arm back down into the misty hollow, passing the lumps and humps Alice now knew to be signs of ancient life. If those people could have made their lives here and been happy, then so could Alice and Callum.

Elspeth and Penny were on the telephone. Michael could hear them from his study.

'. . . and the cost of the school uniforms – can you believe it! Still – we were lucky to get them in; we were so lucky to find this house to get the right postcode . . . '

Penny's mother, Elspeth, was often on the phone. They would chat for what seemed like hours. As Michael expected, the telephone conversation soon turned to the subject of his mother: all the usual complaints.

'She was so stubborn, refused to consider selling that damp little cottage with its hummocky bit of old garden . . .'

Penny felt it was her unequivocal responsibility now to think of the old woman, to telephone regularly to check all was well, to ask – as if she cared – about the stinking dog, to listen to endless droning on about church services, the Women's Rural, and corns; and now this new woman Alice had got herself involved with – some professor, a rambler type just looking for a free bed and a meal whenever she felt like it. They would have to go and visit, drag the children – who would rather go to Alton Towers or somewhere. She knew she would have to bribe them to be nice to Grandma for an hour or two – new trainers would not be enough, it would have to be trainers plus who knew what. Perhaps the promise of shopping at the Metro Centre might work. As if she did not have enough to do. Elspeth agreed and consoled and said yes and no in all the right places.

CHAPTER THREE

The old woman taught me words: 'water', 'fire', 'day', 'night', 'moon', 'sun'. She aged. Her back bent. Her eyes dimmed. Then, when the women came, I learnt – they paid what they could – grain, meat, eggs, hens. We survived. The old woman ailed, her eyes grew grey and clouded, she no longer heard. She died as the sun set and the moon rose between the stones to show the dark nights would soon shorten. I bound her withered body and placed it on the fire set to welcome the lengthening days. The smoke rose in the cold dawn mist and I threw in the herbs to send her to the goddess as she had taught me. I howled. I was alone.

The Sunday began with one of those glorious late September mornings when the air was still as the grave; not a breath of wind moved the thin wisps of mist that hung in the hollow. From the bedroom windows you could look down on to the

21

veil cloaking the lower half of the cottage. The rising sun burnt off the mist by the time breakfast was over. Nipper anxiously looked up at his lead on its hook. Would he still get a walk when there was a visitor? Margaret reached for her walking boots, Alice popped on the Hush Puppies, and Nipper bent himself in half to one side then the other in excitement, woofing loudly.

They took the road along which they had first met that spring.

Alice was pleased that the encounter had led to a few letters. She was delighted that Margaret had taken her up on her genial offer to come and stay. It was lovely to have someone else to think about, shop for, cook for, care for – even just for a weekend. Alice hoped that their friendship could continue and grow, despite their different backgrounds.

Margaret had visited, studied and lectured about many ancient places of human interaction with the spirit – had enjoyed privileged access. Here, in this quiet, still fold in the timeworn landscape, in the company of a woman whose genes led back through generations of ancestors who had probably lived in this area forever – possibly back even to the time of the stones and beyond – she felt the quality of the place deeply.

'Shall we clamber up and visit the stones?' Margaret suggested. Alice had not been up to the stones since Callum's death. She had not wanted to go alone.

'If you like.'

Margaret climbed easily over the fence; Alice found the scramble a bit more difficult than she remembered but hauled herself over with help. They followed the edge of the field round to the nearest point to the stones. The crop had been harvested and the soil ploughed and tilled for winter wheat, so the walk to the top of the hillock was fairly easy. Both women became silent as they approached the stones. Alice steadied herself on the lamp stone – the uphill walk had left her short of breath and feeling a little dizzy. She breathed in deeply and looked around. Tears welled in her eyes and rolled over her downy cheeks as she looked back towards Orby Cottage. Nipper whimpered inquisitively at her feet; he too had not visited the stones since his master went away.

Margaret felt a slight breeze begin to move the still air in the space created by the stones. Feelings of peace and contentment grew in her, she felt a magnetic pull on her feet, a stretching up of her spine, an elongation of her whole being, yet at the same moment she felt so, so small. Here was a place that had retained some of its potency. It was, as it had always been, the centre and focus of the surrounding humble countryside. Margaret remembered Alice and turned to share with her this feeling of potency in the landscape, this link with the past. She found to her dismay that Alice was slumped against a stone with silent tears streaming down her face.

Margaret was not a tactile person. In her spiritually heightened state of mind she forgot this fact and took the few steps across the circle. She took Alice's fleshy, freckled hand in her own bony clasp and quietly asked what was wrong.

Alice told, as she had told no one before, of the day she and Callum had moved into the cottage. She told how they had visited the stones together often throughout their married life, and of how she had not felt able to return without Callum. Margaret was horrified – she knew she had been selfish and thoughtless, dragging the poor woman over that fence and up this hill – as she had stridden on in front she had been so involved in her own feelings that she had not even noticed Alice's distress.

Alice's unfettered outburst of emotion, and the sharing of such personal memories with her, a relative stranger, touched Margaret in a way she had rarely experienced. She reached out and put her wiry arms around the ample shoulders of this woman, a woman as alone in the world as she was – but not by choice.

Dear Alice,

Thank you so much for your kind hospitality last weekend. I am just sorry we did not have much time to spend in each other's company; the Ramblers' group had organised more of my time than I had imagined. I enjoyed walking the section of Hadrian's Wall from Wallsend to Housesteads well enough and the weather was kind to me. Although the wall is such a massive icon to the Romanisation of Britain I have to say that, apart from the more remote sections, it did not manage to affect me as much as the Duddo stones.

The paths were well used and causing some erosion where people had gone around any muddy or awkward stretches. There was the inevitable litter dotting the areas around the main visitor centres at the forts.

I must apologise again for my insensitivity in presuming that the stones had no personal significance for you. I was more than touched by your reminiscence. Without wishing to sound ridiculous I feel that something passed between us there at the stones, something more than words.

Yours truly,
Margaret

CHAPTER FOUR

I stayed at the hovel. I knew of nowhere else except the village. The men fought and died – some brought the wounded to me – some I saved, some not. These outsiders came in droves. They followed our forest lays, cut trees, widened the ways, made great stone straight roads, built vast square stone camps (did they not know how the spirits hide in their corners?). More women came, girls, carrying news in their mouths and children of rape and war in their bellies. Some I cleansed with herb, some with wrappings, some with stone, and some I scraped and hauled from their wombs with the bronze tool the old woman had passed on to me.

The day Michael was due to arrive, the first real snow of winter decided to arrive before him. Alice had baked and made soup. The fire was lit and roaring in the sitting room, the Rayburn was hot in the kitchen and the windows ran with condensation. Michael's old room was aired and ready. He had been expected to arrive by lunchtime. At eleven o'clock in the morning the snow had begun, and it had fallen heavily ever since. Huge soft, white flakes floated down, inexorably covering the whole world outside in a thickening blanket of white. By one o'clock the wind had begun to pick up, piling the soft snow into sculpted drifts along the lane. Local radio was already reporting some of the higher roads blocked, and that snowploughs were working hard to keep the traffic on the A1 moving. Finally at three o'clock Alice saw car headlights through the wintry gloom. Michael's car slowly crunched in through the gate and onto the parking space outside the lean-to.

'Get the kettle on, Mother,' were his first words as he got out of the car, his feet and legs disappearing to his calves in the snow.

'Good job this car has four-wheel drive or I would never have made it. Who says we city dwellers don't need big off-road vehicles?'

Hot tea, two bowls of soup and half a loaf of bread later, Michael sat opposite his mother feeling comfortably replete. Now he was here, he found that without Penny and the children around, it was difficult to know how to start up a conversation. The few times they had visited, Penny had done the chatty stuff, about the neighbours, the church, the Rural. Marsha and Dexter told about school and their friends and what they had been up to.

He knew why he was there, of course. Penny had given him a list of reasons as long as your arm to put to his mother as to why she should sell Orby and move into some sort of sheltered accommodation. That would wait, for now.

'Now then, Nipper,' Michael reached down and hauled the grumbling terrier up onto his lap. 'Still like a good grumble then, eh?' he added, as he ruffled the untidy fur grown thick and stiff since his visit to the dog parlour.

'Still smells of rotting Brussels sprouts then, Mam,' he said as he put Nipper down and fastidiously brushed the shed hairs from his cashmere sweater. Alice remembered the boy who always wanted to sleep in the dog bed because the dog was not allowed to sleep upstairs with him.

Michael went up to his room early that night. He lay in his old single bed in his old room, the wind now howling outside through the branches of the old oak, whistling across the chimney pot and rattling the window. He stretched to his full length and stared up at the room's angled walls and low ceiling. He remembered the day the police had brought him home after he and Grant Meikle had been found drinking bottles of barley wine in Duddo Cemetery. He had been as sick as a dog in the police car, and Constable Blackie had handed him over to his father with a stern reprimand and a wink to Callum. Michael had been sure that this would be the time he would definitely get the belt he had so often been threatened with; however, his father had put him to bed, this same bed, and sat here on that same chair for hours, saying nothing. He had emptied buckets of vomit and wiped the sweat from the grey forehead of his only son and kept watch until he was sure the boy was safe and asleep.

There had been a lecture. His mother had been horrified and ashamed. Drunk in the cemetery. What would the village be saying? His father just hoped he had learnt his lesson and that it would not happen again – and it had not. Michael soon discovered cannabis, again with Grant Meikle, again in the cemetery, and he had come home stoned many times, but Alice and Callum had never realised. At college he had experimented with speed and acid, briefly. He had enjoyed the acid trips immensely. Durham Cathedral on microdots was well-nigh out of this world. He remembered coming down from a trip in his room, the bedclothes breathing; rising and falling like the chest of some paisley-quilted monster.

He had met Penny at a gig, some up-and-coming band from Manchester playing at the university. He had qualified and they had married. Soon he had been promoted at work to a post at the London head office of Bullchurch and Sons, Chartered Accountants. Since then his life had been work and family. A good life, a good responsible job, lovely home, lovely family – beautiful wife, intelligent offspring – yes, it was all lovely, too bloody lovely; lovely enough, sometimes, to make you sick.

At breakfast next morning Michael raised the subject of selling Orby Cottage. Alice had known he would bring it up sooner or later.

'Mum, you know we worry about you, miles from anywhere, especially when the weather's like this.'

'Michael McCleish – who do you think you are talking to? I am not some old biddy who cannot take care of herself. I have lived in this house since the day your father and I were wed, and I do not intend to leave until I'm in my coffin – like your father was. No. No, don't you dare interrupt me. I am sixty-eight, not ninety-eight; I am in good health, I have the car, and I have good neighbours and friends and we all keep an eye on each other as you well know. It's only in your big towns and cities that old people die alone and no one notices for days or weeks. You can go back and tell that wife of yours to mind her own business for once – do you hear me telling her how to run her life? No, and I expect the same courtesy in return.'

The subject was quite obviously closed.

The snowfall had almost stopped, but the wind was still spraying a fine haze of drifting powdery snow into the air. Accumulations of snow fell from branches with a swoosh. Alice said she was just going to give Nipper a breath of fresh air. Michael offered to take him for her. The telephone rang; it was Mrs Meikle, phoning from the village to make sure Alice was OK.

'Yes Eleanor, everything's fine . . . no, Michael's here for the weekend . . . no, on his own . . . yes . . .'

Michael left her chatting. In the porch he found an old pair of his father's wellington boots which fitted him with two extra pairs of socks on. An old waxed cotton coat, with scarf, hat and gloves in the pockets hung there too. He wrapped himself up warmly and reached for Nipper's lead. Nipper lay curled up in his basket next to the Rayburn and did not seem overly keen for a walk this morning. He had been out briefly for emptying purposes first thing and knew how cold it was. Still, it would be ungrateful to turn down the chance of a stroll, especially a stroll with this human. It had smelled vaguely familiar when it first arrived, now its smell reminded him of his old master.

Wyllie Turnbull had cleared a narrow track along the lane down to where it joined the road to the village; the snow-plough had managed to get that road clear too. Michael and Nipper kept to the cleared path. Nipper jumped up onto a snowdrift and disappeared into it, he managed to scrabble out, humiliated by howls of laughter from Michael. Swirls of drift-ing snow were sifting their way from the banks back into the roadway making intricate ever-changing patterns as they wisped along.

The sound of an approaching tractor broke the silence. It grew louder as Wyllie Turnbull rattled towards them, having cleared the lane in the opposite direction to let him get hay out to some beasts in outlying fields. Michael clambered into a snowdrift to allow the tractor room to pass. Nipper wriggled wetly in his arms.

'Young Michael!' Wyllie called out from his heated cab. 'And how are you, then?'

'I'm fine thanks, Mr Turnbull.'

'Tell your mother I'll be along with a few sticks for the fire before lunchtime. I'm sure she'll be needing extra in this weather.'

'Aye, yes, I will; and thank you for keeping an eye on her.'

'No thanks needed, lad; that's what neighbours are for.'

Michael tried to think how many of his neighbours he knew by name. One or two by sight maybe, to nod and say good morning to. Penny knew some whose children were at the same school as theirs; but no, he did not think he actually knew or cared about any of his neighbours.

The tractor rattled off back towards the steading. Nipper's feet had begun to collect great balls of frozen snow on the hairs between the pads, making it difficult for him to walk, so Michael picked him up again, but he was too heavy to carry. Michael unzipped the coat and popped the back end of the dog into the large waterproof poacher pocket concealed inside; he zipped the coat up again until only Nipper's head peered out below the scarf around Michael's neck.

As they turned to walk back along the lane, Michael looked up the mound to the stones that had been the backdrop to his childhood. His father had allowed him free range to explore and play – with the exception of the farm buildings (because of the dangers), the churchyard, the graveyard (which he had disobeyed) and the stone circle.

'You can go up there any time you like, it's not private, and Mr Turnbull knows you won't mither the beasts; but mind what I've told you. It's a special place, older than the church, maybe all those mounds are graves – you must show some respect there.'

He had gone up there of course with mischief in mind many a time, but somehow he always ended up taking his mischief elsewhere.

A sharp crack sounded behind him. Michael turned sharply to see a large limb of a beech tree crashing down across the lane in the very spot where he had stopped to speak to Wyllie. Two minutes earlier and it would have fallen onto them crushing the tractor cab and likely killing them both. Who said the countryside was a safe place to be?

In London Penny was on the phone to her mother once again.

'And now he can't get back for another day because of the snow. I mean, really, we were supposed to be going out for dinner tonight with his boss, and now I've got to phone and make his excuses.'

'Never mind, Penelope; look on the bright side – a quiet night in, kids in bed, long hot soak in a perfumed bath, a bit of pampering and an early night.'

'I suppose so . . . actually, it has been nice having the place to myself – well, me and the kids – and I haven't missed him at all as he is usually either at work or sat in front of the damned computer most of the time. Must dash, make this call to Doug, and then collect the kids from school. Love to Daddy; bye.'

CHAPTER FIVE

The people were defeated. Leaders made pacts with the out-siders. Some began to live as they did, dress as they did, even began to worship their gods. They spread north, but the Pic-tish tribes and the weather forced them back. I stayed in my roundhouse with no corners for spirits, safe, deep in the forest, encircled by the stones that told the seasons.

Mr Fullerton, lynchpin of Durham's University of the Third Age, tried Professor Allerton's telephone number for the third time in ten minutes. The lecture was due to start in twenty minutes and she had not arrived.

'Miss Reynolds, I believe you have some idea of where the Professor lives. I wonder if I might impose on you to give me a lift there in your car? I fear something is amiss.'

Miss Reynolds thought he was being somewhat over-

35

anxious, but she agreed, as it was well known that the Professor was always early for her lectures.

The red Maestro pulled up outside Number 2, Mistletoe Street, and the two hurried to the Professor's door. They knocked loudly, with no response. Mr Fullerton bent over to peer through the letter box.

'Call an ambulance, and the police,' he demanded. 'There appears to have been an accident.'

Dear Alice,

As you will see from the address I am in hospital. I am afraid I had a fall on the stairs and have broken the radius and ulna of my left arm, and several of the small bones in that wrist. I have also damaged an ankle and the calf muscle of my left leg. They say that I am lucky not to have broken my hip at my age. At my age. How I detest that phrase. I cannot tell you how many young doctors and nurses have said 'at your age' this, or 'at your age' that in the last week.

They will not let me go home. Can you imagine, some social worker has apparently assessed my situation and decided that I cannot manage at home – although she may have a point. They are suggesting I take up residence in a nursing home to free up this bed. Alice, I do not think I could bear it. To be surrounded by the ageing process in all its grim glory is more repugnant to me than death itself.

I have a suggestion to make to you, and you are not to feel in the least obliged; I only ask because you are a friend. I have many colleagues and acquaintances, but they are not friends – one could never ask them for help. I can and will, if necessary, hire a private nurse, or companion, from one of the agencies that advertise in The Lady, of which there are many, but I do not relish a matronly stranger bullying me in my own home. Would you come? It will only be for four weeks or so until I am more mobile and can use my hand and arm again. I am prepared to break a lifetime rule of no animals in the house so you can bring Nipper with you. He is no trouble, and I have a small yard for him to sit out in sometimes.

Please let me know soon, as I have to make a decision by the end of the week.

Yours truly,

Margaret

Alice read the letter. She wanted to help, of course, but she did not want to up sticks and move into Margaret's home in Durham. She had built up a mental picture of this home, which sounded so very different from her own homely cottage. It would be one of those old-world places tucked in higgledy-piggledy up some cobbled street, with low door lintels and tiny bottle glass windows. She imagined it full of shelf upon shelf of musty old books, and shrunken heads and graven idols brought back from Margaret's travels. Nipper would hate it.

Dear Margaret,

How dreadful to hear about your accident. I hope by the time you get this you will be feeling much better. I have not had much time to think about your idea, as it seemed urgent to reply. I am not keen to leave Orby, and the idea of the hustle and bustle of Durham all around me makes me quite giddy. I do have another idea, which would suit me much better if it suited you. Why don't you come here to recuperate? Fresh air, peace and quiet would do you the world of good and I would love to have someone to cook for – a good excuse to make your favourite coffee sponge! If the upstairs bedroom is too difficult for you I can get Wyllie Turnbull to move the bed down into the front parlour. The bathroom, as you know, is also downstairs which would be more convenient.

Telephone me when you decide what you want to do.

Yours sincerely,

Alice

Margaret endured the drive from Durham to Duddo stoically. She was not in any pain physically; it was the endless, mindless, patronising drivel from her wonderful volunteer driver she had to endure: Had she seen yesterday's Emmerdale? – You don't have a television! – What do you do? – Do you knit? – Mother used to knit, wonderful Fair Isle and cable jerseys, until her eyesight got too bad, then she just listened to the radio – oh, you listen to the radio? – Radio 2? – that's what mother used to listen to – oh . . . Radio 4 – bit boring – all that talking; Mother liked a good tune – until she went deaf, then she just sat.

Punctuated by brief respites of silence, when the wonderful Mr Whatsisname was temporarily lost for words, Margaret sat and wondered if at seventy-eight she really was old. She certainly did not feel old, apart from a few aches and pains from the fall. She nodded and smiled mostly in the right places, but even if she got it wrong Mr Whatsisname would just smile back and think she might be a bit deaf or senile. Had the journey been much longer she would eventually have snapped and berated this poor kind man for treating her like an old biddy. Did he know who she was? Did he have the slightest idea of the things she had done in her life and the things she still intended to do? Well, did he? The answer would have been no. He had no idea at all. To him she was indeed just a poor old biddy out of hospital after a fall.

Alice, and Wyllie Turnbull, had made the front parlour into a snug bedroom-cum-sitting room. The bed was so placed that when sitting up in it you could look out from the window and up to the stones. Mrs Turnbull, a woman rarely, if ever, seen, had found an old Victorian screen in the farmhouse attic that she had sent down to partition off the bed area from the sitting area nearer the fireplace – for privacy, she said. Alice had placed the best coverlet over the bed, one that had been made by her mother, a Durham quilt of fine needlework, stuffed with sheep's wool gleaned from the hedgerows and fences around her childhood home. The room was spotless and smelt of lavender polish and laundered linen.

Mr Whatsisname drove away from Orby Cottage, worried. He was unsure if he had delivered the old dear to the right place. The other woman was obviously expecting her, but why on earth should the old love want to be stuck right out there in the middle of nowhere? He tuned in his radio to Radio 2 and thought fond thoughts of his own mother as he drove back to Durham.

For the first two days Margaret and Alice both wondered if they had not made a terrible mistake. Both of them had lived alone for too long. Margaret was short-tempered because she hated having to rely on Alice. She believed she would never overcome the humiliation she felt when she got stuck on the toilet and could not pull herself upright. It had been different in the hospital – those people were doing their job, bathing and cleaning her body – it had been impersonal and, she had believed, very short term. Perhaps the doctors had been right: maybe 'at her age' she should have shuffled off to a nursing home and sat and knitted or listened to Radio 2.

Alice felt Margaret was behaving rather like a spoilt child who was not getting her own way; after all, she had wanted to come here to recuperate, to rest and recover, and to do that she had to let Alice get on with whatever needed to be done without being so snappy about everything. Alice telephoned Marjorie Watt, the local district nurse, whom she had known for years. Nice woman: firm, did not suffer fools or spoilt children.

'So that's the situation, Marge. I don't suppose you could just drop in if you're near the village?'

Marge would be changing a dressing for Mr McGregor that afternoon and would certainly stop by. It sounded to her like Alice's new friend needed a firm talking-to.

Margaret had not been expecting Marjorie Watt's visit. Alice took Marge into the parlour and left the two women alone while she made tea and arranged some fairy cakes on a tray. Marge had whispered to her at the door to leave her and Margaret alone for at least ten or fifteen minutes; Marge would come out to the kitchen when she had finished.

Twenty minutes later, with the first pot of tea stewed and cold, Marge emerged triumphant.

'Don't worry about tea for me this time Alice,' she said, although she did help herself to a fairy cake. 'I must be off; and anyway I think your friend has seen and heard enough of me for today.'

Alice tentatively knocked on her own parlour door.

'Margaret, can I come in?' she asked, sheepishly.

She opened the door to find a chastened Margaret sitting in an armchair with her feet up on a footstool by the fire.

'I am truly sorry. I have been such an appalling person to you,' Margaret said. 'No, please don't interrupt, your good friend Nurse Watt has made it quite clear that I must accept my situation as it is, and concentrate on recovery, not brood on the fact that I feel old and vulnerable and take my disgust at myself out on you.'

'I had to ask her advice – I didn't know what to do about it myself.'

'You did exactly the right thing; she is a wise and experienced woman who knows exactly how I feel and has given me what you might call a good talking-to. She also made me realise that if it were not you caring for me it would very likely be someone like her, and I would not want to spend four whole weeks with her putting me firmly in my place.'

Margaret improved day by day. Alice drove her to the cottage hospital where she was given exercises by the physiotherapist. Marjorie Watt stopped by once a week and was pleased with the improvement in Margaret's health and in her demeanour. The four weeks turned into five, then six. Margaret would go home when the plaster cast could be removed from her arm. She had put on a fair amount of flesh with the lack of exercise and Alice's hearty food: the cast was getting quite snug. Marjorie suggested she take Margaret in to the district hospital for an X-ray to see if the bones were knitting well and to change to a new cast if needed.

Alice and Nipper were alone in the cottage for the first time in six weeks. The telephone rang. It was Penny again. She had phoned several times recently for a variety of plausible reasons but underlying each call was the same question.

'How much longer is that woman staying?' revealed itself, thinly disguised, as, 'And how is Margaret coming along?' or 'Is Margaret still with you, Mum?'

Alice wished Penny would call her Alice, not Mum – it

sounded so false. After the conversation Alice put down the receiver with a sigh. She thought it was supposed to be the mother-in-law who was an interfering nuisance, not the other way round. One of these days, she thought, I shall stop biting my tongue and saying nothing for the sake of a quiet life; I shall give that young woman a piece of my mind – one of these days.

A jubilant Professor Allerton returned some hours later with Nurse Watt. The plaster cast was off. The X-ray had shown that not only were the bones beginning to knit, they had finished knitting. The doctor on duty was amazed. The healing process was 'astounding', he had said, 'for someone of your age'. The three women laughed aloud, and celebrated with tea and coffee sponge, large slices.

The two women embraced tenderly on the morning of Margaret's departure. She looked a different woman from the one delivered by Mr Whatsisname six and a half weeks ago. She was upright, walking steadily and alone, and her skeletal form had been clothed with a good insulating layer of flesh and fat. She had ordered a taxi to take her home. An acquaintance, who had been holding the key, had organised her daily lady to go in and turn on the heating, get in plenty of shopping, and air and clean the house from top to bottom.

As the taxi drove away, Alice waved until it was out of sight. The cottage seemed empty. Half a coffee sponge sat in its Tupperware container on the table: Margaret had forgotten to take it with her. Alice went in to strip the bed and begin returning everything to normal. On the coverlet was an envelope; on the front it said 'To dearest Alice.' Inside the envelope was a letter, and a cheque for two-and-a-half thousand pounds.

Dearest Alice,

Please do not insult me by refusing this cheque. I insist that you have it to cover the costs of food and heating during my overextended stay. It is by no means too much: your kindness was offered with no expectation of reward; what you have done for me is from the goodness of your own heart. I do not think I have experienced that kind of congeniality before, except among some of the more primitive and nomadic peoples I have met on my travels.

I would like you to treat yourself to something special – a holiday? – a new something? I will phone you when I am settled in – we do not need to speak of the money again – just accept it is yours, as I had to accept that I was damaged and needed time to mend – time which you gave to me and which is beyond any price.

I feel that 'at my age' I have finally found true friendship.

With love,

Margaret

CHAPTER SIX

I had remained strong; I should have remained strong forever. My curse, strengthened by the blood of all those unborn, lingered, lingered. I screamed it into the face of the Pilus Prior as he lit the faggots around my feet.

'Bane you are, you rapers of women; the blood of Roman bastards drenches the ground of this place. Bane are you, now and forever.'

The bend of my body held my face above the acrid smoke of all I had ever known. They had smashed down the roundhouse, all except the central post, piled everything around it and tied me twisted, growling and biting to the stake.

'Where is it? Tell me before you die,' the Pilus Prior hissed above the crackling of dry wood and wattle. 'Tell me, and I will pray for your soul.'

He pleaded, unheard above the crash and commotion of the crowd. I coughed, and spat my curse between his eyes.

'Die then, you cunning bitch, die,' he muttered; and he turned *to walk away. As he did so, the sky above, darkened already by smoke, grew darker still; the slight breeze stilled, and the sky was rent by a lurid flash of lightning which hit the stag-headed oak, the oldest, most revered tree in the wood. In the silence that followed the crash of the venerable oak to the ground, and with my last breath, I cursed the very land around me as the thunder roared above.*

Summer began warm and moist, the morning sun causing spirals of evaporating mists from road and rooftop. The daffodils were over and the grass badly needed its first cut of the year. The garden had lost much of its charm since Callum had died. The vegetable plot was overgrown with weeds and couch grass and the fruit bushes badly needed pruning back before they became too leggy. Alice had always enjoyed the garden to sit in and to collect vegetables and fruit from in season, but Callum had always done the work. He would spend many happy hours on summer evenings hoeing between the vegetable rows, mowing the undulating lawn, pruning the fruit trees. Margaret's generous cheque had gone into Alice's bank account, but she had done nothing with it so far. Alice made a decision. She would spend the money getting the garden back up to scratch. Callum, if he was looking, would approve, and so would Margaret.

There was a new chap in the village, moved up from down

south somewhere; he had set up his own gardening business. He had taken on Mrs Roberton's garden and she was very pleased with him.

'Aileen . . . Alice McCleish here . . . um . . . could you phone me when you have time. I'd like to know more about your new gardener.'

Horrible, horrible answerphones Alice thought; she felt she always sounded so useless and pathetic burbling away to a tape recorder.

Aileen Roberton phoned back that evening. She could not recommend young Brian Rigden enough: he was very keen, very knowledgeable, and very considerate. He always turned up when he said he would, was never intrusive, quiet-spoken, and Alice had better get in touch with him soon as he had several other gardens, mostly for widow-women like them-selves, that he had taken on, and would soon be too busy to take on anyone else.

Brian arrived promptly at nine fifteen on the Monday morning in his smart white van, with its Brian the Gardener sign painted on, and a Flower Pot Man next to it, thumbs up.

'Morning, Mrs McCleish.' He held out a large hand to be shaken. Alice's chubby hand seemed to disappear within his gentle clasp.

They walked around the garden. Alice explained that she needed to get it looking attractive, but with low maintenance, as she was not quite up to all the bending needed to weed the beds and she couldn't hope to get the vegetable plot up and running again. Brian was fascinated by the undulations in the lawn.

'Ridge and furrow, medieval farming practice, ploughed by oxen and still visible,' he told Alice, who knew already, but feigned surprise.

'You don't want to level this, do you?' Brian asked.

'No, definitely not; my Callum was proud of his ridge and furrow lawn.'

Brian realised that he had been teaching his grandmother to suck eggs, and began to reassess this plump, motherly woman with twinkly eyes. Nipper approved of Brian heartily, especially as he seemed to have an unending supply of doggy treats in his jacket pocket.

'I'd need to do about a week of concentrated work, cutting back, hedge trimming, digging, etc., and then I could probably keep on top of it by coming one day a week during the growing season.'

They agreed: Brian was to come for the whole of the following week to begin – on the understanding that Nipper was only to receive one doggy treat per day, otherwise he would soon be very fat indeed.

Later that afternoon, at teatime, the telephone at Orby Cottage rang.

'Mrs McCleish, this is Brian Rigden the gardener here . . . no, there is no problem, I will be with you first thing Monday morning as we agreed; it's just that there was something I wanted to run by you. I'm passing near you later this evening

– could I pop in for a chat?'

Alice thought it was a marvellous idea. Of course Brian could take over the large vegetable plot as an allotment. Callum would have been delighted. He could come and go whenever he wanted to; of course he could sort out and repair the sheds; and of course he could put up a polythene tunnel. She did not want to charge him any rent, so they agreed a cut-price rate for her gardening, and a share of whatever produce she might want to use.

Over the next few weeks the garden at Orby Cottage underwent something of a transformation. Firstly, Alice's own plot was tidied, pruned, weeded and mown, until it looked almost as good as it had done when Callum was alive. Then Brian began the vegetable plot.

'Mrs McCleish?'

'Will you please call me Alice? Mrs McCleish is so formal – makes me sound like the lady of the manor or something.'

'OK – Alice.' Brian tried the name sheepishly; it felt like calling your mum by her first name – not quite right somehow – but if that was what she wanted . . .

Four weeks later the vegetable plot was covered with dead and dying weeds, turning crisp in the summer sun. The shed had been repaired and treated with wood preservative in a shade of dark green. Alice had been mildly concerned to see Brian cutting a hole in the roof until she saw the woodburning stove and its flue being humped up the garden in a wheelbarrow. Throughout the rest of the summer Brian dug and cleared the vegetable patches, thinned out the old wood from the fruit bushes, summer-pruned the fruit trees and erected the polythene tunnel. He cut a gateway through the hedge onto the lane, and put in a nice wooden gate and arch, up which he planted rambling roses and clematis. He parked his van on the verge outside and it became a familiar sight to Alice on summer evenings.

Sometimes the whole Rigden family would be in Brian's patch. Alice would hear Aaron's laughter as he toddled around the vegetable garden after his father. Faith would be parked in the shade in her buggy, sleeping or gurgling happily to herself while Sarah weeded or hoed. They always waved to Alice in her garden, and often passed the time of day over the fence. Such a lovely family, Alice thought. She had missed so much of her own grandchildren's childhoods due to infrequent and fleeting visits to Orby Cottage, a handful of uncomfortable weekends down in London feeling like she did not belong, and being too far away to babysit or to have the children for weekends.

Under a mass of crisp dead bramble Brian uncovered a large compost heap, untouched since Callum's death, a massive pile of dark, crumbly treasure. Brian scrabbled away at the top layer and reached in with both hands pulling out a mound of the stuff. He lifted it to his nose and breathed in its earthy smell; he rubbed it between his hands and chuckled gleefully.

'Luvverly stuff,' he pronounced to no one.

'Alice, are you there?' Brian tapped on the kitchen windowpane. Nipper roused himself from a heat-induced doze in the shade of the back porch and managed a thump or two of his tail on the floor.

'Hello, Nipper old son; oh, there you are Alice.' Using her name came much easier now they had got to know each other better. 'Sorry to bother you, but I wondered if you would want the contents of Callum's compost heap for your garden? Or . . . ?'

'Of course you must use it for the vegetables; my few flowerbeds can make do with Wondergrow. Is there enough there? You could always speak to Wyllie if you wanted more – Callum used to bring down trailer loads of manure from the cowsheds every year.'

'I'll speak to him next time he's passing; I am going to set up some new compost bins, and the more manure and stuff I can get the better,' Brian replied.

Brian dug out the compost – it extended further than he had first thought; he cleared the dead bramble and ivy back to the hedge. There was enough compost there to fill the raised beds in the polytunnel, and put a good mulch over the vegetable patches. Brian stood back from his work. The ochre–red clay of the local soil had already been darkened and opened up by years of addition of compost by Callum; now it lay beneath a thick blanketing mulch of this last batch of his compost, ready and waiting for Brian to begin growing in earnest. Brian had heard a lot about Callum McCleish from his neighbours in the village, and he knew he was continuing a tradition of growth and production on this spot. The old compost site would make a great place for a potash pit – too shady to grow much in that corner. The new compost bins were going to be installed nearer the vegetable plots to save time and energy barrowing to and from them. Brian had a great pile of garden refuse for burning – any large enough twigs and branches were stacked under shelter to fuel the woodburner; all the rest teetered in a pile. Brian was not going to waste this material by just having a bonfire. He recalled an old Kentish chap on the allotments who always seemed to grow the juiciest and tastiest bush fruits, and eventually Brian had wheedled out of the old sod what his secret was. Potash. Brian had not had a potash pit of his own before, but he thought he would try it out, a sort of experiment.

Brian dug down through the topsoil layer to the clay beneath, throwing the excavated soil into the wheelbarrow at his side. The hole had ended up larger than he had intended, and the sides were crumbling back down onto the clay bottom. He might have to put in a metal liner to stabilise his ash pit. He remembered seeing an old water tank behind the shed and decided that would be just the thing. The tank fitted the hole fairly snugly, so Brian just had to refill some of the clayey subsoil from the barrow down the sides to tidy the whole thing up. He picked up a good spadeful of soil from the barrow and began to infill the gaps. His spade struck something metal the next time it was shoved into the barrow. Brian thought it would be something like an old Coke can, and hauled it out. It was quite heavy, not a Coke can, but metal. Brian spat on the crumpled thing and gave it a rub with his sleeve. The late afternoon sunlight glinted on the clean area, making it gleam golden in the sun. Brian rubbed some more. The sun went behind a cloud, and still the metal thing gleamed. Brian dropped down on his haunches; he sluiced the metal thing in a watering can of water from the rainwater barrel.

'Oh my God,' Brian mumbled. 'Oh, bloody, bloody hell . . . Alice! Alice!' he shouted as he ran up the path to her back door. 'Alice!'

Nipper, cooled down now it was evening, joined in the pandemonium, barking and woofing until Alice emerged from her kitchen to see whatever could be the matter.

CHAPTER SEVEN

H e had promised the cup to me, the Pilus Prior.

His only daughter, whom he desired to marry to the Legate to ensure his prompt promotion, had fallen in love with a servant boy, captured in the south, fair-haired, blue-eyed, tall, strong. The boy had no feelings for the stupid, spoilt child, but he was not going to turn down the chance to take the virgin when she offered herself so freely. She became pregnant, of course. Her mother noted that her moon cycle had stopped and quizzed the child. The father ranted and raved. How could he offer her now to the Legate? Who would want her now, the whore? Yet his desire for promotion overruled all. He wanted more than the vinewood cudgel, the vitis, sign of his status. He wanted much more.

The now truly-spoiled girl had a maid, one of the village girls I had rid of a Roman bastard, who let it be known to the girl's mother that a cunning woman lived nearby; that I might be able to help. Better that, than use a Roman: the news would be all round the camp in days.

55

'Margaret, it's Alice.'

'What on earth is the matter?' Margaret asked, worried by Alice's strained voice.

'Brian's found something in the garden, under the compost heap; we think it could be gold.'

Margaret asked a series of questions which Alice answered as best she could.

'I'm coming up – now; don't speak to anyone else about it till I get there,' Margaret stated. 'Air my room; I shall probably have to stay the night.' Margaret put down the telephone and quickly picked it up again to call a taxi. She arrived at eight-thirty that evening. Brian had gone home for his tea and came back to find the two women sitting at the kitchen table studying a book.

'Look, Brian – look at this,' Alice demanded. 'Isn't it similar? "Found in 1837 on Bodmin Moor, dating from 1700–1500 BC".'

'They found another one of those in Kent just before we put the house up for sale; I remember seeing it on the telly. It was all squashed up like our one – sorry, Alice – your one, after all, it was in your garden.'

'Which is exactly where it would have stayed if you hadn't dug it up, so it's as much yours as it is mine.'

Margaret found the chapter on the Kent cup, found in 2001 at Ringlemere in the south-east of England. The photograph showed a crumpled gold cup, decorated with corrugated wrinkles, looking not so very different from the still grubby example on the table in front of them. The Ringlemere Cup was bought for £270,000 by the British Museum, shared by the landowner and the metal detectorist who had found it.

Margaret was less interested in the value of the cup; she was more curious as to why the cup should be here: this was a high status item.

'Alice, this is really not my field of expertise – I only happen to have this book about gold cups by accident, it belongs to a colleague of mine who specialises in ancient artifacts. I would like to photograph the – dare we call it – Duddo Cup, and send it to him down in London. Would you mind, or do you think I am taking over too much?'

'Oh no, you must do what you think best; this is your area, not mine. I wouldn't know what to do if you weren't here.'

Margaret had pulled out a very expensive-looking mobile phone, taken several photos with it, and sent the pictures in a flash. Text messages whizzed back and forth between Orby Cottage and Margaret's colleague, the eminent archaeologist Professor Mortimer. He was very excited by the find, and would get on the first train in the morning if someone could collect him from the nearest station. Brian volunteered to meet him at Berwick station at eleven-thirty the next day.

Brian went home to Sarah full of news and chat about the cup, the two old women, and the professor coming the next day. He could barely sleep with excitement; in all these years of digging the soil he had found one or two bits and pieces: an old ink pot, stoneware jam jars, a large unidentified tooth, a lead soldier, and a musket ball, all of which he kept in a box in his office room.

Professor Mortimer arrived with Brian at noon the following day. Margaret greeted him with an enthusiastic shaking of hands and introduced Alice. The four entered Orby Cottage kitchen where the kettle was just coming to the boil. On the table, perched on a mound of cotton wool, sat the cup, still dirty with soil, but with the unmistakable glint of gold glowing from the area they had dared to clean. Alice and Brian had been all for giving it a good scrub under the tap, but Margaret had insisted it be left grubby until the Professor had seen it. If it *was* one of these rare ceremonial gold cups, it would need to be cleaned by an expert so as not to damage it further.

The cup was quickly verified by the British Museum. Professor Mortimer had taken it back down with him and great excitement had been caused in the archaeological world. This was the most northerly find, bringing total numbers of these gold cups found throughout Europe and Britain to eight. Local and national media arrived to interview Alice and Brian.

'Who found the cup?'

'Where was it?'

'How did you know what it was you had found?'

Alice was quite dizzy with it all. Fancy living here for almost fifty years and that thing had been hidden there, under the compost, left by one of the ancients whose mounds had become so familiar. The British Museum sent a team up to investigate the immediate area. Duddo stone circle had probably never seen so much activity since the times when wor-shippers had come and gone for the seasonal rituals of the year. Wyllie Turnbull grudgingly gave his permission for the archaeologists to map the field with the stones, and the field that came up to the hedge where the compost pile had been, with a geophysical survey. The results were very exciting, with possible habitation and burial sites dotting both areas of field.

Wyllie Turnbull took some convincing to allow a full ex-cavation to take place. It was planned that the following spring a team of archaeologists and students would spend six weeks excavating the area around the boundary hedge be-tween Orby Cottage garden and Wyllie's field. They were also to dig some test pits around the stones to try to find some sort of dating material. Professor Mortimer himself was to lead the dig, and Alice insisted he should stay at Orby. Wyllie agreed a good price for the rent of the old barn as a headquarters, and the neglected walled orchard next to it for the archaeologists to camp in.

The find seemed, miraculously, to magic Alice's family into visiting. Michael, Penny and the children arrived within days. Margaret had stayed on to support and protect Alice, as only she realised just how much the Duddo Cup would insti-gate world media attention. The first encounter between Penny and Professor Allerton reminded Alice of two cats meeting on neutral ground, circling each other and trying to decide if there was a threat. Margaret insisted on being called

Professor to exaggerate her distance from this young woman, who she knew viewed old ladies as something of a nuisance. Marsha fell for Margaret at first sight; Dexter remained reserved, as did Michael, and treated her with deference.

'Will you be rich now, Grandma?' Marsha demanded to know.

'It will depend if a museum wants to buy the cup,' Alice replied.

'Don't be so rude,' Penny interrupted the conversation. 'You shouldn't . . .'

'Of course she should,' Margaret cut in. 'A curious mind is an intelligent mind.'

Penny's face expressed little, but her eyes . . . if looks could kill . . . She turned and left the room to find Michael in the garden.

'How dare that woman speak to me like that! Who the bloody hell does she think she is, wheedling her way into your mother's life? You mark my words: your mother is so weak that that woman will take over if we let her.'

Alice had followed Penny and Michael into the garden to see if a few well-chosen words might calm the situation. She overheard most of their conversation unseen, and for once she had allowed her anger to rise. She briefly considered quietly slipping back into the kitchen, but really, this time the girl had gone too far.

'Who do you think you are, young woman? No, Michael – don't defend her, I heard every last word. Weak, am I? Just a feeble old biddy?' Alice's voice rose, her face flushed pink and her eyes hardened.

'I have tolerated your unwanted interference and comments about what I should do, and where I should live, for years. I have never once interfered in your life; I have bitten my tongue when you push my son into trying to persuade me to sell this cottage. What is it you want? More money? Have you not got enough? Is that why you have suddenly decided I might be worth a visit? Dear, weak, old Mum, what will she do with all that money from the sale of the cup, a share of a quarter of a million? I'll tell you what she will do with it – make sure you don't see a penny – Penny. Now go back to your B&B – better still, bugger off back to London.'

In the car on the way back to London, Marsha said, 'It's a shame we couldn't stay longer. I liked the Professor; fancy Grandma having a friend who is a professor. Are any of your friends professors, Mum?'

Michael hid his private glee at seeing Penny so outraged at the way his mother had spoken to her. She had been speechless with anger, her self-appointed position of caring daughter-in-law violated. They had returned to the B&B, packed hurriedly and left. Conversation was almost non-existent until they reached York. At the service station Michael and Dexter went off to the Gents.

'Dad,' Dexter called from the cubicle. 'Why is Mum so angry, and why didn't we stay at Granny's for longer?'

'Well, you see, your mum thinks Grandma is . . . in fact

I'm not too sure what your mum thinks of Grandma, but I think she thinks Grandma needs to be looked after because she is old.'

'Does she?' Dexter asked. 'Does she need looking after – is she ill or something?

'No, not as far as I know. Your grandma seems to be doing very well, to me; she has her home which she loves, and lots of friends who care for her, and Brian to take care of the garden – in fact, Dexter, I think your grandma, my mum, has all the things your mum would like to have but hasn't got – if that makes any sense.'

'You mean Mum is jealous of Grandma?'

'Yup, I suppose that's exactly what I do mean.'

In the Ladies, Penny wiped tears she could no longer hold back from her eyes. Marsha noticed but pretended not to.

'Mum, if I go to university, I think I shall study archaeology. Do you think I could go and stay at Grandma's while the dig is on in the spring?'

Penny was unable to reply. That bloody woman – old cow – why can she not just get old sensibly? Penny had imagined that the cottage would be sold after Callum died and the money shared out. It would not have been much, but it might have gone some way to clearing the debts that Penny had accrued. Michael knew about the mortgage of course, he had arranged it – even exaggerated their joint earnings to raise enough to move into the right catchment area for this school. What he did not know, and Penny could not admit to, was the extent of her own personal debt. Store cards, credit cards, and a loan she had taken out shortly after Callum's death in the – so she had thought – sure and certain knowledge that she would be able to pay it off soon. Instead, the old bitch was determined to stay there – she would get old and ill and need to go into a home, and the cottage would be sold off to pay the fees – and now, to top all that, the old shrew had had yet another windfall. It just was not fair.

CHAPTER EIGHT

I was taken to the villa. I had rarely been further than the village. The army camp was set on a sloping hillside facing south. A great wide road led directly into it, through it, and out the other side, off into the distance, through the forest. The villa had been built outside the camp – sure sign that the Romans expected no more unrest among the natives.

There were fields around with crops and livestock. Birds, the like of which I had never seen, wandered amongst the crops: the females, like dowdy hens, soft brown and dappled; but the cocks, vibrant red and green-hued blues, a dangling wattle from the chin, a red ring around the eye, a rattling cry and a long straight tail sticking out behind.

I was afraid of the corners; afraid of the hot floors, where great coloured patterns wound their way around, depicting men, women, strange animals and plants. The walls, too, had painting and colour. No wonder they did not fear the spirits in the corners – they had many ways to drive them out.

The maid led me to a room where a man and a woman lay on soft cushioned beds, propped up on their elbows, eating and drinking. Around them stood servants. The man dismissed the servants and sent the maid to bring the girl.

Professor Mortimer was to lead the dig personally. He had declined Alice's offer of accommodation, explaining that he would need more space than she could offer, but the truth was he was accustomed to living alone and did not want a woman fussing around after him. He had a mobile living unit provided by the British Museum, with satellite Internet access and his own shower and loo: what more could he need?

Wyllie Turnbull looked on aghast as two bright yellow minibuses packed with students, and a flat back trailer piled with wood and canvas came up the lane to the steading, passed the outbuildings, and disappeared behind the barn to park by the orchard wall. Violet Turnbull looked out from her window nervously.

Wyllie pulled on his boots in the cloakroom and went out to greet his unwelcome visitors. He stomped across the yard, following the sound of youthful voices, towards the orchard. The doorway was open and young men and women, in gaudy clothes that stood out garishly against the weathered stone of the buildings, were humping the piles of canvas and wood into the orchard.

The orchard had been Wyllie's mother's favourite place. She had pruned and harvested from the trees, many of which were ancient even in her time. She had known the names of the fruit trees: Keswick Codlin, Stirling Castle, Annie Elizabeth; there were Portugal quince, French pears Beurre Diel and Brown Beurre, and Violette Hâtive peaches trained on the walls. She had nurtured every one of them into fruiting, protecting them from the worst of the frosts with double thicknesses of old fishing net begged from the salmon netters at Tweedmouth. She had planted a few new trees, but her delight was to keep the old ones going despite the ravages of time and insects and fungi.

In the early days of their marriage, before the accident, Violet, too, had nurtured the orchard; since then she had not been near it, and rarely had Wyllie. The students found wildly overgrown apple, pear and plum trees in full blossom; the weedy grass had been chomped down by a few sheep, now returned to their usual pasture with the rest of the flock.

'Funny looking tents,' Wyllie grumbled to a passing boy with hair in great twisted lumps hanging down his back and bunched together with coloured ribbons.

'It's a yurt,' the young man replied.

Wyllie stomped off muttering to himself. 'What the bloody hell have I let myself in for? Yurts, indeed.'

When the yurts were erected, smoke curled up from woodburners within them, kettles were boiling, teas of many different sorts were being brewed and the group of twelve students gathered around a communal campfire with the Professor to discuss tactics.

One student – the one with the dreadlocks, Alex – was too distracted to pay proper attention. His eyes wandered around the orchard. He looked up and was surprised to see that all that could be seen from inside the orchard was the sky: the walls shut out everything else from view. The Professor interrupted the group to get Alex involved.

'Alex, would you mind paying some attention to this discussion?'

'Sorry Prof.; sorry everyone; I was miles away then.'

The first trench was to be along the outside of the hedge near to where the cup had been found. A small digger removed the top surface of ploughed soil until they reached the undisturbed layer where the ploughshare could not reach. Then began the slow work of carefully removing layer upon layer of soil, then sieving the soil for small artifacts – for anything that would give some evidence for dating. Within the garden itself, very little came out in the initial layers, and the roots of the hedge made the going difficult. Five test pits were dug around the stone circle, and one in its centre. Henge Farm became a bustle of activity.

Marsha was to arrive for the half-term week to stay with Alice. Penny had not been best pleased with the idea as she had planned for the children to stay with her parents in Suffolk for the half-term as usual. Dexter had decided he did not want to go there on his own, and he was also adamant he did not want to go to Duddo with his sister.

Michael put Marsha on the one o'clock from King's Cross, and Alice was to meet her at Berwick at around five-fifteen – if there were no delays. Marsha found her seat – Coach F, seat 14, front facing – and put her bag up on the luggage rack above her head. She waved enthusiastically to Michael as the train pulled out. Michael turned away and went down into the Underground to get back to Putney Bridge. This was his baby's first trip alone. She had been on school trips in groups, and had been away on holiday with Penny's parents often, but she had not travelled alone before. He had anxiously scanned the faces of the occupants of the seats around her. An older woman took the seat beside her and summed up the situation immediately. She had caught Michael's eye, and with a look, implied that she would keep her eye on the pretty young thing next to her.

She was tall and gaunt, the woman, with white hair, long and down her back in a thick plaited cord. She removed her coat, folded it carefully and laid it over her small case on the luggage rack. She settled herself in her seat, arranged a bottle of water and a small sandwich box on the table in front of her and, reaching into a large black bag, drew out a book and a pair of spectacles. Once suitably ordered she turned her attention to Marsha. About fifteen years old, she thought; much too thin, rather plain looking, but with large blue–green eyes that could not be ignored.

'Hello, my name is Avian. Was that your father waving you off and looking worried?'

'Hi. Yeah – that was my dad; he still thinks I'm a little kid.'

'Dads are like that,' Avian replied. 'How far up are you travelling?'

'Berwick-upon-Tweed. Dad thinks I'll miss the station and end up in Edinburgh or Aberdeen. Honestly – as if !'

'I'm travelling to Edinburgh, but I shan't make sure you get off at the right station – that is up to you. Sorry, what did you say your name was?'

'Marsha.'

'Well, Marsha, lovely name; almost as unusual as mine, wouldn't you say? What are you going to Berwick for?'

'To stay with my Granny McCleish; there is an archaeological dig thingy going on around her house so I'm going to watch and perhaps even be allowed to help.'

'Was it your granny who found the gold cup in her compost heap? I heard about it on the radio.'

'Yup, that's my gran; she's been on the TV news too.'

'Oh, I don't have a television. Awful things, hypnotic mush for the masses, mostly. I love the radio. You can do other things while you listen to the radio – like make jam, or mix potions.'

Now she will think I'm a potty old thing; why on earth did I say that? Avian mused.

Marsha looked at Avian out of the corner of her eye while pretending to look out of the window. Some of the graffiti was quite good along here; she did not see much graffiti in Putney.

Avian picked up her book, put on her spectacles and began to read, using a long bony index finger to follow the lines in a childlike way. She read very fast, Marsha thought, as the finger whipped back and forth along the lines and down the page and on to the next in double-quick time. They kept a companionable silence for a while until the refreshment trolley squeezed its way along the walkway and came alongside them.

'I would like a cup of hot water please; I wish to use my own tea.'

'Certainly, madam. Milk and sugar?'

'Just the hot water, thanks. Marsha, can I get you anything? Coke?'

'OK – a Coke would be nice; thank you.'

'Something to eat?' Avian enquired.

Marsha shook her head. Avian would have liked to have fed her with something, anything; girls should not be so scrawny, not at that age. The return to conversation allowed Marsha to ask the question that had been in her mind since the last comment the strange woman had made.

'Excuse me, Mrs . . .' She hesitated, realising she would have to use the only name she had for this woman. 'Excuse me, Avian; you said potions: are you a witch?'

The huge blue–green eyes stared from the girl's face with a hint of defiance. Avian wondered what the idea of a witch meant to this girl – something out of Harry Potter maybe –

that JK Rowling had a lot to answer for.

'Depends what you mean by a witch, really; some people might say so, others not.'

'What do you say?'

'I say I am interested in many things: the power of nature, herbal remedies, spirit travel, shamanism; ancient beliefs and old wives' tales to some: witchcraft and magic to others.'

The conversation continued sporadically until the customer services manager announced that they were approaching Berwick-upon-Tweed. Marsha organised herself and prepared to leave her seat.

'Goodbye, Marsha,' Avian said. 'Have a lovely time with your gran. She must be a great favourite of her local spirits.'

'Bye,' Marsha said as she left her seat.

The train swept over the high arched rail bridge spanning the River Tweed as it splayed out towards the sea. Looking down from the vestibule window to the water far below, Marsha could see flocks of white swans cruising the wide water. The InterCity train pulled into the small station with its crumbling remains of a castle wall to one side and large car park to the other. Granny McCleish was waiting with Nipper on his lead at the bottom of the stairs.

'Granny, how are you? And Nipper – hello, boy.'

Alice drove even more carefully than usual with her precious cargo. Neither of her grandchildren had ever come to stay on their own before, and Alice was worried that the child would be homesick, or bored or unhappy to be away from friends; still, she hoped there was enough activity around Orby Cottage at the moment to keep Marsha occupied. There had indeed been times when Alice wished the cup had stayed firmly below the compost heap where it probably belonged. Callum would have been uneasy about the disturbance of the ground. He would probably have thought it best to let the past be, to let the souls of those who had lived there before rest in peace. Still, it was too late for that now, Alice thought. The cup had been found, and it was a very important artifact. The academics needed to find out as much about it as they could.

Marsha chatted away about home, school and friends as they drove towards Duddo. Nipper lay down on the back seat next to Marsha's bag and snored loudly, making both the human occupants of the car laugh. Alice parked under the lean-to and unlocked her front door. Marsha was standing by the car looking around in disbelief at the activity that was taking place around the cottage.

'Granny – can I explore now?'

'Wait two seconds, love. Let's get your bags indoors and let me have a cup of tea and then I'll introduce you to everyone. I hope you've got some sensible shoes or wellingtons in that bag.'

There were no sensible shoes, of course, but there was a pair of new trainers. Marsha seemed quite happy to sacrifice them to the mud of the dig. Alice hoped they were not an expensive pair; perhaps she should buy Marsha a pair of wellies for the week.

The dig was well under way; Marsha thought it was just like Time Team off the telly, but much, much better. Alice introduced her to Professor Mortimer, who was keen to encourage Marsha to get involved.

'Perhaps you could begin tomorrow morning helping with washing and recording finds – that happens in the old barn.'

Alice and Marsha left the main trench behind the vegetable patch and walked along the lane. They passed through the new gate in the fence, along a special walkway running up to the stones to keep erosion to a minimum, and approached one of the test pits.

'Hi, Alice.' Alex was on his knees scraping carefully away at the bottom of a shallow pit outside the circle. 'How are you this morning, and who is this lovely lady with you?'

Marsha blushed scarlet and tried to look deeply uninterested in this very interesting-looking man. He was dressed like one of the hippies who lived in a squat she passed on the drive in to school every morning with her mother. Penny always had something to say as they passed the place.

'Eyesore . . . Probably full of drug addicts . . . Time the council did something . . . See – the police are there again.'

Marsha loved the brightly-painted house – the door had huge sunflowers daubed on, open windows billowed with curtains in purple, orange, pink and blue. Psychedelic people sat on the wall outside; a motley gang of children and infants spilled out onto the pavement with an assortment of scruffy-looking dogs for company. Music could even be heard sometimes over the roar of ring road traffic and the rush of the school run. Marsha thought her life rather dull in comparison. Their home was tastefully decorated and furnished throughout, nothing clashed, every room merged and melded into the next, seamlessly. Nothing stood out, nothing claimed preeminence over anything else – except perhaps the large flat screen television that presided over the sitting room.

'This is my granddaughter, Marsha; she has come to stay for half-term and she wants to help with the dig. Professor Mortimer says she can begin in the old barn tomorrow, washing and recording finds. Marsha – this is Alex, one of the archaeology students.'

Her blush receding, Marsha looked at Alex directly and thought how sparkly and bright his eyes were. She wished Granny had not mentioned half-term, which would mean he would know she was just a schoolkid.

'Hi, Marsha – nice name.'

Their next visit was to the orchard. They walked up the lane to the steading, past the outbuildings, past the old barn and on past the Professor's mobile unit. The gate in the wall was closed. Marsha had never been along to the steading before; she did not know that there was an orchard there.

'It's just like in *The Secret Garden*, Granny; perhaps Dickon and Mary and Master Colin will be there.'

Marsha ran on ahead and opened the gate. Inside was another world. The campfire smouldered, sending coils of smoke upwards to the sky until it reached higher than the walls where the wind caught it and drew it away. Yurts tucked under the spreading boughs of the fruit trees drew Marsha like magnets.

'Granny, can we go in them? What are they? Like tents?'

'Hold your horses, young lady; let's answer one question at a time. Yes, we can go in them if the students don't mind, come on – let's see if anyone's in.'

They walked to the nearest yurt; its door was open but there was no one at home. The second yurt door was also open and as they turned to it a young woman came out.

'Hello Alice, how are you?'

Granny seemed to know everyone, and everyone knew her. Marsha had always thought of Granny as being old and lonely, living miles from anyone or anywhere, just her and her old dog with hardly any friends. That is what Marsha thought growing old was about, because that was what Penny told her. Being old did not seem to be as bad as Penny made it out to be. Granny knew loads of people, even professors. That old lady on the train – she was interested in lots of things, more than she said, Marsha suspected, and she did not seem boring at all; very weird, yes, but not wrinkly and sad.

Marsha was introduced to Maisie; today was Maisie's turn to cook supper for everyone. Everyone took turns except the Professor, and the only reason he did not take his turn was because his cooking was so bad. Maisie had prepared an enormous cauldron of vegetarian chili, and another huge pot of rice was just coming to the boil on the outdoor catering stove. Plates were warming, and a large table set for thirteen stood under a tarpaulin shelter, which housed the stove and food store. The smell of the food made Marsha's mouth water and her stomach rumble.

'What's for tea, Gran?'

Alice had not known what to feed Marsha. Penny had given a list of likes and dislikes over the phone. Likes were chips, pizzas, pasta, tomato ketchup and mayonnaise; dislikes were vegetables, rice and red meat. Alice had looked at the pizzas in the freezer department of the supermarket; she had bought one, and a bag of frozen oven chips, and these were to constitute their tea.

'Pizza and chips?' Alice offered tentatively.

'Why don't you both stay here and eat with us today? There is always heaps of food: I always cook too much.'

Alice looked at Marsha, expecting a refusal as the meal contained two dislikes.

'Oh, go on, Gran – can we?'

'Why ever not? Maisie, thank you; we'd love to. Can we do anything to help?'

Marsha stirred the chili while Alice sliced thick doorsteps of crusty bread from loaves Maisie had baked.

'Don't butter all the bread, Alice; some of the veggies are vegans.'

Vegans, thought Alice; and what is one of them when it's at home?

The archaeologists began to return to the orchard in dribs

and drabs. They washed their hands and removed the grubbi-
est of their outer clothing and arranged themselves around the
long table. Alice sat next to the Professor, and Marsha sat with
Maisie. Alex sat at the other end of the table and Marsha kept
snatching glimpses of him until he noticed and waved to her
which made her blush again. Marsha ate two large platefuls of
chili and rice, and two thick slices of buttered bread. She
drank a glass of cider, and by the time the meal was over she
was feeling full and sleepy.

'Come along, Marsha; time to go back to the cottage. Nipper will wonder where we've got to.'

'Looks like you've got another admirer,' Maisie joked with
Alex that evening around the campfire. He put an arm around
her shoulder and gave her a kiss on the cheek.

'You're just jealous,' he teased.

CHAPTER NINE

The girl stalked reluctantly into the room. She looked at me as if I were shit in her path. Her father, the Pilus Prior, spoke.

'Daughter,' he said. 'This creature can cleanse you of your shame, so do not look at her as if she is lesser than you.'

The maid whispered his words to me in our tongue.

The girl ran to her mother and threw herself at her mother's feet.

'Mother, let me keep the child; I love him, the child's father. Give him his freedom; he will prove himself worthy.'

The mother turned her face away.

'I can't take time off work, Michael; we are snowed under at the minute. You take some time off and look after him.'

'Penny, he is fourteen – he does not need to be looked after. We are both on the end of a phone, and I can be back here in half an hour if there's a problem. Honestly, you are going to have to learn to let go; they are not babies any more.'

'It's all your interfering mother's fault. If she hadn't found that blasted cup they would have both gone off up to Suffolk same as usual – no problem.'

'You can't blame my mother, and you shouldn't expect them to go to Suffolk if they don't want to.'

Penny's real reason for being unable to take time off from her job in the office of a local department store was that she needed the money, and badly.

Later in the week she had yet another appointment with the bank manager to discuss her finances.

'Mrs McCleish, you can go through now; Mr Winterbottom is ready for you.'

Penny felt as if the entire bank staff were watching her, tittering behind their hands, as if they all knew just how much money she owed.

'Come in; sit down, Mrs McCleish. How are you today?'

Penny McCleish sat down heavily in the chair indicated. She clutched her handbag tightly on her knees.

'Mrs McCleish, I am sorry to tell you that head office is concerned about your inability to pay off the loan as agreed. We need to come to some sort of mutual agreement. Have you considered debt counselling? We offer a service here, you know.'

Penny began to sob. Mr Winterbottom made some soothing noises, only making matters worse.

'I don't know what to do – I've been so stupid,' Penny sniffled in reply.

'I think you should discuss this with your husband, Mrs McCleish – don't you?'

Michael came home from work, tired. The Tube back to Putney Bridge had been even more packed than usual; he had stood all the way from the City. Walking along the street towards Number 77 he noticed an ambulance outside. Heart racing, he began to run along the pavement, pushing other pedestrians out of his way.

'What's happening? I live here! Where is my son?'

The ambulance woman led him up the steps and into his home. Someone was being brought along the hallway on a stretcher. It was Penny. Dexter was in the sitting room with a woman police officer.

'Dad, they won't let me see Mum . . . what's happening?'

'I don't know son; I don't know.'

PC Jane Warburton was quite used to such happenings. Middle-aged housewife, change of life, empty nest syndrome; makes unsuccessful half-hearted suicide attempt to gain attention – probably a secret drinker. She had seen it before and would no doubt see it again. Well, it wouldn't happen to her. She had her career. She was going places. She gave the man and his son a moment to embrace and when they separated she proceeded in a most professional manner.

At the hospital, Michael and Dexter waited for news. They sat side by side in silence – together, yet separate – as hospital life rushed past them. Dexter wished his sister were here – he could talk to her. He had come back from school earlier than usual – he should have stayed on for football practice, but the teacher was off sick. The house was quiet but he knew his mum must be there somewhere because her handbag and car keys were on the table. He called, but there was no reply. He went into the kitchen and poured himself a large glass of Coke and pulled a packet of crisps out of the cupboard. Penny was on the sofa – sleeping, he thought. He sat down and turned on the TV. She did not wake; even when he shook her, she still did not wake. Then he saw the spilled bottle of pills on the table. He phoned 999. He did all the right things: the woman on the phone told him to check if his mother was breathing; she was. She asked for the name on the pill bottle and other information. Dexter answered the questions calmly. The woman stayed on the phone until the ambulance arrived.

Michael was in a state of deep shock. Why? The question spun dizzyingly in his mind. He reached across and took Dexter's hand, which was not snatched away. They gripped each other's hand in disbelief. After all, everything in their lives was fine: the new house, the new school, work, money; he had not been having an affair and neither had she – as far as he knew. Their life was wonderful – he had been thinking that only recently when he was at his mother's. 'Be careful what you wish for,' his father always used to say. 'You might get it.'

Penny's parents arrived later. They too joined the vigil.

'Mr McCleish, I am Dr Scott.'

'How is she, doctor . . . my baby?' Penny's mother was desolate.

'I need to talk to Mr McCleish alone; but your daughter will pull through – please don't distress yourself any further.'

'Can my son come with me?' Michael asked.

'I don't see why not,' replied the doctor.

They followed him to an office.

'Your wife, Mr McCleish, has taken a moderate overdose of aspirin. This can lead to complications in some instances. The kidneys can be damaged and we need to keep her in to run tests for a couple of days. She will be seen by a psychiatrist while she is here, but I do not believe this was a determined attempt to take her life; more of a cry for help.'

'Can we see her?'

'Normally, I would say yes, but at the moment she is still somewhat confused and says she can't see anyone because now she will have to tell. Tell what . . . that I don't know. I suggest you leave her with us. I will give her a mild sedative to help her sleep, and I suggest you all come back in the morning.'

'Dad,' said Dexter in the taxi on the way home.

'Yes, son?'

'Will Mum be all right – really?'

'Sure she will – mostly because of you – you were a real hero.'

'But she didn't really want to kill herself – did she?' Dexter felt the sting of salty tears in his eyes as he spoke.

'No, son, she didn't; but there is something wrong, and I don't know what it is. I feel so useless.'

'Marsha will be back tomorrow. Should we phone Granny and let her know what's happened, do you think?' asked Dexter.

Alice had been shocked to hear the news. She was not overly fond of the girl, but that did not mean she would wish her any harm; and how was she to tell Marsha?

Marsha was at one of the test pits, carefully clearing around a darkened area of soil, a posthole. Professor Mortimer had explained that a wooden post had been buried in the earth long ago for some reason – maybe to hold a rush light, maybe the original circle had been a wooden one – they could only surmise at the moment; anyway, the wood had rotted away over time leaving the soil where it had been much darker than the surrounding soil.

Marsha had quickly been promoted from pot washer because she had shown such an interest in everything that was going on. She had posed some difficult-to-answer questions and Professor Mortimer had been most impressed by Alice's young granddaughter. Alice looked out from the front door to see if Marsha was on her way back for tea. She was just coming up the path.

'Hi Granny. I've had a brilliant day – we found a posthole.'

'Hello darling – come along in now – I have a bit of news

to tell you.'

Marsha cried. She said nothing, just sobbed and cried against the comforting breast of her grandmother. Alice let her cry it out. Nipper sat and tipped his head from side to side questioningly.

'Granny,' she whimpered. 'Mum will be OK – won't she?'

'The doctor says she will be fine; they just need to do some tests to make sure her kidneys haven't been damaged by the aspirin, but that is most unlikely. The doctors think she did not take enough of the pills to do any damage, but they have to make quite sure.'

'Granny, will you come on the train with me tomorrow? I don't want to go on my own.'

Alice decided against travelling down with Marsha. For one thing, Marsha had pulled herself together remarkably quickly and had said that it was not necessary – and secondly, once there, she would have had to stay at least until they let Penny come home. Penny's parents were there too and Alice had always felt that Elspeth Buckingham rather looked down her nose at Alice. No, she would stay exactly where she was and not interfere.

Penny was propped up in her own bed. Michael was making tea, again. Marsha and Dexter were being unusually quiet and cooperative. Elspeth and Eric had gone back to Suffolk after some persuading from Michael. Penny's mother had fully intended to stay and take over.

'Of course I shall stay! Who else will take care of everything?' she had stated, plumping up cushions and shaking the curtain folds into position. Michael knew that if that woman stayed another hour he would probably throttle her. He took his father-in-law, Eric, to one side.

'Eric, I really think you and Elspeth should go back home; after all, Penny's home and will be fine. She really needs some space, you know?'

Eric thought of his wan-looking daughter lying upstairs – thought of the panic he had felt, and the anger at Michael, when he first saw her in the hospital. He looked into his son-in-law's eyes and saw the undisguised desperation of a man who really and truly had no idea what the hell was going on.

'You're right Michael: you two need to talk. Should I suggest we take the children up to Suffolk? It would soften the blow for Elspeth.' He knew his wife just wanted to do something.

'No, Eric; I think we all need to be together; we all need to understand what caused this, even the kids. Well – to be honest, if this whole episode has any positive side, it is that I know now that 'kids' is the last thing they are.'

The quiet of the house was blissful: the comfort of her own bed, the smell of the scented candle, the distant sounds of Michael in the kitchen, the soft murmur of the children's voices along the corridor in their den. She had been so ashamed. How could she have done that to Dexter? It was supposed to have been Michael who found her – she should have been just drowsy and incoherent. She never meant to end up in hospital. She felt such a fool.

Michael tapped lightly on the bedroom door and peeked his head nervously round the door.

'Oh good, you are awake. How do you feel?'

'I'm so glad my mother's gone. How did you manage that?'

'I had a word with Eric.'

The memory of her father's expression by her hospital bed sent a physical spasm of emotion through her body that escaped as a huge wrenching sob.

'Poor Daddy – his face was so grey.'

Michael let her cry. The sounds of sobbing drew the children from their den; Marsha peered anxiously round the door to see her father holding her mother as she cried. Not saying anything – not doing anything really, occasionally stroking her hair, he looked up and caught Marsha's eye. The wink and the smile conveyed its message and Marsha whispered to Dexter.

'It's OK – she's having a good cry; that always helps.'

'Really?' Dexter whispered back.

'Oh yes – Granny told me.'

The sobs eventually quieted to silent tears, and those, too, dried up, leaving Penny looking a dishevelled wreck. Her normally immaculate hair had not been washed for a couple of days and needed brushing; there was even a hint of roots showing through. Her eyes were red and swollen; a small crisp of dried mucus clung to the rim of a nostril and her skin appeared translucent. Michael thought she had never looked so awful and yet so lovely. Here, in his arms, was a real person – something like the Penny he remembered who cried at films and forswore make-up and bras.

'I love you,' he said.

'I know,' she replied.

She told him everything then. She didn't know the figures – she had given up trying to work it all out. It did not and would not ever work out, and she was so sorry. She had just wanted everything to be right – to have the right Things. It was all Things and the new Things were soon old Things and not the right Things any more, so she had to get the right Things like everyone else – and there was his bloody mother with all the wrong things – who didn't try at all – and worse than that didn't even seem to care about having the right things and now she has everything and nothing because she's found the cup and now she will have loads of money which she doesn't want and doesn't need and I do because I've been so stupid and I couldn't ask because then everyone will know that it wasn't real, any of it, ever . . .'

Michael listened carefully, sifting the facts from the self-pity.

'Penny – we are real; the kids are real; none of the rest matters – not really; come on, it's only money. Forget it – I'll sort it; but please, Pen, please don't do anything like this again.'

Penny slept. She slept for hours: a deep restful sleep. Michael had found a relaxing essential oil vaporiser in a drawer when looking for her moisturiser; it had probably been there for years, never used. He read the instructions and lit the nightlight with a flourish when he went to tuck her in. Lavender and marjoram with a hint of rose suffused the room; she breathed it deep into her lungs as she slept.

Michael sat the children down and explained the problem. He telephoned Eric and Elspeth to put them in the picture. Eric offered to help, money-wise – after all, he said, it was their fault too: she had always been so spoilt as a child; had whatever she wanted. Michael thanked him but declined. They would manage.

Then he phoned his mother.

CHAPTER TEN

I had only ever cleansed a woman or a girl at her request. To perform the cleansing on a girl who wants the baby and loves the father is against the old ways. I turned to walk away. The Pilus Prior shouted an order to men outside to bar my path and turn me back. If I did not perform the abortion I would be punished, have my tongue cut out so I could not speak of the Pilus' disgrace, and destroy his plans and his wife's desire for social progress. The mother spoke.

'Leave, husband; leave the creature here with me and the girl. This is women's work – it will be done.'

I looked at the mother and daughter, dressed in fine, coloured fabrics flowing from their shoulders, gathered below their breasts, the fine stuff wafting around their long, straight legs, their covered feet, their skin clean, oiled and perfumed, their hair dressed in fantastic braided constructions about their heads. I knew, from reflections in water, that by contrast I was unspeakable.

'Come,' the mother said. *'Before we speak again about why you are here, let us take you to the baths and find you clean garments.'*

Maisie walked from the orchard through the farm buildings and knocked on the large oak door of Henge Farmhouse. Mr Turnbull was out, she knew: he had thundered past in his tractor as she passed the barn and nodded a dour good morning at her when she waved enthusiastically to him. Violet was in her stone-floored expanse of a kitchen when she heard the knocking. Anxiously, she stalked the hallway and peered through the glass panel at the side of the door. One of the students – she had seen her before – a pretty, dark-haired girl – looked directly at her. Violet opened the door a crack.

'Yes?' she asked, nervously.

'Hello, Mrs Turnbull. I'm Maisie, Maisie Quarrenden, one of the archaeology students.'

'Yes,' Violet replied, opening the door the slightest notch more to reveal a sliver of herself to the girl.

Maisie saw a small wizened, elderly lady, in a vast apron dusted with flour, who looked mostly at the floor, only once glancing up to look into the girl's face.

'Mrs Turnbull, I know it's a bit of a cheek to ask, but I wondered if you had such a thing as a griddle iron I could borrow?'

'A griddle iron?'

'Yes, it's my turn to cook again and I wanted to do a huge pile of drop scones for tea break this afternoon.'

Violet had begun to experience the first physical symptom she endured at coming into contact with outside. She felt cold and clammy, a little unsteady; she wanted to slam this door and rush back to the safe familiarity of her kitchen. She did not want to send the girl away, but she could not talk here; not here.

'Come in child, quickly. I need to shut the door to keep out the draught or my dough won't rise; come on.'

As Violet sped to the kitchen, Maisie had almost to trot to keep up through the confusion of corridors. Violet, now calmer, turned.

'Sit child, sit. I must just take these pies out of the oven.' Maisie watched as the fragile-looking woman heaved two enormous golden-crusted pies from the ancient range and placed them on the long pine table to cool.

'Beef and kidney: their favourite,' Violet said to herself, as she did this.

'Have you got family coming for dinner?' Maisie asked.

'Maybe, maybe,' Violet muttered. 'Maybe . . .'

'Now then, young lass, it'll be a girdle you're looking for – that's what it's called hereabouts. Wait on just there and we'll see . . . yes . . . yes . . .' She reached up to a cupboard. 'In here, I think. I can't quite see; I need my steps.'

Maisie got up to move a stubby set of steps, like library

steps, from the corner over to the cupboard.

'Thank you, child,' Violet murmured.

The girdle was huge and old. A blackly crusted circle of iron with a semicircular hinged handle that folded down, it must have been over two feet in diameter and weighed a ton. Yet the old lady heaved it from the cupboard and carried it down the steps to the table quite vigorously. Maisie had been about to offer to help, but she was glad she had not: Violet Turnbull did not need help and would probably have been insulted by the offer.

'Old as the hills, that is,' Violet said. 'Belonged to my great-great-grandmother, who was from the Orkneys; more drop scones made on that than a body could count in a day, I reckon.'

'It's beautiful,' Maisie said truthfully. 'I love traditional cooking utensils.'

'It does the job it was made for, and will do for many years yet, I hope.'

'I saw one of these in a junk shop in London for four hundred pounds. Someone will buy it and hang it on a wall somewhere and never use it – it's criminal. I went in and offered them fifty pounds – it was all I could afford; even when I told them I actually wanted to use it, cook things on it, they wouldn't sell it to me.'

'Right now, child; off you go with it then and get cooking, otherwise your friends will go hungry and thirsty; and mind you bring it back.'

'First thing tomorrow – I promise.'

'When you do you must stop and have a cup of tea with me. I've several lifetimes' collection of cooking utensils in the back pantry you might like to have a look at – will you see yourself out, lass?'

'Really? OK – that'd be brilliant, Mrs Turnbull – thanks.'

Alone again in the kitchen, Violet sighed as she knocked down her dough, which sighed in sympathy as the air was pushed out. She kneaded energetically – more so than was necessary. The honk of a tractor horn brought her back to the kitchen; she quartered the mountain of dough and plopped it into the greased loaf tins to rise again before baking.

The students and the Professor came back to the orchard camp around three in the afternoon, trickling through the tiny door in dribs and drabs, clapping mud from their hands and discussing their afternoon's work. The huge kettle boiled and everyone made their own tea from a selection of Redbush, Earl Grey, Ginseng, Blackcurrant and Vanilla, and good old proper tea. The mountains of sugar-encrusted drop scones, still warm, delicious and liberally sultana'd, dwindled dramatically until all that remained was warm greasy sugar on the plates. Alex wiped a muddy forefinger across a plate and sucked the sweetness off with lip-smacking delight.

The initial dig proved very interesting. The test pits around the stones themselves revealed little in the way of artifacts – a few Victorian glass beer bottles in the upper layers, the remains of someone's party, or picnic, perhaps – then very little until the evidence of the possible posthole. More excavation would be needed to discover if the posthole was just a single post or one of a number creating an earlier woodhenge. There appeared to be a thin, distinct layer of carbon about ten inches below the surface, as if once there had been a large, fierce fire and in the centre a pit – a cremation, with fragments of human bone scattered within it.

The trench incorporating the compost heap contained seven small, flattened stone eoliths of a type of stone not found in the area, carefully engraved on one surface with cup and ring designs. There was also a bronze implement, like a spatula or narrow scoop, possibly used to extract nourishing marrow from large animal bones. These artifacts were nestled together in an area of darkened humus bestrewn with the remains of burnt wood. The collected artifacts and samples had already been sent off to London. The archaeologists and students were due to pack up and leave the next day, Friday. Tonight, there was to be a party in the orchard.

Everyone was invited: Alice, the Turnbulls – even Professor Allerton was coming up from Durham. Brian and Sarah were coming with the children, Mrs Roberton, some interested members of the Women's Rural, and the minister had said he would pop by.

Maisie, Gail and Alan were in charge of the food. There was to be an enormous spread; Violet had offered to help and volunteered the use of her kitchen. No one was more surprised than Wyllie to see a line of students carrying supplies up his front steps, through his front door and into his house. Violet had not mentioned anything at breakfast.

Violet and Maisie had struck up quite a friendship in the last few days: returning the girdle had been the beginning. They had spent hours poring over implements, Maisie wanting to know what this thing and that thing had been used for. She drooled over copper-bottomed pots and pans; she coveted a vast skillet that hung on the pantry wall. Violet had unearthed an old handwritten recipe book and they had salivated over the rendering of dripping, and the mixing of fruits and spices, eggs, freshly-churned butter, and flour into celebratory cakes. Maisie learned of Violet's agoraphobia and showed neither horror nor sympathy. She had an aunt who had had that – didn't go out of the house for years and years – but she was OK now. Violet wanted to know more about the aunt; she wanted to explain to this slip of a girl – to talk about the difficulties, the stigma, about Wyllie's inability to accept that anything was wrong or to talk about it. She could not tell her about . . . the accident; but she wanted to.

Henge Farm kitchen had been a hive of activity all day. Vast crocks of soup simmered on the range; freshly-baked loaves and rolls were piled up by the oven-full on the pine table. The idea of cooking a savoury pie without meat in it had been a novel one for Violet, but she and Maisie had concocted a vegetarian filling of toasted nuts, grated carrot, and swede and potato bound together with fresh eggs and seasoned with herbs and pepper. Maisie tossed huge bowls of salad together with varying dressings, including a tofu one for the vegans. If Violet found the idea of no meat unusual, the notion of a vegan lifestyle seemed to her some kind of self-imposed torture: no milk, no eggs, no cheese; did they use yeast? Violet wanted to know – after all, surely it is some sort of an animal; it lives and breathes.

By late afternoon, the orchard was permeated by delicious aromas wafting and hanging at nose level in the still, balmy air almost as far down the lane as Orby Cottage. Both Alice and Margaret were excited and repelled in equal measure by the idea of a party. Neither could remember the last party they had been to. Should they dress for it? After all, it was outdoors and very informal, but you could be sure the members of the Rural would be in their best bib. They decided on smart, but casual. Alice wore a rather unbecoming shirtwaister dress in a powder blue with the Hush Puppies for comfort, as there would probably be a lot of standing. Margaret wore a pair of chocolate-brown linen slacks with a long, cream, knitted cotton over-sweater.

The two women walked up the lane to the farm, past the farmhouse where Violet Turnbull sat behind her curtains, past the outbuildings, past Professor Mortimer's trailer, through the tiny door and into the walled orchard. The students had decorated the area with vibrant ribbons and bunting hanging from tree to tree.

'Of course, this is all your fault, Alice McCleish,' Mrs Ollerenshaw, secretary of the Rural, piped up. 'Although I must say it's quite exciting. What unusual tents – puts one in mind of pork pies.'

'We should blame Brian, really – he found the cup. If it hadn't been for him it could have stayed under that compost heap for another couple of thousand years.'

'It's all very pagan though, don't you think? Stone Age savages making child sacrifices; devil worship; I mean, who knows what that cup might have been used for?'

Alice felt uncomfortable with Mrs Ollerenshaw's thoughts about the cup, especially here in the orchard. All the time the ancients had been firmly beneath the soil Alice had been quite content with them. She had imagined them living in a way not so different from that which she remembered from her childhood: basic accommodation, no running water, no heating except open fires, smoky, damp; at least there had been a chimney to take out the smoke, and glass in the windows in the tied cottage she had grown up in. She had visualised the women planting and harvesting and raising too many children on barely enough, salting and drying and grinding and clamping, saving for the harsh wintertime. The men, she imagined, had cleared and ploughed patches of land for planting, hunted for boar and deer, snared rabbits and collected eggs from nests. Her picture, she realised, was almost entirely based on the things Callum had told and shown her all those years ago. Mrs Ollerenshaw's picture was startlingly different. Margaret noticed her friend looking as if she needed saving from the twinsetted Rottweiler who was pinning her up against the buffet table.

Alison introduced Mrs Ollerenshaw. '. . . and this is Professor Margaret Allerton.'

Mrs Ollerenshaw was silenced.

'Nice to meet you, Mrs . . . um . . .'

'Ollerenshaw,' Alice prompted, suppressing a smile. She knew full well that Margaret had guessed that this must be she; Alice had described her in detail earlier.

'Oh look, Alice, we must go over and have a chat with that nice girl Maisie.'

Margaret led Alice off towards the yurts, where most of the students sat, eating, drinking and smoking.

'Hello Alex, hello Maisie.'

'Hi Alice, hi Prof.,' the pair replied as they disentangled themselves from each other.

'I just can't believe you'll all be off tomorrow. I shall miss you all.'

'I know,' Alex shrugged. 'Sad, in't it?'

Brian, Sarah and the children came over to join the group.

'Does this mean I can have my veg plot back now?' Brian joked.

Behind her curtains, Violet Turnbull suffered. Wyllie had gone over earlier; he had said he wouldn't be long. She had seen the Ollerenshaw woman and her covey of Rural members pick their way across the farmyard; the minister had arrived in his mouldering Morris Traveller; the gardener chap and his pretty young wife in her long skirts and shawl (surely she could have got a babysitter: fancy trailing little ones around at this time); Marge Watt and her husband – they had all passed the farmhouse.

The evening light was fading and the sky above the orchard on the west side took on a rosy glow. As the sun began to set in the late June sky, slivers of cloud lit from behind made a stained glass fretwork of the horizon and, as the sun sank slowly, an enormous carmine-tinted full moon eased itself above the orchard wall to the east. Violet could see the glow of the bonfire lighting the darkening sky over the orchard. She tried to imagine the orchard, but all she could see was the last thing she had ever seen through that tiny wee door in the wall . . .

It had been a long hot day, the apple trees had been going through the June drop and the ground beneath the trees was littered with foetal apples, nature's thinnings. The twins had been playing in the orchard since midday. They had taken a picnic – cheese and chutney rolls, rock buns, and a bottle of cream soda. Violet had been washing bed linen that morning and she had just gathered the fresh-smelling crisp cotton from the washing line and folded it for ironing the next day. Violet had walked past the outbuildings, where she had waved to Wyllie as he sorted out sacks of feed. She was tired, but very happy: she had a good husband, two adorable sons, and she was going to retrieve them now and cosset them with food. She would bathe the dust and dirt of the afternoon from them, then dry and dress them in their pyjamas. She would tuck them in and finish the story of *Twenty Thousand Leagues Under the Sea* and kiss them, because very, very soon they would be too old for such childish cherishing.

No one had been able to explain how, or why: it was inexplicable. A game gone wrong? The two of them had hung like weird fruit, each in a separate tree. When Violet thought of the orchard she could only see herself – happy, smiling, calling out their names, opening the tiny door into the orchard where they should have been safe, looking around at child height level and seeing nothing; raising her eyes to see . . . Someone screamed, a strangled, ancient cry that echoed around the orchard wall . . . then – nothing, except the bed, the doctor and Wyllie like a tormented ghost in the background, saying nothing.

Violet wanted to go to the party. The girl Maisie attracted her – had got under her skin somehow, the way she talked about the agoraphobia as if it were just another illness – like flu or measles – something that could be cured. Maisie had written down her aunt's phone number for Violet, had suggested that Violet might want to talk sometime. The aunt had been told and would be more than willing to be of help if she could. Talking was the one thing Violet missed. She had the occasional visitor; Marge Watt popped in from time to time – she had come often in the early days. Violet would not see the doctor: after all, she was not ill; she was grieving. The minister, Grigson then, had done his best to help – the boys had been buried properly, in the village graveyard, together – despite mutterings about suicides and burials outside the graveyard wall. The funerals had been Violet's last experience . . . out there. She had remained upright and silent throughout the service and the interment, waiting for it to end. Wyllie held her elbow, supporting her, until the two small coffins were lowered into their shared resting place. He had crumpled to his knees, leaving Violet standing, silent, absent.

Callum McCleish had gathered his boss up from the ground, the mud of the grave sticking to his wedding and funeral suit. Alice and Marge had taken Violet by an elbow each and led her to the chief mourner's cart, pulled by a black horse and decorated with bows of black crêpe paper. There had been a wake of sorts in the farmhouse parlour. Violet had spent the days leading up to the funeral baking pies and bread and a spiced ham and boiled beef for the funeral tea.

Violet knew that this was the time her real life ended; she had stayed, as she had been before, cooking for her two dead babies and terrified of what was waiting for her outside. Over the years, the baking obsession had lessened. In the first few years Wyllie had taken the pies and bread to old people and struggling families, where they had been received with understanding. They were helping Violet and Wyllie – this was no charitable act, it was understood that such a tragedy would affect the poor lass, and if the baking helped her, then they were pleased to accept it. Wyllie had hoped that the self-imprisonment would also end, but it never had. It had taken years before doors inside the house could be left closed. All inside doors had to be open all the time; then there could be no nasty surprises behind them. Doors to the outside were kept firmly shut at all times. She could look out through windows, but to open a door wide to the outside world and look out was impossible. Violet was sure in her heart that – through the open door – would be something . . . terrible.

Still, she yearned to be at the party, to see the yurts, to sit with Maisie, to talk to Alice – Alice, who had tried so hard to help her poor neighbour who had lost her two babies, never truly knowing why. Violet turned from the window and picked up the telephone; carefully dialled the number. The telephone at the other end rang three times before the receiver was picked up.

'Hello?'

Violet said nothing.

'Hello,' the voice repeated. 'Avian Tyler speaking. Who's there?'

'Hello . . .' Violet faltered. 'Hello Miss Tyler . . . your niece Maisie gave me your number. I hope you don't mind me calling like this . . .'

CHAPTER ELEVEN

The woman handed me over to two slave girls; dark they were, eyes like sloes, hair long and the colour of ravens' wings shining blue through the black, glistening with oil. I followed them, my hobbled walk like a broken stick to their willow wand grace. Another square building; smoke seeping through cracks in the walls and from the roof . . . but the smoke was steam. They removed my rags and covered my sallow skin with oils. The heat and steam made breathing difficult; my sweat ran as if my darkest fear hung around me in the moisture-laden air. They took a metal knife from the wall and I was sure that death was near. I shook as they approached and crumpled to my knees. They spoke – but I did not understand. They giggled at my fear and showed that the knife was not for cutting, but for scraping, like the curing of an animal hide. They drew the metal across my skin, scraping away the sweat and oil and with it the filth with which I was encrusted.

After, they led me to a room with water captured in a pool

with straight sides, decorated with monsters, some like fish, some the like of which I had never seen. They pushed me towards the water. Never had I felt warmth from water except for cooking and I was sure they were about to cook me. I struggled and cried but the girls – despite their slender limbs – were strong, and slowly they led me down steps into the water. They entered the water with me, their thin robes clinging to their bodies. My fear became less: they would not cook themselves.

Avian Tyler had replaced the telephone receiver with a sigh. Maisie had written about the elderly woman in the big farmhouse and how she could not bear to go outside. Avian's own experience of agoraphobia had been short-lived by comparison: Violet Turnbull had rarely left her home in over thirty years. Their conversation had been brief and difficult; Avian had picked up very quickly that Violet was holding back, staying firmly behind her doors – physically and emotionally. Avian had offered to come to Henge Farm to see if she could be of any help, but Violet had been very unwilling. Avian had not pushed the issue – after all it was plain that the process was already under way. Maisie had been a catalyst and Violet had begun to consider that her life, what remained of it, could be different. Avian had finished the conversation by pressing home the idea that she would be happy to help in any way she could, and that Violet could phone any time she wanted someone to talk to.

Avian needed to go outside into the fresh air. She threw on a stripy patchwork padded jacket that she had made, slipped her bare feet into a pair of battered red clogs and clonked off along the path to the park.

Violet trembled from head to toe. She stood, still holding the phone receiver in her hand, listening to the buzz of the dialling tone. What was she doing phoning some woman she did not even know, the aunt of some young flibbertigibbet who happened to speak to her during the summer, who pushed her way into Violet's kitchen, who made her be involved with something going on outside, who lived in a yurt, who was young and who could and probably would have a football team of children . . . who had opened a dark door by just a cranny. She replaced the receiver with tears streaming down her wrinkled, blood-drained cheeks, and stood still, holding on to it, pressing it down into its cradle, for a long time.

'I'm sure I am quite the wrong person to help with this problem, Alice.' Margaret had been surprised to be asked. Alice had been invited to appear on a morning television programme, which Margaret had never heard of, GMTV or something, and was in a tizzy about what she should wear.

'If I were you I'd get that daughter-in-law of yours to help; she may have her problems but she is one of the most stylish young women I've seen for quite a while.'

'Perhaps you're right,' Alice replied. 'Anyway, Margaret, how are you keeping? You must come up again to stay soon; it is so quiet up here now that the dig is over.'

'I'm fine, thanks; this damp spell of weather makes my arm stiffen up and my wrist uncomfortable, but otherwise I couldn't be better. I have another session of talks lined up for the University of the Third Age – one of my students is in her nineties; makes me feel almost youthful. Oh Alice, I think there's somebody at my front door . . . must dash . . . speak to you soon. Bye.'

Dear Penny,

I was pleased to hear from Michael that you are feeling so much better. How are the children? It was such a treat having Marsha to stay during her half-term break – she enjoyed the bustle of the dig, and Professor Mortimer said he was most impressed with her enthusiasm. Margaret's solicitors are dealing with the final details about the sale of the cup, and I should be a woman of substance very soon. Margaret has been such a good friend to me over all this; I would never have been able to cope with all the fuss without her help and advice. I hope you are lucky enough to have such a good friend.

You and I both know that we have never exactly seen eye to eye on much – on anything, really. That is such a shame don't you think? Perhaps now it's time for you and me to make a fresh start and try to get to know each other a bit better. I feel guilty about what I said to you the last time you were here, about the money, especially considering what happened later. I am sorry.

I wonder if you could help me with something. Margaret sug-gested you would be just the person to ask. I am going to be on the television, and I don't have a clue what to wear. They are all so glamorous on TV and I don't want to look like a dowdy old woman. You have always had such good taste, just like the magazines. What sort of thing should I look for? When I come down would you prefer it if I stayed in a hotel? I don't want to be a nuisance – the telly will be paying, but I would love to see the children.

Best wishes,

Alice

Penny looked at the postmark; a handwritten envelope – rare, except at Christmas; it must be for Michael. She looked again – no, it was definitely for her, Mrs M McCleish, from her mother-in-law. She read the contents and laughed – a sad laugh – poor old Mum McCleish. Then she cried. That woman, the woman who made no effort at all, who had friends, who had the luck of the devil, who did not care if her furniture and decoration was so old it was almost fashionable again, who Michael loved, who Marsha never stopped rabbit-ing on about, with her stinking dog and caring neighbours . . . was sorry, was hoping that Penny had a good friend. Penny had hundreds of friends; unfortunately none of them had bothered to visit when she was 'not herself' as she put it. There had been a jointly-signed Get Well Soon card from work, and one or two inquisitive phone calls deftly deflected by Michael.

Michael had been marvellous. He had been to see Mr Winterbottom, the bank manager, and re-jigged their finances to something almost manageable. Penny had decided to hand in her notice at work – to save face as much as for any other reason – and to look for a better-paid job, maybe even full-time as the children did not need her to be at home any more.

Penny's first instinct was to say no, she could not really help; but there was a challenge hidden in Alice's letter. For years, Penny had been spouting on about what would be best for Alice. It would be better if she . . . She really should do . . . Your mother should not wear pale blue: she looks washed out and old . . . Have you seen the state of those Hush Puppies? Penny picked up the phone and dialled.

'Hello? Hello Mum . . . it's Penny. I just got your letter.'

'What do you mean my mother's coming down for a few days? She hates London.'

'I have invited her to stay with us when she comes down for the television interview, and get this – she has asked me to help her decide what to wear. Wear! She doesn't know the half of it. I've booked her a hairdresser's appointment with Marco, and a makeover with Carmen, and a manicure and pedicure too. Then we are going shopping.'

'What about the dog?' Michael asked.

'Well, apparently the dog beautician who does its stinking fur has fallen in love with the thing and has offered to take it into her home for the duration.'

CHAPTER TWELVE

The two dark slave girls washed my body with perfumed bars that foamed like soapwort, unwrapped my hair and washed it too. With small bone rakes they teased my hair as if they wished to weave it like sheep's wool – it took a long time, and caused me much pain. They wrapped my shining body in cool, clean linen and tied it at my shoulders. My hair they oiled and braided, looping it around my head, holding it in place with more bone rakes.

It was a whirlwind few days for Alice. She had imagined visiting one or two shops and choosing a nice outfit that would also do for special occasions like the Christmas service, or christenings. She had arrived at King's Cross at lunchtime on Tuesday; Penny had been there on the platform to meet her. Penny gave her nervous-looking mother-in-law a brief half hug of greeting then whirled her down into the Underground and onto a Tube to Putney Bridge.

The new house was indeed just like something out of one of the magazines in the doctor's surgery: cavernous and empty, to Alice; high-ceilinged and large-windowed. Penny had made up the smaller spare room next to the children's bathroom for Alice; it faced the garden, not the road, so it would be quieter. A small vase of white iris sat on the dressing table, the single bed was covered with a matching quilt and cushions in white – the whole room was white except the carpet, which was clotted cream. Very pretty, but not very practical, Alice thought.

Dinner with the children and Michael did not happen until after seven in the evening – very late for Alice, who feared the garlic bread would give her fierce indigestion. Some family gossip round the table followed; the glass of red wine went to Alice's head and knees. She tottered off to bed at nine-thirty and unexpectedly slept like a log.

The following morning after breakfast, Penny explained the shower controls and Alice revelled in the unfamiliar sensation of hot water pouring down her body. A shower hat borrowed from Marsha covered her hair. One wall of the shower was a mirror. Alice tried hard not to look at her body in the mirror; it was many years since she had last seen her naked reflection full-length and even back then gravity had started to make its ravages obvious. Her pubic hair was grizzled, her buttocks and breasts and belly hung weightily, the skin under her upper arms hung down like curtains – like wings, she thought. This was a foolish venture. No matter what anyone did to her or for her she was without doubt a dowdy old woman. She should have known better than to try and be anything but.

The salon was bright and mostly stainless steel; the receptionist was haughty and the music soporific. The smell was the only thing in any way like the hairdresser's in Berwick. Penny swanned in ahead of Alice, waving a dismissive hand at the receptionist.

'Nine-fifteen with Marco; Mrs McCleish. This way, Mum.'

Coats were taken away and hung with care on hangers by a waif with lilac hair. A tall willowy black girl with glistening hair intricately braided, wafted a soft pink coverall over Alice's ample bosom and sat her down in a comfy chair next to the array of marble sinks.

'Your hair is very dry, Alice,' the girl said, as she ran her hands through the grey straw. 'Do you use a conditioner?'

'No,' Alice replied; she was pleased the young woman had used her name like that. 'What is your name, dear?'

'Blossom.'

'No, Blossom, I've never used conditioner. I normally get my hair permed and set every few months at my usual hairdresser. My daughter-in-law insisted I come here and see Marco because I am going to be on the television tomorrow.'

'Really? Cool – what programme?'

Marco drifted over to have a look at this old bird that awkward Penny McCleish had brought in. He knew Penny would complain loudly and publicly if she did not get what she wanted.

'Marco, this lady is going to be on telly tomorrow.'

'How exciting! What programme?'

Alice explained briefly about the cup, the dig and the telly. Penny could see that Alice was settled and happy; she had given Marco and the make-up girl an idea of the transformation she intended to perform on her mother-in-law, so he had an idea of the look Penny was aiming for.

'OK, Mum – I'm off now; I'll collect you about twelve-thirty and we'll get lunch somewhere.'

Alice lay back and finally relaxed as Blossom dampened her hair and began to gently shampoo with some wonderful smelling substance, the fragrance of which reminded Alice of coconut and conkers. Her hair was rinsed and towel-dried a little, then conditioner was combed through and massaged into her hair, then rinsed away gently. Finally, her head was wrapped in a soft warm towel and Blossom led her to the chair where Marco was waiting.

'Now, Alice, what shall we do with you to make you glamorous?'

He looked at her reflection in the mirror intently. Alice wondered what he saw. She saw an old wrinkled face naked under the bright light with nowhere to hide; she looked down into her lap. Marco tilted her head back up.

'You have a heart-shaped face,' Marco muttered, more to himself than Alice. 'Good cheekbones still – good healthy skin tone.' He lifted up sections of hair, ran his fingers through.

'I think we should go for quite short – not quite Judi Dench – too severe; add a touch of colour – not all over, just some warm lowlights – TV lights will make your white hair look yellowy or bluey or even greeny . . . and no perm.'

'No perm!' Alice coughed. 'No perm . . . surely I need a perm?'

'Definitely no perm. Alice, put yourself completely in our hands; we won't let you down. Promise.'

Penny returned at twelve-fifteen. She trusted Marco implicitly, but she was not sure how much Alice would insist on making decisions.

Blossom saw Penny come in. 'Penny – hello; your mum-in-law is just finishing her manicure.'

'How has she been?'

'Great – really good, and she looks great – you won't recognise her.'

Blossom was right: Alice looked wonderful – from the neck up. Her hair lay softly round her face and hung just above her collarbone; subtle hues had been carefully applied to give an all-over honey tone with the merest hints of old gold and copper. Her face had been subtly made up using nothing except a light translucent powder with a trace of bronzing blusher to accentuate the cheekbones. Her eyebrows had been tidied up and tinted, and her eye make-up showed just a suggestion of autumn hues. Her nails were copper coloured and beautifully shaped; her roughened hands looked nourished and softened.

Penny clapped her hands. This was exactly what she wanted; now she had a canvas for the clothes.

'Marco, Marco, you are a genius!' Penny exclaimed loudly enough for the entire salon to hear.

Give her her due, Marco thought: she praises as loudly as she complains.

'Right, Mum – lunch. I thought we might go back home; what do you say?'

'What about the clothes shopping, Penny? We won't have much time if we go back to Putney for lunch.'

'We don't need to go to the shops, Mum; the shops have come to us.'

'What on earth do you mean?'

'Come on back home and I'll show you.'

Alice understood when she got into the car why she had no need to be anxious. The back seats were piled high with clothes shop bags, plain and glitzy, large and small, and several boxes of shoes.

'I thought you might be overwhelmed by choices so I've got all these goodies for you to try on at home and decide.'

'How on earth did you manage that?'

'I just told them I was a personal shopper and stylist for a TV presenter – ran up some cards and false headed notepaper on the computer – easy. What we don't want, we return.'

The two women rushed their lunch and spent a thoroughly enjoyable afternoon trying out different outfits and combinations.

'Remember Mum, you'll be sitting down – so a long skirt like this will not ruck up and show your knees. This one is too tight . . . go on . . . sit down in it; see – it all bunches up around your tummy. That creamy-coloured top is OK but you are going to look very sort of beige all over if you wear that; you need to stand out, not disappear into the background. No, that won't do – don't forget the sofa is blue, and imagine that against the sofa – it would be like camouflage: you'd disappear from view.'

Alice decided she just could not decide.

'You choose, Penny – you know what looks best. I don't look like myself in any of these outfits; you are my personal shopper, you decide.'

Michael, Marsha and a less enthusiastic Dexter sat in the kitchen.

'We want our dinner,' they chorused, childishly.

'Wait, just wait until Granny McCleish comes down,' Penny insisted.

'Bloody hell,' Michael gasped.

Dexter wolf-whistled loudly and Marsha rushed up from the table to hug her Granny.

'Granny, you look brill,' she sang, as she stood back, then circled Alice.

'Well, I've Penny to thank; I could never have done this for myself.'

'Honest, Mum – you really do look so . . . well . . . amazing.'

Penny got the digital camera out and took several photographs of Alice, some close-ups of the make-up, so the TV make-up artist and hairdresser would know the look to aim for. Alice got changed and they all had a late dinner.

The car came to collect a nervous Alice very early next morning. Penny got up to see her off and make sure she had everything she needed. She waved goodbye at the door in her dressing gown as the car whisked Alice off through the still sleepy streets.

Michael, Marsha and Dexter ambled downstairs at their usual times and ate, washed and dressed for school or work. Penny sat down with a large coffee and a chocolate croissant and turned on the television. The video recorder was set ready to push the record button on the remote control to capture the item and show it back to everyone that evening. During the morning she returned the unwanted items of clothing to the stores which had been so helpful.

'Anytime we can be of assistance, Mrs McCleish – anytime.'

Penny arrived home just before the taxi deposited an exhausted Alice at the door.

'Oh Mum, how did it go? You looked wonderful.'

Alice was bustled into the house and into the kitchen and

sat down and fussed over. Alice gulped down a large mug of tea and waited while Penny poured her another.

'It was OK. I was so scared but they made me feel quite at home – Lorraine is especially nice – very down to earth. The lights were hot and there were cameras, and camera and sound men all over. They let me know what questions they might ask so I could have a wee bit think about it before we started. What was it like? Did I make a complete fool of myself?'

'You want to see it now?'

'Do you think I should? Are you sure it was OK?'

Penny led Alice into the sitting room. 'Here, sit here. I'll turn it on and bring us in another cup of tea.'

Penny left her mother-in-law to watch it alone. She came back in with the tea just as Alice's bit was finishing.

... Well Alice, thank you so much for coming in today and telling us about the wonderful gold cup found in your garden under the compost. Now – over to Joanne for the weather.

'She was lovely: after the programme she came and found me in the green room for a chat. Do you know what she said? She said she had been very surprised when she met me, she had seen a couple of the newspaper articles and photographs whilst doing a bit of research for the interview and she couldn't believe I was the same woman. I told her all about you and how you had told a little white lie to the shops and arranged the appointments with Marco and the girls and she suggested you should do it for a living.'

'Really? I'd love to do that; perhaps I could.'

'She really meant it; she said you should get in touch with her – she could do with a change of image.'

Penny smiled at Alice. If only it were that easy.

The family viewing took place as soon as everyone was home. 'Everyone' included two of Marsha's friends from school who wanted to see the granny who had been on the telly. Dexter watched quietly but was not so enthusiastic – after all how uncool must it be to have a granny who found a battered old cup? The cool bit was how much money she might get for it, and how much of it might come his way. Marsha bathed in the second-hand glory of this telly appearance, her new friends thought it was really cool, and they liked her gran and asked her lots of questions. Since springtime at the dig, Marsha had joined the school archaeology group and had become good friends with Ester, and Mairi, whose mum was an English Literature lecturer. Her more girly group of friends seemed a bit silly to her now, and boy bands, designer labels and make-up had been relegated to the background by this new interest.

Alice's appearance on morning TV had made her something of a celebrity locally – after all, anyone could dig up some old thing in their garden, but not any old body gets to go on TV. Mrs Ollerenshaw had been on the phone the moment Alice returned from London.

'Alice dear, I would love you to visit for high tea – say,

Wednesday at four o'clock? Lovely . . . marvellous . . . see you then, dear.'

Dear Margaret,

Sorry to have been so tardy about writing. Fancy you popping round to your cleaning lady's house especially to watch me on the television! Thank you so much for the card you sent afterwards. I was a bit afraid that I had made a complete fool of myself. Your advice about asking Penny to help with what to wear was inspired, and it looks like you may have started her off on a completely new career path. The female presenter of the programme, Lorraine, was very admiring of my outfit, especially as she had seen some photos of me in the newspapers beforehand. She could not believe I was the same dowdy woman! I told her how Penny had helped and she said Penny should take it up professionally. Well, I told Penny of course, but she did not take me seriously, as usual. Anyway, for once, I interfered. I phoned the studio and gave Penny's phone number to the presenter who phoned Penny the same day and wanted to meet her for lunch. That was a couple of weeks ago and I don't know if anything's come of it so far. I expect I have done the wrong thing; still, she has tried to interfere in my life plenty of times so I'm just getting my own back.

You must come up for a visit very soon. The garden is looking wonderful – Brian is such a dear, he is growing enough vegetables and fruit to feed half a dozen families and I need some help to get through my lot. I love to sit in my garden of an evening and listen to him and Sarah talking quietly, with Aaron chuckling cheerfully. Nipper loves the children and is particularly patient with Faith as she toddles about. He sneaks off under the fence to be with them quite often, but they don't seem to mind at all – they don't have a dog of their own.

Write soon. Hope you are keeping well and keeping busy.

Love

Alice

Margaret was not well and she knew it. She read the letter and was glad that her friend seemed to be well and happy. She had been feeling tired; perhaps she had been doing too much – perhaps a short break with Alice was just what she needed. It was hot and the air was still; even opening all her windows had not improved the conditions – the little air brought in from outside was tainted by the fumes of summer traffic clogging up Durham. Margaret fanned herself with the envelope, luxuriating in the cooling wafts she created. She rose steadily from her chair taking great care not to rise too quickly: she had been experiencing dizziness and nausea when getting up from a chair or from her bed, and once, from the toilet. She had an appointment with her doctor for a check-up on Friday, but after that there were no arrangements so vital that they could not be broken. She picked up the telephone and dialled Alice's number.

Alice was in Berwick doing an extra large shop when she bumped into Marge Watt at the cheese counter.

'. . . and a small piece of brie, about six ounces, whatever that is in the new gram thingy – I'll never get the hang of it.'

'Don't worry love, most of our older customers still order in pounds and ounces, and some not so old too. Is that the lot then?'

'Alice, how are you? I saw you on the telly, you know. I wouldn't have recognised you – you looked fabulous,' Marge trilled.

'I knew I recognised you from somewhere,' the girl behind the cheese counter interrupted. 'You found a gold wotsit in your compost heap.'

Alice smiled indulgently and replied to Marge. 'Margaret is coming to stay for a week or two, so I'm getting in some extra goodies; she is especially fond of these French cheeses – smell a bit like they've gone off to me.'

'How is Margaret – wrist and so on not playing her up, I hope?'

'Not this time of year – only when it's damp, she says. You must pop in while she is staying; she's coming up on Friday for a fortnight. She has a soft spot for you, always asks how you are.'

'Really? Hard to imagine Margaret having a soft spot for anyone, except perhaps you. I would love to see her again – maybe Tuesday, that's my half day. I'll phone you beforehand just to make sure you two haven't got other plans.'

'That would be lovely. I'll make sure to bake another coffee sponge. Bye, Marge.'

Marge headed off towards the freezer section and Alice to pet foods.

When Margaret got off the coach on Friday evening Alice was shocked. Margaret looked hunched and pale – and old. Could this really be the same woman she mistook for a youngster clambering over Wyllie Turnbull's fence?

'Hello Margaret!' she called. 'Hello.'

'Alice.' Margaret straightened and laboured a smile.

'You look exhausted – come on, the car's just over here.'

Alice put the luggage in the boot, peering with concern around to the passenger's side to watch Margaret lower herself slowly into the seat. She hoped it was just the result of an uncomfortable journey, yet a warning bell tinkled somewhere in her mind – something was wrong, that was for certain.

Alice drove home slowly, even more slowly than usual, as if she were tending a child or an invalid; a comforting drive, through country lanes on a warm August evening with the breeze through the windows heavy with the smell of newly-cut grass from the silage fields. If Margaret noticed, she certainly never said anything. They were mostly silent; Alice pointed out four buzzards circling lazily on the rising thermals. Margaret breathed in great lungfuls of clean air, and bemoaned the pollution in Durham. Alice said that Marsha was hoping to visit for a weekend just before going back to school.

They arrived at Orby Cottage just as Brian was parking up to spend some time in the allotment. He came over to say hello. Alice saw from his expression that he, too, was taken aback by the change in Margaret. He left to get on with a bit of hoeing, turning down Alice's offer of a cup of tea, leaving the women to enter the house together. Nipper woofed and bounced about a bit as usual and Alice noticed Margaret grab at the back of a chair for support, as if she was afraid of being knocked over. She seemed . . . vulnerable – not a word anyone would have used to describe her before. They ate a light supper of salad from the garden and home-baked cheese scones with home-made apple chutney. Alice insisted they have an early night and the two were in their beds before Brian left for home.

Margaret had the upstairs bedroom, which used to be Michael's. The bed was comfortable and Alice had just made it up with sheets and one blanket because of the heat; there was a light bedcover folded at the end in case Margaret needed it.

Margaret was still recovering from the embarrassment of having to ask if Alice had a commode or some such thing, as she did not think she could make it downstairs in the nighttime. Alice had not batted an eyelid: of course she had a spare gazunder; everyone had a gazunder – Alice herself always kept one in her bedroom, especially in the winter. Who wanted to have to creep all the way downstairs in the cold when you could just hop out and quickly back into a warm, cosy bed?

Both women lay awake for a time, the heat making sleep difficult to attain. A soft breeze gently moved the curtains, and outside, birds sang their evening songs, waiting patiently for the light of the late summer day to fade. Alice worried about Margaret. Tomorrow, when she had settled down a bit and eaten a decent breakfast, Alice would ask her what was wrong. It would be no good waiting for Margaret to offer any information, Alice would have to be quite blunt and say how worried she was, and if Margaret took offence, then that was how it would have to be. She was glad Marge Watt was popping round on Tuesday.

Margaret slept on and on the next morning. Alice was up and about at her usual time, around seven o'clock. She walked Nipper along the lane before the day got so hot that even he would prefer to remain in the shade. Margaret still had not got up when they returned. Alice made some tea and decided to risk taking her guest a cup in bed.

She knocked gently on the bedroom door and carefully opened it. She peered round to see Margaret still in bed, still asleep. Alice decided to chance waking Margaret. She put the cup of tea down on the bedside table and gently shook her friend's shoulder. Margaret's eyes opened and she yawned a gummy yawn. Suddenly she realised that she was not alone, and not at home; she sat up too quickly and any colour she had in her face drained away: she looked grey and about to faint. Alice held her and helped her prop herself up in bed with pillows.

'Margaret, should I call a doctor?'

'No – just pass me my teeth, will you, please.'

'Are you sure you don't need a doctor? It could be a heart attack.'

Alice was afraid. Callum had gone ashen, but he had pain in his arm and chest.

'Is there any pain in your arms or chest?' she fretted.

'No, there is not; now please stop fussing and pass me my teeth.'

'I'm so sorry I startled you like that. Here, have your tea . . . oh, it's gone quite cold. Stay there and I'll brew a fresh pot.' She left the room muttering more apologies as she went.

She brought two cups of tea back up to the room and sat on the chair and watched Margaret slowly drink hers. Some bloom gradually returned to Margaret's cheeks as she sipped the hot, sweet tea.

'It's my blood pressure – apparently it's quite low, and when I move about too quickly I get wobbly and faint. In a quieter voice she added, 'Alice, it can be very frightening, especially when I am alone. Last night was the best night's sleep I have had for several months – because I knew I was not alone. My doctor wants me to get one of those alarm things you wear around your neck which alerts someone somewhere when you press it and they will phone to see if you are OK, and if you don't answer they alert the authorities.'

'Oh, Margaret! Why on earth didn't you tell me this sooner?'

'Tell you what? That I am old and sick and frightened and do not want to be on my own – moan on about not having any family to visit or care for me – wallow in self pity – not my style, is it?'

'When did it start?'

'Not long after I arrived home following the party in the orchard. At first it was just when I stood up too quickly – and just a little dizziness. It became more frequent and several times I thought I was going to pass out – or pass over – I didn't know which.'

'How are you feeling now?'

'Oh, it soon passes. I'd like to get up now.'

'How about some breakfast? You must have some break-fast – you look very thin and fragile.'

Margaret flinched at the word 'fragile'. Alice noticed and wondered if she had gone too far, but Margaret said nothing.

'I'll leave you to get dressed, then,' Alice said, and made to move from her chair.

'Alice, could you stay . . . would you mind? Just in case.'

Margaret was up and dressed and in the bathroom. Alice was making more tea, and thickly buttering some slices of toast and piling them on a pretty blue and white plate. If there was one thing guaranteed to tempt an ailing appetite it was the smell of hot buttered toast. Margaret came into the small kitchen just as Alice placed the plate of toast on the table next to the teapot, steaming away under its embroidered cosy. She turned to the cupboard and produced a pot of home-made, thick-cut marmalade, placing it next to Margaret at the table. In her head she was planning a menu of nourishing food for the next fortnight: her friend needed feeding up and caring for, and Alice was just the person for the job.

After breakfast they sat outside in the garden until it got too hot, then they moved into the shade of one of the apple trees. Here, the two women and one dog dozed companionably until lunchtime. They were woken by the arrival of the Rigden family. Brian's van pulled up and parked by the gate into the vegetable patch. Sarah wheeled Faith in the buggy into the shade of the toolshed while Aaron bumbled along the path behind her. He stopped at the fence that bordered Alice's garden and called out.

'Nipper! Nipper!'

Nipper had barely even bothered to raise his head when Brian drove up – it was certainly far too hot to consider playing with those little humans. He decided he would be better off indoors and out of sight: the kitchen floor, cool and quiet, beckoned. Alice got up and wandered up to the fence.

'Hello, young Aaron; how are you today?'

'Where's doggy gone?'

'He's gone indoors for a nap – it is too hot for him to come and play today.'

Sarah came over. 'Now you leave Mrs McCleish in peace, Aaron. She has got a friend staying for a holiday and they won't want you in the way. Hello, Alice – how's the Professor this morning?'

'Not too bad,' Alice replied.

'Brian was quite worried about her when he came home: he said she looked terrible.'

'She just needs some fresh air and a bit of peace and quiet.'

'Would you rather we weren't here, or that the children weren't here, for a while?'

'Certainly not. Margaret would be horrified if she thought you were staying away because of her; anyway, there is no nicer noise, to my mind, than that made by a happy family.'

'We'll be discreet, anyway. I'll bring a basket of raspberries over for you both, later . . . a few strawberries too?'

'Lovely, Sarah, thank you. I was wondering . . . the children . . . calling me Mrs McCleish. I wish they could call me something more . . . oh, I don't know – more friendly.'

'Hello all!' Margaret called from her chair under the apple tree.

'Hello Professor!' Brian and Sarah called back, waving. Aaron waved too.

CHAPTER THIRTEEN

They gave me a bed in a square room. As the light faded and the room darkened I felt the spirits moving outside, calling me back to my own home, my own bed of bracken and animal hides. I had come with nothing – no herb to burn to cleanse this place, no stones to throw to ask the old ones what to do: seven stones – seven symbols, smooth and soothing, cold to the touch.

I lay on the bed and tried to sleep. Unfamiliar sounds filled my head, yet in the background I heard the wind in the trees, the calls of owls, one sharp coughing bark of a vixen. I woke later to the singing of wolves far in the distance, the bonding cry of the pack. I rose, wrapped the woven cloth that covered my bed around myself and crept from the room. All the world was sleeping. Even the guards snored rhythmically as I slipped past them, my way lit by a sickle moon and star-bright sky.

Avian Tyler returned refreshed and invigorated from her walk in the park, clip-clopping along The Cutting, to her home at Number 7, Railway Cottages. The small front garden was stuffed to the gunnels with herbs. Chamomile and thyme draped themselves over the crazy paving stones of the path to the door. As she passed, Avian trod on and crushed them, releasing heady perfumes into the late afternoon air. She stopped and gathered some sprigs of sage as she neared the postbox-red front door with its brass letterbox and lion's head knocker. The distant telephone conversation with Violet had disturbed Avian.

She opened all the windows and the back door to the rear garden then burnt some sprigs of sage from one of the bunches already hanging by the airing cupboard to dry. She wafted the smoke into all corners of the room and left the embers to smoulder in an old ashtray by the phone. The new bunch of sage was tied and hung alongside the others, to dry. Avian decided to investigate where this village called Duddo actually was; it was quite clear that she would eventually find herself there. She turned on her computer and connected to the Internet, clicked Ask Jeeves on her Favorites bar, and typed in the word 'Duddo'.

One of the sites showed a picture of the stone circle against a setting sun. Avian stared and stared into the picture. She decided to print it out, hoping that her colour cartridge had enough ink in it to do so. The printer whizzed and clicked away until the image appeared on the sheet of A4 that emerged. Avian pinned it up on her kitchen wall. Another site provided her with a section of Ordnance Survey map which covered the stone circle, the grandmother's house, the farmhouse and the village; this too she printed out and pinned onto the wall above the kitchen table next to the picture. Now she had an image in her mind of the place. She knew it was somewhere near Berwick-upon-Tweed, because of where the girl had left the train. Avian began to focus her intent.

Margaret began to perk up very quickly. By Tuesday, when Marge Watt popped in for tea, she was feeling almost back to her usual self. Alice had been feeding her up and some of Margaret's sense of vulnerability had lessened.

'. . . not that I really expected to be able to go charging about the countryside forever, but I had hoped I could keep up the walking for a few more years at least.'

Marge, herself, was due for retirement in several months; she looked at the two older women: not that much older, she realised. This will soon be me, she thought.

'Well, I think you should try and be as active as you can. Low blood pressure is generally considered a good thing you know – better than high blood pressure – now that can be dangerous.'

'Yes,' Margaret replied. 'But it's not so much the dizziness – I understand what is happening, lack of blood and oxygen to the brain – it's the fear of actually fainting, of blacking out. It used to happen to me as a young girl, I remember; one minute

I would be getting ready for school, the next, everything would go quiet, then dark, then the droning noise began and the next thing I knew, I was trying to claw my way back from somewhere towards a distant voice, my mother's voice, calling "Margaret . . . Margaret . . ."'

'Well,' said Alice, with feeling, 'I think you should consider yourself blessed. Imagine being Violet Turnbull along there at the farmhouse. She's barely been out of that house since the accident, about thirty years ago. When she does go out, to the doctor's or dentist, Wyllie has to park as close to the front door as he can and literally carry her out. She's OK in the car as far as Berwick; the problems start when Wyllie can't park close enough to where she's got to go to. Many a time she's missed an appointment because she can't walk the few yards from the car to the door.'

'I'm afraid we are not all as Christian as you, Alice.' Margaret snapped. 'To my mind that is mostly self inflicted: it's not that she *cannot* go outside – rather that she *will* not and now it has become a habit – an addiction, if you like.'

'You may be being rather harsh, there,' Marge interrupted. 'Even if what you say is true, is addiction not an illness? Considering what happened to the twins it is very understandable.'

Somewhat put in her place, Margaret replied, 'I've heard mention of "the accident" a few times now – but nobody seems to talk about it.'

Marge Watt told the dreadful tale of the twin boys while

Alice went into the kitchen to make tea. Even now, talk of those two children brought tears to her eyes. She tried to imagine how she might have felt if her Michael had died, even of natural causes. In her mother's and grandmother's day, loss of a child was commonplace: her own grandmother's proud boast was that she bore twelve children and reared seven. Alice, herself, had lost a brother to measles. Even Alice had lost two babies during early pregnancy and endured the heartbreak of a stillbirth. Violet Turnbull had waited years for those babies to come, had assumed herself barren, and had been elated when the twins finally arrived. She had been the most devoted of mothers.

Alice re-entered the sitting room with the tea tray and coffee sponge cake as Marge was finishing the tale.

'. . . and since the day of the funeral she has not been able to set foot outside her own door for fear of what she might see.'

'Is there no treatment available? A psychiatrist . . . bereavement counsellor . . . or some sort of therapist?' Margaret queried.

'I've tried over the years – so has her doctor, but she maintains she is not ill, and that it is just her way of grieving – which was true for the first year or two. You may have a point in calling it a habit, but it is so deeply ingrained in her now that I don't see how things will ever change.'

'So who did it? Who hanged the children?'

'The verdict was death by misadventure. It was assumed

they had hanged themselves in some sort of game of dare. There was talk, of course, there had been an old tramp hanging around the area at the time: he disappeared soon after; some malicious rumours, too, that Violet had done it herself, which no one, not even the police, took seriously.'

Marge left after tea with a bagful of vegetables from the garden and a jar of raspberry jam. She drove away waving to the two older ladies who stood by the gate waving back to her. Marge was looking forward to retirement: Ron and she were planning a cruise to celebrate, and then they had a wish list of holiday destinations they planned to work through at their leisure.

Penny McCleish had been livid to find her mother-in-law had given her phone number to someone without checking with her first. At the same time, her anger was lessened by the result of that very action. Lorraine Merryweather had called her to arrange to meet for lunch. They had met at the Kensington Roof Gardens and had hit it off from the start. Lorraine crowed with laughter at the idea of Penny running off cards and headed paper and persuading stores to hand over a wide selection of expensive clothing without even demanding a deposit.

'You must have been very convincing. Had you considered doing it professionally?'

'I'd love to, but how on earth would I go about becoming a . . . what would you call it – personal shopper? style consultant? – it sounds so pretentious.'

'Listen, if you had a life like mine – up before the milk-man, busy all day, no time to relax – you would know how valuable a life manager can be.'

'I'm not sure I could do it.'

'What have you been doing over the past ten, fifteen years?'

'Having a family; working part-time later on – not much, really.'

'So – not much, you say! You have been cook, cleaner, shopper, carer, mother, nurse, wife, lover, worker, chauffeuse, and secretary, organising the lives of one adult male and two growing children, liaising with schools and doctors, making sure they get to appointments, paying bills . . . I should say you have all the skills necessary to make you a very valuable com-modity indeed – and on top of all that you have impeccable taste and are very stylish. Alice McCleish came as a complete shock to me when I met her at the studio. A researcher had dug out some earlier news clippings and photos of this elderly lady in frumpy clothes; the woman who emerged from make-up was elderly, yes, but she looked fabulous.'

Penny blushed with delight and pleasure. Alice had been quite right: Lorraine was a lovely person – shame about the colour of that top, however: made her look a bit washed out, to Penny's eye.

'I tell you what, Penny; I am taking a much-needed holiday in a month's time. I am going to Venice with a friend and am going to be really pushed for time to shop for some new outfits. I will pay you eighty pounds per hour to do for me exactly what you did for your mother-in-law,' challenged Lorraine.

Penny beamed. 'OK, you're on.'

'Mum, that's brilliant, that's so cool!' Marsha exclaimed.

'Is it? I can't believe it – shopping for someone else, I do the choosing, they pay the bills and pay me for doing it, too. Eighty pounds an hour! That's almost three times more than I got working in that office. It's a bit scary; though Lorraine has given me the names of several places she shops in already, and they know I am coming, so I just go in, choose a bundle of garments and take them to her flat for her to choose from. What could be easier?'

'What do you think Dad will say?'

'I expect he'll say that spending money is what I'm good at and that he's glad it's someone else's money and not ours.'

'You should phone Granny McCleish and tell her – after all, it's all thanks to her, really.'

'You phone and have a chat and I'll speak to her after you, darling.'

Alice put the telephone receiver back down.

'That was Marsha and Penny. Marsha is definitely coming for a weekend in the middle of September, and Penny . . . well, you won't believe it.'

Alice told Margaret all of Penny's news.

'She says it's all thanks to me, but of course it was you who suggested it in the first place.'

'I'm very glad for her. Rest of the family all right? How about that son of yours? Quiet sort of a chap, decent. Is he like his father?'

'In some ways, yes, you just never know what he is thinking; Callum could be like that too. Sometimes he would seem to be so very far away, even when he was in the same room. I would say to him sometimes, "a penny for your thoughts" and he would look at me and smile,' said Alice.

'Do you wish you'd ever had children, Margaret? Was there never anyone special who you wanted to marry?' Alice wondered.

'No – and no, really – simple as that. There was a chap when I was at university, asked me out to tea and a couple of dances. He was arrogant and handsome; came from a good family. He couldn't believe it when I turned down his proposal. He seemed to think he was doing me some sort of huge favour by offering me, a girl of humble origins, the chance to raise my position in society. I'm afraid I was more interested in my studies and the possibility of travel to settle for married life and a horde of noisy children.'

'Do you fancy a day out tomorrow – weather permitting?'

'Yes, I do – where shall we go? Margaret responded enthusiastically.

'Not too far; I don't like to drive too far,' dithered Alice.

'How about the coast? How about Lindisfarne?'

'Oh dear, I've never driven across the causeway myself,' said Alice, momentarily apprehensive. 'Callum always drove; I haven't been there for years.' Then she rallied. 'Where is the local paper? It should have the tide tables in it.'

On the site of the old sacred spring of the tribe, the newcomers had built a worship house. Tall, stone trunks like dead trees stood thickly around the bubbling waters; on their crowns, a roof – not of thatch or branches but of stone, carved with many symbols. A stone hut nestled beneath. Its wooden door was ajar and soft light glowed from within. It drew me closer, closer, until I stood beneath the stone roof. I crept to the open door and peered into the room. The Pilus Prior knelt before a wooden table draped with cloth. On the table were the lights I had seen from outside; flames flickered from the wicks of the many oil lamps, yet there was a deeper glow. The Pilus Prior raised his arms above his head and the source of the glow became clear. In his hands he held a cup of fire. I knew then that I wanted that cup. It was a cup made of sunlight, of fire, of power. I crept back to the strange room and the strange bed. I knew now what my price would be.

Violet Turnbull could not settle – not in front of the TV; not in the kitchen. She was constantly on the move lately. The big farmhouse was spotless except for the twins' room, the door of which had been locked on the day of the accident by Wyllie and had remained locked ever since. Even if Violet knew where the key was she would not have unlocked that door. Her whole life was within the house, and now the house was more than usually tidy and clean and her everyday occupations of cooking or watching TV no longer distracted her thoughts and imaginings. Several times she had stayed her hand as she reached for the telephone. She wondered what she might say to the woman. Violet looked out of the window. It was a glorious day, the first hint of a change of tint in the leaves, the farmyard parched and dusty. In the orchard the fruit would now be beginning to fall from the trees to the ground. There they would lie and rot again this year; boozy wasps would buzz unsteadily from rotting fruit to rotting fruit. The pears would hang unthinned and unprotected from wasps and blackbirds that would not even wait until they fell before piercing their tough skins and devouring the ripening flesh.

Violet dialled the number.

'Avian Tyler speaking . . . who is this? Oh, Mrs Turnbull – I was just thinking about you.'

When Wyllie came in from the fields that evening, Violet had something to say.

'Wyllie, somebody is coming to visit next week – a woman called Miss Tyler, the aunt of that lovely young girl Maisie who was here for the dig – you remember, she popped in to the house to borrow the girdle.'

'Why?' Wyllie grimaced.

Violet Turnbull lied. She hoped Wyllie would not see it in her face.

'She is very interested in old cooking utensils, writing a book or something, and Maisie told her about the Orkney girdle and some of the other stuff in the scullery.'

'When?'

'Next Wednesday – in the morning, and to stay for lunch.'

Avian Tyler walked the couple of miles from the village. The lanes were empty of human noise except for the clip-clopping of her red clogs. In the hedgerows a myriad of birds, racing against the seasons to raise a late clutch, chattered and twittered their conversations. She heard the sharp kee kee kee of a kestrel and looked across the field to see the red flash of the bird's back as it wheeled and banked low to the ground to escape a gang of mobbing crows. The same gang of crows disturbed a tawny owl from its daytime roost and Avian caught a glimpse of it as it too swooped low over the stubble to escape its tormentors. In the vegetable plot Brian heard what sounded like a pony coming along the lane. He stopped his harvesting and leant on the handle of his fork to watch it pass by. The 'pony' peered over the hedge.

'Good Morning; Orby Cottage, is it?' Avian asked.

'Yes – can I help? Are you looking for Mrs McCleish?'

'No, Henge Farm – Mrs Turnbull – which, if I am not mistaken, is along that lane there.'

'Spot on.' Brian replied.

'What a magnificent crop of carrots – organic?'

'Oh, yes.'

'So, this is where they found the golden cup? You must be the man who found it.'

'That's me – Brian Rigden.'

Alice and Margaret were just coming out of Orby Cottage as Avian turned up the lane to the steading. It was quite unusual to see anyone walking by; this tall, upright stranger with her long white plait and her noisy shoes, the hem of her gaudy skirt trailing in the dust, was an unexpected sight.

'Good morning, ladies. Wonderful weather,' she called out as she strode past.

'Good morning,' the ladies replied in unison.

'I wonder who she was,' Alice mused when she and Margaret were comfortably settled in the car. 'I haven't seen her around here before. Why was she going up to the farm? Wyllie will be at the market today, so she must be going to see Violet.'

'She could have been a Jehovah's Witness – or selling something,' Margaret offered.

'No, if she was selling she'd have tried to sell to us, and the Jehovahs always have either a child or an old person with them to try to make you feel you have to let them in and offer them a seat or a drink or something.'

'True, still – it's none of our business.'

'It might not be any of your business, Margaret Allerton, but it is certainly mine. Violet is my neighbour and she is on her own. You stay in the car a minute; I'm going to phone her.'

'False alarm,' Alice reported as she manoeuvered her posterior into the driving seat. 'Apparently Violet was expecting a visitor – writing a book about old kitchen utensils.'

Alice turned the ignition key and started up the car. They waved and called greetings to Brian as they headed off for their day trip to Lindisfarne. Nipper, a picnic and several flasks of tea, and extra cardigans, hats, scarves and mittens – just in case – took up the rear seat.

Avian Tyler turned in the lane and looked behind her to see for the first time the stone circle of Duddo. Circling low above it, three buzzards waited for the heat of the sun to generate rising thermals, their mewling cries echoing, peeioo, in the still morning air.

'As it was, so it shall be,' she muttered, clasping a small leather pouch that hung between her breasts. She would visit the stones soon; for now, she turned her back on them and continued towards the farm. At the gate she stopped, drew in and exhaled three great gulps of air, spread her arms wide, gathered something invisible to her chest, and entered the farmyard.

Her step slowed. She maintained a wary perceptiveness. She was listening for echoes. As a child she had heard these echoes clearly: they had come from the big trees, archaic musty buildings, antiquated furniture, and hand-me-down jewellery. She had lost the echoes, which were not always voices that spoke in words, but were more feelings that made pictures, sometimes with sounds, sometimes not. She had lost the echoes in the telling of them. No one had believed her. Avian had a vivid imagination, they said; Avian told stories, they said, Avian lied, they said. In the end she chose not to tell and not to listen because the echoes got her into trouble. She may have lost them, but she had never forgotten: her dead grandmother's bracelet, which told of the sadness it had absorbed; the ancient oak tree in the park that remembered a fierce and bloody battle that happened in its youth. For years she kept herself protected from these echoes, filtered, shielded, blind and deaf to them, until this denial became second nature. The protecting itself became habitual, until it was not just the echoes she shut herself off from, but the objects themselves: the trees, the buildings – until she became ensnared within her own four walls. She wondered what had happened to Violet Turnbull to have entrapped her here in this farmhouse.

Walking up to the farmhouse door Avian focused her intent. She muttered a little something under her breath, and knocked. The door opened the tiniest crack, as she knew it would. She placed her hand against the oak timber and pushed gently, peering round to see an arm leading up to a shoulder, joined to the back of a person looking steadfastly back into the house.

'Mrs Turnbull? Avian Tyler – you are expecting me.' Avian pushed the door open enough to squeeze through and closed it behind her.

'I'm sorry,' Violet was flustering. 'It's the door, you see, the door.'

'Shall we go through to the kitchen?' Avian suggested.

'My neighbour phoned, you see; said she'd seen you in the lane, was worried about me, and I had thought perhaps you wouldn't come; after all – why should you?'

'Mrs Turnbull . . . Violet . . . come along. I do understand, honestly. I really, really do.'

'Really?' Violet looked up into the tall woman's face for the first time. Avian's calm, quiet gaze and warm smile, very much like Maisie's, reassured her.

'I'll put the kettle on – actually it's on already – the phone call, you know.'

Avian followed a twittering Violet into the large farm kitchen.

'I can see why our Maisie fell in love with this place,' she said, placing a friendly hand on Violet's shoulder.

Violet flinched.

'Oh, I'm so sorry, I shouldn't have done that; it's just that I feel I know you a bit already from Maisie, and it's just so homely in here.'

The kettle steamed, just about to whistle. The huge old range made the cool kitchen with its cold stone slab floor feel warm but not hot; the breeze drifting in from the open window was warm.

'I see you can have the windows open, Violet; at my worst I couldn't even bear to have a window open, even on the hottest days.'

'No. Windows are fine. How awful not to have been able to open a window.'

Violet and Avian sat opposite each other at the kitchen table with their cups of tea.

'What happens now?' Violet asked directly. 'I mean, what do we do – what do *you* do? What do *I* have to do?'

'Not one to beat about the bush then, Violet? Good. I can tell you about myself – what happened to me – how I found out what it was that was at the root of my agoraphobia. You can listen, and be encouraged to find out that you are not on your own, and realise that there are people who do truly understand and will not judge you out there in the big wide world. That will take up most of our morning and will not make any headway into changing your life. Or, you can do the talking and I can do the listening. I'm happy either way. You may not want to talk yet; perhaps you want to get to know me a bit first. Sometimes though, you tell more to a complete stranger. It's up to you.'

'It was thirty years ago last June . . . excuse me . . .' Violet interrupted herself and got up to get a box of paper tissues which she placed on the table. 'I will probably cry,' she explained.

'It was thirty years ago last June, a lovely drying day and I had decided to wash all the bed linen . . .'

At the mainland end of the causeway Alice parked in the visitor's car park. The tide still had a little further to go down before all of the causeway was water free.

'I'm not driving across there yet; look – you can see the cars spraying up water everywhere in the middle bit.'

'You are so cautious, Alice. When I was in Tibet I crossed suspended rope bridges over raging torrents in precipitous ravines, meltwater boiling and crashing far beneath my feet.'

'Yes, well you are you and I am me, and we are waiting another twenty minutes. Do you want an ice cream?'

'But we haven't had lunch yet,' Margaret said, a little shocked at the suggestion.

'Who cares? I'm having a 99. Go on – you're only young once, you know.'

The two women ate their ice creams sitting at a picnic bench.

'Last time I was here I walked across,' said Margaret.

'Across the causeway?'

'No – across the flats by the original path of St Cuthbert's Way. See that group of walkers over there, the ones with crosses on sticks? They will be waiting to walk across.'

'It must be dangerous, all sinking sand and stinking mud – and how do you know where to walk?'

'See that line of tall posts to the right of the causeway? They mark the pilgrim path.'

'Is that what they are? I always wondered about them.'

'Honestly, Alice, you've lived around here all your life; how could you not know?'

'Too busy just living, I suppose; I don't know. It was never the sort of thing my family talked about when I was young. School was mainly the three Rs with cooking and sewing for the girls, then work, then married, then a family of my own to think about.'

'What about the church? Surely you know about St Cuthbert from there?'

'Yes – and no. I've heard of him of course – well, he is a saint. Still, today's the day to educate myself: we'll go to the abbey.'

Nipper returned from some very important sniffing about just in time to get the two pointy end bits of the ice cream cones.

Margaret and Alice settled themselves back into the car and Alice prepared herself for the drive across.

'I always think it's so exciting, like driving along the sea-bed,' she told Margaret as she slowly negotiated the narrow roadway between the rumpled seaweed-strewn verges.

They drove over the raised section next to the escape

tower, where stranded travellers could take refuge from the seas if they mistimed their crossing and found themselves marooned. The causeway wove its way across towards the towering sand dunes of the island. It clung to the base of the dunes as it reached land and edged its way along until it turned in to the windswept salty sheep-grazed land.

They parked and left Nipper in the car for a few minutes while they visited the loos.

'These loos could certainly do with a facelift; I'd rather pay twenty pence and have an attendant to keep them nice, than have to put up with this. I don't imagine people would leave their own loos at home in this condition,' Margaret complained.

'They've been here for years. No one ever expected this many visitors when they went up – it's no wonder they're in a state,' Alice said, apologetically. 'Let's get Nipper and walk to the abbey. Shall we take the picnic with us? We might find a nice little spot out of the wind and in the sun.'

Nipper was a little surprised to be put on a lead; still, he was more than a little surprised to find himself here: ever since his master had gone, a trip in the car usually meant a bath and a haircut with that nice woman who gave him bacon rinds.

The two women and the dog walked from the car park past numerous 'crab sandwich' signs outside cramped fishermen's cottages, and past gift shops peddling miniature bottles of mead, St Cuthbert souvenirs and Holy Island keepsakes.

Tourists thronged the narrow streets, eating ice creams and crab sandwiches. Alice and Margaret wound their way out of the village towards the castle. They sat on the sea wall and watched the seabirds swooping behind the incoming small fishing boats. Margaret insisted on stumbling across the tussocky grass to have a good look at the herring boats miraculously transformed into the most appropriate type of fishermen's huts – upturned, black-tarred, beached hulls with doors and windows; smoke from extruding flues was being snatched away by the wind from the sea.

'Alice, come over here – it's right out of the wind.'

Alice, struggling with the picnic and an unwilling dog on a lead, attempted to cross the uneven tussocky grass. She stumbled a little and let out a gasp.

'Just a minute . . . I'll bring Nipper first and come back for the picnic,' she called back.

'No, you won't, my lovely; you just give me those bags and I'll make sure you get across all right.'

The man was short and round, his cheeks and nose ruddy and sea-wind burnt. On his head he wore a knitted hat that might once have been a tea cosy; his legs and feet were enveloped in green rubber waders. His accent, so similar to the local mainland accent, but with subtle differences, marked him out to Alice as an islander born and bred.

'You're very kind,' Alice said, happy to get rid of the cumbersome bags.

'I'll take the dog too, if you like,' the fisherman offered.

'Does he need to be on a lead?'

'No, not really, I just didn't want him to be a nuisance, and the sign does say . . .'

'Bugger the sign,' he said; and he leant down to unhook the lead from Nipper's collar.

'Now then, old lad,' he insisted, ruffling the untidy fur on the dog's head. 'You enjoy yourself. Bloody stupid signs.'

They approached a waiting Margaret, who was peering in at the window of one of the herring boats.

'Alice, come and look – these are so fascinating.'

Alice looked at her kind escort, who looked back with an amused smile.

'So, you're local and your friend not?'

'You are quite right. My name is Alice McCleish and I bide at Duddo. Margaret is my dearest friend, and she is from Durham. She's a professor, you know.'

'Fancy that. Now then, Professor; if you're so interested, let's get you inside.' He rattled a bunch of keys. 'Never used to have to lock 'em you know,' he explained, with sadness.

Margaret and Alice never got to the abbey, or the castle. They spent the most charming of afternoons in and around the fisherman's hut. It was clean and shipshape and they sat at a table and chairs in the sun for their picnic out of the wind while their new friend, Andrew, mended nets. Nipper sniffed around at the interesting fishy, seaweedy, salty smells until he had sniffed enough, and then he curled up in the sun on the mended net. The lukewarm tea in their flasks was poured away as they now had a kettle at their disposal.

When Andrew had finished his odd jobs he joined the women, pulling up an old plastic fish crate he had salvaged from the shoreline to sit on.

The conversation went around and around. Alice listened mostly as Andrew and Margaret exchanged travel stories, she of the land and he of the seas. Alice kept an eye on the time: she wanted to get back across the causeway early.

'Margaret, I'm so sorry but we're going to have to get back.' She looked to Andrew. 'I'm a bit nervous of driving the causeway: today is the first time I've ever done it myself.'

'Let me help you back to your car . . . it's no trouble, I'm going that way.'

As Andrew waved them off from the car park, coach drivers were looking anxiously for late returning passengers to avoid the mad rush of the sudden exodus before the tide turned. Alice had timed their departure perfectly; they were across and driving back onto the mainland before the stampede of coaches and cars began.

CHAPTER FIFTEEN

I ate in the cookhouse with the slaves. I asked about the worship house at the spring. The sacred water now was carried from there through gullies to fill the bathhouse and sluice the droppings of the newcomers away from the latrine to the stream below. The power of the glowing cup must be stronger than the power of our goddess who inhabits the spring and the water that flows from it. Perhaps it is the source of the power of these people; if it were mine, perhaps I could use it to make my powers stronger – stronger even than theirs.

Avian Tyler was physically and spiritually exhausted when she got back to the B&B. She could see absolutely Violet Turnbull's problem. The house was not heavy with echoes: she had sensed some instances of disturbance, but they had been faint, and of the long-distant past; some came from the

157

ground beneath – far, far older than the farmhouse. There was sadness – anywhere that had been inhabited had its sadnesses – but she had not been conscious of any recent turbulence within the building itself. There was an emptiness. Violet's story had confirmed the cause of that.

Violet had not touched the box of tissues. Once she had begun her story she had seemed to distance herself from it, as if she told some other woman's story of tragic unexplained loss. She had not held back – she had described her feelings succinctly but not dramatically, as if to herself, as if Avian were not there at all – as if long-practised, much mused-on thoughts had found a chink to seep through.

Avian listened – said nothing – sat still as a stone – collecting impressions.

'My goodness, look at the time!' Violet exclaimed, at length. 'We should have some lunch.'

They silently ate creamy quiche with home-baked bread, which restored them.

'Well, Avian, what do you think, then?'

'I think you are a strong, resilient woman who, instead of erecting invisible barriers around you like most people do to remain in control, has claimed the walls of this house as very real and effective barriers to keep you from confronting the deaths of your twins.'

'So can I change things? Is it possible after all this time?'

'If you want things to change, Violet, they will change; but a word of advice – they may not always change in the way you expect or even want them to. That old saying about being careful what you wish for, as you might get it, is truer than people think.'

'Will you come back tomorrow? I'd like you to.'

'No, Violet, not tomorrow, but I will come back again before I leave.'

'So what do I do now? You can't start something and then just leave me to get on with it.'

'Violet, I haven't started anything – you have. It began before you even telephoned me – it began in this kitchen with Maisie. You need to think – what is it you do want? Do you want change? You can never turn back the clock: breaking through the barriers is not going to bring back the twins; nothing else will change, just you. What about your husband? Does he want change? He may be very happy having you here day after day, year after year – he may be so used to it he will not support you if you change. Talk to him, think long and hard; breaking down barriers is often more painful than putting them up.'

Walking back to the B&B, Avian had thought about barriers. The painful process of breaking down her own was branded on her memory. Breaking them meant letting the echoes return. In childhood she had accepted them as normal, they had always been part of her life, but they became a burden that had to be put aside in order to survive. As an adult struggling to defeat her agoraphobia the echoes had seemed part of the problem rather than part of the solution. For a long time she did not know if she was getting better – or going completely mad. It was only as she reached the end of the slow process of reintegration with the world outside her door that she came to understand that the echoes were both the root of the problem and the key to the solution. She learnt to filter and focus, instead of being overwhelmed by the discordant swell emanating from the environment surrounding her. This took practice. Violet, she sensed, had only desired to cut herself off from one thing on the outside, but in order to do so she had managed to cut herself off from everything. Doors, it seemed, were very important here. She pondered on the significance of doors as she clopped slowly towards Crosshall.

'Ah, Miss Tyler, have you had a nice morning?' Mrs Chambers enquired.

'Um . . . interesting. I walked to Henge Farm – such lovely countryside around here.'

'Henge Farm? Near the stone circle? We are new to the area you see – sold up the bungalow in Tunbridge Wells and bought this farmhouse, so we don't really know the locals. Are they relations or something? I remember . . . Henge Farm . . . where they found that gold cup . . . marvellous thing.'

It was quite clear that if Avian allowed it, this woman would twitter on and on until the cows came home. Avian was drained; her smiling and nodding reserves were at zero.

'I'm going to my room for a rest,' she stated, firmly.

'Dinner is at eight,' an affronted Mrs Chambers snapped. Really, she thought, it takes no effort to be pleasant. Still, she's a bit of a weird one this . . . you get all sorts of guests, running a B&B, and if these walls could talk, they could tell some tales – and some of the items left in rooms – well . . .

The room was pleasant enough, though rather too pink and frilly for Avian's taste, but comfortable and with a nice view over the gardens. She could see Mr Chambers in his vegetable plot. The organic vegetables and local produce had been the deciding factor in choosing this B&B. She wondered if Mr Chambers had met the chap, Brian; she felt they would have a lot in common. She hoped Mrs Chambers' cooking was as good as her husband's obvious gardening skills. He looked up and saw her at her window and waved a friendly wave. Avian had learnt early on not to focus in on people unless it was a real necessity. After all, she had the same senses as everyone else and she preferred to use those. By focusing her intent on a person, she had in the past seen and felt things she would rather not have known about – it could be an invasion of privacy. She waved back. He hurriedly returned to his digging as his wife marched up the path with an empty basket in search of vegetables.

Avian decided to run herself a hot bath. Into it, she added her own favourite concoction of wheatgerm oil, lavender, and clove essential oils. The heady vapours filled the compact bathroom as she lay in the hot oily water breathing in the timeless healing haze.

Violet Turnbull stood at the old stone sink in the kitchen

staring out at the drying green. That was the last place she had been before the accident – the last place she had been ignorant and happy. How would it feel to stand there, to peg washing onto that line unused in so many years? How did the washing smell when it was brought in on a windy summer's day? She had not worn a piece of clothing or slept in a bed with linen that had not been dried stiff from hanging in front of the range on the clothes horse. Her age-spotted, gnarled hands gripped the rim of the sink. I do want to go outside; I do, she thought, fervently. Prayer was unfamiliar to her; once she had prayed so much – firstly to have children, and then to have them returned to her by a miracle. What kind of God was it that made you wait so long for something, gave it to you to be the mainstay of your existence, and then snatched it mercilessly and cruelly away? Even so . . . even so, she thought – perhaps . . .

CHAPTER SIXTEEN

T*he Roman woman sent a serving maid to bring me before the sun had reached half his way across the clear blue sky. I stood before her, and looked her directly in the eye for the first time. At my side stood the girl from our village. She told me that the woman was asking my price. When I gave my reply the girl shook her head and told me that she could not pass my words on. I repeated my price, and the girl, in a low mumble, gave my words to the woman. She stood. She shouted, railed, flailed and made to pull at her hair. I stood firm. I looked in her eyes and she knew that the price of my art and my silence was high, and was set.*

Margaret stayed for three weeks and returned to Durham feeling very much better than when she had left. Alice and Marge had convinced her that having an alarm round her neck was not some symbol of senility or imminent demise.

She contacted Age Concern on her return and a very nice young man had been sent to assist her in her choice of alarm. On receipt of the pendant the young man returned and the system was tested and fully explained.

'Well, Professor Allerton, I am quite sure you will never need to use the alarm, but there you have it, all tested and functioning. If you have any questions do phone or email me.'

'Thank you so much – you have been most helpful.'

As she closed the door, Margaret felt a degree of reassurance. She looked down at the alarm hanging on its cord, held it and looked again before popping it down the inside of her blouse. She phoned Alice.

'You and your bossy friend Marge can stop worrying,' she joked. 'I'm all wired up now; if I feel myself in any danger, I just press the button. Happy?'

'Yes, I am; much happier – except I wish you lived nearer. I shall get lonely without you; we do get on so well, don't we?'

'Yes – yes we do. I'm so glad you provided that cup of tea; and if I hadn't decided to visit the stones we would never have met – now wouldn't that have been a tragedy?'

'I'll phone you next week, Margaret. I must go now because young Sarah Rigden, Brian's wife, is coming round for a lemon curd lesson.'

'Have fun, and save a jar for me. Bye, Alice.'

The sterilised jars and lids stood in a neat row on a wooden board waiting to be put on the warm shelf of the Rayburn. The eggs were at room temperature, the sugar warming in a stoneware bowl on top of the range, where the kettle was just about to come to the boil. Sarah parked the buggy with a sleeping Faith snugly wrapped within it, knocked on the kitchen door, opened it and popped her head round.

'Hello, Alice – are you there?'

Alice appeared from the hallway.

'Sorry, my lovely. I was on the phone to Margaret. She's got her alarm thingy and its all working.'

'You must be pleased. I know she's very capable and all that, but she's no one to check on her except her cleaning lady. She's so indomitable I'm quite amazed you managed to get her to agree to the alarm.'

'Well, I think she'd had a few frights with this low blood pressure business, and Marge – you know Marge, the district nurse? No? Oh I am surprised – I'll introduce you sometime – anyway, she managed the convincing, not me.'

The kitchen smelt of lemons, zesting, juicing and cooking.

'I've tried before to make lemon curd, but never been able to get it to set,' said Sarah.

'The trick is not to try and make too much at one time, and to have everything at room temperature to begin with. Just watch. Have you tried making jellies?'

'No – I don't have a jelly bag to begin with, and it seems quite a wasteful process.'

'I suppose it is, but it's so nice for those seedy bitty fruits, especially if you've a glut, and especially if you've got false teeth: all those pips get right under the plate.'

'Where is young Aaron today?' Alice asked as she stirred the warmed sugar into the lemon mix.

'At nursery. Brian will collect him today, so there's no great hurry to get back, although I don't want to be too late.'

The two women talked and stirred and potted and covered as the citrus smell billowed out of the kitchen doorway and out into the lane. Nipper slumbered noisily in the porch; he roused himself and raised his head to listen to a noise coming down the lane from the farm – clip, clop, clip; he quizzically tipped his head from side to side, stood and began to softly growl under his breath. The noises stopped and he sat down; then they began again, leaving the lane and coming ever nearer to the back door of Orby Cottage. A woman appeared. The fur on Nipper's back stood on end; he retreated back-wards into the kitchen to stand by Alice's side. The woman tapped on the glass of the door.

'Hello.'

Alice and Sarah turned to see Avian Tyler in the doorway. Alice recognised her as the woman she and Margaret had seen on the morning of their trip to Holy Island.

'I'm so sorry to just barge in on you like this, but it was the smell of the cooking. Please tell me it's lemon curd,' Avian explained.

'Yes, it is. I think we've met before, briefly, in the lane. Have you been up to visit Violet? She said you were a cook, or writing a cookbook, or something.'

'I have been to see Violet, but I'm not a cook, or a writer.'

'I'm sure she said . . . still, would you like to come in? The kettle's just about to boil.' Alice asked politely.

'The kettle's always just about to boil in this house. My name is Sarah, and I'm having a lemon curd masterclass.'

'Avian – Avian Tyler, and this must be the famous Alice McCleish – it's very nice to meet you in person.'

'How . . . oh, I suppose Violet mentioned me.'

'No, actually she didn't. I'm Maisie's aunt – Maisie, from the dig; and I have met Marsha, your granddaughter – we travelled up on the train together when she visited you during the dig. Oh, and you were in the newspaper too. I'm afraid I never saw the TV appearance, but I heard all about it from Maisie. By the way, the child outside is just beginning to stir from its nap.'

The three women sat round the kitchen table drinking tea and chatting while the jars of lemon curd cooled and thickened on a shelf. Alice thought her unexpected visitor strange but very compelling; there was something about her that put Alice in mind of Callum, but she could not put her finger on what it was. Sarah jiggled a contented Faith on her knees.

'I'm leaving tomorrow, so I'm really glad I was cheeky enough to invite myself into your cottage or we might never have met,' Avian said. 'I shall be visiting again, I expect, but I can't stay any longer this time.' Avian stood up and Nipper grumbled.

'Stop that, Nipper! I'm so sorry – he's not usually so

grumpy with people.'

'Don't worry – dogs often find me perplexing; they usually come round when they get to know me. Thanks so much for the tea and the chat.'

Avian was pondering on Wyllie Turnbull. He left little of himself in the house that she could pick up on; she felt him as something like a dusting of snow, or years of dust – covering, enshrouding everything but not concealing. His sphere of existence was outside: the farm, the fields, the crops and live-stock; she would meet him in time.

At Crosshall, Avian enjoyed her final meal with Mr and Mrs Chambers. They sat together in the conservatory looking out across the rolling open countryside.

'Mrs Chambers,' – they had never got as far as first names – 'that was truly the most delicious meal I have eaten for a very long time. The vegetables were beyond description, straight from soil to pot to plate and cooked to perfection.'

Mrs Chambers puffed up with pride. She had softened to the strange Ms Tyler during her stay. She enjoyed the chal-lenge of preparing interesting vegetarian meals, although she and hubby were voracious meat eaters themselves – her roast rib of beef was 'fit for royalty' as Mr Chambers often said.

They finished their glasses of wine as the sun sank – the red of the wine echoing the flush of sunset.

In her pink-infused room, later, Avian mused over her

visit to Duddo. She lay on the unfamiliar bed remembering the people she had met, the homes she had entered: Henge Farm, Orby Cottage, Crosshall – Violet, Alice, Sarah, Brian. On the surface they lived in happy isolation from the modern world. Here there was no rush and hurry, the air was clean and fresh, the countryside unscarred except by a line of ever-decreasing pylons marching towards the Cheviot Hills. But there was something here, underlying this rural idyll, casting a shadow . . . that was it: something casting faint shadows.

CHAPTER SEVENTEEN

The Pilus Prior was called. He and his wife dismissed the guards and servants from the room and I stood there as they shouted and argued. I understood not one word, but the stance of their bodies and the anger in their eyes and mouths was clear. The woman began to beg, her body bent, her hands held out in supplication. She cried and wailed – but the Pilus stood firm. Then the woman looked at me with pure hatred; she spat on the ground at my feet. The Pilus looked from his distraught wife to me. I saw him. He took the woman's arm and led her to the side of the room. They talked urgently, voices lowered, stealing glances at me as they plotted.

The postman knocked on Margaret Allerton's door. She rose carefully, giving herself time to stand without getting dizzy. The impatient postman knocked again more loudly.

171

Margaret drew back the security chain and opened the door cheerfully.

'Good morning, postman.'

'And a very good morning to you too,' he replied. 'Here's your post, and here's a parcel for you – no chance of getting that through the letter box,' he quipped, winking at her cheekily.

'Thank you very much,' Margaret answered, smiling. Time was when she would have had no interest in passing the time of day with a postman; there had been far more important things for her to be doing. She had come to see that her life had been more about things and places than people; but without people there would have been no things or places for her to study.

The parcel was from Alice, marked 'Fragile'. What on earth could it be? Margaret carefully carried it over to the table and laid the letters down beside it. Inside, carefully packed with straw, was a jar of lemon curd, and a note.

Dear Margaret,

Thought you might like a jar of this. Do you remember that strange-looking woman who walked past towards Henge Farm on the day we went to Lindisfarne? Well, she appeared in my kitchen yesterday, drawn like a Bisto Kid by the smell of lemon curd cooking. Strange soul – very nice – not a writer at all as it turns out. Odd name – Avian Tyler.

Heard from Prof. Mortimer this week – money from sale of cup to British Museum should arrive very soon. What on earth am I going to do with it all? It's a bit like winning the lottery.

Much love, enjoy the curd.

Alice

Margaret sifted through the remaining post: a letter from U3A asking if she would consider a series of lectures at the museum for the next session, a Damart catalogue, a postcard sent from Peru by a former student, a hearing aid circular and a kind offer to provide her with a platinum credit card. She emailed U3A to gently decline, binned the catalogue and circulars and concentrated on the postcard.

Margaret would have given anything to return to Peru where she had studied religious beliefs and the practice of child sacrifice. The bodies of these children were found mummified by the dry high air amongst the peaks, accompanied by votive offerings of tiny gold and silver llamas. The preserved fabrics wrapping their tiny frames were almost identical to those still in use today – the dyes, the style of decoration, the patterns of weaving. Margaret sighed. Never again would she feel the intoxication of the thin air of the mountains; the smells, sounds, sights and experiences of her more active life were stored away in her memory. She sat back in her comfortable chair and reminisced. This was how she spent a great deal of her time – travelling the world in retrospect, trying to see past the academic to the human aspects which she had disregarded at the time.

She was just drifting into a mid-morning doze when the door opened. She had forgotten to put the security chain across. Through half-closed eyes she saw a man peep round the door. He looked at her closely, decided she was fast asleep, and crept in, closing the door behind him. Margaret closed her eyes tightly. He must be a burglar – a drug addict or even a rapist – her heart raced within her outwardly somnolent body. She decided to play possum. Let him take what he wanted, as long as he left her alone. She made a mental note of his appearance: jeans, trainers – dirty-white, shirt – green with orange stripe across chest, height – taller than doorframe – he'd had to duck to get under, peaked cap thing – worn back to front – also dirty-white with logo, white, late teens to early twenties, barbed wire tattoo around left wrist. The young man looked around; he could not see what he was looking for: TV, video. He looked along the bookshelves and passed by tomes worth more than ten TVs if he had but known it. He spied the computer and looked again at Margaret. He bent to unplug the machine.

'Young man.' A soft woman's voice paralysed the burglar.

'Young man,' Margaret repeated a little louder. He swung round to face Margaret, angry at being caught out.

'There are many things in this house worth a great deal more than my computer – I will willingly part with something more valuable if you would kindly leave that alone.' Margaret's voice sounded authoritative despite her inner fear.

'Oh, fuck,' the burglar hissed.

'There is no need for that sort of language, thank you.'

'You sound just like my gran,' the burglar grumbled, and he sat down on the chair in front of the computer.

'And how would you feel if some good-for-nothing crept into her house and stole her TV? No, don't tell me, I dare say you would "sort him out" somehow or another.'

'Look, missus.'

'I am not a missus. My name is Professor Allerton, but you may call me Margaret.'

Now the burglar was completely confused. He was not a career criminal – he owed a bloke for a bit of speed and a few Es – nothing heavy. It was not as if he were a crackhead or heroin junkie; he just needed fifty quid, and he needed it today – or else.

'Look, mis . . . whatever you call yourself – I don't want any hassle. I'll just leave now OK? I won't take nothing, OK? I won't rob you.'

'So what will you do? Go and rob some other poor soul? Really, it's just not good enough. Why not get a job, earn some money instead of stealing?'

'Oh, and I s'pose you think it's that easy, do you? "Go out and get a job." What the fuck would you know? Old bitch.'

'You may have a point there, young man, but there is no need to swear in order to put it across. Now then, I do not want you to go and rob one of my neighbours; how much do you need?'

'Fifty quid,' the burglar replied – too quickly, realising he should have upped the ante.

'Pass me that handbag if you would,' Margaret requested.

The burglar picked up the handbag and momentarily considered doing a runner with it.

'Bag please, young man,' Margaret insisted. She fumbled around in her purse, muttering under her breath.

'Right, here you are – fifty pounds. You now have a choice. You can steal this fifty pounds from me, and I shall call the police and give them a very full description of you, and you may get caught. Or, you can take this as payment for doing a day's work for me before the end of this week. If you don't come back and do the work, I shall then inform the police: entirely up to you. Off you go then, and if you have not appeared by ten o'clock on Friday morning I shall be reporting this as a crime.'

The burglar stood up, bemused by the whole incident. He had only wanted to nick a TV or a video to sell at Barnwood's Second Hand Emporium to pay off the debt quick before he got a pasting. He snatched the money from Margaret's hand and stomped towards the door, turning before opening it, just to check that what he thought had happened had really happened and was not some kind of nasty hallucination. The old bitch was real enough, sitting there all wrinkly in her comfy chair, staring straight into his eyes, daring him not to come back and do a day's work. He walked away. No way was he

going back there, not a fucking chance – no way, not in a million years.

When he had gone, definitely gone, Margaret began to
sob. What she felt was anger at the violation of her home and
privacy. She should have chased him off with a poker or a
broom. What had she done? Stupid, stupid old woman; she
had given a stranger, a burglar – probably a drug addict – fifty
pounds. However, he had not harmed her, he would happily
have gone off and robbed someone else and left her alone if
she had let him. Alice would have seen something good in
that; Alice would have tried to understand the human circumstances which had led to the incident. With her heart still
racing, Margaret picked up the telephone and dialled her
friend's number.

'My goodness, Margaret! But you're all right? Physically I
mean? You are bound to be shook up!'

'Yes, I'm all right now I have spoken to you. I think I shall
write down the description now so I do not forget anything. I
am going to give him until Friday, as I said – although I don't
hold out much hope of him turning up.'

'You may be surprised. Stranger things have happened.
Now make sure you're all locked up properly, and phone me
any time. I mean that – any time at all. You will do that, won't
you Margaret?'

Alice put down the receiver. Her friend was terribly brave,
she thought, to confront a burglar like that.

'Dear old Nipper,' she said to the dozing dog. 'You would

see off the nasty burglars, wouldn't you my old love?' Nipper managed a heavy thud of tail on carpet in response. 'Well, perhaps not, but you would put them off, I hope.'

On Friday morning at five minutes to ten there was a tap at Margaret's front door. She gently levered herself up from her chair and crossed the small room to open it.

'Glad to see you put the chain across, missus.'

The burglar stood sheepishly on the step.

'Good morning,' Margaret said, a quiet smile hidden behind a firm exterior. Alice will be pleased, she thought. 'You had better come in. You can tell me your name now, I suppose, seeing that I shall not need to telephone the . . .' she hesitated; 'Old Bill,' she said, her face breaking into a grin.

Marcus Mooney had stuck to his intention to never, no way, go back to the old dear's house – until Thursday night. Thursday night his old gran had a fall and he had found her on her kitchen floor when he popped in for his tea – after all, Gran's was the only place he got a decent cooked meal. He had gone with her in the ambulance; his mum arrived three hours later – someone had found her in the pub. She was drunk, emotional and useless as always so Marcus had put her in a taxi home. He knew the taxi would take her straight back to the pub.

His gran was OK – not dead anyway, not yet – but suddenly he had realised that she would be, one day, dead.

'I have to say, I am somewhat surprised that you came.

What should I call you?'

'Marcus – Marcus Mooney. Would you have rung the Bill?'

'Honestly . . . yes, Marcus; I would have. On the table there, you can read it if you want, is a description of you and of what happened and when.'

'You don't mess about, missus; you're just like my gran.'

To Margaret's total astonishment the burglar, or not burglar, as it were, began to shudder, his cocky shoulders drooped, his arrogant chin quivered and his sharp eyes began to flood with tears. What on earth should she do? Before she had finished the thought she had begun to move towards the boy – not that much more than a child, really. She found herself with her tiny frail arm around the waist of this stranger – who had tried to rob her – who she should have reported to the police the instant he had left her home.

'My dear boy,' she crooned. 'What on earth is the matter? Sit . . . sit here . . . yes, good.' She steered the sobbing boy to a chair and sat him gently on it.

'Now then, you had better tell me all about it. Drink? Cup of tea?'

Margaret sat back in her comfy chair, a cup of tea on the table at her side. Marcus had pulled his chair round to face hers; he balanced a sherry glass of ancient brandy in a large and clumsy hand. They talked – or rather Marcus talked and Margaret listened.

'Oh, Marcus, I just do not know what to say to you.'

''salright, missus, I shouldn't have said nothing – after all, why should you care?'

'Twelve months ago I would not have cared a jot, I promise you. If you had tried to rob me twelve months ago this would never have happened. However, lately I have discovered that you are never too old to change – or too young, I suspect.'

Marcus was embarrassed by his outburst.

'What do you want doing then? I usually do me gran's windows once a month; that do you?'

'That will do very nicely indeed, and while you do that I will prepare us some lunch. I was going to have couscous.'

'What?'

'Ah, well – then perhaps pasta?'

'Like spaghetti? Yeah, I like spaghetti.'

The spaghetti was not exactly as Marcus had imagined it. For him, spaghetti was long, thin stuff with meaty sauce and grated cheese on top – Gran made it sometimes. This spaghetti was long and flat and green, like it had gone funny. There was no meat, and the sauce was creamy. He tentatively moved it around on the plate. It did smell nice. He cut off a small segment of the pasta and carefully placed it on the tip of his tongue; he closed his mouth, then his eyes for a second and smiled.

Finishing his second plateful at a speed that alarmed Margaret, Marcus sat back in his chair and belched loudly.

'Pardon me – was that rude? That was a brill dinner, missus . . . Margaret.'

'I am very glad you enjoyed it, and – no, belching is considered a great compliment to the cook and host in very many cultures.'

'Gran never minds – better out than in, she says.'

After lunch Margaret dozed in her comfy chair. Marcus slipped out into the yard for a cigarette. The yard had been neglected for some time. The cleaning lady only did inside. Margaret woke with a start and was surprised to hear someone crashing around outside. She almost got up too quickly to go and see, and then she remembered Marcus. She rose from her chair sedately and went into the kitchen to wash up, only to find it already done. She put the kettle on instead. Every time she put her kettle on she thought of Alice – imagined Alice in her very different kitchen putting her kettle on, too.

Margaret followed the sound of the banging out into the yard. She stood in her doorway and gasped.

'Marcus.'

The small, walled yard, unswept, untidied and neglected for too long, was a picture. Accumulated rubbish whooshed in by the wind, crisp packets, drifts of last autumn's leaves, carrier bags – all had vanished. The stone slabs had been swept and the worst of the weeds pulled from the cracks between them. Two black plastic bin liners stuffed to bursting were all that remained of years of detritus.

Dearest Alice,

Thought I should update you on Marcus and his grandmother. Granny is fine in herself now, but they will not let her go home. She probably will never be able to live independently again, but the council has offered her a flatlet in a sheltered housing scheme. Marcus says she is 'cool' about that. His mother, of course, is useless – not capable of looking after herself most of the time, let alone a son and an elderly mother.

Marcus is still coming two afternoons a week. He truly does not seem to mind what he turns his hand to. He has painted the bathroom ceiling for me; always phones before he comes to see if I need any bits of shopping brought in. He is to me what Brian is to you; I wonder how I ever really managed before he came along.

Dear Alice, I fear this may sound somewhat effusive, but there is something I have to tell you. Before I met you, before we became friends, I was never really engaged by people, not as individuals. I thought I was, but really I was interested in peoples, groups, tribes, nations, cultures – considered something of an expert in my field, but I understood little of people. Meeting you, and all your wonderful friends and neighbours, has given me something beyond value. What I am trying to say is thank you. Thank you so much for being my friend.

I hope we can get together soon; love to Nipper.

All my love,

Margaret

Alice McCleish sat quietly in her kitchen, Margaret's letter clutched in one hand, damp handkerchief in the other. She mopped away a last tear, resettled her reading glasses on the end of her nose and read the last part again. She was surprised to discover that Margaret, her erudite and professional friend, had learned something from her, Alice McCleish, housewife and mother.

'Well, well, Nipper; fancy that. Who'd have thought it?'

Nipper wagged enthusiastically; he had not been out for his walk yet, and was hoping Alice wouldn't be long in getting her shoes and coat on.

'Just you hang on a minute; I need to go to the bathroom.'

Nipper was sitting waiting by his lead when Alice emerged and sat down to lace her shoes. He woofed as she pulled on a coat; and he bounced stiffly round her feet as she wrapped a scarf around her neck.

There was no wind today: the smoke from the cottage chimney went straight upwards in the cool, clean air. Alice decided to walk up to the steading and back, just as far as the gate – it was too chilly for a lengthy stroll. Trees were taking on their autumn colours: cherry leaves had begun to turn deep red; the first few had already fallen to the ground.

Alice walked as if in a trance. She was deeply concerned about the money from the sale of the cup. A price of two hundred thousand pounds had been agreed on, to be split equally between Alice, and Brian Rigden. One hundred thousand pounds was a great deal of money, and truly Alice felt she did not particularly want it all. She had her house, she had her car; her garden was looking lovely. Alice knew she wanted to do something for her grandchildren. She needed some advice – she needed to speak with Michael.

Nipper had found a fresh rabbit burrow and was energetically digging, spraying soil out behind him, and grunting malice into the hole.

'Come on, Nipper; leave the rabbits alone. Save your energy for getting the blighters that sneak into my garden and eat my plants.'

Alice looked up towards Henge Farmhouse. Wyllie was just leaving, shotgun tucked – the barrels hanging safely broken from the stock – under his arm. He saw Alice and waved, then beckoned her to come towards the house.

'I've got Nipper with me!' Alice called.

'That's all right,' he shouted back. 'The collies are tied up in the barn.'

Nipper was generally very amiable with other dogs – bitches were always warmly greeted – but collies of either gender just brought out the worst in him. Alice could understand why: grovelling, cowering creatures, she felt, always so desperate to please, looking up imploringly for direction. Alice put Nipper on the lead anyway, and opened the gate. She and Wyllie met halfway along the track.

'Morning, Alice – how's the fettle today?'

'Oh, you know . . . mustn't grumble. Nip in the air now, Wyllie – and the nights are fair drawing in.'

'Aye, well – harvest's in, ewes are tupped – that new tup I got at the Kelso Ram Sales is a beauty. Callum would have appreciated him.'

'How's Violet?'

'Now, that's why I called you over. I'm not sure. She has had some very strange moods lately. I was hoping you'd pop in for a cup of tea – see if you could drag the cause from her. She'll not speak to me about it, whatever it is.'

'I can't just now, Wyllie – she won't have the dog in the house and I won't tie him up outside. I'll phone her later today and arrange to see her before the week's out, but don't hold your breath, she's not one to pour out her troubles to others, as you well know.'

'Thank you, Alice – you're a good woman,' Wyllie said. As he ambled slowly away, he turned to watch her walk back to the gate. She turned, and they waved.

Alice was glad to get back indoors. She should have worn a hat, and an extra cardigan under the coat would not have gone amiss. At this rate she would be getting her winter coat out of the wardrobe before long . . . now there was something she could treat herself to: a new winter coat! She made herself a pot of tea and picked up the telephone.

'Violet, it's Alice. How are you?'

'Alice . . . och – you know – can't complain. Did I see you talking with Wyllie earlier? I suppose he asked you to phone?'

'Well, yes he did; he seemed concerned about you.'

'Did he now?' Violet replied. 'Did he indeed?'

'Violet, he asked me to visit. I'd love to see you anyway; do you know we haven't spoken since I saw Miss Tyler walking up the lane and I was worried about you – and that was on the phone.'

'Did you speak to her?'

'Not that time, but she did appear in my kitchen later that week, drawn in by the smell of lemon curd that Sarah Rigden and I were making.'

'Can you come tomorrow afternoon? Wyllie will be away at a vintage ploughing competition with the Fergie.'

'Yes, about two?'

'Lovely – and bring me a jar of lemon curd if you've one left; I haven't had that in years.'

Alice's next phone call was to Michael. She had searched her address book and found a work telephone number for him, a number she had never used before.

'Good morning; may I speak with Michael McCleish, please?' she asked the woman who answered.

'Who's calling please?' came the efficient reply.

'I'm his mother.'

'I'll put you through, Mrs McCleish; hold the line please.'

'Mum, what's wrong?' Michael's worried voice asked.

'Nothing, dear. I'm sorry to call you at work, it's just . . . I need some advice, financial advice. The money for the cup is about to come through and I need help deciding what to do with it all. Can you help?'

CHAPTER EIGHTEEN

T he serving maid and the girl were called back. As the serving maid gave me the words of the Pilus and his woman, the poor child stood, her hands resting on the gentle rounding of her belly. This must be done soon, or the herb will not be sufficient and the binding or stones may be needed. To enable me to win the cup, the girl must keep her health, of this I was certain. The Pilus would pay, he offered coins, but I stood firm. He offered land and animals, but I stood firm. He offered slaves, oils and wines, but I stood firm. Finally, he offered the cup.

Michael sat in front of his computer screen at home. For once, the house was empty. Marsha was staying over with her new friends, studying for her A level mocks: next year she would be finishing school and was planning to study Archaeology and Prehistory at university. Dexter was the worry. He

187

had never settled into his new school properly. He had lots of friends, was representing the school in the Year 11 football and basketball teams but he was not a natural academic. Michael was reminded of himself at that age – not much of a scholar but good at maths. Dexter was good at sport and biology. They had discussed careers like sports physiotherapist, or physical education teacher. Dexter's lack of enthusiasm was worrying. Penny had suggested the two of them spend some time together – male bonding, she called it. Perhaps she was right; he would ask Dex if he wanted to go to Granny McCleish's for a few days, which he probably would not be excited by, but the lure of tickets to the Newcastle v. Sunderland match at the Stadium of Light might just be enough to swing a decision.

He heard the door open and Dex's individual stomp approach the kitchen; the fridge opened, bottles rattled.

'Hi Dex!' Michael shouted through. 'Put the kettle on, mate.'

Michael made a large strong cup of coffee and sat at the dining table with his uncommunicative son.

'How do you fancy a few days away, just you and me – men stuff, you know?'

'Doing what? Not fishing or camping or something – no ta.'

'As if. When have we ever done fishing or camping? No, I thought we could go to the Newcastle–Sunderland game; maybe stay at Granny's for a couple of days – not long.'

'OK.'

Dexter stomped off up the stairs to his room. Michael sat in shock. Dex had agreed. No arguing, no grunting – just an 'OK'. An 'OK' was good enough, and Michael booked two tickets for the game on the Internet. He phoned his mum to tell her the good news.

Conversation was sparse on the drive north. Dexter was umbilically attached to his MP3 player, and his only comments were in regard to service stations, food, drink or needing a pee. Michael quite enjoyed the companionable silence, despite the tchh tchh tchh sounds that leaked from Dex's headphones as his head nodded in time to the music. Michael turned off the A1 sooner than Dexter expected.

'Why're we going this way, Dad?'

'Just for a change; the main road is so busy, I thought we'd take the country route. This road goes over the moors towards Chillingham – do you remember we went there with Granny when you were small – Wild White Cattle, remember?'

Dexter grunted in the negative, and they drove on.

Alice had been busy getting the spare room ready for Michael and Dexter. This was to be a real treat: her two favourite boys all to herself – even if it was only for a few days. While she had been airing the room and making up Michael's single bed and an old camping bed for Dexter, she had been mulling over her strange visit with Violet Turnbull. Violet had seemed different, somehow. They had talked about the same things they usually talked of – village gossip, births, marriages, deaths, and Michael and the family; yet Alice had felt that Violet had been trying to say more, wanting to communicate something else but unable to do it with words. They had tea – Alice had brought the lemon curd, Violet had baked an enormous cake heavy with dark, dried fruits. Alice had risen to leave, expecting Violet to stay in the kitchen as she normally did, but Violet walked with her through the maze of passageways to the front porch.

'Bye Violet . . . no . . . don't come too near the door; I'll see myself out.'

Violet grabbed Alice's hand with both her tiny bony ones. Alice looked into Violet's eyes and was shocked to react to her mute appeal in much the same way she might to a grovelling collie dog. Alice felt awkward – was sure the shock had shown in her own face; Violet turned away, also embarrassed. Alice turned the handle on the big old wooden door and opened it. She turned to say goodbye, expecting to see her neighbour's bent back retreating from the glimpse of the outside world and was amazed to see Violet steadying herself against the door frame of the inner door, looking out. The expression on Violet's face, so unexpected, was not her habitual expression of dread, but had changed to one of longing.

Brian came to give the lawn one of its last cuts before

growth stopped for this season. When he had finished, Alice called him in for a cup of tea before he sloped off to his vegetable patch for an hour before going home. She had wanted to talk to him about the money but felt uncomfortable about bringing the subject up. Brian saved her.

'Well now, Alice – what on earth are we going to do with all this dosh then?'

'It's so much – quite unbelievable.'

'Alice, love, it's not so much nowadays; some people could spend that much in the blink of an eye.'

'I know – it's just that I don't feel I did anything to deserve it – does that make any sense?'

'Sarah and I have decided to tie a fair amount up in trust funds for the children, for their education mainly – who knows how much it'll cost for kids to go to university by the time Aaron and Faith are old enough.'

'Michael is coming at the weekend, with his son, Dexter – you haven't met them, have you? Michael will advise me on what's best, that's what he's good at.'

'Very wise, Alice, very wise; might even speak to him myself if he can spare the time. Thanks for the tea, love. Do you want a few Brussels or do you like them to get a touch of the frost first?'

Michael and Dexter drove the winding roads over the moor, wended their way down the high steep escarpment down to the lower ground and on to the Wooler road. It had been many years since Michael had driven on any route other than the A1, but even so, this was all very familiar. Dexter removed the earphones from his ears and turned off the MP3 player.

'Where are we now then, Dad?'

'Nearly there. I'm surprised you don't recognise this bit – the Heatherslaw Railway – Thomas the Tank – the little trains that run along the river to the ruined castle?'

'Oh yeah, I do remember that; Mum's got some photos of us on the train somewhere.'

'Seems like yesterday to me,' Michael said, more to himself than to Dexter.

Alice looked out of her sitting room window, waiting to get the first glimpse of the car bringing her visiting menfolk. From her kitchen the smell of a roasting chicken permeated the house. It had been a while since she had cooked a full roast dinner – stuffing, tatties, carrots, peas, broccoli, and there was apple crumble and custard for pudding. There was something about feeding men, especially ones with hearty appetites, that Alice missed so very much. Callum had been a great eater, always cleared his plate with a flourish and a compliment to the cook; Michael had followed him. She saw the car turn the corner and dashed into the kitchen to put the kettle on the range; it would be whistling merrily by the time they were inside. She opened the front door and waited with Nipper worrying at a rabbit scrape in the border to the left of the door. The dog heard the car draw up and came away wagging and woofing to see who the visitor was. Michael parked the car in front of the lean-to, then he and Dexter emerged to be hugged enthusiastically by Alice, and jumped up at and licked by Nipper.

'Hiya, Gran,' Dexter said as he disentangled himself, rather embarrassed, from Alice's embrace.

'Hi Mum – gosh, you are looking well. Look at your garden – it looks almost as good as when Dad was alive.'

'That's all Brian's work, except for a bit of weeding now and again when I feel up to it.'

Nipper and Dexter disappeared off to the back lawn for a game of catch and fetch leaving Alice and her son to walk arm in arm into the kitchen where the kettle was indeed singing merrily.

'Something smells good, Mum – you shouldn't have gone to any bother.'

'Bother? How could it be any bother to cook a dinner for my two favourite men? To be honest, lovey, cooking proper meals is one of the things I miss most of all. It's not much fun cooking for one.'

'But you're all right though, Mum, aren't you?' Michael's expression showed his concern. Alice could see straight through him.

'Don't you worry, my boy; I'll not be moving in with you for a long time yet – hopefully never.' Alice put hot water into the saucepan with the broccoli in it and set it on the range.

'You sit there and tell me all your news while I get on with this dinner.'

As she moved the broccoli off the hotplate to simmer, checked the carrots, took the chicken out to stand before carving and turned the crisply roasted potatoes just one more time, Michael filled her in with their news: Penny's new clients and busy lucrative life, Penny's parents' new holiday apartment in Spain and the rumour that Michael could be up for a promotion.

'And what about our Dexter? What's he going to do?'

'I wish I knew,' Michael sighed. 'I really wish I knew.'

Dexter stood in the doorway and overheard the end of the conversation.

'Bloody hell, Dad, I thought this was a holiday! All you keep on about is, "What are you going to do? What are you going to do?"'

'Mind your language, son – especially in front of your gran.'

'That's all right; let's not argue now. Michael, will you carve this bird? Dexter, stir this gravy for me and keep stirring while I pour this vegetable water in there; Michael, pour some of the chicken liquid in here too, you can never have too much gravy.'

They sat in silence and feasted. Michael and Dexter exchanged glances and lip-smackings that spoke of how long it had been since they had sat down to a proper home-cooked meal at a table. The apple crumble and custard was scrump-

tious: both boys had second helpings. Alice looked at the pair
of them, contented and replete, as she began to clear the
dishes.

'Leave that, Mum – Dex and I will do the dishes in a bit,
when we can move again.'

'That was a brill dinner, Gran – really scrummy.'

Alice put the roasting tin down on the kitchen floor for
Nipper to scour.

'Don't you look at me like that, Michael; our dogs have always had the roasting tins and it's never done me or you any
harm.'

Dexter was delighted; he would have loved to have seen
his mother's expression had she seen that.

Michael and Alice took their cups of tea into the sitting
room. Dexter found a can of Coke in the back of the fridge
that had probably been there since their last visit.

'Granny, can I take Nipper out for a walk?'

'Yes, but take his lead, just in case you meet Wyllie
Turnbull's collies – or any collies, for that matter.'

'OK; won't be long.'

'Now, Michael, you are not here for long and I don't want
to waste too much of our precious time on this money business. There will be a payment into my bank account of one
hundred thousand pounds by the end of the month. What on
earth should I do with it all?'

Michael had been thinking hard about this conversation.

'OK, Mum – we need to start by forgetting I'm your son

and you're my mother. I have come up with some suggestions – they are exactly the suggestions I would have given to a complete stranger – a client with similar requirements. I don't want you thinking I am trying to diddle you, OK?'

'Good, that's exactly what I wanted you to do.'

Michael had devised a simple plan that he knew his mother would understand. He retrieved some paperwork from his overnight bag and went through it step by step with her. She said very little, which he found a bit discouraging, but he continued until he reached the end of his notes. Alice sat back in her chair and thought for a moment.

'I'll need to read through it again, and then go through any questions I might have, but it seems to be just the sort of thing I wanted. Thank you, son; the bank manager had contacted me about it, wittering on about offshore this and tax efficient that, and that I should arrange a meeting to talk about it with him. He'll be very surprised when I turn up with a plan already decided.'

Dexter and Nipper returned to find Alice and Michael at the kitchen sink – Michael washing up and Alice drying and putting away. Nipper was exhausted; it was a long time since he had played fetch and catch and had a long walk in one afternoon. He flopped panting into his bed.

'Dry him off a bit will you Dexter, otherwise he'll end up stiff jointed when he's old.'

Nipper rolled reluctantly onto his back to allow access to his sodden underbelly.

'Can I go and watch TV, Gran?'

'Surely. Off you go.'

Saturday morning Alice waved the men off from the gate as they headed to the football match. Callum had taken Michael to every home game they could manage. He would have been horrified at the price of a ticket these days. She sat herself down with a cup of tea and reread Michael's notes on how to manage this windfall.

Twenty-five thousand into an account that paid a monthly interest into her current account – it would not be very much, but the money was really safely locked away and would be part of her estate when the time came. Ten thousand was to go into her current account for spending money, for a holiday, for anything she needed. Five thousand was to go to the Duddo Church Restoration Fund. The remainder was to be divided between the grandchildren, thirty thousand pounds each for their higher education if they wanted it. Marsha was to have hers now; Dexter when he reached eighteen. She knew the bank manager would huff and puff and try to change her mind. Let him try, she thought: I shall not be budged.

The telephone rang. It was Margaret.

'Is everything all right, Margaret?' Alice asked.

'Everything is cool,' Margaret replied. 'I am becoming very au fait with youth-speak.'

'I take it that young Mr Mooney is still a reformed character?'

'I wouldn't know about that; still, he has started doing a few odd jobs for one or two of my cleaning lady's other elderly clients. She was not at all sure about him to begin with, but he has proved himself reliable and trustworthy. She gets quite motherly about him nowadays.'

'I am glad to hear that. Now, what else have you been up to – and more importantly – when are you coming for a visit? You must be able to fit in a long weekend before the weather gets too cold,' Alice insisted.

Michael and Dexter returned from the match flushed with the excitement and hoarse from the shouting.

'It was great, Gran! Dad showed us where he used to stand to watch with Gramp. Dad knew all the words to the songs, even the rude ones.'

'There's a surprise,' Granny answered with a wink. 'Now then: dinner. I'm afraid I didn't feel like cooking today. I was thinking perhaps we might go to the pub – my treat.'

Sunday dawned bright and warm, one of those Indian summer days of autumn, a slight breeze gently stirring the air. Dexter and Michael woke as the sun poured in through their bedroom window.

'Dad . . .'

'Yeah, son?' Michael yawned in reply.

'What'll we do today? There's not much to do round here

'cept walk the dog.'

'Maybe take Granny for a drive in the car?'

'Oh, brill.'

'Come on Dex, your Granny just wants to spend a bit of time with us – with you; it's not too much to ask now, is it?'

'S'pose not . . . can I smell bacon?'

The two were up and dressed in a jiffy, racing to be first to the kitchen. Alice could hear the laughter from downstairs.

After breakfast Dexter took Nipper for a walk. Michael and Alice sat in a sheltered, sunny part of the garden where Michael dozed. Alice smiled at him, this grown man, her and Callum's only son. He followed her in looks, not as dark and rugged as his father, but he followed Callum in his ways. Steady, reliable, strong, supportive – Callum had been very proud of his son, but always said of Michael that an office in a city was no place for a man born and bred in the country. Alice could hear his echo, 'He'll come back to it one day, mark my words; it's in his very marrow.' Well, for once, Callum had been wrong. Alice heard a car pull up by the vegetable patch. It woke Michael.

'Who's that?'

'It'll be Brian, maybe the family too; I'll take a look.' She stood and looked up over the hedge. 'Morning, Brian!' she called out. 'Michael's here – come and say hello. I'll put the kettle on.'

Michael stood up to shake Brian's outstretched hand. They exchanged pleasantries and sat down as Alice appeared with a tray of tea and biscuits.

'You sit down here, Mum; I'll pop round and get another chair from the shed.'

Dexter and Nipper returned in time for tea, which Dexter refused, preferring something fizzy and sweet. Nipper never said no to a saucer of warm tea, a great treat, especially when accompanied by a few custard cream crumbs.

'What's the plan for today, then?' Brian asked Dexter.

'Don't know, really.' Dexter looked from his father to his gran.

'I would like a really lazy morning sitting in this blessed sunshine,' Alice declared.

Michael nodded in agreement. 'Perhaps a jaunt out in the car for an hour or two this afternoon?' he suggested.

Dexter looked appalled at the idea.

'Tell you what, Dexter, how would you like to earn a few quid and have something to fill up your time too . . . if nobody minds me whisking you off for a few hours?' Brian proposed, looking to Michael for approval.

'Doing what? Not digging vegetables?'

'No, I've got another job to do which needs an extra pair of hands. I've been putting it off for a while, but if you're up for it. . . ?'

'OK.'

'You might want to change those trainers; it could get grubby.'

'See if one of those old pairs of wellies in the porch fit,' Alice advised.

The pair of them left, ten minutes later.

'I wonder what they'll be doing,' Michael said.

'Knowing Brian it's probably best not to think about it,' Alice replied.

CHAPTER NINETEEN

The serving maid led me to the edge of the forest. I needed to go back to my home and read the stones. I needed the bronze scraper and the herbs. The forest was cool; I left the straight, stone road of the newcomers and turned towards the stag-headed oak that rose tall above all the other trees. I climbed up the tor to the stones. I looked around at my home and found it wanting. It was dank, dark and smoke stained; the skins on the floor and walls stank. The hearth was cold and dead. I had seen another life – and wanted it.

Sunday afternoons at Henge Farm were a ticking, silent time. After a large traditional Sunday lunch, Violet and Wyllie would adjourn to the parlour. The rest of the week this room sat empty, gathering dust. On Friday mornings Violet would polish the large dark pieces of furniture she had inherited from her in-laws, wind the clocks and put the vacuum cleaner round in preparation. The windows faced the rolling countryside behind the house. Once, the fields had all been theirs as far as the eye could see, but over the years Wyllie had sold a field here and a field there to neighbouring farmers as it had become too much for him to manage. He should have taken on a new hand when Callum died but he had never got round to it; he sold off a few more fields until the farm was little more than a smallholding, a few hectares of arable, some silage, the rest mostly grazing for his sheep.

Wyllie sank into an old overstuffed armchair covered in dark maroon brocade trimmed with faded cut ruche, his feet propped on a matching footstool, its ancient fringing sun-bleached and perished. Habitually he hid behind a copy of *Farmers Weekly*, occasionally grunting his agreement or otherwise with various articles. Violet usually read her weekly women's magazines. This Sunday, however, she just sat and looked out of the window.

'Wyllie, can you put your paper down for a while – please.'

Wyllie slowly lowered the pages down until he could see Violet over the livestock price section.

'Wyllie, I need to attend to the twins' bedroom. I want you to give me the key.'

His reply was short and definite. 'No,' he said, and raised the paper again.

Violet said nothing for a time; she just looked hard at the front and back pages of his paper. She tried to look through it, to see his face, to judge his reaction. Wyllie knew she was staring at him; it made him feel very uncomfortable. He could barely believe what she had just said. He could have just imagined it; no . . . he peered surreptitiously over his paper to see Violet's waiting expression.

'No,' he said, more forcibly.

'Don't you dare hide behind that paper again. I am serious, man. I need to do this . . . *we* need to do this. They are never coming back, my babies, never.'

'You couldn't take it, woman – you're too frail, too delicate.'

Violet Turnbull stood up from her chair. She rose to her full height, all four feet and eleven inches of her. She strode determinedly across the room. She bent, and ripped the *Farmers Weekly* from her husband's gripped hands.

'Look at me.' She spoke in a voice like breaking ice. 'Look at me, Wyllie Turnbull. Who do you see? An old woman, an old, sick, frightened woman, a grieving creature unable to face anything outside of her own front door. Now look again. Think back man, think back to the young woman you married – strong, hard-working, barren – yes – for far too long, but happy. I poured my life into this farm then – our farm, our home, our lives. Then – a miracle. Our miracle – two miracles; and I poured my life into them.' She hesitated, filled her lungs with air for her next tirade. 'I do not want to die a frail, grieving, old woman – and what if you die before me? It's very likely, you know. I'll be a sad, mad, old widow-woman with a locked room like a shrine, like something out of a Victorian novel. I want to hang out my washing on the drying green, I want to go to a Women's Rural meeting, I want to be able to walk out of the door to the car without having to cover my head and eyes almost collapsing with terror at the hugeness of it all.'

Wyllie looked up at her face from his seated position. For years he had looked down, down into a sad, distant face: an empty face, a loveless face, a fearful face. This face was different. From beneath the massed wrinkles and downy, soft hair a face from the past glared down at him – not beautiful certainly, but striking: striking green eyes and black hair flying in the wind.

'Violet . . . I . . . what do I do?'

'Where is the key, Wyllie? Get me the key, now, while I have the strength.'

Wyllie rose slowly. He took Violet by the elbow and began to steer her gently back to her chair. She shook him off.

'The key,' she demanded.

Brian Rigden deposited a filthy, dishevelled, exhausted Dexter back at Orby Cottage in time for tea.

'Cheers, Dex. Here's twenty-five quid – will that do? I couldn't have got that job finished without you.'

Dexter was very pleased with the cash – not bad, not bad at all. He limped down the path and round to the back door where Nipper and the smell of cooking met him simultaneously.

'What's for dinner, Gran? I'm starving.'

'Goodness me, look at the state of you! What have you been doing?'

Michael ambled in from the sitting room.

'Hedge laying. Well, Brian did the hedge laying really; I cleared up the brash and burnt it all. I had a go at the laying, too – look at my hands – real blisters and thorn gouges.' Dexter was quite proud of his war wounds. He had learnt that the blackthorn and hawthorn were vicious brutes, that the elder was a pain to burn, that there was a proper way to set a bonfire, that designer jeans were not for working in, and that wellington boots made his feet sweat and stink more than trainers did.

'You've time for a quick bath before dinner. The water's nice and hot; clean towels in the airing cupboard,' his gran told him.

'Great – haven't had a bath in years.' Dexter noticed his granny's raised eyebrows. 'Showers, Gran, showers.' He tootled off upstairs to get some clean clothes, chuckling at his own joke. As he passed back through the kitchen Alice and Michael both held their noses in fun, pointing at his sweat-sodden socks and the prints they left on the kitchen lino. They all laughed together.

After dinner they sat in front of the television to watch *Antiques Roadshow*.

'Here Gran, it would be just your luck to find out that some old bit of china you'd got was worth a bundle.'

'I certainly hope not,' Alice replied, truthfully.

Dexter dozed off; Alice nodded sleepily in her chair. Michael rose softly and left the room, gesturing to Nipper to follow.

'Come on, boy, it's a lovely evening – let's have us a short stroll, eh?'

They walked up towards the steading, Nipper following a fresh scent under the hedgerow. Michael walked slowly, thoughtfully; he remembered doing a bit of hedge laying with his dad, years ago. He was, he realised, faintly jealous of his son, tired from a hard day in the fresh air. He was also more than faintly jealous of Brian Rigden. He turned in the lane and looked back towards his childhood home. The sun was setting, and on the horizon the stones still stood. Nothing here had changed, yet everything had changed. He had left – been desperate to leave – done a bit of this, a bit of that, married, settled down, worked hard, provided for his family – they were still together – a miracle in itself these days. He should be happy. Once again that feeling he had experienced before, that feeling that his existence was too nice began to come upon him. Last time he had felt this way Penny had ended up in hospital. Last time he had felt this way, things had not been as 'nice', had not been as 'lovely' as he had imagined. Penny was happy now, the money problem sorted, she was making a very decent income, as he knew from keeping her books.

Things were looking up. Things might have been looking up, but Michael was not. This time, he realised suddenly, standing in the lane, lit by the last gilding rays of the sinking sun, he was the one with the secret. He grasped at wisps of thought stirring in his mind. He wanted to come home.

That same Sunday, Avian Tyler sat in her kitchen. She was thinking about Violet Turnbull. Maisie had visited Avian the week before, in transit from the orange farm in Spain to a festival in Scotland. Maisie had asked after Violet, and Avian had told her about the visit to Duddo.

'Great – do you think you'll be able to help her? She is such a nice old lady – maybe a bit scary on the surface, but underneath . . .'

'You think so? I get the feeling that underneath lies an even fiercer person than you might imagine,' Avian had replied.

That sentence had stayed with her. What had she meant by that?

The telephone rang. Avian was not surprised to find her caller was Violet Turnbull; such synchronicities were commonplace and not unexpected.

'I've got the key – the key to the twins' bedroom. It's here, on the table in front of me.' Violet's voice was high and breathy.

'Good afternoon, Violet.'

'Yes, sorry . . . it's me – I've got the key.'

'Yes, you said. Why have you phoned me?'

'I don't know; I did it without thinking. Wyllie gave me the key and walked out – said he had to clean off the tractor. He's just gone – I just phoned.'

'What do you want from me? You know I will help if I can, but you have to know what it is you really want.'

Violet did not reply immediately. Avian listened to Violet's breathing slow down as she composed herself.

'I am afraid,' Violet replied, eventually, her voice returning to its normal pitch. 'I am afraid that when I open that door, when I open those windows, that the last remaining echoes of the twins will escape like wraiths. I am afraid that I have trapped them in that room in the same way I have trapped myself in this house.'

'Violet, listen to me. The twins' wraiths are not in your house. They are trapped, and – yes – it may well be you who is not letting them go, but they are absolutely not in the house. I promise you, I would have known if they were.'

'Are you sure? Do you have the Gift? I should have known.' Violet's childhood had been permeated with stories of the old land, the old time; the Gift was something she could accept without misgiving.

'So, will you open the room?'

'I will. I will do it now. Avian, will you be with me, please?'

'I will. I will be with you. Imagine my hand gently pressing into the small of your back, supporting you. Can you do that? Can you feel it? Keep it there. Be strong, be unafraid, gather your strength; pick up that key.'

The phone went quiet; Avian heard the click as the receiver was replaced, then the hum of the dialling tone. Avian left the phone off the hook. She sat herself comfortably in a chair and focused her intent on Violet Turnbull. Through the palm of her right hand she shared and bore some of the intense emotion this woman was experiencing: her palm sweated, it shook; she felt the droop of the spine as Violet reached the bedroom door; she felt the cold shiver as the key was turned; she gave a gentle push forward. The connection fractured then. Avian was momentarily fearful for the elderly woman so distant from her. Had she collapsed? Avian focused again, harder; she felt sure Violet had severed the connection – rejected the support.

Avian smudged the room with smoke from burning dried sage, opened all the windows and doors to cleanse the space, and waited.

Violet stood just inside the doorway of the room she had not entered for so many years and looked around her. The room was tidy; she wondered who had tidied it. Thick, soft dust covered every surface, lacy cobwebs danced in the draught from the opening of the door. The late afternoon sun angled in from the windows lighting the air in blocks full of dancing dust motes. It fell on the hand-knotted rug on the floor; it clipped the patchwork quilt at the end of one of the two single beds with their heavy, carved, wooden headboards.

It lit the long dangling legs of a golly that Violet had made, which sat on an Orkney chair. Violet slowly walked around the room, her slippered feet shuffling up wafts of dust as she moved. She opened the windows wide, and the fresh, sun-warmed air entered in gusts, gradually replacing the stale air of decades. She picked up a small pair of leather shoes and rubbed the dust from them with her sleeve before she replaced them. She opened drawers to find pyjamas, vests, pants, socks, hand-knitted cable jumpers, Fair Isle tank tops, little checked shirts and pairs of worsted shorts. She brushed over the clothes with the tips of her gnarled fingers, remembering the buying, the knitting and the sewing. She walked over to the Orkney chair and lifted the golly, brushed the dust from his red felt waistcoat, blew the dust from his round black face and his curly sheep's wool hair. She sat in the chair; its straight hard back held her upright, the rough weave of its fibres dug into her thighs, buttocks and spine. She sat, holding the golly to her shrivelled bosom. Slow large teardrops rolled over her wrinkled cheeks forming deltas of moisture that seeped down her neck to wet the collar of her blouse.

Wyllie found her there later. He had hosed down the tractor, and if his face was wet it could have been from spray; he wiped the wetness off on his sleeve. The redness of his eyes told another story. He had hoped to find Violet still in the kitchen, still looking at the key – she was not. He checked the downstairs rooms, he cautiously went up the first flight of stairs to see if she had gone for a lie down or a nap in their bedroom – she had not. He opened the door at the bottom of the attic stairs and called her name. He crept up the stairs and turned the corner to see the door of the twins' room open; afraid, he entered. Violet did not hear him; she sat with her back to him, hidden behind the Orkney chair, only her frail arm hanging over its armrest told of her presence. Wyllie walked round to the front of the chair, terrified of finding her dead – dead of shock, heart attack, broken heart. If she was dead, that too would be his fault; again he would be guilty – after all, he had handed over the keys, he had walked away and left her – he was the one who was too weak to face this room. He trembled, silently keeping his eyes firmly on his wife until she looked up.

'Wyllie,' she said, in a voice surprising in its fortitude. 'Did you tidy the room?'

'Yes,' he replied simply. 'Tidied the room and locked the door.'

'And you've never been in here since?'

'Never.'

'They weren't here. There is nothing of them here; toys, clothes, yes – nothing of them; no wraiths.'

'No, Violet; not here.'

'Where, then, Wyllie? I have to find them – to let them go.'

'They've gone, Violet, gone.' It was not a question, or a suggestion; it was a statement of fact. Violet rose from the chair, the crumpled damp golly falling to the floor, raising dust as it landed.

She gripped her husband's arm tightly, and looked deep into his eyes. 'No. You are wrong.'

Together they closed the windows; Violet smoothed the quilts on the two beds, Wyllie picked up golly and put him back on the chair. They left the room hand in hand. They did not lock the door.

Avian waited patiently. Sure enough the phone did ring. A man's voice spoke.

'Miss Tyler?'

'Yes, this is Avian Tyler; can I help?'

'My name is Wyllie Turnbull. I believe you know my wife, Violet?' The voice was calm; it held no note of panic or distress. 'She asked me to telephone to let you know she is OK.'

'Good, I am glad to hear that. Thank you so much for letting me know, Mr Turnbull.'

There was a brief silence broken by Avian.

'Was there anything else?' she asked.

'No . . . no, just to let you know she's all right. Goodbye, Miss Tyler.'

'Goodbye, Mr Turnbull.'

CHAPTER TWENTY

I threw the stones. Four landed with the ancient scratch marks, already worn by generations of the old woman's forebears, facing the sun; two with their marks facing the earth, and one on its side, its marks towards the cold hearth where the fire had gone out for the first time in my remembering.

Four to the light, two to the dark, and one to the place of fire. The odds seemed in my favour. I collected my stones and placed them in the skin bag along with the dried herbs – rue and fern, madder and watermint for the child, plugs of root of the wild carrot for the girl, and a stick of saltwort. The bindings and the scraper I placed in my bag. I turned my back on my past and walked back to the villa.

Monday morning, as Michael and Dexter said their good-byes to Alice, Wyllie Turnbull arrived at Orby Cottage.

'Back off down to the smoke then, young Michael?' he asked.

''Fraid so, Mr Turnbull, 'fraid so,' Michael replied. The tone in his voice made Alice turn from a snatched hug with her reluctant grandson. In the car, she safely stowed away a flask of tea and numerous sandwiches and cakes, plus a large bottle of Irn Bru, a local delicacy from north of the border which Dexter had discovered when working with Brian.

As they drove away she turned to Wyllie.

'Now then, Wyllie, what brings you to my door of a Monday morning?'

'Alice, do you think you could make a brew?'

'Yes, of course; you had better come in. Is anything wrong, Wyllie?'

Over tea Wyllie told Alice the bare bones of the previous day's events.

'And how is Violet this morning?' Alice asked.

'It's hard for me to tell. She needs a woman friend to talk to. Will you pop along Alice, please – today?'

'Aye, I will; don't fret Wyllie – it'll all come right in the end.'

Later that morning Alice walked up the lane to Henge Farm. She rang the bell and let herself in, calling Violet's name loudly to announce her arrival. Violet was in the kitchen. When Alice came through the door Violet turned and embraced her neighbour. Alice was quite taken aback by this embrace; Violet had always been a body who liked to keep a bit of space round her.

'Alice, has Wyllie told you? I opened the room, the twins' room; Wyllie had tidied it all those years ago. They weren't there, the twins – the room was empty.'

'Do you mean the room was empty? Had Wyllie cleared it out without you knowing?'

'No, everything was still there – clothes, toys, beds – all the things were still there, but the room was empty of them . . . of the twins.'

Alice worried briefly for her friend's state of mind: she was certainly rambling, confused maybe. Alice sat Violet down and made them a pot of tea. Violet exhumed a huge cake tin from a cupboard and cut two slices of rich, dark fruit cake.

'Now, Violet; start from the beginning, you've lost me a bit.'

Violet went through the story of what happened the previous afternoon. Alice interrupted occasionally if she had misunderstood or lost the thread.

'So what happens now, Violet?'

'I wish I knew, Alice. I think I need to invite Avian Tyler back here; she has the Gift, you know.'

'Does she indeed?' All Alice's fear of the unchristian was expressed in those three words, and Violet felt it keenly.

Violet Turnbull looked Alice straight in the eyes. 'There's no need to look at me like that, Alice McCleish. The Church does not have all the answers, you know. What sort of God is it that snatches a woman's babies so cruelly? Just because you have had a charmed life does not give you the right to be so all-knowing.'

'I'm sorry, Violet – I didn't mean it like that.'

'Oh yes, you did – it was written across your face. I was raised on the Islands, surrounded by grave mounds and standing stones, and steeped in legends of the past. My mother's sister had the Gift, as did my grandmother, and great-grandmother. They had to keep it a secret to avoid persecution – some of my ancestors were probably burned at the stake, for all I know. Those stones out there were a link to my homeland when I first moved here to marry Wyllie. Whenever I felt lonely, I would look out and feel a connection between me here and my family home in sight of the stones I grew up with. Don't you dare to tell me it's all nonsense, just don't you dare.'

Wyllie was quite right to be concerned about Violet. Since the Tyler woman's visit, Violet had been changing. Alice had never heard her express such a heartfelt opinion about any subject for years – not since the accident.

'I have upset you, Violet, and I am truly sorry. I had better be getting back along now – Michael promised to phone me when they got back to London.'

'I am not upset really, Alice; it's just that you . . . oh, it doesn't matter, really it doesn't. Thank you for coming. I am not quite myself at the moment – I haven't been myself for such a long time; bits of me feel like they are coming back – it doesn't make sense; I only know I need Avian's help. I will telephone her this afternoon. Go on, off you go; I'll see you to the door.'

I reached the villa before nightfall. The woman and the girl were waiting in their private quarters; only the maidservant knew the reason for my return. I ground the herbs to a paste with the juice of ramson and smeared the paste onto the fire-hardened saltwort stick. This I passed into the womb of the girl as she lay, legs apart, on the low table. I pierced the sack, and the waters, tinted red, ran from the girl's body. She moaned. I pierced again, feeling the flesh of the infant, first withstanding, then breaking under the pressure of the sharpened stick. The first stage was complete. The plugs of wild carrot root I inserted into the girl's anus; the seaweed paste I smeared into her birthing passage. Then I bound her, and sat with the woman and girl until the labouring began.

Just before dawn, the girl's anguish was over. The small dead infant, curled and bloody, was expelled. I wrapped it in the bindings from its mother's body and threw it into the fires that heated the floors as the sun rose over the horizon.

Michael McCleish sat staring out of his fourth-floor window at the other office blocks surrounding him. Up in the top left-hand corner of his window he could glimpse a triangle of blue sky. In the air-conditioned environment it would have been impossible to guess the season: the temperature and humidity were kept at the optimum for maximum efficiency of the workforce. His secretary popped her head round the screen sectioning off his workstation.

'Michael,' she said. 'Top floor are on the phone – Angela Smith-Gore wants to see you about the Branxton account.'

'Tell her I'm free after my two thirty video conference with Euan Mathieson; should be finished by three fifteen at the latest. I'll see her at three thirty if it suits.'

The secretary's sleek blonde bob disappeared behind the screen, shortly reappearing when she confirmed the meeting for three thirty.

Michael missed the privacy of a proper office. His company had adopted the workstation ethic in the late nineties. He was one of the fortunate few with a permanent station which was for his use only; other, lesser members of staff were constantly mobile, able to access their information from any of the computer-linked stations within the building, or through hand-held devices. He sat back in his chair, his hands linked behind his head, and sighed. He tried to imagine himself somewhere else. He could only envisage the area around his childhood home. During rare moments for contemplation snatched since his return from Orby Cottage, he had daydreamed about escaping the rat race, buying a French farm-house, travelling the world with just a backpack – Australia, Nepal, the Aztec trail. Woolgathering, his father would have called it; pipe dreams. He wished his father were still alive; he could have talked to him – Callum would have understood. Whatever unlikely scenario Michael imagined, his reverie always seemed to bring him back to Duddo, the place he had tried so hard to escape from, the place where nothing much happened.

He remembered that pang of jealousy he had felt when Dex had had such a great day with Brian Rigden – he should have been the one teaching his son something. His chest tightened; he could have found himself in tears if his computer diary had not chimed its reminder that his video conference was in five minutes. Michael thought to himself that he would have to do something about this ridiculous situation – and soon. The computer screen changed from screensaver to conference mode and Michael resumed the efficient persona he inhabited for work purposes.

The meeting with Angela Smith-Gore went well: she was impressed by his work on the Branxton account, which had been causing some concern higher up. He had negotiated a package ensuring Branxton's continued use of their services for the next five years with an option to extend. There had been more hints of a promotion in the offing – nothing definite, just a strong possibility – was Michael interested? she wanted to know. He had said yes – and meant no.

If he were to escape, what the hell would he do? He could hear Penny: 'What could you do there, for Christ's sake? There's only fields, trees and bloody sheep – gonna be a shepherd are you?' Marsha would not care, she would soon be away to university and it would not matter to her where her parents lived any more. Dex. How could I move him to Duddo? Why should a city-raised kid want anything to do with the country life Michael lusted after? Just because he had one good day getting filthy and scratched did not mean he was a country boy at heart. Penny would be right – what could he do? Start up his own accountancy business? No, thank you; change one office for another? Might as well stay where he was.

No, it was pointless, he thought, as the train rattled into Putney station. He walked past the art college on his way home, decided to pop into Waitrose for a bottle of cheap bubbly, and arrived to find the house empty, a scrawled message from Penny by the microwave:

Nobody due back till after nine, M&S Cantonese Chicken meal for one in top of freezer, enjoy, love Pen.

A whole hour to himself. 'Great,' he groaned. He did not like the emptiness of the house. He fished out the frozen meal and threw it into the microwave, heat on full for eight minutes. As the meal spun slowly round and round in the brightly-lit oven he opened the bottle of champagne. The microwave pinged a reminder that the food was ready. Michael sat at the breakfast bar eating the meal from the container and drinking champagne while scribbling down initial notes for his great and cunning plan.

Dexter had been out with a gang of his mates: they were just hanging about. They had bought several bottles of Ice White cider, super strong and mega cheap from the supermarket. One of the lads was very hirsute for his age – good moustache and goatee beard – never got asked if he was eighteen or not. They also had fags, skins and a nice bag of weed that Natch had 'borrowed' from his dad's stash. They mooched off down to the park and sat under a plane tree on the sparse grass. Dex liked a smoke now and again – he had never really got into the booze. Natch rolled up a couple of joints and passed them round. Dex took several good lungfuls and lay back on the grass to watch the clouds puff by. The sky above was full of aeroplanes – some low, coming in to land, some higher, waiting their turn, some higher still, heading off into blueness, leaving contrails of white, which dissipated slowly behind them. He half registered his mates getting steadily drunker on the Ice White; Josh Dempster turned up with a bottle of buckie. Dex smoked the next joint to pass his way and drifted into a stoned pipe dream. He came to, later, at the sound of raised voices – shouting – a drunken argument. Natch had accused Josh of nicking what was left of the weed. The row had become physical and Josh, so pissed he could barely stand, was waving the broken empty buckie bottle in Natch's face. Someone had called the police on their mobile and two policemen were approaching dressed in protective knife-proof jackets, wielding their as yet unextended batons menacingly. Sirens were heard in the background as other officers rushed to the scene to provide backup. Some of the others legged it sharpish, disappearing into the back streets and alleyways. Dex, still a bit stoned, stayed just where he was. He sat up.

The next thing he knew he was in the arms of a large policeman. PC McLaughlin was really quite nice. Dexter was sent off with a caution: he had not been drunk, he had not been involved in the fight, he had not run off; but he had been stoned – although not actually in possession. PC McLaughlin's family came from Sprouston, a village near Duddo, just over the border into Scotland. He had, it turned out, known Michael McCleish from the good old days, and he asked Dexter to pass on his regards.

Michael finished the Chinese meal and was on to his second glass of bubbly when Dexter strode in.

'Hiya Dex – good day?'

'Different.'

'How different?'

'Don't lose your cool, Dad, but I nearly ended up at the police station. Do you remember a Malcom McLaughlin? He sends his regards.'

'Police station! Where? Why? Mal McLaughlin . . . big bloke . . . beard.'

'No beard now, but big – very big. There was a fight in the park – not me, I was in the wrong place at the wrong time – and probably with the wrong people. PC McLaughlin just gave me a telling off . . .' Dexter faltered. 'Dad, I don't want to stay round here, I don't want to do A levels; it means another two years round here.'

'Not do A levels? Your mother will be pleased.' Irony tinged Michael's reply.

'I think I want to go to horticultural college . . . you know, be a gardener or something . . . like Brian Rigden.' Dexter was hesitant; he was expecting a huge row about this as it had always been assumed he would go to university. Marsha would probably fulfil all their parents' expectations and then some, bloody golden girl, with her high hopes of a place at Durham. His father's reply was unexpected, to say the least.

'Go for it.'

Dexter's jaw dropped.

'Here, have a glass of this bubbly, let's celebrate.' Michael poured a frothing glass for his son; the boy's confusion was plain to see.

'Dex, look – if that's what you want to do then you go for it. Let's get on the Net and find out some more information; if we present your mother with a good proposal it will be harder for her to argue about it.' The two of them took their glasses of champagne into Michael's office where they entered 'horticultural colleges' into Ask Jeeves, and pored over the results.

Penny crashed in through the door at nine forty-five, throwing her handbag down next to the microwave.

'Hello? Don't speak to me!' she shouted, to anyone within earshot.

Michael and Dex looked at each other, their expressions showing that now was probably not a good time for their news.

'I have had a shit day – really, really shitty. You wouldn't believe . . .' Penny continued, crashing and thrashing about in the kitchen. '. . . Oh! cheap bubbly – and there's a glass left.' She poured the remaining liquid into a glass and drank deeply, put the glass down and belched. 'Oops . . . sorry.'

Michael and Dexter appeared from the office.

'Hi Mum,' Dexter said cheerfully. 'What's for dinner?'

'Whatever you can find in the freezer, and I'll have the same.'

Dexter dug deep into the chest freezer, 'M&S Sweet and Sour prawns?'

'Lovely; don't suppose there's any more bubbly, Michael?'

'No, but there's a nice dry white if you fancy it.'

As she ate, Penny entertained the men with tales of the quirkiness of today's client. '. . . and still she insisted on the short-cut jacket over the trousers with the line right across the widest part of her hips . . .' A prawn. ' . . . So she looked shorter and dumpier than ever. Unbelievable.' Some rice and another prawn. '"Why do you employ me?" I said to her. "I am supposed to tell you what does and does not work."' A slug of wine. "'That jacket makes you look fat; it cuts you in two at your widest part." But no, she would not listen; what can you do? Short-cut jackets are in – all the weather girls wear them, so madam has to have one. Anyway, how was your day?'

They both replied that their day had been fine. Dexter disappeared off to his room, leaving Michael and Penny sitting opposite each other at the table. For a while they sat in silence, Penny pushing the remains of her food around her plate.

They spoke each other's name simultaneously.

'You first.'

'No, age before beauty,' Penny replied.

'Well, I was just wondering . . . a bit, you know, about . . .'

'Come on Michael, you're making me nervous; what is it?' Penny hurried him.

'Well, I know everything's fine – you and me, and the kids – that's all fine; and your new job and stuff – but I was wondering.'

'So you said,' Penny interrupted, firmly, looking Michael right in the eyes.

'Are you happy? Sort of in yourself, I mean, with who you are and what you are doing?'

'Why? What do you mean? It's a bit deep, that.' Penny raised an eyebrow.

'I mean, well – it won't be long until the kids have left home to do whatever it is they do, then it'll be just us, which will be lovely, but . . .'

'How long have you been mulling this over, then? This is

not something that's just occurred to you, is it?' Penny's tone was one of curiosity, and this surprised Michael. He had not meant to get on to this conversation so soon; he had not had time to think it all through himself. He had assumed she would be dead against any dramatic change to their lifestyle.

'Not long, really; only since Dex and I came back from Mum's. I haven't got some mad midlife crisis idea about dropping out and walking to India or anything. It's just that the one thing I do know is that I do not want to go in to that office day after day after day until I reach sixty-five, to retire with a reduced pension, if the current situation is anything to go by, to live out my days here in the city with one or two Saga holidays a year to keep me sane – or not.'

'Do you hate your job that much, really? I often wondered how you could bear it. Hasn't there been a hint of a promotion?'

'Yes, there's a meeting next week, and I think they are going to offer me Bob Jenkins' position – he's leaving for health reasons. I don't want it, Pen; more client handling, more lunches, more pretending; it's not the real me, it's the work me; the work me could do the job – that's not the problem – but can the real me live with that work me? Sorry, that makes no sense at all, and you have had a long shitty day, and it's getting late.'

'Don't accept it if you don't want it. Just say thanks, but no thanks.' Penny read the look on Michael's face and realised there was more to it than just the promotion. She put her well-manicured hand over his and turned his hand to face palm up. His hands were big and square, her small hand was hidden beneath. His hands were soft to touch, clean: incongruous to see such a masculine hand so unblemished. She kissed his palm.

'It's late – let's not worry about the promotion now – don't take it if you don't want to. The real problem as far as I can tell is working out what it is you – well, both of us, I suppose – what we *do* want.'

They went to bed and quietly made love. Michael slept soundly, afterwards; he was relieved to have begun this new conversation – relieved and surprised by Penny's response.

Penny lay awake.

CHAPTER TWENTY-TWO

I stayed with the girl for two days. The servants were told that she had a fever and that I had been called to heal her with my art. All believed this, except the one who spoke my words for me. On the third morning the girl rose from her bed. She looked at her mother and at me with bitter hatred in her eyes. The woman left us. To lessen my guilt, I showed the girl how to stop the coming of another infant with the juice of onion or ramson soaked onto a pad of wool flock, or with mashed willow leaves. My words were given to her by the serving maid. I walked to the worship hut, where the Pilus Prior was waiting.

Avian Tyler replaced the telephone receiver and sighed. She went into her kitchen and put the kettle on. Waiting for it to come to the boil, she constructed an open sandwich of organic wholegrain bread, cottage cheese and sun-dried tomatoes, over which she dribbled a little Greek olive oil. She poured the boiling water into a one-cup-sized brown earthenware teapot to infuse the herbal concoction waiting within. Musty, earthy steam perfumed the room. She ate the sandwich slowly, savouring each mouthful. She pushed the empty plate aside and poured the herbal brew into a cup. Sitting back in her chair, she allowed herself finally to consider the content of her conversation with Violet Turnbull.

Violet had certainly begun her journey. Opening the children's room was monumental, and something Avian had not expected would happen so soon. Avian once more realised that she had underestimated the old woman.

Violet had asked Avian to return to Duddo. There was something Violet needed her to do – and she had been very cagey about exactly what this 'something' was. Avian was unsure. In the past, with other people she had helped, she had kept a certain distance, avoided bonding, feeling instead that it was not her place to share in the person's journey; rather, to provide signposts and the occasional resting place along the way. Perhaps it was Violet's age that had hastened the pace; in her eighties she may not have the luxury of a slow, gradual recovery. Maybe Violet's journey was to be short and turbulent; maybe Avian should make herself more accessible.

Avian arrived at Orby Cottage within the week. Violet had arranged for Avian to stay with Alice McCleish for a few days. Violet had initially offered to put Avian up at the farm, much to Wyllie's disgruntlement; he could not begin to understand why his wife should suddenly want the company of this woman, whom he had never met, but who sounded like a bit of a weirdo to him. Avian had Michael's old bedroom; Alice had made it pretty with some flowers picked from the garden, and she had placed the Durham quilt, folded, on the end of the bed, in case Avian should feel chilly at night. Avian sat in her room on that first evening after an inventive vegetarian meal. The room spoke to her mostly of restful sleep, children's conversations, secrets shared; it had a slumberous, yet mischievous voice. She hoped she would find rest easy in this room. She stood and wandered over to the window. On the skyline the standing stones jutted up in silhouette.

Avian had discovered long ago about the voices of such places. On a family caravan holiday, they had taken the road across Salisbury Plain and parked higgledy-piggledy, along with a few other vehicles, in a field. They had all disgorged from her father's old Austin Healey. On the Primus her mother brewed up a pot of tea and they ate a picnic of bacon sandwiches outside at the fold-up table, all sitting on vivid, striped nylon fold-up chairs. The whole family – Mum, Dad, Nan, Granddad, Avian and her brother – crossed the narrow road and walked towards the stones, her brother running like a puppy off its lead, round and round, shouting.

'It's the Flintstones, Daddy! Look, it's the Flintstones!' Avian had felt what she described to her mother as 'earachey' during the picnic; the nearer they got to the stones, the more she tried to drop back.

'Hurry up Ave, it's the Flintstones,' her brother had cajoled, running back to take her by the hand.

'It's too noisy.' Avian had resisted his pulls. She had allowed herself to be drawn closer to the stones by her father – she felt a little braver holding his hand.

'Daddy, why is it noisy?' she had asked, looking up into his face so far away from hers.

He picked her up and sat her on his shoulders. She was a strange one, this daughter of his; fancy thinking it noisy. He listened. He could hear the soft whisper of a gentle summer breeze, he could hear skylarks and curlews, he could hear a car in the distance; how could she think it noisy? Avian had sat firmly on her father's shoulders, her little feet, in blue Clarks sandals, held in his strong hands, her own hands tightly around his forehead, her bare summer knees clasped to his ears. The sound grew stronger as they approached an enormous arch of stone. Nan and Granddad had found a smaller stone, just the right height for them to sit themselves down on comfortably. Granddad was slipping off his jacket in the heat, revealing his braces; under his shirt his string vest showed. Nan struggled out of her cardigan and flapped a piece of paper at her face to cool herself down. Mum was keeping an eye on the puppy boy.

'Dad, I don't like it. Put me down.'

'Don't be so silly. Let's see if we can find Barney Rubble,

shall we?'

He lifted her down from his shoulders. She wheeled through the air and felt she was flying. The noise, a deep, resonating, physical thrumming beat into her whole body; her vision began to see beyond what was there: the plain became forested, the noise became a tumultuous gaggle of untold number, the knapping of untold flint, and the roar of furnaces and kilns, as if this place were a repository of every echo of local existence. When her feet touched the ground her knees buckled, she collapsed like a rag doll on the grass, she was sick, she wet herself, and her bowel emptied.

She came out of the faint to see her grandmother's face and hear her voice.

'Avian – wake up now, Avian.'

A wet flannel was being wiped over her brow and she was back in the caravan, lying on the bench seating by the table, naked and sweating. Outside, she could hear the voices of her mother and father, but she could not focus on what the words were.

'Nana, it was so noisy.'

'Never you mind, my lovely. My mother always said such places weren't put there just for visiting; she always said they were special places best avoided by ordinary folk.'

Avian realised now, as an adult, that her Nana – her father's mother – might have understood a lot more than she ever let on. She had died when Avian was nine, just a few years after this holiday.

Avian's mother had come up the step into the van and peered round the door.

'Do you think she needs to see a doctor, Mum?' she asked.

'No, love, it's just the heat and the travelling, and she probably gobbled her food too quickly. A lie down in the shade and a bit of quiet's all she needs; you lot get back off to the stones, we'll be fine here, won't we, Ave?'

'Yes, Nana,' she had replied, feeling the cooling draught of air wafting from behind the closed caravan curtains. Her clothes had been rinsed and hung out to dry, and Avian drifted off to sleep with the gentle flap of the clothes and the slow, rhythmic breathing of her grandmother as a lullaby.

All these memories rushed to the fore as Avian contemplated the simple circle on the hill. There was a scratching at the bedroom door, and Avian moved across to open it. Sitting at the threshold was Nipper – just sitting: neither growling nor wagging, he was just waiting, as if he had decided it was time to make up his mind about this strange person.

'Come in if you want to,' Avian offered.

Nipper stood and looked up into her face. He walked stiltedly into the room, sniffed around her shoes and bag, and then sat down again looking directly at her.

'So, you don't trust me then?' Avian asked. 'Suit yourself. Don't you go thinking I am going to try and woo you into being my friend with titbits or belly scratching – not my style; take me as I am or not at all.' And she sat down on her bed.

Nipper sat a moment longer, as if contemplating this situation. He gave himself a quick scratch behind his left ear, stood up, wagged his tail, and jumped up onto the bed next to Avian.

'Smart move, dog.' Avian said.

Later Avian heard Alice calling in the garden. 'Nipper! Where are you? Nipper!'

Avian called down from her window. 'I'm afraid he's sneaked up here with me, Alice. I'll send him down.' She gave the dog a friendly shove and sent him on his way.

Alice called up the stairs. 'Fancy a cup of cocoa before bed?'

'I'll come down,' Avian replied, closing the door of her room behind her.

They sat in the kitchen over their steaming mugs of cocoa.

'Yes . . . it was very strange,' Alice recounted. 'Violet told all about the key, and opening the room; she said the boys weren't there – which of course they weren't. She seemed very confused – rambling, almost.'

'What was she like before?' Avian asked.

'Before? Before the accident, you mean? Well . . . what would be the word . . . hang on a mo,' Alice said as she got up and went to a drawer in the dresser. 'Somewhere in here should be some photographs.' She pulled out a large old maroon cloth-covered photograph album stuffed to the gunnels and overflowing. Alice shuffled through the album pointing out any pictures with Violet in them. 'Here – here's a good one, this shows what I mean.'

There was a photograph of a barn, and in the barn huge Belted Galloway cattle milled around. Behind them, a small figure in overalls and wellington boots waving a stick was herding the stragglers in, waiting to close a gate behind them.

'There's Violet; my Callum said she was as good a stockman as he had ever come across. See this one here – this is Violet at the Glendale Show – there, in the white coat, showing that Galloway bull; won prizes all over the north, she did, with that one. Well, all those years with no sign of children, she had to put her energy into something. The farm was much bigger then.'

Avian looked at the dwarfed figure of the young Violet Turnbull leading the enormous beast around the show ring. She had misread Violet Turnbull entirely: the real Violet, this feisty, dominant woman, had been, until recently, so completely entombed in the fearful Violet that even Avian had not sensed her presence.

'That was the other thing she said that was strange,' Alice recalled. 'Bits of herself were coming back, she said. What do you make of it?'

Avian was silent. She looked down at the scattered photographs on the table. Alice sighed deeply and sadly.

'Look, here are the twins.' She took a tissue from her sleeve and dabbed away a tear. 'Such a tragedy: such a mystery. Violet was never the same. Couldn't stop grieving, I suppose. I know what it is like to lose the person you love the most, but Callum and I had lived a life together, had our own son in the end, then the grandchildren . . . shared memories. Violet had them for such a short time and they were so precious: her miracle babies, she called them.'

Alice found one more photo of Violet, the only one in close-up, where Avian could see into her eyes: a defiant woman. Thick, dark eyebrows sat straight across her brow, unshaped. Her hair, only partially tamed by a headscarf, still sprang out in dense black coils lying thickly on her shoulders; her eyes were dark and clear, looking boldly into the eye of the camera. Her mouth was slightly open, as if she was just about to speak, or had just spoken; there was a hint of a smile on her lips.

'Thank you, Alice, for the cocoa, for showing me the photos; you really are very kind.'

'Not at all: don't even think on it. I just hope you can help poor Violet.'

'Do you mind if I borrow this last photo, just for a day or so? I promise to give it back before I leave.' Avian held the photo in her hands.

'As long as you like, dear, as long as you need it.'

Avian rose to go to bed.

'Goodnight, Alice, see you in the morning.'

'Goodnight Avian, hope you sleep well.'

Avian slept fitfully that night. Half-dreams and spectres choked by unintelligible hints of voices leapt suddenly, or wove themselves intricately, in her semi-conscious mind. A small dark-haired woman stood in the shadows of her sleep, always just out of view, intangible. At sunrise she woke suddenly to the sound of children's voices which faded away in echoes. Avian sat up in bed. The house was silent. Outside her window the birds were just winding down from the exultant summons of their morning chorus; a blackbird still trilled in the oak tree beyond her window. Avian wrapped an old dressing gown, which hung on the back of the door, around herself, and tiptoed along the hallway past Alice's room, down the stairs to the kitchen. Nipper raised his head, huffed at the visitor, and snuggled back down into his bed.

'Good morning to you too, dog,' Avian whispered. Leaving the bathroom, concerned that the rattling of pipes would wake her host, Avian decided to take a stroll in the garden. She tied the threadbare gown securely around her middle, taking up some of the excess length that trailed on the floor behind her. She shoved her feet into a pair of enormous cold, clammy wellington boots and drew an old waxed jacket around her shoulders. 'Coming?' she asked the dog.

He hesitated, then stood up and stretched luxuriously, shook himself and nonchalantly walked over to the door.

The morning promised a clear day. Wisps of cloud hung like streamers high up in the sky; a slight mist, already beginning to burn off in the sun, remained, and the grass was wet with dew. Avian slushed around the garden in the enormous wellies, leaving long shuffling tracks through the bloom of dew. Nipper chased a baby rabbit out of the garden through a hole in the fence – the rabbit had been munching happily in

Alice's flower bed. The hole was too small for Nipper to follow; he worried at the fence. Avian marked the spot with a cane so that the gardener could repair the gap.

Avian felt she needed to connect with a guiding voice. She was somewhat lost; she felt she could be dealing with something more unfathomable than Violet Turnbull's agoraphobia. The megaliths stood timelessly on the horizon, the low morning sun casting long shadows that ran like liquid down the sides of the mound. They stood above the retreating mists. Avian's musing was interrupted by the unmistakable sound of a kettle whistling from the kitchen of Orby Cottage. Alice was up and about. Nipper scooted back indoors to see his mistress, anticipating his morning biscuit. Alice peered out from the kitchen doorway.

'Good morning, Avian – my, don't you look a picture! Brian Rigden's scarecrow looks better dressed than you do.'

They sat in companionable silence in the kitchen crunching toast thick with butter and home-made dark marmalade laced with a drop of whisky.

'Are you going along to see Violet this morning?'

'Not yet; there's something I need to do first,' Avian replied.

'Can I help?' Alice offered.

'You can point me to the nearest rowan tree.'

Alice felt herself bristle. Rowan . . . and what does she want that for? As if I didn't know, she thought to herself.

'Down near the burn, in the wee valley behind the mound:

I used to collect the berries to make a jelly.'

Alice was intrigued by the woman sitting opposite her, still wrapped in the old dressing gown – Michael's, she thought – or was it? Never mind. The idea that the woman – who seemed very pleasant, if unusual – had the Gift, second sight, made Alice feel most uncomfortable. Did she know what Alice was thinking? It may be a gift, but from whom? Not from Alice's God; her God had removed all such gifts when Adam and Eve were cast out from the Garden of Eden.

'Thank you, Alice; I realise that I am a somewhat unwelcome guest, and that it is only because of your deep concern for Violet that you have been kind enough to put me up like this. I understand your misgivings, truly, but there is nothing evil in what I do. I just listen. My gift is my ability to hear more than most people do. I can't explain it; it has been both the plague and the pivot of my life.'

'My Callum always wanted to plant a rowan by the gate "to keep the witches at bay". He kept a lot of the old lore and beliefs fast in his head. Learnt it from his grandmother, he said. Heathen nonsense I called it. We agreed to differ. I hope you and I can agree to differ. You go and collect your herbs and do what you do. It's my turn to clean the church this week; I shall pray for Violet, for her peace of mind.'

'It's a deal.' Avian smiled with relief.

Alice drove off later into Duddo, to the church, a new pack of dusters and a large tin of lavender beeswax polish in her bag. She hoped Mrs Ollerenshaw would not be there.

That woman took it upon herself to organise everything nowadays . . . and such a gossip.

Alice parked and walked to the church. She took a large old key from the ledge above the door and let herself in. The building was quite plain: functional, not adorned or ornamented, except by the two stained glass panels and the altar cloth. A huge venerable parish Bible lay closed on the simple lectern, a soft green felt bookmark identifying the place of the last reading hanging from the top and bottom of the book, beautifully embroidered in silk thread. Alice closed the door behind her and dipped almost imperceptibly in the direction of the altar. Alice swept and dusted; she took the rugs out and gave them a good shake; the few cobwebs she could reach, she swished away; others lurked higher, covered with a soft layer of grey dust, swaying gently. The aired rugs replaced, the worst of the dust removed, disturbed motes filling the air, waiting to settle, Alice began to polish the pews. The smell of lavender began to pervade the building as she rubbed the sticky, transparent brownish substance onto the pews.

Alice placed the used tea bag and two of the plastic milk pots into a rubbish bag, and took her cup of tea outside. She sat on the little bench with its plaque in remembrance of the old minister. The sun was warm and Alice felt sleepy; she had almost nodded off when a voice disturbed her. It was Sarah Rigden.

'Morning, Alice – you look very relaxed there.'

'Sarah . . . oh – and little Faith; how are you, my little

sweetheart?'

'Off to mother and toddler group at the village hall; not really my thing, but it's so good for Faith to spend time with other children. It was different with Aaron, there were lots of young mums along our street and we used to pop into each other's houses for tea and a chat, or tea and a good cry – whatever. It's the one thing I miss, that and having my mum nearby.'

'You look a bit strained, if you don't mind me saying,' Alice remarked, immediately wishing she had not – that was probably the last thing the girl needed.

'It's nothing . . . nothing to worry about, anyway. How are you?'

'Very well; I have that Avian Tyler woman staying with me just now – only don't say anything in the village – you know how the gossips are.'

'The Ollerenshaw Mafia, that's what Brian calls them.' Sarah and Alice giggled.

'Right, that's us off to the village hall now, or we shall be late. Bye, Alice.'

'Bye, Sarah; bye-bye, little Faith.' Lovely names, those children; shame the family never went to church – still, not so many people did any more. Alice returned to the cool interior of the church. With a new duster she polished the oak pews until they gleamed golden in the muted light.

As Alice left the church, carefully locking the door behind her and hiding the key in the frighteningly obvious place it had been kept for as long as anyone could remember, Sarah and Faith walked past on their way home. Sarah was walking fast, head down, did not notice Alice; Faith wailed miserably. Alice noticed Sarah's shoulders were held high and tense, her eyes screwed almost shut. Alice watched her fumble blindly for her keys, struggle to unlock her door, and eventually wrest the door open and let herself and Faith in. They disappeared from view, but the door remained open. Alice was concerned. She was not one to interfere. However, she walked past her parked car, down the village street, and into the Rigden's house.

'Sarah!' she called from the hallway. 'Sarah, are you all right?' She heard a sobbing from another room and she followed the sound of it. Sarah was on her knees in front of the buggy, weeping uncontrollably, trying to undo the clip of the safety harness to get Faith out. Her hands shook, she stopped to wipe the tears from her eyes to see, and saw Alice standing there.

'Sarah, sweetheart – what's wrong? What on earth is the matter? Here, let me.'

'It's time for her lunch,' Sarah sobbed.

'Just you sit yourself in that chair there – don't argue with me, young lady. Now then . . .'

Faith was extricated from the harness, whisked away to the kitchen by Alice, fed and popped into her cot upstairs for a wee nap. Sarah had been furnished with a pot of tea, a jug of milk, a mug, and a tray with biscuits; a blanket was wrapped around her quivering shoulders, and her feet were raised and similarly wrapped.

Over the baby alarm Sarah could hear Alice crooning the child to sleep, an old local lullaby Sarah had not heard before. Despite the crippling pain in her head, the soft singing soothed her, too, and when Alice came downstairs again, Sarah was fast asleep. What to do? Alice thought. She could not just leave them. Alice phoned home.

'Orby Cottage,' a voice replied.

'Oh Avian, I am so glad I got you – it's Alice. I'm at young Sarah Rigden's house. There's something not quite right . . . I mean . . . it's OK now, they are both sleeping, but something is definitely wrong.'

'Do you need me? I was just about to leave to visit Violet, but I can phone her and explain, if you need me there.'

'No, don't worry about that, I just wanted to let you know what was happening, in case I'm not back until much later. Could you let Nipper out? And feed him around fiveish if I'm not back – one mugful of the dried food in the pantry is all he needs. He could probably do with letting out for a pee.'

'He's fast asleep, Alice; he insisted on coming out with me this morning, so he has had plenty of exercise. I hope you don't mind.'

'I'm very glad indeed; thank you. I can stop worrying about him and get on with finding out what the problem is here.'

Alice had been quietly peeved that Nipper had spent his

morning with Avian – after all, he was her last link with Callum, he had been Callum's wee dog. However, the dog was generally a good judge of character, and if he had taken to the Tyler woman, then perhaps she was not as strange as Alice had first imagined.

Alice wondered about phoning Brian, but decided against it; men, she had found, were never much use in such situations. They tended to panic. Faith woke up before Sarah – Alice heard her over the baby alarm. Alice got the child up, took her downstairs to the kitchen and gave her a cup of some apple juice she found in the fridge. It was strikingly cold, so Alice poured a little hot water in to warm it up and dilute it. Funny, she thought, how the old knacks of childcare just come back to you, like it was yesterday. She remembered her own, rather more substantial, boy baby and how it felt to feed a child at the breast, wean it, watch it grow to manhood. Poor Violet, she thought. Sarah slept on. The poor girl must be exhausted, Alice thought. She dressed Faith in a warm cardigan and took her out into the garden, where Alice found an old deckchair in the shed and settled herself to wait for Sarah to emerge.

An hour or so later Sarah did appear at the back door. Her face was sad, her eyes still red and puffy from so many tears. Alice sat her in the deckchair and made them both some tea. When she came back outside, Sarah was cuddling a happy little Faith and all seemed peaceful and calm.

'Sarah, what was the problem?' Alice asked tentatively.

'Tell me to mind my own business if you want to, but you were very distressed.'

'I keep getting these dreadful headaches – truly, truly awful; unbearable, like someone sticking needles into my head – big, fat hot needles. I have been to the doctor – he gave me some strong painkillers – migraine, he said – but I've never had migraines before. I don't like taking the pills – they make me drowsy; I'm afraid I'll drop Faith, or forget to collect Aaron from nursery . . . which reminds me – what's the time?'

'Ten past three – but don't you worry: I'll collect him in my car – it's just over the road.'

'Thank you, Alice; but I'll have to phone the nursery and tell them, or they won't let him leave the building with you – Stranger Danger policy.'

Alice finally left for home when Brian returned dirty and hungry at five o'clock. She had reheated a casserole she had found in the freezer, sat him down to his dinner and told him why she was there.

'I'll send her to a specialist,' he told Alice. 'I hadn't realised it was as bad as this – it never seems to happen when I'm around.'

'Do that,' Alice said. 'Just make sure you do that – and soon.'

Alice parked under the lean-to and wondered why she could not hear Nipper's usual woofs of excitement at her return. She wandered round to the back door – and still no woofing. The door was open and Alice called out.

'Avian! Nipper! Anyone about?' No reply. Then Nipper appeared from outside wagging and twisting around Alice's feet. 'There you are, boy – where have you been?'

Avian walked in slowly behind the dog.

'My goodness, Avian, you look washed out.' Alice declared. 'Have you been up to the farm to see Violet?'

'Oh yes, I didn't get back until gone five, so I thought I should give Nipper a quick stretch and a bit of fresh air.'

'You are kind, but you shouldn't have – a toddle round the garden on his own would have been fine.'

'No, it's OK – I needed some fresh air myself if the truth be told.' Avian had no intention of discussing the events of the afternoon with anyone, she needed to mull it over, to try to piece together their conversations and make some sense of what had occurred. She changed the subject.

'How is Sarah now? What was the problem?'

They discussed Sarah Rigden's headaches as they prepared a light supper of salad from the garden and some hard-boiled eggs.

'What has the doctor said?' Avian asked, as they sat down at the table.

'Migraine. He has given her stronger pills, as the last ones didn't help much.'

Avian knew she could help Sarah with more natural remedies, but not just at the moment; for now she was preoccupied with events at Henge Farm. She had collected the plant material she needed to shield her and prepared an amulet of sorts that morning wrapping the charm in plantain leaves and tying the bundle with woodbine tendrils. This was to strengthen her and provide some protection from the cacophony of voices and echoes she expected to encounter at the stones.

'Did you find the rowan trees?' Alice asked, as if she had grasped something of Avian's thoughts.

'Yes, I was hoping to go up to the stones this evening at sunset, but I am so tired, I don't think I can.'

'It's not far; I could come with you if you like.'

Avian knew perfectly well that it was not far, and she certainly did not need Alice for company. Her tiredness was not physical.

'Thank you, but I must go alone. I shall go tomorrow morning at sunrise.'

In a way Alice understood what Avian meant. Her last visit to the stones, with Margaret, had been so unexpectedly emotional, she had not imagined that she could have felt so touched by whatever it was that was there.

The two women spent the evening in quiet companionship. Alice sat and did some mending she had been meaning to do for ages, while Avian read. They exchanged soft words now and then. Alice made tea. At nine thirty, Avian closed her book and stretched her arms high above her, yawning.

'Bed, I think . . . early to bed, early to rise, etcetera.'

'Cup of cocoa before you go?' Alice offered. 'Always helps me sleep.'

'Mmm – lovely – how kind. Isn't your missus kind, Nipper?' Avian answered, rubbing the upturned belly offered by the dog.

'He's taken to you now, Avian, the silly old sausage.'

Avian stood naked at her bedroom window, looking out and up at the stones. As always, in these circumstances, she was afraid. Who would not be? She took her leaf-wrapped amulet and held it to her brow, her chest and then her belly, asking the plant spirits to grant her a clear night's sleep and that she should wake with courage. She focused her intent on the stones, trying to imbue them and their eldritch echoes with something of her purpose. Maybe there would be more of a welcome if they knew who she was – and why she was coming. Avian was hoping to find the guiding voice she needed. The moon rose, and Avian greeted the sliver of waxing light.

'Sister, grant me gentle reviving sleep; Sister, carry the burden of my unease for a few hours; I will accept its return when I wake.' She placed her charm on the windowsill, drizzled two drops of lavender oil under her pillows, and lay down in the comfortable bed.

CHAPTER TWENTY-THREE

The cup was in my hands. It was heavy beyond my imagining. My fingers fitted into the pattern of grooves that decorated it. For a cup of fire it felt very cold. I put it into my bag and walked away. As I passed the private quarters of the woman, I saw the serving girl who had spoken my words. Her tongue had been cut away, and she screamed unintelligibly as she lay on the ground. Her blood soaked the ground – there was no one to staunch it; she was close to death and I could not help her. She saw me and shook her head in anguish, pointing away from the villa. I ran as fast as my broken body would take me, ran to the forest and towards the stag-headed oak.

Violet and Wyllie Turnbull sat to their supper in silence. Violet avoided Wyllie's inquisitive glances across the table. She had not spoken of the Tyler woman's visit and he had not

255

dared to ask. Violet rose to clear away the empty plates. Wyllie could bear it no longer.

'Well then, woman – are you going to tell me what she said, then?'

'Who's "she"? The cat's mother?' Violet snapped back from the sink.

'Mrs Tyler, of course.'

Violet spun round.

'Miss Tyler – Miss. Don't you ever listen? She's not so stupid as to have got herself wed.'

'Don't you get all Emily Pankhurst with me, Violet. What did Miss Tyler have to say? Leave that washing-up and sit down, woman. Talk to me.'

Violet wiped her hands on the linen dishcloth, hung it on the rail of the range, untied the strings of her floral apron and returned to sit opposite her husband at the table.

Violet had been anxious before Avian's arrival. She had stood by the window and looked down the lane. Avian's unmistakable figure appeared at the gate. Her hair today was loose, hanging heavily over her shoulders and down her back to rest on her buttocks. The gentle breeze lifted the finer hairs around her face and wafted them like gossamer, the fine silver hairs reflecting the light of the sun, and sparkling. Her long, full skirt was a patchwork of multicoloured tiny fragments. A flowing cotton shirt in a shade of muddy orange floated around her and her red clogs peeped from beneath her skirt.

Violet watched her open the old gate and walk through, closing it behind her. Somewhere in one of the outbuildings the collies set up their warning cry.

As Avian walked up the steps she was surprised to see the door already open a crack, and Violet peering around it.

'Good morning, Violet. Why don't you open the door wider? What difference will another few inches make now?'

She stood still on the step and waited. The door creaked open a little further . . . then a little further still, until half of Mrs Violet Turnbull was visible.

'Come in, girl; what are you waiting for?' she snapped.

'The same thing you are, Violet; I'm waiting for you to come out.' Avian offered her hand to the old woman teetering behind the half-open door. She envisaged the photographs of the young Violet Turnbull, the determined stare into the camera, the tiny woman goading the great belted beast round the show ring. Avian sensed a moment's hesitation. She held her hand out still, willing the older woman to take it.

In the silence, Violet could hear the beating of her heart, the rushing of blood around her body, the throb of it at her temples; a nerve twitched in her neck, her fingers began to tingle, she held tightly to the door handle but could not feel it in her hand.

'I can't. You know very well I can't, you cruel girl,' she snapped.

'Violet, just take my hand to steady yourself and open the door right up, you don't have to cross the threshold – think of it like an open window,' Avian urged.

Violet felt a great surge rise up from her abdomen. From somewhere deep within, strong emotions reared up in response; the old eyes suddenly looked out at Avian with a fierce other glare. Avian caught her first glimpse of the formidable character lurking deep within. The door began to move . . . at first it almost shut, with Violet disappearing behind it; Avian thought the moment was lost and was just about to push the door open and enter when she heard a sound. It was very slight to begin with, like a whine – a whimper; Avian froze. The sound grew to a moan . . . a wail . . . a mewl. Inhuman, it rose until it became a keening: the unmistakable wild, unhindered howls of grief and anger. The door, the heavy oak door with its brass and iron fittings, crashed back into the porch to reveal to Avian's eyes one elderly lady being held by many glimmers of wild, black-haired women in all of whom Avian perceived the Gift. Violet looked deep into Avian's stunned eyes: this was Violet, the part of her that had been absent, interred within the older Violet, and as the dark women supported the frail body, the young Violet smiled at Avian and returned emancipated.

The shades faded and Avian stood face to face with Violet; each stood on opposite sides of the wide open door and the threshold. Neither moved for a second; neither spoke. Avian reeled – she was used to sounds, echoes and voices – rarely since childhood had she been granted sight before. She noticed Violet begin to sway slightly and quickly stepped into the porch to catch her. Avian began to steer the frail body into the house.

'And where do you think you are taking me?' Violet gasped in a breathless whisper. 'Do you really think I can turn back now, after what has happened? Outside girl, take me outside. Now.'

Gently, Avian turned Violet round by the shoulders; she took one frail elbow in one hand, and placed her other arm around the thin back to support it. One tiny step . . . the body in her arms trembled and pulsed with vibrant energy. Another . . . another . . . until Violet Turnbull's slippered left foot crossed the threshold of her home for the first time in many, many years. The right followed, Avian close behind. In their shed, the collies set up a howling; ragged black crows and jackdaws screeched and flew up from the trees; a sudden wind whipped up and blew whirlwinds of dust around the yard . . . then silence – except for the gentle sobbing of two women – each holding the other on the doorstep. They stood apart, looking into one another's tear-reddened eyes.

'Are you all right?' Avian asked.

'I don't know . . . I think so.' Violet looked away from Avian's face; she looked up at the sky, she scanned the farm-yard, she reached up and stroked Avian's shoulder. A shudder ran the length of Violet's body from head to toe.

Wyllie Turnbull sat speechless at the table opposite his wife as she told him about the events of the day. She had been outside. He could not believe it. He repeated it to himself over and over. She had been outside – his Violet – outside – today. He did not hear the rest of the story, how Avian had held her while she shook for an age when they had returned indoors. How the strange woman had listened for echoes of the dark women, how she had burned herbs and brushed Violet down with owl feathers, how she had rubbed the ash from the herbs over Violet's hands, forehead and feet.

'Wyllie, are you listening to me?'

The silent man looked at his wife. In her eyes he saw an old sharpness, a clarity he had missed and almost forgotten. He stood, pushing his chair back behind him on the flagstone floor, his hands gripping the table's edge. He groped his way around the table, his eyes not leaving hers; he took her hands and raised her from her chair. He led her from the kitchen, through the scullery to the back door. Wyllie's hand reached for the door handle, Violet nodded, the door creaked open on stiff hinges. Together, the grizzled pair, arm in arm, walked out to the drying green.

Avian was granted a seamless night's sleep. The moon, her sister, arced across the sky, her faint glow illuminating the bedroom; the voices of the mischievous children and the echoes of the past remained silent. She awoke before the sun rose and crept downstairs, eating and drinking nothing before she left. She noticed nothing – the wagging of the dog's tail, the time on the clock. She wrapped a coat around her naked body, slipped her feet into the old wellington boots and quietly left the house. In one hand she carried the amulet, in the other a branch of mountain ash. She found herself just outside the perimeter of the stone circle without being aware of distance or time. The sky had changed from dark grey to soft violet and on the horizon a thin line of gold heralded the rise of the sun. Avian held the amulet up to the sky; her head was full of echoes and voices. She called out. 'I am here. May I enter?'

A whorl of sound whipped around her. She felt tendrils of it coil out from the spaces between the stones; they lashed across her body, winding her in spirals of archaic fury, tossing her from side to side, rising to a crescendo of almost unbearable volume as if to test her determination, or worth, or both. Avian stood her ground. The cacophony ended abruptly. A voice rumbled out from the sanctum.

'You may enter.'

Avian stepped boldly into the circle of stones.

'What do you seek?'

'I seek a guiding voice.'

'For what reason?'

'Not for myself – for another.'

'Prepare yourself.'

Avian stood tall, her long grey hair loose in the wind; she raised her arms above her head, the amulet and branch held high. At that moment the sun rose. Avian was warmed instantly, she felt encompassed by a gentle supportive spirit. They spoke without words and Avian knew that the spirit was that of a man, a kind spirit, who knew the land and where the vixen raised her cubs and the badger dug its sett.

Avian returned to Orby Cottage wrapped in old coat, boots and a sense of deep content. Nipper greeted her enthusiastically, sniffing her hands, licking her naked legs and feet.

'Yes, yes . . . your master still loves you as you know full well.' She hung the coat in the porch and tiptoed back upstairs. She lay tired and elated on her bed until she heard Alice on her way downstairs.

Alice was very, very curious about Avian's early morning visit to the stones; however, as she felt such heathen goings-on were intrinsically wrong in the eyes of the Church, she had decided not to enquire. She thought perhaps she should talk to the minister about all this. In her imagination she had visions of heathens calling on false gods – she could see the picture from the Old Testament of people making false idols of golden bulls' heads, and Moses on the Mount receiving the Ten Commandments in stone. Thou shalt not . . . Thou shalt not.

'Are you going up to see Violet today?' Alice asked. It seemed a safe subject.

'Oh yes – now I have the answer.'

Alice steadfastly ignored the opening she had been offered. Avian knew she would have to convince Alice to listen somehow – after all, there was a message for her, too.

'More tea?' Alice offered.

She was not sure how she felt about this strange woman, sitting there opposite her over her kitchen table. She was very nice, there was no doubt about that – polite, and she had got Violet Turnbull to set foot outside her front door for the first time in . . . well, since the twins' funeral. If the minister had achieved that, Alice would happily have regarded it as some kind of miracle.

Avian was not offended; she understood how Alice McCleish thought. Here was a rare creature: a Christian who truly lived within the tenets of her faith.

'No thanks, Alice – I promised Violet I'd be early this morning, and it's nearly nine already. Will you be here when I get back?'

'Yes, I should think so; I've nothing planned.'

'See you later then, in time for lunch I expect.'

Avian's clogged feet clopped off up the lane in the direction of Henge Farm. She breathed the clean morning air deep into her body, letting the breath out slowly. She turned in the lane to look back at the stones.

They must have been a strange couple, Callum and Alice, she thought as she gazed – he deeply rooted in the land, she striving for Heaven. He had loved her, and she had exasperated him with her narrowness, and encompassed him with her unquestioning love. She had loved him, yet she feared for his soul and tried to be good enough for both of them.

'She knows, somewhere deep inside her she knows. Yet this fear of hellfire, of purgatory, of fire and brimstone smothers everything.' Callum's spirit had told Avian.

Enough of them for now, Avian thought; and she began to focus on the events to come. She turned to continue to the farm and was surprised and thrilled to see Violet waiting by the farm gate, hanging on to it with one hand, and waving the other high in the air.

'Well, look at you, Mrs Turnbull!' Avian greeted her with a beaming smile.

'Avian,' was all Violet could say. She stretched out both hands in welcome and gratitude.

The two walked arm in arm to the front porch. Here, Wyllie had put the two chairs from the parlour; in the sun, they looked even more maroonly shabby.

'I just want to be outside,' Violet said, as if in explanation.

Wyllie drove past in his tractor; he blew a kiss in the direction of his wife, grinning like a schoolboy. Violet and Avian sat themselves down in the two chairs.

'Do you know?' Violet asked.

'Yes.'

'Where?'

'Shall I tell you, or show you?' Avian enquired.

Violet rose creakily from the chair; Avian stood and took her by the arm. They went down the steps and walked together in silence through the farmyard, past the barn where the dogs barked at them both. Violet realised she was being led towards the orchard. She stopped. Avian turned and looked down into the wrinkled face. They said nothing. Violet wanted to refuse, to cry out, 'not the orchard . . .' she could not. The last time . . . She shook her head slightly. Avian smoothed the steel-grey hair as if Violet were a child, patted her hand and turned to continue. Violet was drawn along, despite herself, by herself – by her old self who had re-emerged as a fire in her belly.

The orchard had been left unused since the dig. The yellowed circles of grass left by the yurts had recovered and the grasses and wildflowers had grown waist high. Wyllie had sprayed weedkiller around the perimeter of the wall, and a dead yellow ring of dry herbage clung to the circumference of the orchard. Dead sprays of bramble arched across the small doorway. Avian pushed them aside. She could feel Violet's tension through the frail arm: one word now and the moment would be lost. She turned the black metal circle of the handle, lifting the latch on the inside with a rusty scrape. Avian had to duck slightly to enter; Violet resisted. Avian snapped her intent onto the young Violet Turnbull, that shade which had returned with the support of her sisters.

'Help her,' Avian pleaded wordlessly. 'Help yourself.' The frail arm unhooked; Avian feared that Violet would turn away, that this was just a step too far. Avian stood aside. Violet must make her own decision.

For a moment Violet wavered. The door was open in front of her and this strange woman was there, waiting. To step inside was to see those trees, those two big central Keswick Codlins where they had hung. One in each, facing each other, their heads cocked, their bodies limp, their knees knocked and their little rumpled socks and scuffed shoes dangling on coltish legs. Alastair and Angus, her angels: her precious babies.

She took the two small steps from outside to within, her eyes cast down. Avian was strong and tall beside her, listening. Boyish laughter echoed softly around the wall, among the trees. Two voices whispered back and forth; they stopped suddenly as if realising they were not alone.

'Mummy's come – look, Angus – Mummy's come; I told you she would, one day.'

'Violet,' Avian spoke softly. 'Violet, they're here – I can hear them.' She took Violet's arm again and led her to a fallen cherry, its striped red and bronze bark peeling; it lay caught in the lower branches of its neighbour and made a perfect seat. The air was perfumed by the crushed grasses and plants they had trodden on; all they could see was the sky and the treetops, as if the rest of the world had disappeared.

The voices of the boys came closer. They were not sure that this elderly lady, sitting on the fallen cherry was their Mummy. She had been younger, her hair blacker and wilder, but when she raised her eyes to look around her, they knew: those were Mummy's eyes. The other lady was different – she could hear them, perhaps she could see them.

'Poor Mummy; she's got very old.'

'We must have been here an awfully long time.'

Avian let the words tumble repeated from her mouth as

the tears tumbled silently down her cheeks. Violet sat smiling; yes, she thought, just like them not to go unless they'd asked me first. She wished she could remain here just like this forever; the love she felt replaced the fear; she found unexpectedly that she no longer wanted to know why, or what had happened: it did not matter, not anymore. The boys had waited for permission to go – she had held them there – left them there for years. Avian rose to leave. Violet looked up with the black eyes of her youth.

'I have to leave you to say your goodbyes,' Avian bent and whispered into her ear.

Violet nodded. 'Do you think they can hear me?' was all she wanted to know.

'Even if you say nothing, they will hear you.' Avian squeezed Violet's offered hand and turned to leave.

Avian waited patiently outside the orchard wall. Wyllie returned on the tractor and parked it near the pressure hose to wash it down. He came round the corner and was shocked to see Avian standing by the open orchard doorway. He hurried forward.

'She's never in there? On her own? My God, woman, what are you thinking of!' He ran to the doorway and stopped – fear made him cautious – he peered around the door, expecting . . . who knew what. Violet saw him. She waved him over to her, called him. He entered steadily, walked across to where she sat, still smiling. Briefly he thought she had perhaps gone mad, sitting here, smiling, after all this time. Violet patted the fallen trunk and he sat, taking her hand in his.

'They were here you know, Wyllie, all this time, because I didn't give them permission to go; but I have to let them go – we have to let them go. It won't be many years before we'll all be together again.'

Wyllie nodded and pulled her into his arms.

CHAPTER TWENTY-FOUR

The stag-headed oak was old and I knew its nooks and crannies, having often hidden or placed tokens within it as the old woman had shown me. Beneath its roots, below the thick layer of crisp leaves and dark humus, a fissure hid unseen. Carefully I removed the dry leaves, then the moist, dark, rotted layer to reach the hole and carefully placed the cup deep within it; the leather bag of stones went next, then the bronze scoop. I would return for them.

Alice had spent the morning making vegetable soup and granary bread. She was just lifting the tray of bread from the oven as Avian appeared at the back door. Nipper no longer woofed at the clip-clopping approach of his new friend, he just wagged happily to see her.

Avian's eyes were red and puffy; she looked tired, but was

smiling.

'Hello Alice, hi Nipper.' She kicked off the red clogs in the porch, walked into the kitchen and sat down. 'That bread smells amazing – I hope it's for lunch.'

'That and vegetable soup – hope that's OK?' Alice had felt a twinge of guilt for her treatment of Avian at breakfast; she had just been trying to make it clear that she did not approve of some of her goings-on – nothing personal – just, well . . . just like Callum.

'How was Violet this morning?'

'She was waiting for me by the farm gate, she has made Wyllie put chairs – big comfy ones – out in the front porch with the doors wide open.'

'I have to say, I don't know how you did it, but for Violet's and Wyllie's sakes I am very glad you did.'

'I don't do anything, Alice. I don't cast spells or call upon dark spirits. I just look for the root of the problem and try to help people deal with it, that's all.'

'So why the sunrise visit to the stones, then? Why the rowan twigs? Why the sage?'

'I think you know why perfectly well. They are props – like the Church, the Cross, the incense, palm leaves, the rosary – all just a means to an end, an attempt to contact a spiritual aspect of life which we all know exists and call by thousands of different names – always have done and always will do. It doesn't matter what you call it – God, Goddess, Green Man, Kali, Ishtar: it's all the same.'

'You sound just like my husband . . .' Alice faltered; 'and Margaret, and Violet . . . what about Jesus? He was real. He was the son of God.'

'He was the son of his God, as I am the daughter of mine. He thought his was the only God; I do not.' Avian did not want to antagonise her hostess – Alice was so kind and caring, putting up a stranger to help a neighbour: a good Samaritan; a good Christian; a good person.

Avian told of the day's events, but she did not name the spirit of the stones who had guided her; not yet. Alice might not understand – might not want to. She did not go into detail about what happened in the orchard, just that they had entered, that she had left Violet alone to say her goodbyes to the children, and that Wyllie had returned and she had left.

Alice had not interrupted, although she had raised an eyebrow at the idea of the children still being in the orchard. They were in Heaven: she had been at the funeral. They were innocents. 'Suffer the little children . . .' she thought, and saw the image of the seated, haloed man surrounded by little ones.

'I don't think Violet will be needing my help any longer,' Avian concluded. 'So you should have your lovely home back to yourself very soon; I may leave tomorrow.'

'Don't think it's anything personal, Avian – you are a lovely person, you have gone out of your way to help someone you did not even know. Whatever our differences I have enjoyed having you to stay and getting to know you better.'

'Thank you, Alice. Actually, I think you and I are very

much alike.'

The two smiled and Alice reached across the table to take Avian's hand in hers and squeeze it gently.

Later Avian asked Alice if she could phone Sarah Rigden.

'Of course, her number's in the book by the phone.'

Avian dialled the number and Sarah answered.

'Sarah, it's Avian Tyler here . . . I'm fine, it's you I am calling about . . . They sound worse than headaches from what Alice has told me . . . Look, why don't I pop round when the children have gone to bed and we can discuss some alternative treatments? OK . . . about six-thirty . . . Dinner? Oh well, I don't know what Alice has planned.'

Alice overheard this bit of the conversation and indicated that Avian must have dinner with Brian and Sarah.

'Lovely, see you at six-thirty then.' She replaced the receiver.

Penny left home early the next morning to meet with a potential client who wanted someone to organise his single life for him. She woke Michael with a cup of coffee before she went. Sleepily, he mumbled his thanks and reached out for her hand.

'Oh no you don't, Michael McCleish. I have work to do and it's time you were getting up anyway. Dex is in the shower, and Marsha is on study leave, so let her wake up in her own time.'

'Go on . . . just a little cuddle.'

'Absolutely not,' Penny giggled. 'You'll mess up my hair.'

She drove away, thinking of their conversation of the evening before. She wondered what was on his mind. At the traffic lights she stopped on red and was so engrossed in her thoughts that she did not notice the lights change. Cars behind her hooted indignantly. She put the car in first and pulled away, shaking her head to clear it of its musings, and tried to get her working head in gear. This potential client was a Swede, Thor Jansson, who lived mostly in Gothenburg, but who kept an apartment in Kensington for when he was in London. He needed an organiser. This was a little different from previous clients, mainly women, who had needed a wife/friend/confidante to take some of the strain and deal with the boring things like shopping and finding a reliable cleaner. Thor Jansson had made it clear that he expected to arrive at his apartment – always with at least twenty-four hours' notice, often with guests, to find everything – and he meant everything – ready, waiting, and of the finest quality.

Penny had soon grown tired of personal shopping. This had surprised her. The women were addicted to the latest fashions, even when quite unsuitable. They wanted to change their look, the style of their home interiors, their lampshades, carpets and curtains constantly, but did not have the time or the taste to achieve the desired result. They employed interior designers, life coaches, cooks, nannies, housekeepers: a veritable army of extras in their lives to enable them to follow their careers and have a family. They were never satisfied. Nothing was ever good enough. Penny had seen shades of herself in these women – had been brought face to face with the nonsense of the whole charade. She had once aspired to their lifestyles, but now, gifted with inside knowledge of the truth of their existences, she began to see the absurdity of it all.

The interview went well. Herr Jansson – Thor – insisted on first names, but this was his only diversion from anything other than a formal working arrangement. He made it quite clear that he did not expect to see Penny except in exceptional circumstances. He expected to arrive to an immaculate apartment. Penny was to liaise with the cleaning lady who had been with him for years. Penny was to make sure the food and wine was ordered and delivered. Dinner party meals were to be delivered ready prepared by Thor's personal cook; champagne and vodka delivered ready chilled. Penny was to check the apartment on the day of arrival, accept deliveries, arrange the masses of fresh flowers in every room, ensure the table be laid fit for royalty – the silver gleaming – exactly the correct distance between each setting. For this service, Thor was happy to pay top-notch wages – not by the hour, as Penny had imagined, but by a constant retainer that could house and feed a family of four easily if they were not overly greedy. He had offered her a three-month trial period there and then, which she had accepted. His staff, he said, once hired, usually stayed with him for many, many years, even though he rarely saw or spoke to any of them.

Penny drove away in a trance. This seemed a dream job; after three months, if all went to plan, she would be able to drop her three existing clients to concentrate on Thor Jansson and his opulent lifestyle. She headed for Kew. The Honourable Mrs Annabel Maitland needed her wardrobe cleared out for next season's rags, and a discreet listening ear lent to her trifling bleatings. Three months, Penny plotted – three months and you can find another mug to mother you.

Dexter waited for the postman. The prospectuses should begin to arrive today. There was one college he particularly wanted to find out more about – it was not far from Durham, so he would be close to Marsha, and to his Granny McCleish. The postie still had not arrived by nine, and although he had a free period to begin the day, Dexter could not wait any longer. He flung his heavy schoolbag over his shoulder, left the house, first looked hopefully up and down the road for a sign of the postie, then slouched off to school.

Michael had already left for the station, laptop in hand, umbrella rolled – sometimes he felt he should have a bowler hat. He stood on the platform at Putney Bridge surrounded by the usual heaving mass of humanity . . . pushing and shoving to get into the train . . . standing to Waterloo . . . crossing the labyrinth of corridors to get to the right platform for the Underground to Blackfriars. As he hung by a strap, strangers' elbows and bosoms pressed against him, always someone sneezing, spreading God knew what germs.

Michael closed his eyes in self-defence. Where would I really like to be? he meditated, allowing his senses to delve inwards. As the sounds around him muffled, he groped inwardly for a true answer. As before, he found himself thinking of home, his childhood home. Hopefully, Marsha was going to be at Durham; Dexter was very keen on the horticultural college at Valley Spire. Penny had not flown off the handle at his not wanting the promotion, or at the hint of his need for some sort of dramatic change of lifestyle. He tried to imagine her living a country life. He was jerked out of his reverie as the Tube stopped at his station. He hustled out with the crowd, glided up the escalator and emerged into the fug and fumes of the city. Standing there, people rushing past on all sides, Michael McCleish made two decisions. One, he was not going to accept the promotion. Two, he would be out of London, with Penny or without her, within the next twelve months.

All day in the office he was preoccupied with these two ideas. Refusing the promotion would be liberating. Getting out of London was exciting, intoxicating, but the prospect of a life without Penny was something he could barely conceive of. He remembered the overdose; he recalled his fear of losing her. By whatever means were necessary, Michael McCleish would convince his wife to go with him.

His pager bleeped. Angela Smith-Gore would like to have a meeting with him at three, if he was available. Stage one of the McCleish plan was about to get under way.

Dexter rushed home to scour the post for the prospectus from Valley Spire Horticultural College. He ripped it out of its brown envelope and locked himself in the loo to read it in peace and quiet. The courses were very varied, from NVQ's to degree level, and even if you had not passed any A levels, you could get a place and work your way up through various grades to get either a degree or the prestigious RHS Master of Horticulture. The college had its own farm, it ran agricultural courses too, it had extensive gardens open to the public, and undertook field trials of new hybrids for seed companies. Dexter needed to get five GCSEs with at least one science subject to be considered for a place. There seemed to be only one minor hiccup: they gave preference to students who had shown an interest and been involved in some way with horticultural work. One day's hedge laying was hardly enough to convince them that he was really interested. He'd talk it over with his dad when he got home. Dexter flushed the loo, hid the prospectus under his jumper and exited the bathroom. Marsha was on the landing.

'What's up your jumper then? Porn, I expect – honestly – boys . . . '

'It is not porn, and even if it was it's none of your business.' Dexter stomped off to his room to wait for Michael to get home.

Penny was back early. The Honourable Annabel had been more vituperative than usual, and in anticipation of ending their relationship, Penny had bought an Indian feast of microwaveable goodies. Michael arrived home later flourishing two bottles of Bollinger, ready chilled. He bounced in through the door.

'Get the glasses out – we're celebrating.'

He hugged Penny, picked her up and swung her around in the kitchen, which was redolent with the smells of several regions of India. Marsha and Dexter followed the smells and the laughter down to the kitchen to see what the fuss was all about. Michael was skipping round the kitchen like a child, glass of bubbly splashing about in his hand.

'Children! Look, Penny, it's our little babies. Have champagne, babies – Daddy's celebrating.'

The children looked to their mother for explanation for this strange behaviour.

'Your father has refused a promotion which would have set him on course for a directorship,' she said, without a trace of malice.

Marsha and Dexter exchanged bemused glances and accepted the proffered glasses of champagne. The family feasted and guzzled, and chatted amiably about this and that. Granny McCleish's trust fund money was toasted by Penny. Michael proposed a toast to 'Unpredictability', Marsha toasted 'The Romans', and Dexter toasted 'Hedge Laying'.

Penny told of her successful interview, and toasted 'Rich Swedes'. Michael was astounded at the retainer his wife was to receive.

'How much? My God, Pen – he must be worth a fortune!'

'He must, and he believes good staff are worth a fortune too.'

Penny and Marsha began to clear the plates and glasses and put them into the dishwasher.

'Dad?' Dexter asked, 'can you spare us a few mins? There's something I want you to see – men's stuff – nothing to do with girls.'

'We need a glass of port and a big cigar while the ladies withdraw – except it's us doing the withdrawing: to the office!'

Dexter had not seen his father in such a good mood for a while – probably since they had visited Granny; it was nice.

CHAPTER TWENTY-FIVE

I ran through the river shallows to keep the dogs from follow-ing my scent. I knew the way of a hound's mind. All day I could hear them bay in the distance, confused. As evening fell I found myself far from all I had ever known, with nothing. I found a yew, its branches thick and hanging to the ground; I scraped the dry needles and soil into a hollow between roots and rustled down into them. Fitfully, I slept.

A knock on the door brought Margaret back from a spell of nostalgia. She drew back the chain and let Marcus in.

'Morning, how are you today?' he enquired, smiling down at her.

'Good morning Marcus; I am very well – thank you for asking,' Margaret answered with a warm glow. Marcus always asked after her health. Once upon a time she would have been furious at the impertinence of it.

'Now then, you've got me all day if you want me. Mrs Compton has gone to stay with her family down south for a week, so I've only to pop in and feed the cat for her later on.'

'There is some shopping I'd like to do this morning – I could do with some help carrying bags.'

'No probs Maggie.'

Margaret feigned disapproval at this truncation of her name. She had always been Margaret to family and her few friends, Professor Allerton to everyone else; however, she had a secret liking for this display of affection which Marcus used only when they were alone together. Marcus helped Margaret into her coat and the unlikely pair wandered off into the morning.

'I want to move into the village, Wyllie.'

Wyllie Turnbull raised his head in surprise. This was a bit sudden; totally unexpected.

'Did you hear me, man? I want to . . .'

'Yes, I heard you; you want to move into the village. What's brought this on then?'

Violet had been churning this thought over and over since her visit to the orchard. She had been back each day since, and knew the children had left.

This farmhouse was too big for the two of them, it needed a family – it needed new life. The farm, even with its presently diminished acreage, was too much for her husband – not that he would ever admit it. They had to face the facts: they were old; they had no children to pass it on to; very soon it would become just too much of a burden for them. Better to move on now, while they could. Just weeks ago the thought would never have crossed her mind. Just weeks ago she was trapped here . . . waiting.

'We don't know how long we have left, Wyllie. Do you want to die of a heart attack or something away in the top field and lie there for hours until someone finds you? I certainly don't want to find myself here alone. It's well past time you retired – you can keep your hand in judging at local shows or entering sheepdog trials or growing vegetables in a back garden.'

'Sell the farm? Sell Henge Farm? But . . .' The ties of the land pulled at parts of him he had forgotten; his hands and arms ached at the thought of not touching it; his feet and legs weakened at the thought of not walking it; his eyes watered at the thought of not seeing it every day, every season. His heart thrummed fit to splinter. Violet saw his turmoil.

'Wyllie, it makes sense; surely for what we could get for the farm we could buy one of the terraced cottages on the outskirts; there would be enough left to live on comfortably for as long as we are going to last. We would have neighbours; I could walk along to the shop, catch a bus to town, maybe we could go away for a holiday; I would love to see the Islands again. Think about it – but don't take all day: we are not getting any younger.'

Wyllie left the house a confused and worried man. For years he had lived a life of total predictability; it had become a habit – Violet was indoors and he had the farm to work. The seasons had run their courses, coming late or early, being too dry or too wet, but he had always known where his place was in the grand scheme of things. Climbing into the tractor he noticed how old and gnarled his hands were, how grey the hairs on his arms had become; he noticed how stiff his knee was, and how much harder it was to climb the steps to the cab than it used to be. In the wing mirror he caught a glimpse of an old man. He looked behind himself briefly before realising the old man was himself. He drove past the farmhouse – windows and door wide open, and Violet, a blanket over her knees, sitting in the porch in one of those old, old armchairs. The paint on the window frames was peeling off, the guttering was broken on the north wall, several slates had slipped and lay caught in the guttering; the flashing around the chimneystack needed replacing. Once, Wyllie would have tackled all these things. He drove to the top field to check on his small flock; all was well: the salt lick would need replacing soon but there was one in the shed.

He climbed down out of the cab and stood on the highest point of top field. He looked down at the farm buildings; sheep nudged and bleated around his legs. Tears welled up in his eyes as he began to accept the sense in Violet's observations. He did not want to break up what remained of the farm, but who would want it as it was? It was not big enough now to make a living. Maybe he could sell off the fields and house separately, but that seemed somehow wrong – and what about Alice McCleish? Who would keep an eye on her? He felt he owed that to Callum. He must talk to Alice; she deserved to know. He took the tractor down the back track to come out along the lane by the stones. Alice heard the tractor coming along and was surprised to hear it stop outside Orby Cottage. Nipper woofed as Wyllie trudged round to the back door and peered into the kitchen.

'Wyllie, come on in, the kettle's on; time for a cuppa?'

Wyllie kicked off his wellington boots in the porch and sat down at Alice's kitchen table.

How many years had he known this woman? He always thought of her as Callum's buxom young wife, and there she was – grey-haired, lined face, widowed, standing opposite him, curious.

'Alice.' He was not a man to waste words. 'Alice, Violet wants to sell the farm and move to the village.'

Alice sat down heavily. Henge Farm without Wyllie and Violet? Almost unthinkable; yet . . .

'That's very sudden, Wyllie. How do you feel about that?' Alice's voice remained calm.

'How do I feel?' The poor man held his head in his hands. 'How do I feel . . . I don't know what to feel. One minute she's sick, indoors, permanently; the next that woman arrives from out of the blue and suddenly she's better – she's talking about the children, opening up their room, going outside, smiling.'

'But that's all for the good, surely?'

'Yes – yes of course, but – selling the farm . . . She's right of course – I am too old, she is too old, and . . .' he added sheepishly, remembering Callum's unexpected death, 'we do still have each other, for now. But I don't want to see it built on – everywhere you look nowadays it seems every old barn is ripe for conversion – every old pig shed, every bit of land is up for grabs.'

'I know – the village dower house has sold off half of its garden and they are building four new homes in there – Brian Rigden told me, just yesterday.'

'I don't know what to do for the best, Alice; I just don't know; I wish there was someone I could trust who could explain it all to me simply. I don't trust solicitors or estate agents – just out to make money for old rope.'

'You could try our Michael, he helped me organise the money from the gold cup. Would you like me to phone him this evening, to see if he can help?'

Wyllie lifted his heavy head from his hands. 'Would you, Alice?'

'I'll speak to him tonight and let you know what he says.'

Alice was happy to see her neighbour leave looking a little less shell-shocked than when he arrived. She was not sure that Michael would be any help, or if he would have time to help – he was busy, and there was the prospect of promotion. She put the matter from her mind for the time being and washed up the cups in the kitchen sink.

Wyllie felt a little more hopeful after his visit. Alice McCleish took everything in her stride: she was strong and capable and had been more than a friend to Violet and himself over the years. Their Michael was a good lad; Wyllie would wait and see what advice Michael might have for them, if any. The tractor roared into life and Wyllie drove up the lane to the steading.

Violet sat on the porch. Her skin, once transparent and sallow, was now nearing the shade of nut brown it used to have; her eyes were closed, and she was still smiling, smiling, smiling. A wave of love washed over Wyllie, he recalled their closeness, their passion: once he would have crossed the world over and over to give her what she wanted; now all she wanted was a quiet life, with him nearby. If it could be done, without breaking up the farm, he would do it for her . . . for them both.

Dexter answered the phone. 'Oh, hiya Gran . . . yep, Dad's here, I'll get him for you. Dad! Gran's on the phone!'

Dexter heard just one side of the conversation.

'Really? Well, they would certainly get enough to do that, and get some kind of income from the residue. Would it help if I phoned him and had a chat? OK, give me the number.' He scrawled down a number on a Post-it note. 'How are you anyway, Mum?' Several ums and ahs and the odd 'Yes, I see,' followed. 'OK Mum, lovely to speak to you.' Michael put the phone down and looked very thoughtful.

Penny arrived home to find Michael and Dexter, heads together, poring over some paperwork.

'What's all this then?' she asked, taking them by surprise. She walked into the office and peered over their shoulders. 'Horticultural college? But you haven't even started your A level courses yet.'

Dexter's heart sank. He knew his mother expected him to go off to university – study something sensible, like accountancy, or law; he was in for a lecture for sure.

'Dex,' his father said. 'Do us a favour and go and put the kettle on, make me and your mum some coffee – go on.' Dexter slumped off into the kitchen, the vision of another two years at school hanging above his head like a storm cloud.

'Sit down love, and listen.'

Penny sat. Michael explained how he and Dexter had discussed the possibility of Dexter leaving school after GCSEs and going to horticultural college.

'He's not happy at the school; he doesn't want to stay in the city. We should be glad he knows what he does want to do at last – so many kids don't. Look here, he can get a place at this college with five GCSEs – he'll easily get those, then he can work his way through from diploma right the way up to Master of Horticulture if he wants to. It's a good life: fresh air, exercise. Gardening's the new rock and roll don't you know. He could be the next Alan bloody Titchmarsh for all we know.'

'I don't understand,' Penny whimpered. 'He wants to be a

gardener? Where the hell did that come from? We don't even have a garden, not even a window box.'

'I think it began when I took him up to my mum's – remember he spent the day with Brian Rigden, her gardener – ruined that ninety pound pair of jeans?'

'But surely there's no money in it . . . no prospects?'

Michael tapped a few keys on his computer. 'Here, look, one of those staff agencies – I looked it up days ago. See "Gardener, two-bedroom cottage with costs, use of a car, and twelve thousand pounds per annum"; here's another for a Head Gardener: OK – it's not a white collar salary, but it's not bad.'

Dexter came in with the coffee. Michael winked at him and, catching his eye, nodded him away again. Penny was reading the prospectus; flicking through the pages, she looked up and smiled. Dexter disappeared to watch TV with a seed of hopefulness germinating and beginning to take root in his imagination.

'I need to think about this properly,' Penny stated firmly.

'How about if I get dinner on while you look through this stuff in peace?'

'That is too good an offer to turn down; if I didn't know better I'd think you were up to something yourself, Michael McCleish.'

Michael retreated quickly before his expression gave him away. He was indeed up to something. A ridiculous idea was forming in the back of his mind. He wanted to buy Henge

Farm.

In the kitchen he tossed ideas and salad; he almost burnt the pork chops under the grill; the new potatoes in the pan boiled over and hissed and spat on the hotplate. He wanted it, he really, really wanted it . . . but what on earth would he do with a farm? This required serious thinking time.

Over dinner the three of them discussed the horticultural college idea. Penny's immediate horror was overcome by the possibility of her son studying for The Royal Horticultural Society's Master of Horticulture, which sounded quite grand. The fact that Dex's first choice college was within miles of Marsha at Durham, and in easy reach of Granny McCleish eased her maternal compulsion to keep her last baby near at hand for as long as possible. He was obviously keen, had done a fair bit of research – had discussed it with Michael.

'Why didn't you talk to me about it?'

'Come on Mum – you had great plans for me, wanted me to be a lawyer, or an accountant like Dad; it just sounds so boring. Brian said . . .'

'Yes, well, I shall have to have a word with Brian,' Penny said, adopting an angry tone which alarmed Dexter.

'Mum, don't do that.'

'And why not? It says in this prospectus you have to show some enthusiasm by getting your hands dirty. If it's all this Brian Rigden's fault then the least he can do is give you some experience – you'll not get much chance around here.'

Marsha swanned in after dinner.

'Sorry I'm late Mum, there was a discussion that went on and on after archaeology club – it was so interesting.'

'There's new potatoes left, and some salad; Dexter ate your pork chop. You could have a few prawns if you like.'

'Brill, I'll defrost them in the micro.'

Marsha was worrying needlessly about her ability to live up to her predicted A level results: would she get the grades she needed? She was so looking forward to uni – to leaving home; some of her friends were also applying to Durham.

'Not long now,' Penny said, guessing at her daughter's thoughts. 'You'll be fine, all your teachers expect you to pass with flying colours.'

'Yeah, I know, but I really, really do want to get into Durham. I don't know about staying in halls though Mum; me and the girls were talking about sharing a flat, a student flat you know, but doing our own cooking and stuff.'

'Let's wait till your results arrive and we'll talk about it more then. As soon as your place is confirmed we'll go and visit and check everything out.'

'It looks like you may not be the only one leaving home at the end of next summer,' Penny said at breakfast the next morning.

'Your brother is applying to Valley Spire College, just outside of Durham.'

Marsha looked very surprised.

'Really? You're not staying on for A levels? What do they

do there then?'

'Horticulture.' Dexter said, with a touch of defiance.

'Gardening,' Penny and Michael said in unison.

'It looks like we'll both be digging about getting our hands dirty then,' Marsha laughed; 'and you won't be too far away – or too close for that matter.'

Michael thought to himself that they may not be the only ones getting their hands dirty, but he kept quiet about that for the time being.

Dexter disappeared off to his bedroom to watch his TV, Marsha commandeered the bathroom and would be gone for some time, leaving Michael and Penny in the kitchen clearing up after dinner.

'How do you feel about this horticulture business then, Pen?' Michael dared to ask.

'It's a bit of a shock, to be honest, and I wish you two had discussed it with me sooner.'

'The boy didn't want to disappoint you – it matters very much to both of them that you – especially you – are pleased with them. He has made a choice, a brave choice I think.'

'And what about you, Michael McCleish – have you made a choice?'

'I'm working on it,' Michael replied with a wink.

Michael had to come up with a viable plan to make Henge Farm into a serious business prospect with which he could convince Penny – who was going to take a lot of convincing.

Various ideas had crossed his actively seeking mind: continue to farm? That was a non-starter; even with Wyllie's help, Michael would never become a farmer. Turn it into a campsite, and be inundated with noisy families and roaring bikers from Easter till the end of summer? Somehow he could not see Penny getting even mildly enthused by that idea. Maybe start a garden centre – Dexter could help in the holidays – maybe Brian Rigden would run the practical side of things for him. But there wasn't much in the way of passing trade around Duddo. Michael knew he could run the business side of almost anything – books and figures were his forte. He would telephone Wyllie Turnbull – that was the first thing to do. He dialled the number. At Henge Farm, Wyllie picked up the trilling telephone.

'Hello?'

'Hello, Mr Turnbull; Michael McCleish speaking. Mum said you wanted some advice.'

'Oh, Michael lad – good of you to phone. It's like this . . .'

Michael sat and patiently listened to the old man struggle to explain his situation.

'And so you see, lad,' he concluded, 'I need to sell the farm, but I don't trust these estate agents. Can you help?'

'Mr Turnbull – can I call you Wyllie now, do you think?'

'Yes lad, I wish you would.'

'Wyllie – unless you can find a private buyer I don't see how you can avoid using an estate agent. They are not all bad, you know.'

'I know, lad, but I need help. I can't face all the legal stuff; dirt and animals is what I'm good at, dirt and animals, not office types.'

'Leave it with me for a day or two, Wyllie. I'll do a bit of research this weekend and see what I can come up with. I'll get back to you Sunday evening if that's OK?'

Michael put the phone down and began a search of farms and smallholdings for sale on the Internet. There were not many in the north Northumberland area, but it seemed that prices were high, higher than Michael had imagined. The area was no longer the quiet backwater it had once been. Alnwick had been voted the best place in Britain to live, with the best quality of life, the Castle had been used in the Harry Potter film as Hogwarts, and the young duchess had put the gardens on the international map. Prices were on the up. Michael soon realised that selling the land off in plots for building would be Wyllie's best move financially speaking; however, Wyllie had been definite about one thing – he did not want the land split up. It seemed an impossible situation. Michael would have to come up with an idea to use the land without farming and without building.

Marsha slopped into the office in slippers and dressing gown, her hair wrapped in a towel turban balanced on top of her head.

'Hi Dad. Busy?'

'Never too busy for you, sweetheart. What's the problem?'

'No problem really, Dad – just a question.'

Marsha had been pondering this topic for some time. She had decided she did not believe in God; that was OK - that was not the problem. She knew Grandpa McCleish had not believed in God, and that Granny McCleish did, and went to church and stuff. She stood quietly trying to formulate the question tumbling around in her mind. 'You know when people die.'

'Yes . . .' Michael replied. This might be more difficult than he first imagined.

'You know they either get buried in the graveyard or cremated.'

'Yes . . .'

'What if you don't believe in God – and – you don't want to be cremated? What happens then?'

'What on earth has brought this on?' Michael asked.

'It's just that we've been studying ancient burial rites at club, and it made me wonder why Grandpa McCleish was buried in the churchyard even though he did not believe in God. It doesn't seem right somehow – as if Granny was being a bit selfish about it.'

'I think Granny didn't have much choice; Grandpa did not believe in cremation, he always said he came from the earth and wanted to go back to it. Granny will be buried in the graveyard next to him so they will be together again. I think there used to be a law or something about burials only being allowed in consecrated ground . . .' at this point Michael's voice trailed off.

Marsha looked at her father. He seemed deep in thought. Perhaps I should not have asked – perhaps I've made him sad, she thought. Suddenly her father clapped his hands, jumped up from his chair, rushed round his desk, grabbed his towelling-shrouded daughter round the waist and spun her round until her turban fell off and her wet hair whipped drops of perfumed water around the room.

'Dad, Dad, stop it – you're making me dizzy!' she laughed aloud.

Michael deposited her back onto the floor.

'You, Marsha Penelope Anne McCleish, are a genius: a complete and utter genius.'

He whizzed back round to his computer, typed 'alternative burials' into a search engine and an array of sites appeared. He clicked on one.

'Look, here's the answer to your question,' . . . and mine, he thought. 'Green burials, woodland burials, non-religious ceremonies. Here, Barrow Farm, Dorset. An alternative burial ground near to a Saxon burial ground. They bury you and plant a tree over you, and eventually there is a beautiful new woodland filled with wild flowers.'

'That's lovely – Grandpa McCleish would have liked that.' Marsha's question was answered and she skipped off to dry her hair. Michael clicked on more sites: this could be it – this could be the answer to making a go of Henge Farm. There would be problems, no doubt, but nothing that could not be overcome. The only neighbour was his mother, and she would never complain if it meant her Michael living just up the lane. He closed his eyes and imagined. He could see himself – running the office, doing the books, cutting the grass. He could see Brian Rigden and eventually Dexter running the landscape side of things; the place would be beautiful. The ancient burials and the stone circle would be a huge marketing device, especially for pagan and non-religious burial. Marsha would one day be able to advise on that side. The one bit of the jigsaw he could not fit into place was Penny. He could guess her reaction: 'Live in the middle of a graveyard, all those dead bodies rotting away under our feet? Michael McCleish – you have finally gone gaga. If you think for one minute I am going to live surrounded by corpses you have got another think coming . . .' etcetera, etcetera. I am going to have to be very careful how I go about this, Michael pondered; what would be a good way to win her round? Barrow Farm website had a 'contact us' icon. That is the first thing I must do, he decided. He drafted an email there and then and hit the 'send' icon. Now all he could do was wait.

He rang Wyllie Turnbull on Sunday evening. Marsha and Penny had gone together to see some new romantic comedy starring Hugh Grant at the Multiplex. Dexter was round at a mate's house for a video fest – several of them were staying over to watch all the Star Wars movies back to back.

'Hello, Mrs Turnbull, it's Michael McCleish. How are you?'

'Michael, how lovely! I am very well; did your mother tell

you I can go outdoors now? It's wonderful.'

'Yes – yes she did. Is Mr Turnbull there?'

'Hang on just a minute; I'll get him for you. Wyllie – telephone. He's just coming, Michael.'

The two men talked earnestly for some time. Michael had done his research and could give a reasonable estimate of the value of the farm and its buildings. Wyllie had been taken aback by the value of the farm. Things had certainly changed in the last ten years. Michael gave sound advice, suggesting the sale in plots would bring the highest return. Wyllie refused to even consider it. Finally Michael dropped his bombshell.

'Wyllie, I have a confession to make. I want to buy the farm.'

There was silence at the other end of the phone, followed by a throaty chuckle.

'Pull the other one, lad. What on earth would an office boy like you do with a farm?'

More chuckles.

'I'm serious, Wyllie. I think I have an idea to make it pay and keep the whole thing together – improve on it, even.'

Wyllie stopped chuckling.

'I need to do a bit more research into the idea; can you give me a couple of weeks before you contact a land agent?'

'Michael, you can have a month; longer, if need be. If there is any way, any way at all that you and your family could take on Henge Farm . . . well, it would be almost like family taking over, almost family. You would make me a very happy man indeed.'

They agreed to speak again in two weeks' time.

'Please don't mention this to my mother for the time being, Wyllie; I should hate to raise her hopes and then nothing comes of it.'

'Certainly, lad; this is just between us two for the time being.'

Wyllie went back to the kitchen.

'Well?' Violet enquired. 'What did he say?'

Wyllie explained almost all of Michael's advice. Violet was excited by the unexpectedly high value of the farm.

'We could buy a nice cottage and have plenty left over. Michael could advise us on the best way to use the left over money. Oh, Wyllie . . .'

Tears welled up in her eyes; she knew how hard this was going to be for her husband – for both of them – but a new home, small, easy to keep; a holiday – a trip to the Isles. She anticipated their last few years together as the Indian summer of their lives.

The email in reply from Barrow Farm was short and sweet.

Dear Michael McCleish,
I think your best course of action would be to come down and

visit us here. The local pub does a very good bed and breakfast, and if you let us know when you would like to come I will be very happy indeed to give you a guided tour and some explanation of planning regulations and how the whole thing pans out.

Yours truly,

Johnathan and Celia Evans

Pub is called The Dun Cow.

Email - theduncow@hotmail.com

Penny and Marsha arrived home arm in arm. Michael beamed to see them.

'Pen, I've got a surprise for you.'

'Goody goody, what's that then?'

'I've booked us a winter break in Dorset, where the cider apples grow – or is that Zummerzet? I'm assuming Marsha and Dex can cope without us for a couple of days.'

'Lovely, as long as Thor does not phone. Maybe I should email him to check that he will not be needing my services.'

'You do that now, while I make the coffee,' Michael offered.

Herr Jansson did not need Penny's services, so the weekend was on. Michael hoped that Barrow Farm and the Evanses would be so inspiring that even Penny would see the possibilities.

CHAPTER TWENTY-SIX

I awoke to the sound of many voices nearby. Not Roman. I crept nearer to see a band of men. They were armed and painted for war.

I joined the women following in their wake. With them, they had wounded from battles, but they had won, and were pushing the Romans back, fort by fort. I cleaned and bound wounds and made draughts of herbs to dull the pain while the men and many of the young, strong women travelled ahead. Many clans and tribes and defectors from the Romans, they said, had joined them as they drove the incomers south. And at the head of this wild warrior quiverful was a woman: Cartismandua, Warrior Queen of the Brigantes with her husband, the Warrior Venutius.

Marcus Mooney was waiting at Durham railway station for Margaret Allerton to arrive on the ten-fifteen from New-

castle. He had missed her. He had had bad news. His grandmother had died. The station announcer's voice droned out
that the ten-fifteen had been delayed by livestock on the line
and would arrive some thirty minutes late. Marcus went to
get a takeaway coffee. He found a corner of an empty bench,
sat down, lit an illicit cigarette and waited. As he waited, he
thought of his grandma, of everything she had done for him as
a child – raised him, really, from when his father left and his
mother turned to the booze. His gran had tried to get him to
go to school, scraped up enough money for shoes, football kit,
the day trip to Beamish. He had never thanked her for all that
– never sat down opposite her, face to face, and said it in
words; now he could never do that. Then there were all the
questions he had wanted to ask but had not. What was his
father like? Why did he leave? What did Granddad do for a
living? Why did his mother drink? Why didn't she love him?
Grandma never volunteered any of this information – she
must have been waiting to be asked, and he never had. Nobody thought he cared, nobody guessed that he might want to
know these things – might *need* to know them – to have the
slightest chance of becoming a complete person. Now it was
too late; there was just the funeral to get through with tight
throat and choked-back tears, his mother wailing, flailing,
needing to be buttressed upright throughout the proceedings.
He needed Margaret to come, to be there, even just somewhere in the background.

The train now approaching is the delayed ten-fifteen from New-

castle. We apologise . . .

Marcus stood. Wiping his eyes with the back of his sleeve he put on a cheerful face. He saw Margaret before she saw him as the train slowly passed him on the platform. He ran alongside to be waiting when the doors opened. He helped a young woman out with a child in a pushchair, then lifted Margaret's luggage from the train. He looked up into her face and she immediately knew something was wrong.

'Marcus, you are wonderful,' she said, as he helped her down the step and across the gap to the platform. He gathered her luggage and led her out to the taxis waiting in the queue. Once they were settled inside, Marcus gave the address and they were soon at Margaret's door.

The house was aired and spotless; the cleaning lady had been in and had left a casserole in the fridge to be heated up. She had left a note.

Dear Professor Allerton,

Welcome home. I hope you had a lovely holiday and are not too exhausted by the travel. In the fridge is a lamb casserole – plenty for two, as I know Marcus is collecting you from the station. It just needs heating through. Please tell Marcus I will be thinking of him on Friday, and tell him I am sorry for his loss. I never met his grandmother, but I understand she was a remarkable woman. Will be in Tuesday morning as per usual.

Jenny

Margaret read the note and turned to look at Marcus. 'Marcus, I am so sorry about your grandmother; why didn't you tell me straight away?' She walked to him and put her arm around his waist, led him to a chair and sat him down. 'Let me make some tea and put this casserole in the oven and we can talk, OK?'

Friday morning arrived, and Margaret Allerton was smartly turned out in sombre, respectful shades of navy. She had promised Marcus she would be at the crematorium and was waiting for a taxi. For a second time, the young man had crumpled before her – expressed his confusion. Margaret understood. She, too, had spent most of her life hiding behind a sanctuary wall of donnish, detached academia not so different from Marcus's own screen. She, too, had lately been surprised to find cracks in her wall, crumbling areas she could no longer refortify.

She remembered her father's funeral, an inhumation after a service in the university chapel. She had maintained an aloofness from her own grief and that of her mother, despite knowing that recognising and accepting it was a necessary part of the mourning process. She had, by then, studied the funeral rites and practices of many cultures, and considered those of the Church of England to be based on the manipulation of the grief of the bereaved – grief which must be discreetly displayed in the right way, at the right time and place. Margaret had admired the outward, uncontrolled demonstration of grief she encountered in some cultures, although she herself could never have expressed herself in such a way. She liked the idea of professional mourners, but the harping on about 'ashes to ashes' and 'he who believeth in me shall not die' had left her cold and unmoved . . . until the coffin was lowered into the ground; then, from some deep animal cave lurking in her depths, a moan had emerged, it had risen through her body, vibrating every bone, muscle and organ; it had rushed up towards her mouth bursting for release, the tendons in her neck taut, the muscles of her face strained. Margaret had stifled the cry. The unbridled ferocity of this emotion – unwanted, unexpected – had almost pushed her into a faint. She had gasped in several great lungfuls of air and clenched her fists, determined to remain outwardly in control and upright. She had never forgotten that feeling; she had buried it deep.

The taxi beeped outside and Margaret gathered herself together for Marcus's sake.

Margaret sat to the rear of the chapel on her own. She had seen Marcus briefly when she arrived and saw the look of relief on his face that she was there. The poor boy was trying to deal with his mother. He had arranged the funeral first thing in the morning in the hope that she would be fairly sober at that time of the day. She had been a good-looking young woman once – Margaret could see that. Those rheumy eyes had once been fine and clear without the shadowy circles beneath; her cheekbones were high and prominent, with a dainty nose and well-proportioned mouth, but her skin was now sallow, greying – blushed with finely broken veins and fissured with premature wrinkling. Her hair hung limp and unwashed.

The service began. It was short: one hymn, one prayer, the curtains closed. Margaret wished she had been around to help Marcus arrange this; she knew how much the old lady had meant to him. The family, such as it was, went back to Marcus's mother's home for drinks. Margaret declined the slurred invitation and, taking Marcus aside, told him that if he needed to escape he knew where she would be.

The drive back from Dorset was a quiet one. Michael was feeling like a tightrope walker as he gripped the steering wheel like a bar in his hands to help maintain his balance. If he lost his balance there was no safety net. Penny had been furious: how dare he disguise this as a holiday!

They had arrived at The Dun Cow in fine spirits, had a smashing meal and a couple of drinks, and were snugly ensconced in an old pew by the open fire in a romantic frame of mind. A man, a local man, had come into the bar and ordered himself a pint of cider. He had a ruddy complexion and a loud voice; he was tall and his hands were massive: the pint glass looked more like a half in them. He chatted amiably to the landlord, who pointed out Michael and Penny by the fire. The man had walked over.

'Hello – Michael McCleish?'

Michael stood up and shook his hand.

'Yes, I'm Michael – and this is my wife, Penny.'

'Nice to meet you,' the man replied.

Penny thought how friendly the people here must be, just to come up like that.

The man introduced himself. 'My name is Johnathan Evans, from Barrow Farm.'

Michael immediately looked shifty and embarrassed.

'Oh . . . yes . . . nice to meet you too. Ah, I'm afraid I have not yet had time to fill my wife in on the underlying agenda of this weekend away.'

'What agenda? What on earth are you on about, Michael?'

Johnathan Evans excused himself with dignity, sloping back off to the bar knowing he had surely put his very big wellingtoned foot firmly in it.

The rest of the evening was less than romantic. Michael firmly led a spitting mad Penny out of the pub and down by the river where her strangled, angry voice would not be overheard. In the taut atmosphere, everything Michael had thought to say for the best effect came out twisted and wrong; and it did sound like an extremely stupid idea: give up a well-paid job with imminent prospects and a top-notch pension scheme; sell the London house; move to a run-down farm right next door to his mother in the middle of nowhere; bury dead bodies in the fields.

'Is this some kind of midlife crisis?' Penny squawked. 'Male menopause? My God, Michael, I knew you were ruminating about something – but this! Buying Henge Farm . . . truly I had no idea. Where do I come into this cosy little plan then? What about my job? I suppose that doesn't matter at all? What do you expect me to do – make funeral teas – cucumber and fish paste sandwiches – serve small glasses of sherry to the bereaved?'

They had slept with an uncomfortable distance between backs that night, eventually. Both had lain in pretence of sleep, unmoving and unmoved. Michael thought he had cocked up the whole business. If only he had told Penny before – on the drive down, even – he would have been in control then, his prepared spiel would have made sense. Damn Johnathan bloody Evans, damn him.

Penny's chest was tight with anger. Yet another secret kept from her: was she such a harridan that her own family could not confide in her? First Dexter leaving school early – they had connived together over that one, not included her in their discussions, as if what she thought just did not matter. Now this. Unbelievable. He was prepared to turn down promotion and a significant salary increase for this – to live in the middle of nowhere with 'that woman' at the end of the drive, surrounded by rotting corpses. No, no, no – not in a million years. She had, however, agreed to keep the appointment Michael had made with that yokel to save face. The man and his wife had been good enough to set a morning aside; the least Penny could do would be to go along. It would be short and sweet, just enough to be courteous. Michael had better not expect her to try and look happy about it though.

Celia and Johnathan Evans met them at the farm gate. Two curved low walls, mirror images of each other, marked the entrance to Barrow Farm. The iron gates stood permanently open; a sign discreetly announced:

BARROW FARM
WOODLAND AND ALTERNATIVE
FUNERAL GARDENS

The grass verges and hedges outside were neatly cut. The place had the look of a country estate or country house hotel. Michael and Penny followed the Evanses' Range Rover along the manicured, newly surfaced drive, which split some distance along. The left turning was marked 'Farmhouse – Private'; the right, 'Funeral Gardens'. They took the right turning and pulled up alongside three family saloons and a people carrier in a gravelled car park. Penny slung Michael a frosty look before she got out of their vehicle to meet the Evanses, a forced smile clinging to her lips.

Johnathan had told Celia of the meeting in the pub.

'Typical man,' she had declared. 'Typical; she must be livid – I know I would be. Are they still coming, do you know?'

'Unless I hear different I assume they must be; 'twill be an uncomfortable meeting, I imagine.'

Celia strode up to Penny and took her hand firmly in both

of hers.

'Mrs McCleish – I can call you Penny, can't I? I am Celia. I understand this has all come as a complete shock to you.'

She led Penny away from the men. They could just hear Johnathan trying to apologise for his indiscretion the previous evening.

'I am quite sure this is the last place on earth you want to be this morning; still, why don't you just come for a walk with me and we'll meet up with the men back at the farmhouse later?'

Penny was relieved: Celia understood how she felt. How was it, Penny mused, that a woman, even if you had only just met her, was a better judge of your mood than a man you had lived with for far too many years? Celia turned and waved dismissively to Johnathan, who got the message and led Michael off in the opposite direction. Celia did not mention the burying business for the first half hour of their walk through the winter woodland. They strolled beneath the latticework of bare branches and talked of their children, life in the city, the trouble with men. They came to a small hill and walked through the frost-rimed grasses to its top. Here Celia stopped and turned to look back the way they had come.

'This little hill, or barrow, gives the farm its name. It is said to be Saxon, although there has been no archaeology done here for as long as my family have owned the land.' She noticed Penny's raised eyebrow. 'Oh yes – the farm is in my name; I inherited it from my mother. There has been a long family tradition of passing this particular holding down on the distaff side. There are other farms in the family, but this one has always been somewhat different.'

There was a circular seat on the top of the hill and the two women, warmly wrapped against the winter chill, sat in companionable silence for a few minutes.

'It is very beautiful here, Celia. I'm not much of a country lover, but this is so peaceful. Where are all the graves?'

'Oh, Penny – don't you realise? The woodland we have just walked through was the very first field we used for burials; under every tree we passed are the remains or the ashes of someone or other.'

'But there weren't any headstones.'

'Of course not – that's the whole point: people who choose to be buried and remembered here don't want headstones; they don't want church services – although some do have a service before they come here for interment.'

'But isn't it eerie . . . weird . . . being surrounded by . . . ?'

'Penny, look around you and answer that question for yourself.'

Celia Evans was not what Penny had been expecting. Short, dark, Celtic-looking, her face was brown and softly wrinkled; she was older than Penny, but not by much. In fact, nothing about Barrow Farm was quite what Penny had been expecting. It was a place full of life.

One field had become a huge orchard: fruiting trees were the choice of the customers for this area. The two women left the mound and headed for the orchard. Many of the trees here were well grown. Newly planted trees in neat plastic shelters marked the most recent arrivals.

'Families come and pick the fruit every year. Planting something that either fruits or blossoms about the time of the anniversary of the death is very popular. This is a fairly recent arrival – see – this one has a small plaque; some of them do.'

The plaque said 'Baby Nathan, born 1st January 2002, died aged seven weeks'.

Penny had begun to soften under Celia's kindness; the plaque for Baby Nathan was just enough to make her eyes water. She turned away so that Celia might not notice – but Celia did.

'Penny, a lot of tears are shed here; that does not make it a bad place. Nathan's family visit often; when the weather is good they usually have a picnic in the sun beside his tree.'

Penny and Celia walked back in the direction of the farmhouse. When they arrived, Johnathan and Michael had not yet returned.

'Great,' Celia said. 'We can have a cup of tea in peace.'

'What do you have to do, Celia? I imagined having to make sandwiches and pour sherry for the bereaved.'

'No, nothing like that; we do have a small contemplation area – it's a converted stone barn; it has a churchy feel to it but is not consecrated; I keep that nice – put in fresh flowers every day, but only because I enjoy it. Sometimes someone will be in there; sometimes they want to speak; mostly they don't. It doesn't affect my life at all really – no different to having fields of sheep or cows – or crops even. We separated the farmhouse off from the business side of things: nobody gets buried within the farmhouse gardens area. Except us of course, when the time comes.'

Penny had insisted they cancel the booking for the rest of the weekend at The Dun Cow. They had left Barrow Farm with the intention of driving straight home. She sat in the car, next to a silent Michael, thinking. An hour and a half into their hushed journey she turned to look at him. His brow was furrowed, his hands showing tension, veins standing out.

'I need a pee; stop at the next services please,' she said in a surprisingly calm voice.

Michael nodded, and turned off at the next Little Chef. They both got out of the car and Michael locked it.

'Do you want to eat?' Penny asked.

'Do you?' Michael replied.

'This is crazy,' Penny sighed in exasperation. 'Crazy – you are a crazy man, do you know that?'

'I know – let's have some lunch; don't suppose it'll come up to Dun Cow standards, but we should eat – and talk.'

Michael found a table while Penny found the loos. When she came back she sat down heavily in the uncomfortable plastic chair.

'So, what did you find out from him, then?'

'You aren't interested; the whole idea is a huge no-no as far as you are concerned – you've made that perfectly clear.

I'm just sorry I ever mentioned it.'

Penny looked out through the steamy window at the traffic rushing by: cars and lorries, lorries and cars, hurtling from one place to another. She remembered the tranquil moments she had spent with Celia Evans sitting on the top of Barrow Hill. A waitress arrived with two cups of tea and the two bacon rolls Michael had ordered. They ate in silence.

'Michael,' Penny said as she put her empty cup back in its tea-puddled saucer. 'I am interested in what he might have said – I mean . . . is it a viable business?'

'Oh yes, people never stop dying; graveyards are full, and consecrated plots expensive to buy. Some parishes have had to dig up the oldest untended areas of their graveyards to make more space; the idea of a plot being yours forever and ever amen is becoming a thing of the past. The alternative plot is yours until your tree dies – could be hundreds of years – and you can arrange it so your family members have space to be placed next to you, or even share your tree.'

'Does it make money?'

'Oh yes – not a fortune, but it makes enough for them to drive fancy four-wheel drives and live a fairly middle-class lifestyle.'

Penny thought back to the large stone-flagged, Aga-warmed kitchen with its pair of lazy Labradors lounging in huge wicker dog baskets, the family photos lined up on the mantlepiece. There was something to be said for the country life – but could she imagine herself living it? She had never been inside Henge Farm; all she knew of it was its rutted muddy lane, its noisy tractors, smelly sheep, snarling sheepdogs; all mud and smells and falling down outbuildings. Barrow Farm was well tended – beautiful, even. It was going to be hard to admit, but she had been impressed – despite trying very hard to maintain determined opposition to the whole idea.

'Michael, I've changed my mind; I don't want to go straight home. The kids aren't expecting us till Sunday night, so we might as well make the most of it. Let's make a deal: we won't talk about this whole thing until we get back. We'll book into some nice hotel for tonight, and forget all about it till next week. It will give us both a chance to think.'

Michael was surprised and grateful for a break in the atmosphere. They popped into the tourist information kiosk at the services on the way back to the car and arranged a luxury dinner, bed and breakfast at Mossingham Manor, twenty miles or so off the next motorway junction.

CHAPTER TWENTY-SEVEN

I followed with the women for days, moving ever southward, not knowing where I might be. A hand touched me on my shoulder and I turned from the arm I was straightening with strong straight sticks and bands of leather. It was the slave girl; she smiled and waved a greeting. How she had survived she could not tell with word, but in a mime she showed that she had been found by villagers, taken to their home, hidden, and given the chance to survive.

Avian Tyler was considering the best way to pass Callum's message to Alice. The woman was church-going, religious, and was bound to be shocked by the idea that her dead husband's spirit had been chatting to a strange woman at dawn. She had considered telephoning, but somehow that seemed inappropriate; this was something she should have dealt with face to face before leaving Orby Cottage; a letter, perhaps? Avian searched out some matching writing paper and envelopes and sat at her kitchen table, pen in hand, unsure how to begin.

Dear Alice,

I had to write to say how very much I appreciated your hospitality when I last came to visit Violet. She is very fortunate indeed to have such a good friend and neighbour in you.

I realise some of my antics seemed heathen and irreligious to you; despite that, you made me feel most welcome in your home – even Nipper decided I was not such a bad soul. So, thank you again.

I have a second reason for writing to you, not so easy to unravel as my first. Please believe me when I say that I must continue with this as I made a promise, a promise I cannot break. That morning, up at the stones, I made contact with the spirit of the place. All such places have a spirit, or the echo of one. The spirit, which waxes and wanes, is the spirit of someone who loved and cared for the area. Sometimes, it is so long since a living person has truly cared, that the resident spirit becomes a mere shadow – until someone living, who does care, dies and takes on the mantle. Your Callum is the spirit of the place, but I don't think that will come as a complete surprise to you. He said that deep down, you know that – especially since your visit with your new friend; and he wants you to know that he was right. He would not elaborate, he said you would either know, or find out very soon, what he had always been right about.

He sends you his deepest love.

There, I have kept my promise. I hope I have not offended you in any way in the doing of it. There was one last thing – he did say you should visit the stones again soon, and often, with Nipper.

My very best wishes to you. I hope we meet again sometime.

Love,

Avian Tyler

Sarah Rigden was packed and ready to go – physically. Mentally, she was nowhere near prepared. She had never left her children for more than an afternoon, not even with her mother before they moved. Sarah could not begin to imagine how Brian was going to cope for three whole days. Yes, he could change a night nappy; yes he could bath them – in his way. Faith would only have her hair washed if you sang a particular song and poured the water over her in a particular way; she liked her food cut up in certain shapes. There were rituals to the smooth running of a day that Brian had no idea of. She had left lists pinned around the house.

Faith likes to be put down for her nap just after lunch.

Put on nappy; cuddle and story downstairs. Upstairs singing 'Baa Baa Black Sheep'.

Put her down; she will whimper; pick her up and give one last cuddle; put down firmly waving bye bye, and leave; shut door.

Make sure two-way baby alarm is on.

All over the house, sheets of written instructions flapped

in the breeze from open windows. Through clenched teeth Brian nodded and smiled at repetitions of how to do this, and when to do that.

'Honestly Sarah, it'll be fine – we'll be fine. You are going to miss your train if you don't get in that taxi now; the poor man's been waiting fifteen minutes already.'

He hustled her out of the door, Faith wriggling in his arms, and Aaron wailing for his mummy.

'Just go, woman – he'll stop wailing as soon as you've gone. Go.'

He gave her a parting kiss and shoved her out of the door towards the taxi. When she turned round he had shut the door. Aaron's wailing could still be heard. Tears welling up in her eyes, Sarah managed to fight the instinct to dismiss the taxi and go straight back indoors.

'Where to, missus?'

'Berwick train station,' she said – in as solid a voice as she could muster.

Avian hoped she had not made a big mistake in inviting Sarah Rigden to visit. This was something she had not done before. However, she could not imagine any way she could have helped Sarah at home: the children consumed her every waking and sleeping moment; there would have been no way to break through, to find time and space to listen.

Avian had given the spare room, previously used only by Maisie on her impromptu visits, a spring clean. She had collected lavender from the garden and placed several sprays in small vases and jugs about the room: the air was permeated with the fragrance. Mediterranean-style vegetables were roasting in olive oil and garlic in a baking tin, and the aroma wafted out through the open kitchen window. Avian heard the taxi pull away, and had opened the front door before Sarah had made it down the path with her luggage.

'How long are you planning to stay?' Avian laughed. 'A month? Two?'

'I know, I know – it's just that I haven't been away for so long – I got carried away.'

'I am glad you are here – welcome,' Avian declared as she relieved Sarah of two smaller bags.

'I am glad to be here . . . I think. Sorry, that sounded so rude. I mean – it's the children.'

And the tears that had been waiting for the whole journey broke through and rolled down Sarah's tired white cheeks.

'Now then, get in here and phone Brian – set your mind at rest; come on, hurry up.' Avian took charge – bustled Sarah indoors, pointed out the telephone, and left her to make her call while Avian bundled the luggage up to the spare room. She sat on the bed and compared Maisie's travelling light kit of one small backpack – enough for her to cross the world with if she wanted – to Sarah's pull-along monster, her handbag and another bag about the same size as Maisie's single one. Three days: how on earth could she begin to help this confused creature in just three days? She would need help from Sarah, yet she did not expect that help to be forthcoming.

Sarah called up from downstairs. 'Everything's fine; they are both in bed and fast asleep, and Brian sounds like he won't be far behind them.'

'Good, that means we can settle down to eat in peace. Hope you are hungry.'

They ate the meal slowly, talking often, sipping the red wine Avian had bought especially. They mopped up the delicious juices from the meal from their plates with chunks of home-baked bread, then sat back in their chairs, satiated. They were quiet for a while. Avian knew Sarah was thinking about the children. She had better start as she meant to continue – she would have to be quite firm with Sarah.

'Now then, stop thinking about Faith and Aaron. We have three days – only three days – and I can't work with you unless you can at least try to clear your mind of other people. This break is about you.'

'I know . . . it's so hard,' Sarah whined.

'No. That's where you're wrong. It's not hard at all. You have to let yourself do it, allow yourself, be selfish for once. We'll make some tea and go and sit somewhere more comfortable and you will begin to tell me all about you.'

Avian went to bed exasperated. Sarah seemed only able to place herself in relation to other people. Talking of her childhood, she talked of how her mother felt; her brother, sister;

how what she said and did affected them. At school, she had been an able student – would have been anyone's ideal best friend – always agreed and always put others first. It had been like pulling teeth getting any inkling as to how anything much had affected Sarah until she had the children. Her natural (unnatural, Avian thought) concern for everyone around her, and her strong maternal instincts and urges focused every ounce of Sarah Rigden away from herself and towards her children. Avian dripped a few drops of marjoram essential oil onto her duvet cover. Maybe she would be inspired by dreams.

Sarah looked at her room. It was relaxing – she could close the door and know that nobody and nothing were going to disturb her sleep. No baby alarm by the bed. No Brian coming up late after watching telly, her pretending to be asleep, him trying so hard not to wake her. He would slide into the bed and be asleep within minutes; she would lie there, listening; listening to his breathing, listening to the baby alarm, listening for Faith in the next room. She slept listening, any slight sound snatching her back to alertness. She was sure she would not sleep here, in a strange bed, in a strange house – yet she felt strangely tired. She undressed and climbed into the high bed. The mattress was soft and she sank into it; it felt like a nest, cradling her. The room smelt of lavender; the bed smelt strongly of lavender. She breathed in deeply and stretched herself out in the cosseting embrace of feathers, and slept.

'Good morning, Nipper,' Alice yawned as she opened the

back door to let the dog out into the garden.

The kettle boiled, the toast popped up from the toaster and Alice sat down to read her mail. Mostly bills – circulars – the bank, offering her yet another credit card. Then Alice came to the envelope with the unfamiliar writing. She wondered who it could be from; not Michael or Penny or the grandchildren; not Margaret. She slid her forefinger along the envelope and extracted the sheet of paper within. She read the letter. She read the letter again.

'Well I'm blowed,' she puffed. 'Would you believe it? What nonsense! What a cheek.'

She screwed the letter up in one hand and was about to place it firmly in the bin when she had second thoughts. She sat back down at the table and smoothed the wrinkled paper out and read the letter again, slowly. Avian could not have known of her visit to the stones with Margaret – only Alice and Margaret knew. Alice was aware that she had felt something there that day – she had crumpled, cried; it had been the incident that had drawn her and Margaret together. She had spoken of it to no one. She shivered, despite the warmth of the morning wafting through the open kitchen door. Nipper waddled in.

'Well, Nipper – what to make of all this? I'm sure I don't know. Perhaps I should talk to the minister. Perhaps I should talk to Avian first.'

The little dog rubbed his body against her leg and woofed.

When she was washed and dressed Alice felt more herself

again. She decided to telephone Avian Tyler. She dialled the number from the top of the letter, the phone rang in Number 7, Railway Cottages and Sarah answered it.

'Hello, Avian Tyler's phone – can I help?'

'Sarah? Sarah Rigden – is that you?'

'Yes, who is this? Has something happened?'

'This is Alice McCleish. No, nothing has happened. What are you doing there? Not that it's any of my business . . .'

'Avian is trying to work out the cause of these headaches, and it's a break for me.'

'Oh well; good luck. Is Avian there?'

'Well, she sort of is, and she sort of isn't. What I mean is, she's busy – trying to pick up echoes or something – not to be disturbed.' Sarah hoped this made sense.

'Can you tell her I called? Just tell her I'm not offended, but I am confused. There's no rush – tell her to call me after you have left – then she can concentrate on you. Bye, my love.'

'Bye, Alice.'

Sarah put the phone down with her hands shaking. Any sense of relaxation she had found had disappeared. She wanted to phone Brian, to make sure that everything was OK, but she had promised Avian that she would not – at least not until this evening when the children would be tucked up in bed – hopefully. Avian had been doing whatever it was she was doing for three quarters of an hour, since their late break-fast; to Sarah it seemed like hours. She had nothing to do, nothing. She would normally be getting Aaron ready for nursery and Faith ready for mother and toddler group, and attending to all that that entailed: Faith's spare clothes, wipes, bottles of juice, little healthy snacks like dried bananas or carob drops; finding shoes, doing up jackets or cardigans, strapping into the buggy, finding Aaron's little bag; then, lastly, organising herself, brushing her hair, finding the keys; guaranteed Aaron would want the loo just as they were about to leave. There would be washing in the washing machine by now churning endlessly round and round.

Here – nothing. She had been glad of the phone call – something to do. Where was Avian anyway? Sarah decided to take a look out in the tiny backyard. It was overcast, grey, but warm and there was no wind. Hesitantly, as if she were entering a forbidden room, she opened the back door. The paved yard was full to bursting with pots. Anything that could conceivably be used to put a plant in was there. An old leather boot, old paint tins, their outsides coated in the original contents, all the colours of the rainbow. Terracotta pots did exist in this strange jungle of recycled receptacles alongside old chimney pots, an old mangle, a dented lead water tank, one rolled-down blue wellington boot. The plants, dead in their myriad containers, were mere ghosts of the previous season's riotous floral disorder. Brian would hate this, Sarah thought. There is no order here, the newer the container and plant, the nearer the front of the group it would be, regardless of height or growth pattern. Trailing plants that would have hung gracefully down from the top of the wall lay in tangled confusion over other plants, containers and the ground.

Sarah noticed a chair beneath the kitchen window, almost hidden by the leaves of a native sunflower growing in an old washing up bowl. She sat down. She had expected Railway Cottages to be noisy with trains rushing past, the sound of the city perpetually grinding away in the background. She had been wrong. The siding had been unused for many years and the city was far enough away behind the invading hedge of privet and the high metal fence to be almost inaudible. Certainly here, in this strange backyard, the hum of human life did not compete with birdsong and the droning of insects.

Avian brushed herself down with owl feathers and smudged the room she had been using with sage. She looked down at the object she had been focusing on. It was a rather timeworn, much-loved bear, ten inches or so tall, one button eye missing, one ear sadly chewed – by Sarah, it seemed. Avian had asked Sarah to bring something, something that had always been hers, was personal – jewellery maybe, but not inherited. She had brought the bear. Known only as 'Bear', it had been a first birthday gift from her grandmother on her mother's side. Bear had kindly given Avian the lead she had been looking for. Bear carried with him echoes of all Sarah's childhood woes – he had been hugged close to a face wet with tears, laden with all Sarah's secrets. Sarah could not have chosen a more intense concentration of herself than Bear, who apparently still sat on a chair of his own in Sarah's bedroom in Duddo – still collecting her innermost thoughts.

'Thank you, Bear, you have been most helpful,' Avian said as she collected the moth-eaten thing ready to hand it back to Sarah. The kitchen door was open; Avian and Bear entered to find Sarah fast asleep on a chair, her feet propped on an upturned box. Avian popped Bear gently onto Sarah's lap and left the room. So. How to deal with this one? Avian had heard of lost twin syndrome – sometimes due to separation at birth, sometimes to infant death of one twin. In this case, Sarah, it seemed, had no idea she may have had a twin.

It may be that many people begin life as a twin: the zygote splits into two separate cells, these then begin to divide; when they come to embed themselves in the uterine wall maybe only one is successful. Both may embed, but both may not reach full term – the mother may never even have known that she began a pregnancy with twins.

Sarah had an intense friendship with an invisible friend throughout her early childhood. Sarah, Bear, and Angela, invisible to all but Sarah, had struggled through childhood. The family tried to accommodate Angela: a place would be set at table sometimes but Sarah's insistence on Angela being everpresent in family life began to take its toll. In the end, exasperated beyond belief, her mother had finally put her foot down.

'Sarah – it's time you grew up – you are ten years old now. Big girls don't have imaginary friends. I don't want to hear Angela's name mentioned in this house ever again. Do you hear me? Never again.'

Sarah, Bear and Angela had rushed away upstairs to their

room. Sarah had cried and cried and Bear had become sodden; as she calmed down she sucked on Bear's ear. Angela had stood by the bedside and watched her in her anguish. Angela sat on the bed and stroked Sarah's hair.

'Go away,' Sarah sobbed. 'Go away now. You heard what mummy said.'

'I will always be with you; don't forget, Sarah – always,' Angela murmured, and she left.

When Sarah withdrew her face from the moist mess of her bear and her pillow she was – except for Bear – alone, quite alone, for the first time she could remember. She had been afraid.

When she awoke she found the kitchen table set for tea. In the chair sat Avian; on the table, tea and cakes. Sarah ate and drank quietly, asking no questions as Avian explained something of what she had been doing, and something of what Bear had revealed.

At the end, Avian added, 'I have one question to ask you, Sarah. Cast your mind back, and describe to me what Angela looked like.'

'That's easy – she looked just like me: we always wore the same clothes, had our hair the same, same shoes; she even had a bear of her own, just like mine,' Sarah said as she held Bear against her cheek. 'How could you know all that? It's spooky.'

'Not spooky; Bear is the repository of your childhood, it's all in there just as if you had kept a diary. I am lucky; I hear it, like someone else might read it. In fact Bear is the repository of your whole life, even up to today.'

'What has all this got to do with my headaches?'

'You have shut out what should have been a big part of your life. That takes a lot of effort for your brain, mind, soul – whatever you want to call it – to maintain, constantly, like a pressure. Do you dream of Angela?'

'No – never.'

'Then you have maintained that effort twenty-four hours a day since you were ten. Is it any wonder you have headaches? Then there's the family to care for. I think the effort of maintaining both has just become too much – you need to give up some of the effort,' Avian suggested.

'How can I give up anything to do with the children? Who else is there to do it?' Sarah snapped, irritated once again by Avian's intrusion. She had expected help with her headaches – massage, more of the potions – not this. She felt somehow naked, betrayed by Bear, exposed to this woman in a most uncomfortable way.

'Who is looking after them now?' Avian spoke firmly.

'You know who – Brian is who, and I expect he's making a right pig's ear of it. I bet he hates it.' Sarah's voice rose by an octave.

'Really? You imagine he hates the closeness, the intimacy of children, the innocence of their affection; those big round-your-neck tight hugs and wet kisses? Being told by Aaron how much he loves him? You imagine he hates that, do you? If he hates anything I imagine it's being shut out, not being the person his children come running to if they scrape a knee, or are frightened by a leaping frog. You cannot be a perfect mother, Sarah – or a perfect wife, friend, daughter or sister – you just have to be good enough.'

'How would you know? What makes you such an expert? You're not married; you haven't got any children,' Sarah blurted out angrily, her chest heaving with emotion.

Avian knew she had touched a nerve. Calm, gentle, earth mother Sarah was losing her cool. How far should Avian go? How much could Sarah handle? An echo, like an echo of Sarah's own voice sighed some distance off. Avian almost didn't hear it; she focused her intent momentarily away from Sarah. Again, the sigh: stronger. Angela – Angela was nearby.

'What about Angela?' Avian pressed.

'Imagination. Silly, childish imagination. Nonsense. This is all nonsense – I should never have come here.'

Sarah began to cry. She hugged Bear, then threw him away; she turned fiercely away from Avian in her chair, drew her knees up, clasped her arms around them and wailed. Avian sat patiently waiting for the storm of pent-up anger to decrease.

'And you can stop stroking my hair,' Sarah sobbed.

'I haven't moved an inch; I'm still in my chair – five feet away from you,' Avian replied.

CHAPTER TWENTY-EIGHT

*W*ord– of a great council to come – at the place of the
Caledonians called Laggharn. Leaves turned and fell,
as from all directions the peoples of the Islands – from north and
south, and east and west – and many deserters from the Roman
ranks, Gauls, Usipi and more, merged upon the ever more menacing high land.

Alice McCleish put down the telephone handset. She was
glad Sarah had gone off to visit Avian – the break would do
her good. Alice had offered tentatively to babysit, or have the
children for the odd hour or two to give Sarah a break. Sarah
had always sidestepped the offer – very politely, but firmly.
Alice had spoken to Brian about it. Brian had explained that
Sarah found it very difficult to leave the children, even with
him – it was just a thing she had – nothing personal. Brian

333

would have happily taken advantage of Alice's kind offer. So Alice had stopped offering. She was mildly concerned, come to think of it, that Avian might influence the girl, yet at the same time she hoped Avian would have some kind of influence – the kind she had with Violet.

Honestly, Alice McCleish, she said out loud to herself. All those years with Callum – you should be used to this sort of thing by now. But she knew she was not. Callum kept his beliefs close to his heart. He had no desire to confront his wife's religious faith. They had long ago agreed to disagree, and had rubbed along with that for years. Avian Tyler was so much more obvious – wafting stuff around, using twigs from certain trees, hearing things . . . Now she maintained she had spoken with Callum. Alice did not believe this. Her faith taught her that when you died you went to one of two places, and she had fervently prayed that Callum's spirit was up there, not down below. She had spoken to the minister about it after Callum died. The minister had been thoughtful in his reply.

'Callum was a good man. I never heard him say a bad thing about anyone, and never heard of him doing anyone a wrong turn. Our Lord himself preached in the open air – the Sermon on the Mount, for instance. He did not worship his Father, The Almighty, in a building. I'm sure Callum will be judged favourably – aren't you?'

Alice's mind had been put at rest, the minister had buried Callum in the graveyard, and all was well . . . more or less. Until now. Perhaps she should take Nipper out for a walk to clear her head. Maybe she should go up to the stones – after all, since the dig, there was a gate and a rough path – it would be much easier now. Nipper moved and sat beside his lead hanging on the back door.

'You are a knowing little soul. Just like your master,' Alice said, as she ruffled the shock of stiff, soft hair on the little dog's head. She sat to put on her Hush Puppies, laced her feet firmly in them and pulled on a cardigan.

'Come on then, dog – off we go.'

As they walked along the lane, Wyllie and Violet pulled up in the Land Rover.

'Morning, Alice. How's the fettle?' Violet asked, leaning out from the open grubby window.

'Grand; it's a grand morning. Where are you two off to then?'

'Estate agents in Wooler. There's nothing for sale in the village at the moment,' Violet answered.

'I don't know if I should say anything, but Marge Watt was talking to me in the shop last week – she's just coming up for retirement you know – can you believe it? Where does time go? I got the impression that she and Ron might be considering moving away, nearer to family. I could be quite wrong, of course.'

'Should I phone her, do you think?' Violet asked, some excitement showing in her voice. The Watts' cottage was very nice – Ron had kept it lovely, and it had a decent-sized garden for Wyllie to play in. She could see herself living there, right opposite the bus stop.

'Well, I don't know – she didn't say anything definite, just a hint. You could lure her out to you with the offer of tea and fruit cake – see what comes of it – after all, no one knows you are thinking of selling the farm yet – do they?'

'Just us and your Michael; he was a great help. Such a nice lad. Still, Alice, we must be off,' Wyllie said, revving the engine of the noisy vehicle. These two would chatter on all day if he didn't put a stop to it. Nipper scooted up onto the grass verge at the sound of the engine and sat waiting for the filthy noisy thing to go away.

Alice opened the gate to the field, edged through with Nipper at her heels, turned, and closed the gate. Nipper darted off – rabbits beckoned, their white retreating tufts irresistible. Alice stood, hands on hips, girding herself for the uphill path, getting a good lungful of air to start off with. She was apprehensive. This was the first time she had ventured up here since Margaret's visit, and the first time ever – absolutely ever – that she had come here alone. She walked slowly, her gaze mostly on the ground. Now and then she would stop, look ahead, upwards, at the silhouettes of the stones on her horizon: so familiar, so much a part of her life. She had been happy to think of it as some kind of farming calendar; there was sense in that. To think of it as a place with something of her husband haunting it was another thing altogether. She was confused. She had experienced several happenings lately, which were making her question beliefs she had steadfastly stood by all of her life.

She took a deep breath, folded her arms across her bosom, looked directly at the stones, whistled for Nipper and walked forward. What did she expect? She did not know. A breeze curled lazily around, first this way, then that; the stones were set, as they had been for thousands of years: a dull sky meant they cast the merest of shadows. Alice entered the circle and stood still; Nipper cocked his leg up a stone, a curlew mewled in the distance. Alice knew that with Wyllie and Violet away in Wooler, she was the only human being in the landscape for several miles around – but she did not feel alone. Avian's rowan twigs lay at the foot of the lampstone, the leaves crisp red brown. Alice bent down to pick them up. There was no great inrush of emotion as there had been before, with Margaret. She felt a calmness – the feeling she would have when Callum slept in the armchair beside the fire on a winter's evening; the chores done, she would sit and sew, watching him slumber, a dog at his feet, the contentedness of long habit.

'Callum?' she spoke aloud. It felt so different from speaking to him at his graveside – somehow blasphemous. 'Callum, I don't understand all this. It's all wrong. I'm being pulled this way and that, like this breeze. It's cruel. How could Avian speak with you when I can't? Everything seems topsy-turvy.'

Nipper waddled over, looking around to see who missus was talking to. He sat sullenly for a moment beside her legs. The breeze ceased its meanderings and all was still. Alice was just about to leave when the dog yipped excitedly, rolled over on his back and wriggled energetically from side to side, leapt to his feet, and began to run back and forth, back and forth as if retrieving thrown sticks.

Alice watched; the dog was behaving oddly. 'Come on, Nipper. Here, boy,' she called.

The dog stopped and looked at her. Alice began to walk back, whistling the dog as she went. She turned; the dog sat in the centre of the circle, tail wagging, head to the clouds.

'Nipper, come here! Nipper!' she shouted.

The small dejected dog slunk slowly back to Alice, stopping and looking behind himself more than once. Alice tried hard to convince herself that the dog was just being daft, as dogs are sometimes. She dropped the bunch of dead twigs still held in her hand and put the reluctant animal on his lead. She almost had to drag him back down to the gate and home.

When Alice got home the telephone was ringing as she opened the back door. She hurried to pick it up, breathless.

'Hello? Oh, Michael, hello . . . No, I'm fine – I've just come in from walking the dog – puffed out. Yes, yes of course – your room is always made up, just needs an airing . . . That's fine – just you, is it? OK, see you then. Bye.'

Sarah Rigden arrived back at Berwick railway station at two-thirty one day earlier than planned. There had been no phone call from home to bring her back early – Brian, it seemed, had coped very well and had enjoyed himself. She took the lift up and down again to the station entrance, where

Brian, Faith and Aaron were waiting. Her first feeling on seeing them, Aaron's hand tightly in Brian's, Faith clinging around his neck clutched in Brian's other arm, was one of intense jealousy. Like a tight knot in her stomach she wanted to snatch the children from him: she was their mother, they needed her. *Her.*

'Mummy, we had fun – where have you been?' Aaron rushed towards her.

Sarah dropped her bags and grasped the happy child tightly. Mine, she thought to herself, all mine.

Brian came across to hand over a wriggling Faith and pick up Sarah's bags, but the child clung to him, burying her face in Brian's neck, clinging tightly with her pudgy legs around his chest.

'Come on Faith, it's Mummy,' Brian said as he tried to prize the arms free. 'You go to Mummy, and Daddy can carry the heavy bags. Off you go now.'

Faith was not best pleased to leave Daddy: she whined and wriggled in Sarah's embrace.

'Faith, darling, did you miss me? Mummy's home now. Mummy's home.'

At the car, Sarah had to overcome a huge urge to keep Faith on her lap for the journey; she knew the child should be strapped firmly in her seat – knew that was best, safest – yet she did not want to let go, ever. She wanted to drive. Suddenly she did not trust Brian to drive them all safely home. Her fingers began to tingle uncomfortably; her head began to swim.

'Brian . . . Brian – I . . .'

She came to in the waiting room. Brian was holding her, his arm round her back, supporting her, wiping her forehead with a damp cloth courtesy of the tea room attendant.

'The children . . .' Sarah mumbled.

'It's OK, love – you didn't drop her. I got to you just in time – caught you both. You fainted. Just sit still there; drink some of this water.'

Sarah woozily saw Faith and Aaron over near the lift with a station employee. She closed her eyes and waited to come back to herself properly. Brian wiped the cold sweat from her forehead; the tea lady brought over a fresh cold cloth.

'Happens a lot to women in her condition,' she said in a comforting voice to Brian.

Brian looked up at the tea lady standing before them. She winked knowingly.

'I can always tell – so could my mother – always tell.' She chuckled and went back off to her kiosk.

Brian got Sarah to the car. The station guard enticed the children away from the great game they had been having of going up and down, up and down in the lift with him.

'Look – ' he smiled, dropping down on his haunches to get nearer to their level. 'Look – Mummy's feeling better now. Let's go and see her, shall we?'

Brian strapped the children in and turned to the guard. 'Thank you – thanks so much for looking after them.'

'No problem; no problem at all. I look after my grandchildren two afternoons a week to give their poor mum a break. She's all on her own you know; so many of them are, these days.'

Later, when the children were bathed, in bed, and had been read to by Daddy, Brian took Sarah a cup of tea in the front room, where she was resting.

'Thank you, Brian,' she said, without looking at him.

'Sarah . . . Sarah – look at me please.'

Sarah slowly turned her head and looked up into Brian's concerned face.

'What on earth happened at Avian's? I thought you were going about the headaches, to get better, not to come back and faint like that. Why did you come back early?'

Sarah sighed deeply. 'You know she's a witch, or something, don't you?'

'What?'

'Psychic or whatever – so she says. Says my headaches are my own fault.'

'There's a lot of it about,' Brian said thoughtfully.

'A lot of what?' Sarah snapped. Brian did not seem to be taking her very seriously.

'Being psychic. Didn't you hear what the tea lady said?'

'No, I wasn't listening.'

'She said you were pregnant – said "it happens a lot to women in her condition", meaning you. Are you pregnant?'

'I'm a few days late I suppose – probably just the upset of being away or something. Anyway – how would she know?

Silly old woman.'

Three weeks later, Sarah bought the pregnancy testing kit. She looked at it sitting on the cistern top, waiting. They had not planned for another baby, not yet. Sarah raised her eyes from the kit to her reflection in the bathroom mirror. She thought of Angela.

When they visited the hospital for the ultrasound scan they were in for another surprise: they were expecting twins.

CHAPTER TWENTY-NINE

*W*e wended our weary way, eating what we could find:
there were many berries and fungi, swollen root, seed
and nut, and all collected as they walked. The land was thickly
wooded with tall trees with fissured bark that glowed pink and
lilac and orange in the autumn twilight.

*Day by day we walked; the hills around grew high and cut the
light from the valleys, which ran with turbulent streams and falls
where only an angry water spirit could wish to live. We took the
high path, taking direction from the inhabitants where we could.
Above the tree line, we crossed open moorland through mist and
rain and wind. From pass to pass, with more ahead and more
joining us behind from every settlement, we passed on our way.*

Michael and Penny arrived home to find the house
tidy(ish), clean(ish) and empty. A note on the table informed

them that Dexter was at a friend's for a *Lord of the Rings* fest and would not be back until sometime tomorrow. Marsha had gone to a talk at the local TA hall called 'Out of Africa: The Work of Louis and Mary Leakey' and would be back around eleven.

As agreed, they had not mentioned anything to do with green funerals, buying farms, and keeping secrets, but both knew they had to talk about this sometime. Michael had more or less come to terms with the fact that the whole idea had been stupid. How could he ever have thought that Penny, his Penny, might have even considered the idea?

Penny opened a bottle of wine and poured two large glasses. She popped a microwave paella in the machine and laid two places opposite each other at the breakfast bar. The microwave pinged; she warmed two plates on full for a minute, and then served the food.

'Michael! Food! Such as it is . . .' she called to him. He shuffled in, prepared for the worst: prepared to eat humble pie and just keep plodding on in the same old way – after all, why should he be any different from all the other accountants in the world?

'Michael . . .' Penny broke the silence halfway through the meal.

Michael looked up from his plate.

'Michael, listen. I don't know quite how to tell you this, but . . .'

Michael's expression halted her; he looked terrified, as if

she were about to tell him something awful, like she was leaving or something.

'Don't look at me like that. I've been thinking – really properly thinking about everything – about the kids growing up, about us, about the future. You see, I thought I knew what the future would be: you would work then retire with a good pension – even join the golf club, like my dad. I would meet friends for lunch; we'd have lovely holidays abroad; all that stuff – don't interrupt me,' she said, raising her hand to deflect a comment from Michael. 'But I can see now that that is not what you want. The question is – what do I want? Do I want a busy city life, with places to go, people to see, things to do – or do I want to be stuck in the middle of Northumberland surrounded by decaying corpses? Except it's not like that at all. It's being away from the dirt and filth, the crime, the used needles in the bus shelter, the endless splats of chewing gum polka-dotting the pavements, the dog crap, the litter, the traffic, the beggars, the noise, the homeless. I'm trying to say, Michael, that perhaps you should find out more. Just how possible is this crazy idea? How will the money side of things work? I can still carry on working for Thor – I can take the InterCity and be there almost as quickly as I can drive in from here on a bad day. I want to know more. In fact – I want to know everything as and when you know it: no more secrets – OK?'

Michael's mouth hung open during this outburst: food particles were visible.

'Shut your mouth, Michael, swallow your food – and then

say something, will you.'

Michael shut his mouth, but could not think of a word to say. He got up and walked round the end of the breakfast bar. He took Penny's hand, and led her up the stairs to the bedroom.

The next morning he phoned his mother.

'What did she say?' Penny asked.

'She said, "your room is always made up; just needs airing,"' he replied, emphasising Alice McCleish's accent, the twang of which still clung to his own voice. 'I'm going up next weekend.'

'She is going to be so shocked,' Penny giggled, imagining Alice's expression.

'Say that again,' Alice said slowly to her son across the kitchen table at Orby Cottage the following Saturday lunchtime.

'Penny and I are thinking about buying Henge Farm.'

A familiar voice echoed in Alice's head: 'Mark my words, it's in his very marrow'. She raised her hands from the table to her chest and clasped them together.

'I don't believe it – you and Penny – Henge Farm. Why?'

Michael laughed and took his mother's hands in his. 'Why not?'

'The . . . the children?' Alice stuttered.

'Will both have left home. Marsha is bound to get in to university, and Dexter is applying for a place at Valley Spire

College – so we'll be nearer to them, and to you.'

'But what will you do? You're no farmer.'

'We have got something in mind, Mum; but it's just an idea at the moment – nothing definite; there's a lot to discuss and to think about, but we thought you should know.'

'Have you spoken to Wyllie?'

'Hinted, only hinted; that's another reason why I've come up. I'm seeing him tomorrow.'

'Oh son, you know your father always said . . .'

'Yes, I know what he always said. Don't get too excited – it could all be a pipe dream.'

Michael rose early next morning and took the dog for a short walk along the lane. As he walked, he thought and re-membered. He thought of himself walking with Penny along here sometime in the future; he thought of how it would feel to own these fields, the fields he played in as a child, the lanes he cycled down. He remembered his father teaching him to ride a bike along this very lane – how long ago? Forty years? – more? He remembered falling off and skinning his knee and elbow quite badly; the faint scars were still there. He stood still. Nipper scuttled around the hedge bottom busy on a scent. A pheasant rattled its cry and flew off, disturbed, in the near distance. He wondered how he should tell Wyllie of his plans. Should he be discreet – keep the burial ground scheme quiet for the time being, or should he just come straight out with it? He ambled back slowly, feeling very small in this landscape. The trees towered over him; the sky was huge and uninterrupted by anything man-made except the stones.

When he returned, Alice had cooked a big bacon and egg breakfast with fried bread, and as usual a pot of tea steamed away beneath its knitted tea cosy.

'Cor, Mum! That's a treat – its muesli or toast at home.' He sat down and tucked in.

Alice sat opposite and watched her son eat. Feeding a family was the one thing from her busy earlier life that she missed more than any other. There was no point baking bread for one. One person did not need two dozen jars of bramble jelly or green tomato chutney. In that kitchen she had baked and preserved. The autumn chutney would last through until the next autumn; the bottled plums dark with burst skins had been used for crumbles in the depths of winter. If the family were going to be nearby, she would have people to ply with jars of preserves. Perhaps she could help out; cook meals. The children would be home for holidays for a few years to come – they would be near enough to come home for weekends. Alice stopped herself mid-daydream: she must not get too excited; she could end up very disappointed indeed.

Full to bursting with breakfast, Michael went upstairs to his room to collect the briefcase and files he had brought with him to show Wyllie and Violet. He had a wash, cleaned his teeth, brushed his hair and adopted his professional persona.

'You've scrubbed up well,' his mother said as he walked past her at the kitchen sink.

'See you later, Mum – wish me luck.'

'Bye son; good luck – not that you'll need it.'

As Michael walked up the lane to the steading his mother prayed. Dear God, please be with Michael today; please guide his path and that of Wyllie and Violet. Amen. A twinge of guilt racked her for two reasons: one, because she had suffered doubts about her faith of late which the Lord would know all about; and two, because this prayer was really for herself.

In the kitchen at Henge Farm, Wyllie and Violet sat at one side of the huge pine table and Michael sat at the other. The pleasantries had been gone through and it was time for Michael to put forward his plans. He leaned down and opened the briefcase.

'Before we go any further, I want you to know that Penny and I are very interested indeed in purchasing Henge Farm in its entirety – the house, outbuildings and fields – and we do not intend to split the property up to sell it off for housing or anything similar.'

'Oh, Wyllie!' Violet gasped, grasping her husband's hand.

'However,' Michael interrupted; 'as you know, we are not farmers, and it's too late for us to learn now.'

'Never too late, son – I've enough years left to teach you – help you on your way – if you wanted.' Wyllie spoke from the heart.

'No, farming is not for us, especially not for Penny – she's a city girl, not over fond of mud and muck.'

Wyllie and Violet exchanged glances. Neither could begin

to imagine what else you could do with a farm other than farm it. Michael reached into the suitcase and brought out several colour brochures and leaflets, laid them out on the table, then spun them around and pushed them across towards the Turnbulls. Violet put on her reading glasses; Wyllie squinted at the papers in front of him.

'No, don't say anything yet: read through them together. I'll take a breather outside and leave you to talk for ten minutes. OK?'

Michael rose and left the kitchen out through the back door and onto the drying green. He wished he had a packet of cigarettes: he could smoke one now, even though he had given up years ago. He paced back and forth on the drying green. Through the window he could see the two heads bent over the paperwork. He could see them talking, shaking their heads, gesticulating; he was desperate to know what was being said. He turned away and looked across at the rolling landscape. His father had known this land inside out. Michael remembered nocturnal walks – silent – to the badger sett, to watch the young tumble and play. His father had not been a talkative man – he had worked long hours and was tired when he got in – but thinking back, Michael remembered that Callum had shown him the wren's nest, the fox earth, and the otters sliding and playing at the stream edge. Michael had forgotten so much – it had all seemed so unimportant then – there was so much more to life – television mainly. *Thunderbirds* and *Stingray* were far more entertaining than boring old birds' nests and as he had grown he showed less and less interest in his father's way of life. As a teenager his only thought had been of how to get away – yet now, here he was, negotiating to buy his father's old boss's farm. He wondered what Callum would have made of that. Would he have been proud?

Wyllie called from the back door and broke Michael's reverie. 'Come on in son – the kettle's on again and Violet's cutting a fruit cake.'

That sounds hopeful, Michael thought. He turned and walked back into the farmhouse kitchen.

Violet poured three cups of tea from the huge old brown teapot and handed one to Michael. She offered him a slice of fruit cake that was bursting with glacé cherries and succulent sultanas.

'Right, son. I'll tell you now that I've never in my life heard of green burials, woodland burials or the like, but, seems to me – to us,' he said, looking to Violet for approval, 'that it's a fine idea. I'd like to be buried here myself, lad – so would Violet. There's one condition . . .' Wyllie hesitated.

Violet spoke for him. 'It's the walled orchard. We wouldn't like to think of anyone being buried there, what with the twins.'

Michael nodded. 'Of course: I understand.'

'And there's the stones to think of; I doubt you'd be allowed to disturb that field.' Wyllie added.

'Wyllie, there's bound to be a million and one things the powers that be will not allow me to do. They may not even be prepared to consider the idea, in which case I don't think Penny and I could continue with the purchase; the alternatives are not what we would be interested in doing – bed and breakfast, camping, that sort of thing.'

'So, what happens now, son?'

'With your support I'd like to sound out the people at the local planning office – get some idea of the lie of the land.'

The meeting ended with all parties enthusiastically in favour of Michael's seemingly crazy idea. Michael left the Turnbulls feeling hopeful; however, there was one more person to consult: his mother.

'A graveyard, but it's nothing to do with the Church, it's not hallowed ground . . . surely you can't just bury people in fields willy-nilly like that?'

Michael showed his mother some of the information he had brought for the Turnbulls.

'Listen, Mum. Things have changed in the world – even here in Northumberland. Not everyone is Christian. Lots of people choose not to have a religious service at all these days. Other religions would use the place, and people with no religious beliefs at all.'

'I don't know that I want to be surrounded by graves. What would the minister think?'

'The minister would probably be as pleased as punch – after all, his graveyard is almost full – so full that most of his parishioners opt for cremation, with the service at the crematorium I imagine. Not good business for him, is it? Imagine – I bet plenty of people would still want some sort of religious service. Maybe I could do a deal with him and put some work his way.'

'Michael, don't speak that way; really, you sound just like your father sometimes. I can't for the life of me imagine your Penny living in the country. Surely she does not really want to live . . . well you know.' Alice had a mental picture of Penny picking her way up the rutted, muddy lane to the steading, Penny with her car spattered with thick, clinging winter mud.

'Mum – see this one here. Barrow Farm, Dorset. I took Penny down to see the place, to meet the owners. It is beautiful; it's not muddy because there are no tractors or sheep or cows to churn the place up. The early fields are now semi-mature woodland; there are no graves to see as such – just trees, all sorts of trees – a whole new environment free of chemicals and fertilisers – except for the departed, that is.'

'Well, I don't know about all that.'

'Mum, I need you onside. You are the nearest neighbour – the only neighbour – in fact you are probably the only person who could throw a spanner in the works by opposing the plans.' Michael's face had the same expression on it she remembered from his childhood. Before her again was the boy who really, really wanted a Chopper bike; who really, really wanted . . . any number of things boys wanted then. She had always found that expression and its implicit request particularly difficult to refuse.

'I need to think about it,' she said; 'to talk about it with someone – Margaret maybe, and definitely the minister.'

'OK, Mum – talk about it with them, but no one else for the time being. Wyllie and I are going to sound out the planning people on Monday – I might need to stay an extra day or two – if it's OK with you.'

'Well I think it's a marvellous idea,' Margaret Allerton said enthusiastically down the telephone to her friend. 'In fact – I'd very much like to be their first customer.'

'Margaret!' Alice replied, shocked by both responses. 'Is there something you haven't told me? Are you all right?'

'Yes – of course I'm all right. What I mean is I would like to be the first to book my plot. I was planning on a cremation, but a woodland burial really appeals.'

'Does it? Does it really, Margaret? I don't know about it at all, I really don't.'

CHAPTER THIRTY

Rumour had it that Calgacus himself would speak. It was whispered that the last of the free – an army, raised in secret, deep in the impenetrable depths of the Highlands, would be seen there – the myth of their existence exposed as truth.

Never before in living memory had so many gathered. He spoke, this leader, not just to the chieftains, the queens, the princes, but to the people. His Celtic words echoed across the silent crowds by callers, transformed in the callers' mouths into each tribe's tongue or dialect so that all who were gathered should know his words. Behind him, in an arc of hundreds, stood the last of the free. Men, women and children of fearsome look gathered in clans, each wound around with peculiar cloth; and so many voices of ghosts a-wailing, their spirits coiled within the mists that wreathed the ancient fort.

The following Sunday, the service was at Duddo Church. Afterwards, Alice waited behind to speak to the minister. He listened carefully to what she had to say.

'Indeed, it is legal, and acceptable in the eyes of the Church. So many of our graveyards are full – in the cities they are removing the remains of those who were buried years ago and have no living descendants, in order to make room for the new. A grave is not a place one will remain in forever any more.'

'Surely that won't happen here, minister – digging up the old to make way for the new? It can't be so. Do you mean that one day, when I'm gone, Callum could be dug up like that? Could I?'

'In theory, that is quite possible,' the minister replied. 'Quite possible. Now Alice, if you'll excuse me, I have to visit Mrs Ollerenshaw . . . something to do with the Rural.'

Alice did not feel like driving home. The world suddenly seemed to be changing at an alarming rate around her. She decided to walk down through the village to the graveyard to visit Callum.

Since Marcus's grandmother's funeral Margaret had been musing on the subject of her own disposal. She had written off burial years ago, had been sure that a quick cremation with no service would be what she wanted; no fuss – there did not even need to be anyone there. Now she thought she might like Alice to be there – and Marcus, maybe – and maybe her cleaning lady. Alice's phone call had caused her to reconsider. She turned on her computer and went online, typed in 'alternative burials' in a search engine and scanned the sites. She was particularly taken with the handmade wicker caskets designed to rot away along with their contents – so beautiful – even tiny ones for babies. She thought the whole idea was charming. Margaret checked her emails. There was one – from U3A: would she like to give a one-off lecture on something or other? She replied at once in the negative and logged off.

The years, she felt, were slowly catching up with her. Her health was reasonable, her GP informed her – for someone of her age. She was still careful not to rise from a chair or from her bed too rapidly, but apart from that she was fine. She no longer walked. This irked her. Inside, she felt quite fit enough to march the length of Hadrian's Wall, or attempt less hilly stretches of other paths. A knock on the door roused her from her ponderings. Margaret opened the door to find Marcus, a large bunch of flowers in his hands.

'Morning, Maggie – how are you today?'

'I'm very well – thank you for asking. To what do I owe this pleasure?'

'First, I got you these. It's a sort of celebration.' A grin spread across Marcus's face.

'You had better come in then. I will put them in a vase, if I can find one.'

'That can wait. I've got something to show you.' He turned from the doorway and pointed behind himself at a small red car.

'Whose is that?' Margaret asked sharply.

'Oh, I haven't nicked it, Mags – no, no. My gran left me some money – not much, but enough for a few driving lessons and a car. I passed my test yesterday.'

Margaret was given a quick tour of the little red car. She made all the right noises, she hoped. She was thrilled for the boy, for the freedom it would give him. They went indoors and Margaret found a large old jug lurking beneath the sink into which she placed the cut flowers. The smell of the lilies in the bunch permeated the room with a thick air of decadence that Margaret did not really like, but the colours brightened up the corner where they stood.

'I thought you might like to go out for a drive.' Marcus suggested.

Margaret was a little apprehensive. 'You only passed your test yesterday; perhaps you should get a little more practice before you . . .' she tailed off as he shook his head.

'Maggie, I've been driving other people's cars since I was eleven, on and off. Admittedly they didn't usually know about it till afterwards. Never got caught for that – nearly did once so I stopped.

'Marcus,' Margaret tutted, 'that's nothing to be proud of.'

'I know, I know,' the young man teased, putting his arm around Margaret's disapproving shoulders. 'But I'm a changed man now, thanks to you.'

Marcus helped Margaret down into the low seat of the

Mini.

'Promise me you'll not go too fast. Promise,' Margaret insisted as she did up the seatbelt.

'I promise. Right, where does her ladyship want to go, then?' Marcus was so thrilled to have someone to share his joy with. His mother would only have wanted a lift to the pub.

'Could we drive along through Weardale, do you think?'

'We could indeed. Maybe get some lunch out? My treat?'

Margaret got as comfortable as she could. Marcus started the engine and they were off. Soon they were out of the busy town traffic, which Marcus threaded his way through with ease, sliding off on little back streets to miss the worst of the holdups. At Crook, they took the A689 and were soon out in the open country. They did not speak much; they caught each other's eye and smiled, or Margaret would point out a particular view. As they travelled unhurriedly along, Margaret was filled with a desire to get out of the car and walk. They stopped at Stanhope for lunch in a tea room. Going back to the car, Margaret noticed the tourist information kiosk. She wandered over with Marcus in tow.

Margaret perused the display of leaflets on offer, then she noticed a map of the area pinned up on the wall. She peered at the map and found Stanhope; several footpaths wove out into the hillsides.

'Marcus – do you think we could go for a short walk? I'm a bit stiff from sitting in the car and sitting during lunch; I need to stretch my legs a bit.'

Marcus wasn't too keen; however, if Margaret wanted a short stroll then she should have one. He imagined a leisurely toddle along the road a bit, and back to the car. How wrong he was. They crossed the Wear over the picturesque bridge, but instead of following the old road along its southern bank, Margaret veered off to the right along a marked footpath. The sign said Black Hill, and the footpath became steep very quickly. Margaret took the lead and clambered off like a mountain goat, with Marcus trailing behind. At the top of the first incline Margaret stopped and turned, hands on hips, to catch her breath and admire the view. A little behind and a little below she could see Marcus hauling himself up the last stretch, panting for breath. He reached her position, sweat pouring off his brow, legs like jellies.

'How. . . ?' he gasped. 'How on earth. . . ?'

Pant . . . loud inhalation . . . hands on thighs.

'Maggie . . .'

Margaret laughed out loud – not at the young man beside her, beginning to recover, but at life. She was bursting with pride at the relative ease with which she had clambered up the path. Since her fall, and the unsettling dizzy spells, she had curtailed any outdoor adventures.

'Oh, Marcus!' she chortled. 'Have you got your breath back? You should give up smoking, you know.'

Marcus regained a degree of his usual cool. However, he could not ignore the fact that this lady had made him look very unfit – very unfit indeed. How old was she? Must be almost eighty, if not more; and he, twenty-something.

'Oh God,' he groaned.

The pair ambled back down the path together admiring the views across and along the valley.

'Marcus, I can't tell you how good that felt, really I can't. I thought I would never really be able to walk – as in Walk with a capital w – like that again. I could not do it on my own,' Margaret said, as they approached the car again.

'I feel so ashamed,' Marcus joked. 'Beaten up the hill by an old lady like you.'

'You need to get fit, young man! Perhaps we should do this again – a proper walk next time, a bit longer and a bit flatter?'

'Right,' said Marcus. 'You're on, Maggie – you're on. Next week, if the weather's OK.'

When they returned, Marcus dropped Margaret off in Mistletoe Street outside Number 2.

'Thank you so much, Marcus – I have not enjoyed myself so much for an age,' Margaret said before waving the young man away. She could have had him sent to prison, that young man; she was very glad she had not.

Marcus came as usual on the Friday – did a few bits and bobs – mended a broken handle on a cupboard, swept the yard, got a few cobwebs the cleaning lady had been unable to reach. At lunchtime, he and Margaret pored over a Landranger map for the area and found a walk to attempt on Sunday, weather permitting. Marcus was a bit worried that something might happen to Margaret – she could slip and turn an ankle, break a leg or hip or something. Margaret was all prepared for that. She had survival blankets, flares . . . a whole practical ensemble that packed down into a small Bergen, leaving room for flasks, food, and some waterproof gear for Marcus.

'Of course you will have to carry the pack – that's one thing I can't manage any more. We'll inform the local police station of our route and expected time of return.'

'How far are we thinking of going then, in a day?'

'Well, I think I can manage two one-hour stretches with a tea break in the morning, stop somewhere for sandwiches at lunchtime, then two one-hour stretches to walk back.'

Marcus felt the weight of the Bergen. It seemed OK. The walk was not too hilly: they had decided to head for the Derwent Reservoir and head along the valley towards Nookton Fell and back.

Dearest Alice,

I just had to write and tell you about a lovely day out I had with Marcus. He has passed his driving test and has got a small red car, not terribly comfortable, quite low down to get into. Nonetheless, we have had a couple of trips out. The first time was just to have been a drive in the country, but after we had stopped for lunch we decided to have a short stroll to stretch our legs. There was a footpath heading off upwards and I could not resist. I was very surprised indeed to

*find I could still manage to make my way up with little trouble –
much slower than I used to be of course, but still quicker than poor
Marcus managed. He was puffing and panting like an old man
when he caught me up. I can't begin to tell you what it meant to me,
to be able to get out into the wilds again where there are no noisy,
smelly cars and hustling, bustling people.*

*We planned another trip to Derwent Reservoir, and walked the
valley. This time we were much better prepared, with flasks and
waterproofs just in case. Marcus was my mule, and carried everything. He is surprisingly unfit for a young man, so I have decided it
is my task to improve his fitness. Actually, I got the impression that
despite his groans and grumbles, he quite enjoyed himself. Once he
got the hang of the compass, his map reading soon improved – to
begin with, he hardly knew east from west and north from south.
We are planning another little jaunt at the end of the month. I could
never do this alone – I am indeed a fortunate woman to have the
company of an able young man to assist me.*

*What news of the burial ground? Have you told Michael I wish
to be the first person to book my plot? Do keep me informed.*

Much love to you and Nipper,

Margaret

*PS Perhaps Marcus could drive me up to see you one day – then
you can meet him at last.*

It had been a while since Alice had heard from Margaret.
Alice was pleased her friend had found a way to get out and

about after the fall and things. She hoped Margaret was not pushing herself too hard – even with Marcus to keep an eye on her, anything could happen out in the hills – the weather can come down in the blink of an eye and people get lost. Still, she was sure Margaret would take all the precautions she could, and it was not as if they were heading off to the top of the Cheviot or some other dauntingly high summit.

It seemed to Alice that everyone except herself found the idea of the burial ground totally acceptable – even her fusspot daughter-in-law seemed happy with it. Margaret, Wyllie and Violet all wanted to book plots; the minister was more than happy. Why, then, did Alice still harbour doubts? She should be pleased – pleased that the family were going to be near her as she inevitably aged. The grandchildren would be around – maybe one day great-grandchildren, if she kept her health. The ancient burial mounds had never disconcerted her; why should new ones? She imagined streams of hearses passing her home day after day, like at the crematorium. Surely that would be depressing, gloomy? She wondered for the umpteenth time what Callum would have said – even though she knew full well: he would have been right behind the idea; he was probably right behind the idea now. There were endless legal mazes to be gone through but Michael and Wyllie seemed fairly sure that there would be no insurmountable difficulties. Michael and Penny had put their house on the market, Wyllie and Violet were keen to buy the Watts' cottage in the village – it all seemed destined to be.

There was to be a party at Henge Farm. Change of use had been granted. The local council had been very supportive of the whole idea – in fact the application had solved a problem they knew very well would soon have meant them providing a site and a service in the region. The Monuments Commission had insisted on various provisions: the stones and the mound were not to be disturbed, neither were the burials already obvious above ground. Any ancient graves that may be uncovered must have full archaeological investigation. Michael's plans were that the whole field where the stones stood should not be part of the burial ground anyway. Marsha had told him how they imagined such sites might have looked in the past. Michael had decided to let the field become a wild flower meadow, with a spiral path mown through it, curling up the mound to the stones. It was to be a place of contemplation. Wyllie and Violet had already sent all their remaining livestock to market, and there was to be a farm sale of all the machinery at the end of the month. Marge Watt had retired – she and Ron had found a smashing little bungalow on the coast – near enough to the family, but not right on their doorstep. Marsha had excelled in her mock exams. Dexter's place at Valley Spire was conditional on his working with Brian Rigden for the summer. Mr Winterbottom, the bank manager, had been extremely impressed with Michael and Penny's business plan and the bank was generous in the overdraft facility they had offered. Everything was ready: what could go wrong?

CHAPTER THIRTY-ONE

Food for so many was scarce. We turned around and returned south in the vanguard of the greatest army since Boudicca of the Iceni. We were weak, the fighting force had priority over all – over children, over the sick, over the old men and women – and many were left where they lay or were taken in by clanswomen if they could earn their keep. We left the highest land behind us and the valleys spread wider, where wild fowl, and rush root, and bilberry could be hunted and gathered – and once, a wild goat that had outwitted the front line.

We were far behind the front. We did not see or hear the Romans, as they gathered in their thousands behind the ridge tops, until they showed themselves, the gold of the eagle they carried glinting in the sun. We did not believe the Romans would come so far north in such numbers; they did not believe there could be so many of us.

It was a massacre. Roman bodies littered the valley. Some of us, those followers unfit for the fight, watched from the hills.

Sarah Rigden was enormous. Faith and Aaron had both been big babies, eight pounders plus. These two creatures writhing about in her womb had stretched her stomach to obscene proportions. She could barely walk; she could not bath herself, dry herself or put on her own knickers and she still had almost three months to go. She could only sit and watch gratefully as Brian cared for the children and for her. Sarah's mother had been able to come and stay for a week, which gave Brian the chance to catch up on his jobs. Thankfully, young Dexter McCleish had arrived in Duddo before the rest of the family were due to move. He was staying with Alice at Orby Cottage and was, thank heavens, a fast learner. Brian would collect him in the morning, deliver him – along with any tools he would need – to a particular garden, tell him what wanted doing, and leave him to get on with it. The customers liked him too – after all, Alice McCleish's grandson must be a nice lad – not as if he were a stranger. Usually, Brian would return to collect Dexter to find him in the kitchen having a cup of tea and being force-fed cake or sandwiches. At the moment he was only allowed to cut grass, dig over vegetable plots and trim hedges; no weeding or suchlike as he did not yet know his fat hen from his fuchsia.

Sarah had struggled early on in the pregnancy. She had been even more determined to cling to her children, to not allow anyone else near – even Brian. But she became so tired she had come close to fainting several times and Brian had finally insisted that he spend much more time at home to help with the children and the chores. Sarah's visit to Avian had left its mark. Her initial anger with Avian had mellowed to disgruntlement. She was annoyed that the woman had found a way through – seen through. In quiet moments, when Brian was taking the children to nursery or playgroup and the house was empty, Sarah would allow her enormous self to settle into a bovine state, just huge and growing, natural, about to calf, chewing over the cud of life. She allowed herself to think of Angela – Angela, who was not real, who was imaginary . . . but she *was* real. Sarah had known that once, and she knew it now. Avian Tyler had not stroked her hair – why would she? – she had kept her distance physically at all times. Sarah had asked her mother if there was a history of twins in the family; her mother said she did not know. Confused, Sarah had probed further to find that her grandmother had actually been her step-grandmother. Sarah's natural grandmother had died in childbirth and her grandfather had quickly remarried to keep the family together: he could not have raised three children on his own.

'So Nana Marsh was not your real mother?' Sarah had asked.

'No, but she might as well have been – she raised me from a baby.'

'And your mother died giving birth to you?'

'So many questions, girl! Yes, she died giving birth to me.'

The tone of her voice made it clear that Sarah's mother thought she had gone far enough with answers and would go no further. Sarah wanted to ask why no one had ever told her about it. Here she was, thirty-two years old, about to have her third and fourth babies in one go, and nobody had thought to tell her these things. She had filled in questionnaires at the doctor's, the clinic, the hospital. Those 'is there a family history of . . .' questions, which she had answered to the best of her knowledge, she had answered wrongly. It was not as if it were a big lie – an important lie, just that it was not the truth. People deserve the truth – after all, what if there was some sort of hereditary condition that Sarah should know about? Sarah was too tired to press her mother any further.

Alice also came to visit once or twice a week. She would keep an eye on the children and Sarah while Brian took a break. She loved her mornings with Sarah, Faith and Aaron. She would make endless cups of tea and drinks of juice for the children. If there was a pile of ironing waiting to be ironed, Alice would iron it. She would arrive with batches of cakes, and pies for the freezer. Sarah told her she should not bother: just being there was help enough. Alice insisted that the freezer needed to be full to the top: Sarah was not going to have much time for cooking with two newborns as well as Aaron and Faith to care for.

Penny McCleish stood, hands on hips, surrounded by the collected memorabilia of half a lifetime. The house was sold, contracts had been exchanged and the move date was in two weeks. Many times Penny had overseen the winnowing of chaff from corn in the wardrobes and lives of clients. Now, faced with her own life harvest, she understood why those women had needed her. I need someone just like me, she whimpered to herself. It all seemed insurmountable – and on top of that, Dexter was already up at Duddo and Marsha was leaving for university at the weekend. Penny did not have the words to describe how she felt. This was what it had been for, after all – those years of parenting, good and bad. Their daughter, their fairy child, was leaving, going away into the wide world. Her bags were packed and stacked along the hallway outside her bedroom; she had decided against going into halls, and was sharing a student flat. The lump in Penny's throat tightened as she thought about Marsha; tears welled behind her eyes, she pushed back a strand of loose hair with the back of her hand and slumped into an empty armchair.

Dexter was digging. He straightened his back and looked around him. No concrete, no tall buildings blocking out the sky, no rumble and grumble of traffic. He could see far into the distance, the autumn sharp blue sky streaked by high brushstrokes of cloud. A robin hopped about near him, sitting chirping on a snowberry twig, fluttering down to collect worms and grubs turned over as he dug. A treecreeper scurried up and down a nearby oak bole. A deep contented sigh escaped from the young man, his breath like smoke in the cold morning air. Soon the sun would rise higher and the day would warm; by mid morning he would be tearing off his jumper. He had never realised there was so much change in the course of a country day: the light changed, the temperature, the sounds, and smells – in the city these had been constants. At his granny's, night-time was dark: there were no street lights. Dexter had been amazed to see so many stars – he had never been aware of just how dark the night really was.

Michael McCleish sat in his office. This was to be his last hour in front of the humming, buzzing, flickering screen that had ruled his working life for so long. Angela Smith-Gore had been down to the office after lunch; the speeches and presentation of a leaving gift had passed with the normal uncomfortable procedures of any office. The secretaries had cried softly, briefly. His associates had shaken his hand, patted him on the back, praised his bravery, and said they wished they could be as daring – by which they meant they thought him either mad or reckless or both. Michael threw his suit jacket over one shoulder, turned off his computer for the very last time, collected his few personal items from his desk, and left the office.

On the Tube everything was as normal – people pushed and shoved, but Michael was oblivious to everything. He felt like bursting out into song – and as the Tube approached his stop he did just that – stepping off on to the platform and turning around to face his unsettled fellow travellers he bowed in a theatrical fashion, turned and walked home.

Penny and Michael drove Marsha up to Durham. They

settled her into her flat, hugged their daughter, and drove away. Around the corner Penny made Michael stop the car while she had a jolly good cry. Michael held her tightly until she stopped sobbing, wiping away tears of his own as they rolled silently down his cheeks. They blew their noses and dried their tear-stained faces together in silence until Michael said, 'Ready?' Penny nodded, and they headed north. There were one or two things to organise before the move.

'Cheer up love, at least we'll get to see Dex again – it's been weeks since we've seen him.'

Alice McCleish's life had changed so much she could hardly believe it. Having Dexter to stay had been wonderful. Cooking meals, baking bread, the extra shopping, housework and laundry, and helping with Sarah and the children had kept her so busy she hardly had time to think. Today, Michael and Penny were arriving to finalise the last details for the move. In two weeks' time they would be moving in to Henge Farm.

The last days and nights of the pregnancy seemed an endless attempt to get comfortable. Brian slept on a camp bed on the floor to give Sarah some room. She had pillows on either side to prop up the lump, pillows under her knees, pillows raising her feet. When her pains finally began, Brian called Alice, who drove over to look after Faith and Aaron until Sarah's mother could get there. Brian eased Sarah into the van and headed off for the maternity unit.

There were some complications: the umbilical cord of one twin had managed to wrap itself around the neck of the other, but both babies and their mother were healthy and well.

Sarah lay in the ward, one little cot on each side of her bed. Brian came in – the first time he had met both babies since the delivery. He stood by the bed and cried, just as he had when Aaron, and then Faith, had been born. Tears of joy and pride ran unashamedly down his face.

'You soft old thing – come here.' Sarah held out her arms to her husband who buried himself in her neck. 'Oh, Brian, mind my bosoms – they are starting to swell and dribble all over the place already.'

'Sorry, love. Can I pick one up? This one is awake, almost.'

The winter months were spent in a turmoil of builders, tarmac layers and fencers. The pandemonium involved in transforming Henge Farm from a working farm to something almost ready to become a woodland burial ground lasted throughout the winter. Some days the rain and mud made the place look like a primeval swamp; later, snow and ice held up work for days. Somehow, despite setbacks, the work progressed. As spring approached, nature began to heal the scars of the radical surgery the farm had undergone.

On the first day of May the new sign was delivered and put in place.

HENGE FARM
WOODLAND BURIAL GARDENS
VISITORS WELCOMED

Michael, Penny, Alice, Dexter, Brian, Wyllie and Violet were there to watch. Wyllie patted Michael on the back.

'Well done lad, well done – you've done it.'

Violet hugged everyone; Michael opened a magnum of champagne and they all drank and toasted to the success of the new Henge Farm.

There was still much to be done – some of the outbuildings still needed either renovation or pulling down. Brian had started off a tree nursery for Michael and Penny to raise their own trees rather than buying them in, and Dexter had spent days collecting native seed of oak, rowan, beech and field maple, and planting them up in pots. Germination had been excellent and there were now almost five hundred seedlings ready to plant out into nursery beds. The website was up and running, a local wicker worker was making caskets for display and would make them to order. Margaret, Violet and Wyllie had all booked their plots and there had been several enquiries by email and phone already.

'What you need now, lad,' Wyllie joked, 'is a few dead bodies.'

Avian Tyler had been busy. Fate and word of mouth had led her in many directions since Sarah Rigden had stayed for those few days last year. Avian often thought of the young woman – curled, distraught – in a chair in the kitchen, her hair being stroked by an invisible hand. It had been difficult for Avian to hear Angela: she was silenced, had been silenced for so many years. Avian had thought of telephoning Sarah, and then had thought better of it. The girl had left dramatically: the stroking of the hair had been the last straw for her; she had packed her bags and ordered a taxi to the station first thing the next morning. They had been polite on her parting, but Sarah's hurt and confusion had shown as cold anger in her eyes.

Penny was daubing paint on to the walls of the scullery. She was completely spattered with the stuff herself – globs of it stuck drying in her hair, under her nails were wedges of the stuff, her face freckled with it. She turned the radio up and danced paintily around the scullery to an old Joan Armatrading number she had loved years ago. She did not hear Michael come in from the drying green; he stood in the doorway watching his wife dance and sing, using the dripping, painty brush as a microphone. She stopped suddenly, feeling she was being watched, turned and saw Michael leaning on the doorframe, smiling hugely. She was about to turn the radio down when Michael took her in his arms: he danced with her and they sang together.

The winter had been a hard time for them. The farmhouse was big – huge – when the Turnbulls had emptied it of their possessions. Apart from a few smaller pieces of furniture, some paintings, and some of Violet's collection of kitchen implements including the girdle, most of the Turnbulls' possessions had gone to auction. Some had raised a surprising amount of money, which they had spent on furnishing their new home. Wyllie had kept the Land Rover in the same way someone might keep an old horse – out of sentiment and loyalty; however, he had bought a new Range Rover in which he drove Violet wherever and whenever she wanted. Michael and Penny had kept the enormous pine kitchen table and some of the old bed frames, including one four-poster that was in their room waiting to be newly curtained. Every room had needed redecorating – that was after the windows were replaced, central heating installed, the damp-proof course renewed and woodworm treated in the attics. The cost of revamping the house had soared, and Penny had had to cut back on some of her schemes for redecoration – hence she was doing some of the painting herself.

Joan Armatrading's voice was cut off by the nasal interruption of the DJ. Penny disentangled herself from her husband and turned the radio off.

'Cup of tea then, is it?' she asked.

'Come on now, Michelangelo of the Scullery, what else does a hard-working man come indoors for in the middle of the afternoon?'

Penny put the kettle on the ancient range. This range was very lucky to have kept its place in the kitchen. Penny had struggled to understand its moods, the warm oven, the hot oven, how to light the bloody thing when it went out, how it was unhappy when the wind was in the east. One day, Michael had found her on her knees, crying, begging the thing to light. Sooty and sobbing, she demanded a new electric one with thermostats and everything.

Michael had phoned Wyllie and Violet, who arrived and tamed the beast in no time. Violet wrote a list of instructions – these Penny had pinned on the wall – and despite a few hiccups, she had managed to bring the thing under control. She was still determined that one of these days she would change it for a new one, and would threaten aloud the purchase of a brand new Aga any time the range showed signs of misbehaving.

Alice's misgivings were mostly behind her. There had already been several non-religious burials at Henge Farm; there had been no – to her mind – 'proper' Christian burials so far. The bishop had not yet agreed to consecrate the top field, but the minister had assured Alice that the bishop was considering the request and intended to visit as soon as his duties allowed him to before making a decision. The non-religious burials were either inhumation of the body, topped with a tree of the family's or the deceased's choice; or burial of a small casket of ashes post cremation, also with a tree planting; or the scattering of ashes in the wild flower meadow surrounding the mound with the stones. There was an increase in traffic past

Orby Cottage, but it was sedate, respectful traffic most of the time. People would come back often to visit their loved ones: they parked in the car park past the cattle grid, and many would walk down the lane to visit the stones.

Alice's garden was often admired, and many people stopped to talk to her over the fence. They would tell her who it was they were visiting – a mother, father, son, daughter, aunt, uncle or friend – share anecdotes, and invariably, Alice would invite a lonely soul into her kitchen for a cup of tea. Her life had not been this full since before Michael had left home for college all those years ago. Callum would have enjoyed this, she thought; he would have been retired now, pottering in the garden, helping Michael out where he could, talking to visitors and telling the interested ones the history of the area and the stones. There were more visitors at weekends, and often Alice would look up to the stones when walking Nipper to see small groups of people walking up the closely-mown spiral path that Brian had marked out and cut. There were seats arranged looking north, south, east and west near the top of the mound, lower down the slope than the stones on the crest. The meadow had been planted up with daffodil bulbs, crocuses, primroses and cowslips. In summer it glowed with poppies, cornflowers and ox-eye daisies, and in autumn all the growth was mown back down to green velvet. Margaret Allerton had visited several times during the summer, driven up by her friend Marcus, a lovely boy who had become a good friend to Dexter. Margaret had chosen her plot in the burial ground, and had decided to have a crab apple tree planted in remembrance. Alice sat and pondered on the past year's comings and goings, and with hindsight, realised how misplaced her anxieties had been.

Michael sat in his office. He had converted the twins' old room into a large office-cum-den. Wyllie's old roll-top desk had been hauled up from outside and swung in through one of the windows and had pride of place opposite the door. Wyllie had insisted Michael have it as a goodwill gift, despite its considerable value. It had belonged to his father and grandfather, and had always contained all the farm documents in a state of mucky disarray. Clearing it out, Michael had found no end of interesting bits of paper – copies of old land maps showing the extent of the farm in its glory days, and later maps showing how fields had been sold off here and there. The names of the fields were fascinating. Top Field was so named because it was the highest point of the farm, Stone Field held the stones, and Well Field held an old capped well, disused for years and years. Michael's father had known all the fields by their names – once Michael must have known some, but he had forgotten. Wyllie and Violet had chosen a plot in Top Field, at the very highest point, where their ghosts could oversee the land they had loved and worked together. Margaret Allerton had decided, after much consideration, on a plot close to the crossing of the two footpaths that intersected Henge Farm land, as near as was allowed to the little bridge which crossed the stream where the rowans and willows grew.

The phone rang.

'Hello, Henge Farm.'

Michael had got used to the different tones of voices. Some were lighthearted – these were mainly those prospective customers who wished to visit and maybe reserve a plot – such conversations were normally entertaining. The others were the washed-out voices of the bereaved: voices with no colour – sad voices, often close to tears. This was one of the latter.

'I would like to . . .'

Having quickly learned that certain skills he did not possess were required in this business, Michael had contacted the local funeral parlour. Mr Solomon Arkwright, the proprietor, and his son, also Mr Solomon Arkwright, had been reticent; they were traditional purveyors of funeral services. Arkwright senior was dismissive. He considered that there would be little, if any, call for 'green burial' around here. Arkwright junior, away from the gloomy influence of his father, was more enthusiastic. Michael had managed to lure Arkwright junior to Henge Farm and had given him the hard sell.

Solomon Arkwright junior had been impressed. He could imagine one of their elderly, but very stylish, hearses gliding up the newly tarmac'ed drive to the farm. He could see himself in full regalia, walking, head respectfully bowed, top hat held against his breast, slowly leading the hearse up the drive, mourners following in their wake. Solomon Arkwright junior had secret plans for the funeral business once his father finally retired and handed the reins over to him. Michael and Solomon junior were chalk and cheese. Michael remembered Solomon from school: he had been several years older than Michael, and had been mercilessly teased for his name, and for his father's occupation. Solomon had never responded to the teasing. He had maintained a solemn dignity that must have been inherited from the long line of previous Arkwrights who had dealt with death for generations. They had never been friends: just nodding acquaintances.

Solomon had shaken Michael's hand firmly, and looked him straight in the eye when he left.

'Leave it with me, Michael; leave it with me. Things are changing in the funeral business – Father just does not want to see it; I do. You just leave it with me.'

Michael had thought no more of it, assuming that the old man would have his way for some years to come. He had been surprised to receive a call from young Solomon several weeks later. Arkwright senior had been told by his doctor to take a back seat or become one of his own customers: his blood pressure was dangerously high; he risked a stroke. Things had to change at Arkwright and Son. Young Solomon now offered a green burial package to their customers, and there had been many takers. The two younger men had become close as business associates, and as friends. Solomon's years of experience in the trade was shared with Michael. Both benefited from their alliance.

Despite everything, despite Michael's efforts with local advertising and networking, they needed more bodies to make a profit. Short of going out and murdering some of the prebookers, Michael had sat at the roll-top desk pondering options. Perhaps he should advertise further afield – Newcastle was the biggest urban population. Would people really travel to Duddo from Newcastle to be buried? He had to find out. Michael phoned the advertising desk of *The Journal*. The girl on the phone was very interested.

'Well fancy that,' she said, chattily. 'Me mam and me was just talking about that the other day; she don't want a cremation, but she don't want no churchy thing neither – no time for God and such, me mam. Tell you what, when I've taken your details for the advert I'll speak to Gina on the features desk, she might like to do an article about you.'

And Gina had wanted to do an article. She had come up to Henge Farm with a photographer. They gave Henge Farm a half-page spread on page four, with colour photos of Michael and Penny by the entrance sign, and one of the stones at sunset. The response had been immediate. Visitors began to arrive – mostly at weekends; many had holiday homes or caravans in the surrounding area on the coast at Berwick, Bamburgh, Alnmouth or Beadnell, or inland at Kelso and Wooler, and were delighted with the idea of being buried outside and away from the city many of them loved and hated with equal intensity. Bookings were on the up.

Dexter McCleish had been accepted for a place on the RHS Dip. course at Valley Spire Horticultural College. His enthusiasm at interview had surprised his prospective tutors and his reference from his summer job was excellent. Several of Mr Rigden's regular customers had also provided references as to the boy's good nature. Michael and Penny had driven him down to begin the course the previous autumn.

CHAPTER THIRTY-TWO

D ays later, when I dared to emerge from the crack in the rocks where I had hidden myself, the first sounds I heard were the eagle's call, and the buzzard, and raven – their noise filled my ear as the smell of death filled my nose and mouth. There were moans, and cries of voices in the air: the death rattle of hope; the hopeless keening of women wading through bodies to find lost ones. I could not help them. I had to save myself. I had to get back to Dadda's lands to dig up my cup, stones and scoop.

Dear Alice,

I simply had to write and tell you my news. Last weekend, on Sunday, Marcus arrived to take me out for a drive in the car and a short walk. We drove helter-skelter down the motorway to Scotch Corner (not like your careful driving) – thankfully it did not take long. Then we headed into Arkengarthdale. The road went up and up and the views were breathtaking. We parked at Langthwaite and walked up the narrow lane between rows of stone cottages with white painted doors. Stone-edged narrow beds along their fronts were planted prettily, honeysuckle and roses scrambled up trellis, clothing the walls. The signpost said 'Booze', which made Marcus laugh – he never knew there was a place called Booze – his mother should live there, he said. Past the cottages the gradient climbed steeply, but only for a short distance. I needed my stick to lever myself up the last section; however, we arrived at the top to look out over a bird's-eye view of the Dales. We continued to Booze where we left the lane and turned onto a narrow track skirting the ridge of hills. In places the countryside still bore scars of the lead mining industry that once prospered there. The path took us down to Slei Gill, a peaty tumbling stream running down off the hills into shady woodland. The path led us along its bank, then back again to Langthwaite. It was a mere two and a half miles, but took us almost three hours including a picnic lunch of tea and sandwiches.

Of course I could not have done it without dear Marcus. He is getting quite keen on walking in the hills. I have left him all my maps and equipment in my will. He is thinking of undertaking an access course to give him the right qualifications to go to college and study. If he was my own grandson I could not be more proud of him than I am.

How lovely for us that he and Dexter have struck up such a friendship! I have told him he should bring Dexter on one of our weekend walks, but he says Dexter always goes home at weekends to help out at Henge.

I wonder – how would you feel about Marcus and me coming up for more than a day trip? Maybe Marcus could stay at the farm-house? Have a think and let me know. I can think of nothing I would enjoy more than a long weekend at Orby Cottage with you.

Much love,

Margaret

PS Decided to write rather than phone – I do so miss our letters.

Dear Margaret,

I miss our letters too. It was a real treat to see an envelope on the mat with your handwriting on it. I put the kettle on, made myself a nice cup of tea and sat down to read it in comfort in the sitting room.

Dexter always speaks of Marcus when he is home for weekends – of how they have been to the cinema, or a pop concert together. How lovely that they should get on so well. I think it would be lovely for you and Marcus to visit, why not make it longer? Marcus could bring you one weekend, he and Dexter could go back to Durham for the week, and you and Marcus could go home the next weekend. I'm sure Michael and Penny would put Marcus up at the farmhouse – they have plenty of room. I'll speak to Penny today – she said she would pop in on her way shopping to see if there was anything I needed.

She has been quite a revelation. I can tell you that I had my doubts that she would fit in with country life. She has been too busy to interfere in my comings and goings, and that suits me just fine.

She pops up and down to London – commutes, she calls it – to work for this foreign gentleman, and when she is here she spends most of her time decorating.

I have to admit she has transformed the downstairs of that farmhouse. It always used to be so dark – dark polished wood, dark paintwork, heavy curtains at the windows. Now the rooms are bright, cheerful and airy – the heavy pelmets, curtains and flock wallpaper replaced by white paintwork – ivory she calls it, light floaty blinds at the windows – and beige carpets – taupe she calls it. Mind you, I would not have a plain, light-coloured carpet – can you imagine the dog paw prints! Still, it's muddy boots and shoes off in the porch or scullery now up there. The upstairs is next on her list and number one is a new bathroom.

I got a postcard from Marge Watt last week, just to say she and Ron were very happy in their new bungalow. She asked me to pass on her regards to you.

The Ollerenshaw woman is still ruling the Rural with an iron rod. I don't go along so often now, what with the family being nearby I find I don't have the need for the company so much.

The minister has announced his retirement.

I think that is all the news from Duddo.

Let me know which weekend (or week would be even better) you would like to visit.

With love,

Alice

Alice had cleaned and aired the spare room, and placed the gazunder discreetly by the bedside so that Margaret would not have to ask for it this time. Marcus was to stay at the farm: Penny had been quite enthusiastic. Michael was hoping the lad would make himself useful: they could do with an extra pair of hands to knock down a couple of old pigsties. Marsha was also coming for the weekend. She was very interested in Granny McCleish's erudite friend who had been at the end of dig party in the orchard, and she was determined that she was not going to miss the chance to get to know her better. Marsha had uncovered a cache of Professor Allerton's old papers and lecture notes in the university online archive and was amazed to discover just how influential the woman had been in her time.

Dexter, Marcus and Margaret, in the little red car, arrived on Friday evening. Marsha had arrived by train earlier in the day. Penny had insisted she cook a meal for them all at Henge Farm. The range, now almost tamed, had behaved splendidly and a mammoth meal was served on the huge pine table in the sparkling kitchen. Wyllie and Violet Turnbull had also been invited.

Conversation rattled noisily around the table, punctuated by bursts of laughter. Violet wiped a silent tear from her eye as she thought of how things might have been. Alice noticed and took Violet's hand, giving it a gentle, knowing squeeze. Marsha sat next to Margaret and the pair became deeply engrossed in a conversation of their own. The men sat to one end of the table; the women, the other. The men discussed cars, Marcus's little red boy racer being ridiculed by Michael and Wyllie, who then disagreed between themselves on the benefits or otherwise of Land Rover versus Tata. Penny found herself face to face with her mother-in-law.

Penny had softened towards Alice. Since living here she had begun to discover just how much her mother-in-law did. She was not the silly old woman to whom good things just happened. In the village, according to what was left of the local population, no one had a bad word to say about her. Mention Alice McCleish and people would say, 'Oh, Alice – such a kind person: when my Bob was in the cottage hospital she drove me in to visit every day for a week,' or 'Alice McCleish's daughter-in-law? Such a nice family – she . . .'

It seemed Alice had done something, at sometime, for almost every household. Penny could not think of anyone who might say such nice things about her if they were to be asked. The clattering of cutlery subsided. Alice stood up to begin to clear the table. Penny's first instinct was to ask her not to, to tell her to sit down while she, Penny, cleared the table. Instead, Penny rose to join Alice, and the two of them left the others to their gossip.

'Penny – that was a scrumptious casserole.'

'Thanks, Mum . . .' Penny hesitated. 'Look – I know it sounds daft now, after all this time, but do you think I could call you Alice?'

Alice turned from the sink to look at Penny. 'Why?' she

asked, curious.

'I don't really know why – just . . . maybe it would be a bit more friendly. It doesn't matter if you'd rather not – honestly.'

'You know, once, I used to wish you wouldn't call me Mum. I used to hate it. I was not your mum and I tried very hard not to behave like a mum-in-law. You used to interfere so – always trying to get Michael to talk me into selling up. You treated me like an old nuisance.' Alice could barely believe what she was saying.

'I was jealous: simple as that – jealous. I thought you sat here on your fat bottom doing nothing, and everybody loved you, and money and love just fell into your lap. I kept the children at a distance – I can't tell you how much I regret that – because I knew they would love you more than they love me,' Penny admitted, painfully.

'Jealous? You – of me? You had – have – everything: lovely home, all the new things you wanted, you sent the children to the best schools, and Michael adores you.'

'Yes, but it was such hard work to keep up. It was all a show, a façade – the house, the clothes – all that stuff and nonsense; but I felt it made me better than you, because I was working hard, trying hard for it – whereas you . . .'

'But it was never a competition, Penny; life is not a competition. Life is life: you do what you can.' Alice was amazed. All along, the interfering, the looking down the nose, the keeping of distance was because the girl was jealous. That thought had never entered Alice's head. Poor Penny, she thought. She put a heavy arm around the girl's drooped shoulders.

'Call me Alice,' she said; 'or Mum – or both – whatever you feel like, but don't be jealous of me. I don't want – have never wanted – to take anything from you, or anyone. I just wanted a share, that was all – and don't you dare cry on me, or you'll start me off as well.' Alice dried a tear from Penny's cheek with the corner of a tea towel. 'Silly girl. What's for pudding?'

Marsha and Margaret were discussing burial rites. Marsha had been studying alignment and its significance. Margaret was able to answer one or two queries that Marsha's tutor had struggled to explain clearly.

'But of course, Professor! Now it begins to make sense!' Marsha exclaimed.

Alice and Margaret left shortly after Wyllie and Violet.

'Are you off now, Mum?' Michael said, rising from his seat. 'Shall I walk you down the lane, or would you like a lift?'

'Oh, I think us two old dears can manage to stumble down the lane – don't you Margaret?'

'Yes, Alice dear – I'm sure we can, even at our age,' Margaret agreed, with a raised eyebrow.

'Sorry,' Michael mumbled.

Michael helped his mother on with her jacket. Alice briefly hugged the children, Marcus, Michael and finally, Penny, who responded enthusiastically, without embarrassment. Margaret said goodnight to Marcus and the others, all of whom waved from the front porch as the two women strolled arm in arm away from the farmhouse.

'You and Marsha had a lot to talk about,' Alice said, as they wandered along in the gloaming.

'Yes, an enquiring mind; she will do well. She has been reading some of my old papers at the university. Never mind me, what was going on with you and Penny over by the kitchen sink?'

'I'm not sure . . . she's the same Penny – wants the best of everything – but something's different. She more or less apologised for keeping the children away from me so much. She said she did it because of jealousy – in case they loved me more than they loved her.'

As they walked along in silence, Alice tried to recall more of what Penny had said, but the fact that Penny had said anything at all overawed Alice – muffled her memory. She remembered something about her 'sitting on her fat bottom'. Alice looked up from the lane to the stones silhouetted against the darkening sky; a barn owl screeched overhead, dropped soundlessly from its perch and drifted noiselessly away across the fields. Rabbits scuttered into the hedgerows as the women neared.

The first crunch of a footstep on the path set Nipper off into a passion of barking.

'Shut up silly boy, it's us,' Alice called, as she reached the door.

The next morning Alice rose early and made tea. She took

a cup in to Margaret and placed it on her bedside table, waking her friend gently.

'Margaret . . . Margaret,' she shook her shoulder gently.

Margaret stirred.

'Good morning – here's your tea – don't let it go cold.'

Margaret gently manoeuvered herself into a sitting position while Alice opened the curtains. Low early sunlight poured in through the window gilding the room and the two ladies within it.

'It's going to be a lovely day: we must do something later. First, I have to do the flowers in the church for tomorrow's service. I know you won't want to come, but I must go this Sunday. It's the minister's last service in Duddo.'

'I'll not go to the service, but I would like to come with you this morning when you do the flowers – as long as you don't expect me to wax the pews.'

'Oh no, I did those in the week.'

'Really, Alice – I was only joking.' Margaret could see from Alice's expression that she had indeed waxed the pews during the week.

They drove to the church with the car full to overflowing with foliage. Great skeins of ivy lay across the back seat; the boot was full of spindle bush, holly, teasel heads, and great umbrellas of seeded cow parsley flower heads, crisp and brittle.

'Do you realise the Pagan significance of some of this greenery, Alice?' Margaret asked.

'Well actually, yes – I do,' Alice retorted. 'Callum . . .' she began – but faltered. 'Callum was always bringing in bits and pieces, sprigs of this and that, hanging them up around the house. I didn't like it at first. "What if the minister comes round?" I used to say. Callum didn't care about the minister. He did care about me, though, and began to hang his things in the shed. Christmas was different – not that he believed in Christmas – he gave it another name, but then the greenery would come in, the tree would be decorated with lights and lametta and shiny baubles. In he would come with armfuls of ruby-berried holly and shiny ivy leaves, and they would be hung from the beams; great tangles of mistletoe from Henge apple trees in the walled orchard would hang above every door. I thought I would decorate the church for Callum, in the way he would have liked it, just this once.'

'And what will the Ollerenshaw woman make of that, I wonder?' Margaret twinkled.

'To be quite honest with you Margaret, I don't care. She volunteered herself and her cronies to take charge of the minister's last service in the parish, which is in one of the other churches – the larger one, at Berwick – in four weeks' time. The new minister will be there too, so she is going hell for leather to make a good impression.'

'So there'll just be the two of us then.' Margaret envisioned herself climbing on pews to dump greenery around.

'No, Wyllie is coming with his stepladders to help reach any difficult bits and do any heavy stuff.'

Alice had invited Violet, too, but Violet had not returned to the church since her recovery, and Alice did not think she would come.

They pulled up outside the church. Wyllie's ancient Land Rover was already outside. He heard Alice's car and hurried out to meet her.

'Alice! and Margaret too – the more the merrier . . . shall I?' He indicated the back seat full of plant material.

'Yes please, Wyllie; the boot's full, too. Be careful with the cow parsley – the heads are quite fragile.'

Alice led Margaret into the church. The building smelt of lavender, beeswax, turpentine, dust and faintly mouldering fabrics. Rainbows of refracted light that flooded through the stained glass panels bounced off the gleaming oak pews to echo on the stone walls. Margaret found its simplicity calming. No screens to separate congregation from celebrant, no artifice to distract the worshipper from worship: just the two long panels behind the pulpit depicting the beginning and end of the life of an extraordinary man. Margaret believed in the person of Jesus Christ – there was much evidence to prove his existence.

'Enough dawdling, Professor: work to be done!' Wyllie shouted.

The three of them unloaded the car. Just as they had finished doing so, Violet arrived, a huge flat wicker basket hanging over her arm.

'I've come to help,' she called to the others.

In the basket were fungi – all sorts of woodland and meadow fungi that Violet had collected early that morning, and fir cones and glossy conkers. Wyllie took the basket. Alice and Margaret marvelled at the natural arrangement, and Alice decided to place it, exactly as it was, at the foot of the pulpit.

An hour and a half later the florists sat down on the bench outside the church enjoying a well-earned cup of tea with real milk. Alice had brought a pint with her. She could not bear any more tea made with that other stuff in little peel-off pots. Wyllie stood up and rubbed his lumbar region.

'Everything all right, Wyllie?' Margaret asked.

'Aye, I'm fine. I should never have given up working: ever since, I've been stiffening up,' he replied.

'You've been stiffening up for years, man; you'd rub your back like that after harvest in your forties, let alone now,' Violet teased. 'Don't you pay him no mind Margaret, he's just an old man.'

'Right, troops,' Alice enthused. 'Back to it – not much more to do now.'

The four of them stood in the church porch and looked back at their work.

'Happy with that, Alice?' Wyllie asked.

Alice stood and looked a minute longer. She nodded her head. For Callum, she thought. Margaret nodded in silent understanding and agreement.

Sunday morning, Alice rose, took in Margaret's tea and was surprised to find her awake already.

'Did you not sleep well?' she asked, concerned.

'Like a baby,' Margaret replied. 'I'm up early because I've changed my mind; I will come to the service. After all that hard work I think I should.'

'You are not just doing this for me, I hope?' Alice queried.

'Not at all.'

The minister's voice rose and fell above the small congregation. He had been surprised that a few non-churchgoers had turned out for this last service in Duddo. Alice McCleish had that friend of hers from Durham with her, the Turnbulls were there, and one or two other faces he usually only saw at Easter and Christmas. He was pleased Mrs Ollerenshaw was absent. She had phoned to tell him she was busy with arrangements for the final service. He was dreading that: the Berwick church would be a riot of expensive out-of-season flowers ostentatiously arranged. This, he felt, was very much nicer. He must thank Alice.

Alice sat next to her friend. Her thoughts were of Callum, of the fuss she had made about the things he brought home, the things he believed. He had been a good man. She missed him terribly; time had helped, of course – but she still missed him. The Church was right – she knew that – but was Callum right too? and Avian Tyler? and Violet? Could more than one thing be true? What was truth? She prayed for understanding.

Violet Turnbull had not been to a service since the twins' funeral. The Church was wrong. The innocent spirits of children did not go straight to heaven, nor did the spirits of good men like Callum McCleish. Equally, the so-called wicked spirits of her maternal forebears who had been burnt or drowned did not languish in the pits of hell – no, not at all. The twins had waited, overseen by Callum, before they did what they did and went wherever they went. Beside her, Wyllie began a gentle snoring. Violet jabbed him in the ribs with a sharp elbow.

Margaret let the meaningless words of the minister wash over her. The sounds merged into a distant chanting, leaving her in a world of half awareness. Her eyes open, she looked over the minister's head at the windows. The panels were well executed: the family responsible had not been mean with this one aspect of decoration. Above the panels hung the blank round window. Why had it been left empty? Was this clear view to the sky for the congregation to look out to their God on high? Margaret stared up through it. Crows flew past, fleetingly providing an image. Alice nudged Margaret, the congregation stood for the hymn.

The minister said his goodbyes outside the church; regulars would probably see him one last time at Berwick. Alice was the last to leave.

'Alice – will you be at Berwick?' the minister asked.

'No, I don't think so. This is my little church and I am happy to say my goodbyes here. Thank you, minister, for everything . . . Callum, and . . . well you know. Do we know who is replacing you?'

'No, not yet: I have heard they are considering a couple of people, but nothing definite.' The minister looked round; the congregation was drifting away. It seemed to him a representation of the state of the Church he was leaving, with people just drifting away.

'The floral decoration is lovely, Alice, very natural,' he said.

'I did it for Callum,' Alice said, without thinking. She stumbled over an apology.

'No, Alice, don't apologise; I can't think of a better reason. I shall always remember Duddo Church like that – full of nature.'

'Minister, are people part of nature, like trees and cows, or are we something different . . . special?'

'That, Alice, although simply put, is one of the biggest questions there is. I wish I knew the answer. Once, I thought I did – unquestioningly; now? I trust in the Lord: what more can we do?'

After lunch Alice and Margaret set off in the car with Nipper excitedly fidgeting about on the back seat.

'Have you made a will?' Margaret asked, out of the blue.

'In a way,' Alice replied, surprised. 'Callum and I made one years back. When he died everything came to me, and when I die Michael inherits everything.'

'I keep changing mine,' Margaret admitted. 'I'm sure my solicitor thinks I am a barmy old dear. I want to leave something to you, Alice.'

'Don't talk like that – you won't be going anywhere for a good while yet.'

'Alice, be realistic. I am getting old: I won't last forever. I was looking around my home, wondering what I could leave you. The books I'm leaving to the university library; Marcus is to have all the maps and walking equipment and enough money for him to walk around the world if he should want to; Professor Mortimer – George, you know – is to have my collection of artifacts to do with as he pleases; that just leaves the house.'

'Don't you dare leave me your house. What would I do with another house?' Alice was horrified by the idea.

'You could sell it,' Margaret stated, bluntly.

'Leave it to a charity or something; please Margaret, don't leave it to me.'

'Fine. Well, I shall have to think of something else then,' Margaret muttered under her breath.

'Let's talk about something else, Margaret; it's a beautiful day and we should be happy to be alive – not talking about dying.'

Alice parked in a lay-by on a country road where she, Margaret and Nipper got out of the car and stretched their legs. Nipper's tail fell when the berry basket was pulled out of the boot. The three walked up a footpath until Alice stopped.

'Well, there's no sign of brambles here.' Margaret looked around. 'None at all.'

'Good,' said Alice. 'Because we are not out for brambles; look here, on this blackthorn – sloes.' The hedge was dripping with sloes and they soon filled the berry basket. Fingers perforated by the sharp thorns of the blackthorn, and clothes covered with the burrs of sticky willy, the two women weaved their way back along the path to the car. Nipper appeared at a whistle from Alice, great clumps of burdock burrs stuck around his nose and shoulders giving him a grotesque appearance.

Penny was cleaning the range when the phone rang. She laid the scrubbing brush down, wiped her hands with an old cloth, and slopped in her oversized overalls to the ringing phone in the kitchen.

'Hello, Henge Farm.'

'Hello, is that Violet Turnbull?' Avian asked, not recognising the voice.

'No – I'm sorry – but the Turnbulls moved some time ago. I can give you their new number if you like.'

'Thank you; that would be most kind. I'll just get a pen.' Avian laid the receiver down and got a pen from the jam jar on the sideboard.

'Hello.' She picked up the receiver. 'I have a pen now.'

Penny gave Avian the Turnbulls' new number, adding, 'I could give you the address if you like . . . on second thoughts, maybe not – after all, I have no idea who you are – you could be a burglar for all I know.'

'No, I'm not a burglar – my name is Avian Tyler, if that will put your mind at rest.'

'Oh yes, I've heard about you; I'm Penny McCleish, Alice's daughter-in-law.'

Avian wondered what Alice's daughter-in-law might be doing at Henge Farm, but did not ask.

'Thanks, Penny; I'll try Violet later.'

'I shouldn't bother if I were you – she and Wyllie have taken a trip up to the Orkney Islands. They are due back at the weekend – you could try then.'

'Goodbye and thanks again.' Avian put the phone down and made a note to phone Violet next week sometime.

'Avian, I'm so glad you phoned. Wyllie and I have been up to the Islands – have you been? You really must go; I had forgotten how otherworldly the place is.'

'No, I've never been; I would like to one day. Anyway, how are you? How is Wyllie? Has he settled into retirement or is he missing the farm terribly?'

'He moans sometimes, but I am keeping him busy. He spends half of his time up there anyway, helping young Michael where he can. How did you get this phone number? Have you spoken to Alice?' Violet was curious: she had not kept in contact with Avian – certainly she had not thought to give the woman her new address and telephone number.

'I telephoned Henge Farm just to see how you were getting on and a woman answered – Penny McCleish, Alice's daughter-in-law. It sounds like a lot has happened in Duddo since my last visit.'

Violet filled Avian in on all the details: the selling of the farm, the woodland burial gardens, Michael and Penny, the new cottage in the village. Avian sat and listened, smiling hugely to hear Violet so full of village news and tales of her holiday.

'Well, Violet, it sounds as if all is well with you and yours. Truly, I am so happy for you.'

Violet replied firmly, 'It's all down to you, Avian – all down to you. I can never repay you; never.'

'The joy in your voice is the only kind of repayment I need,' Avian replied.

'By the way, Penny McCleish dropped in some post last week, and in with the bills and advertisements was a postcard from your Maisie – from somewhere exotic. She said she was coming back to England for Christmas and would like to visit. How can I get in touch with her to let her know we would love to see her again?' Violet had been worrying about this. She had very fond memories of the girl: in truth, it was Maisie who had begun her process of healing.

'Don't worry, Violet – Maisie will just turn up out of the blue. You are lucky to get a postcard as a warning – she just turns up on my doorstep with no warning whatsoever.' In the background Avian could hear the frantic barking of collie dogs.

'There's Wyllie back for his dinner; listen to those dogs! It's a good job we have understanding neighbours,' chuckled Violet.

'Violet, it has been lovely to hear your news; you had better get that man of yours his dinner.' Avian could feel the magnetic attraction of the area even through the telephone. She said her goodbyes and promised to keep in touch.

Somehow she had a feeling of unfinished business at Duddo. Somehow there was more for her to do.

CHAPTER THIRTY-THREE

I skirted the field of death; I followed goat path and deer track south – always south towards the sun – following the return of the remains of the decimated Roman army as it staggered back. I felt home before I knew it: my step felt a part of the soil it fell on, the trees more familiar, although now bare. I followed my feet and came to a bend in the track that ran around the base of a rise in the folding landscape. I knew before I looked up that the stones would be there. I scurried up the bank to see what remained of the hut. It had been ripped apart.

Margaret Allerton could not get rid of the image of the empty round window of Duddo Church. During the service she had seen it, filled briefly, passingly, with the images of whirling crows. She lay in her bed at Orby Cottage, listening to Alice rattling about below in the kitchen, knowing that

407

soon a cup of steaming tea would make its way to her bedside table. She had come to love this cottage – its silence. The view of the stones from this bedroom had become her view, a view representing both permanence and change. She felt an unaccustomed surge of something which must be a kind of love: it washed over her like a wave, rising as a lapping ripple from her toes, strengthening as it laved over her body, crashing in a frothing lather across her chest and over her shoulders and fading to stillness as it swirled around her head. Maybe she was experiencing the love of God? Margaret lay still. No, this was no judgemental power: this feeling could not be accounted for in such a way; it was a natural, spiritual connection with this place. It was a feeling she had experienced in high or remote places – in moments of weakness, she had thought then – and she had dismissed it as altitude sickness, lack of food or sleep – illness, even – but had never been able to admit the incorporeal nature of the experience.

A gentle tap on the door and in came Alice, Nipper at her heels.

'Morning, Margaret – it's another lovely day.'

'Alice – morning to you, too.' Margaret sat up in bed. 'What is on the agenda for today then?'

'Oh, I don't know; what do you fancy?' Alice asked.

Over breakfast the two women decided to visit Holy Island.

'Perhaps we'll make it to the castle and abbey this time – unless we get led astray by our friendly fisherman again,' Alice joked.

Together they prepared a picnic, checked the tides and crossing times in the local paper and set off to spend their last day alone before Marcus and Dexter arrived that evening for the weekend. Alice had been very pleased to see that Margaret's health was much improved. She seemed stronger, more enthusiastic – almost back to the Margaret she had first met in the lane – how many years ago was it? It seemed to Alice they had been friends forever.

Michael and Penny sat in the huge kitchen. The kettle steamed on the range, the room smelt of frying bacon and a new dishwasher hummed away, busily de-griming several days' worth of washing up.

'How many today?' Penny ventured, a touch of humour in her voice.

'How many what?' Michael mumbled from behind his newspaper.

'Bodies of course – how many bodies?' Penny giggled.

'Why is the number of bodies a constant source of amusement, my beloved?' Michael controlled an urge to grin in unison with Penny.

'Well, it is funny in a way – I mean us – living here, and people being buried all around us. How many is it now? Almost two hundred of them?'

'Yep, and pre-booking is on the up; the website is getting a good few hits every week.'

It was true: the deal with Arkwright was paying dividends; the newspaper article had caused a flurry of enquiries. Henge Farm Woodland Burial Gardens was finding its feet.

Michael reached across to get the teapot to pour himself another mug of tea. Penny intercepted his reach and took his hand in hers. She turned the hand over, remembering the white smoothness, the neat clean nails of past days. His hand was weathered brown; dirt ingrained the whorls and creases of his fingers; his cuticles were ragged, stained rust colour by the clay-rich soil; beneath the chipped fingernails clods of earth clung despite the scrubbings of a nail brush.

'Look at these hands . . .' Penny said. 'Just look – filthy even before you set foot outside the door.'

Michael's ruddy face beamed back at her across the table. 'I love you, Penny McCleish.' He pulled her hands towards him and kissed the backs of both. 'Are you happy? I mean, I know you are happy, but are you really, really happy?'

'I am – really, really I am. I'm not sure why, living here in the middle of nowhere, with the mother-in-law next door, surrounded by corpses, both my children flown the nest. But yes, funnily enough – unbelievably enough – I am happy.'

'You haven't made many friends: I worry about you.'

'Look, Michael, I didn't make many friends living in London. Yes, there were the girls at the department store – they were . . . well – it was a hierarchy thing, you know, like in the office. Then there were my 'clients' – what an eye-opener that was. It was great at first – you know, after Alice was on the telly; but it was all show. I learnt a lot about myself doing that: I could see myself in their obsession with the newest, the best, the most expensive; and in fact they were never – would never be – content.'

'What about Herr Jansson?'

'Him? What can I say? Money for old rope. I enjoy it: I enjoy the independence it gives me. I mean – he's paid for almost all of the redecoration work and the dishwasher,' Penny grinned.

Michael was satisfied. He gulped down the last of his mug of tea and stood up. 'Right, lass – time to go and dig a grave or two.'

He scuffed his way in his slippered feet to the scullery, pulled on his wellington boots, grabbed a sleeveless jacket and a pair of leather gloves, and clomped out across the drying green to the machine shed. The mini digger lowered in a dark corner. Like Penny, with the range, Michael had taken some time to domesticate this clawing animal.

'Right, you – I'm the boss round here, and today we are going to dig graves.' Michael addressed the machine firmly but kindly, opened the cab door, climbed in and turned the key. The mini digger responded grudgingly and trundled out of the shed on its tracks. Michael drove up to Fescue Field. This was their first major planting area; anyone who was either not fussy or did not specify or book a particular site on the farm would be placed here. Around these plots, saplings radiated outwards and downwards: those nearest the hedgerows were the most mature. The leaves of these young trees were just hinting at their autumn colours. Michael did a few sums in his head. He was forty-nine; if he were lucky he might live to be eighty-seven, say, in another forty years. He tried to imagine Henge Farm in forty years' time. The trees, many of them, would have reached full maturity. He tried to imagine the swaying saplings at full height: tall oaks still with generations of growth to go; cherries, not so long-lived, branches bent to the ground in forty years – bark peeling, drenched with spring blossom or hanging heavy with dangling red fruits.

He looked north over the fields, over the roof of the farmhouse and outbuildings, over the roof of his childhood home where his mother's car sat parked on the gravel. The stones stood on their mound; Michael could see the spiral path winding its way upwards towards them. Brian Rigden appeared from the far side on the big mower, meticulously following the path as originally laid out. He wished his father had lived to see this: Callum McCleish would have been very proud. Momentarily, Michael felt he was not alone. He shook the feeling off immediately. 'Right then, machine – plot number 196, John Altman, Field Maple.'

Marcus and Dexter arrived late on Friday. They went straight to Henge Farm, ate a huge meal, drank one or two cans of beer by the fire and crawled exhausted into their beds.

Next morning Michael woke them with mugs of coffee.

'Right lads, today we demolish the pigsty. Bacon and eggs

in the kitchen in fifteen minutes.'

'And fried bread?' Dexter yawned.

'And fried tomatoes?' Marcus muttered from beneath his duvet.

'If you like – and don't bother with showers: you are going to get filthy.'

In the kitchen Michael fried the breakfast. Penny had received a late phone call from Herr Jansson – most apologetic – unavoidable situation, he explained: he and a friend would be arriving late Saturday; could Penny organise the flat and put the heating on? He would need armfuls of flowers but it was too late for the florist to help. He exhorted her to do her best – he would be so grateful. Penny had driven in to Berwick early and caught the six-thirty train to London.

Michael aimed the mini digger at the crumbling pigsty. Dexter stood ready, sledgehammer at his side, while Marcus reversed the tractor and trailer close by to tow away the rubble. The next few hours were noisy, dusty, sweaty and smelly. At eleven, Michael called a halt.

'Tea break, lads – anyway, there's a burial due at a quarter past eleven, so we should try to project an aura of peace and tranquillity – at least until the mourners have left.'

Marsha McCleish had decided to attend an evening lecture. She arrived alone, notebook in hand, and found herself a seat at the end of a row of chairs arranged in a semicircle around an overhead projector. The lecture was to be given by a Professor A Willis; the subject, 'Alfred Watkins – Genius Terrae Britannicae?'

The row of seats gradually filled with a selection of diverse individuals. An elderly gentleman settled himself next to Marsha, turned, and introduced himself.

'I do believe we have met before. My name is George Mortimer – Professor Mortimer; and you, if I am not mistaken, are the granddaughter of that lovely lady who discovered a gold cup beneath her compost heap.'

'Granny McCleish.' Marsha smiled, looked again at the gentleman, and recognised him. 'How lovely to see you again, Professor. It's thanks to you I'm here, you know.'

'Here – at this lecture?' the Professor asked with surprise.

'No, here in Durham, at the university, studying archaeology,' Marsha corrected him.

'How satisfying . . . how satisfying,' he mumbled.

The general conversation died away when a young man walked up to the projector, his hair in vast dreadlocks that spiralled madly down his back and lay heavily upon his shoulders. His baggy jeans and Bob Marley T-shirt hung loosely on his spare body. Marsha thought he must be a technician adjusting the projector or something. The lights faded down, the young man pressed a button, and the projector whirred into life. On the screen, in black and white, appeared the image of an elderly gent, his hair sparse and white, with a neatly-trimmed moustache and pointed beard. On top of his large nose perched a pair of round black-framed pince-nez; a thin string hung down from them and around his neck. Beneath his untidy collar he wore a cravat, knotted and clasped by a thick metal ring.

The voice of the speaker broke the silence; Professor Mortimer groaned quietly under his breath. Why, he wondered, had he bothered to come? Why, oh why? The answer was that he had been invited, and that he still found young Willis difficult to refuse.

The lights went up and the young man with the dreadlocks still stood beside the projector. He turned, and in the voice Marsha had listened to throughout the presentation but had imagined belonged to someone else, said, 'I expect there will be plenty of questions. Professor Mortimer – nice of you to come. Have you a question?'

Marsha looked hard at Professor A Willis. Where had she seen him before? When he looked in their direction to reply to Professor Mortimer's initial bone of contention it came to her in a flash – Alex. She felt herself blush and felt silly. She remembered the pang of jealousy she had suffered when she realised Alex was with that other girl, the nice one – Maisie something. By the end of the question and answer session, during which she had remained silent, Marsha had regained her composure. She was just saying her goodbyes to Professor Mortimer when Alex came over.

'Professor, thanks so much for coming, I take it I still haven't convinced you totally – I'll keep trying though.'

'Alex, my boy – good lecture, well prepared, well argued:

nonsense of course. Still – you keep at it. Do you remember this young lady, I wonder?'

Alex turned from the professor and looked straight into Marsha's eyes. She was very glad indeed she had got the blushing phase over and done with earlier. She returned his look.

'I look at you and I think of postholes – Duddo – the gold cup – am I right?' Alex's head tilted inquisitively; he pushed a stray dreadlock back over his shoulder.

They went for a drink, just the two of them – the untidy young man who looked like a dropout, and the elegant, composed young woman who felt like a schoolgirl on the inside.

Sunday morning, Marcus and Margaret set off to walk a section of St Cuthbert's Way. Michael, Penny and Dexter all enjoyed a long lie in bed. Alice saw Margaret off, making sure she and Marcus had plenty of supplies. They had asked her to join them – they were not walking the steep section from Kirk Yetholm, they were following the path from Yetholm Bridge back towards the coast through the valleys and lower ground.

Alice had declined. 'No thank you, Margaret. I haven't recovered from following you round Holy Island at a cracking pace yet; you go with Marcus. I still have to prick the last of those sloes, and I've promised to help Penny later. She's doing a big dinner for us at about six.'

'Well, it had to happen sometime, Michael – be realistic,' Penny yelled back from the utility room, previously known as the scullery.

'But she's our baby! How can she have a boyfriend? Is it separate rooms, or what? Do you think they are sleeping together? Penny – bloody answer! This is important.'

Penny sat the iron back in its cradle on the ironing board. She turned it off at the switch and walked into the kitchen. Michael was pacing about; he turned and opened his mouth, about to continue with his tirade.

'Stop!' Penny commanded. 'Stop right now. Sit down; don't say another word until I have made us some coffee.'

Grudgingly Michael obeyed. He sat and fidgeted while the kettle came to the boil. He rubbed his hands together while the coffee granules went into the cups. He almost spoke, but Penny anticipated this and stopped him with a raised hand. She turned from the work surface with the mugs of coffee, placed them on the table and sat opposite her husband. She had to make a real effort not to laugh at him out loud.

'Listen,' she said; 'and don't interrupt until I'm finished – OK?'

Michael nodded his head.

'Our daughter Marsha is eighteen years old – nearly nineteen. She is a big girl, a grown up woman. She has very high self-esteem and is not, I repeat not, going to do anything which will stand in the way of her long-term plans to travel round the world digging stuff up. She is not going to get pregnant; she is not going to be an old slapper – you know all of this. Your lack of trust in her is unfounded and insulting:

insulting to her – and to us as her parents. Look me straight in the eye and tell me you would feel like this if Dex had a girl-friend – for all we know he might have; if he was having sex you would be proud of him – admit it. I thought we tried to bring our children up as equals; I thought our relationship was founded on the fact that you and I are equal. How dare you dredge up these antiquated, outdated, chauvinistic opinions now! What Marsha does with her life and her body is her business – OK? Her business – not ours: not mine, not yours – hers.'

Michael's mouth opened.

'Don't interrupt, I said. I am so disappointed in you. This bloke is a professor – and you can stop imagining some lustful old Svengali figure luring her into a world of tantric sex – because he's twenty-something – about the age you were, and I was, when we first started going out together.'

During Penny's rebuttal of his worries, Michael began to see that he was indeed being very foolish. The remainder of Penny's speech fuzzed in his brain. Of course Penny was right – how could he think that of his daughter? And yes, Penny was right about Dexter, too.

He heard Penny say, 'So, is that clear? Are you listening?'

'Yes, I'm listening – yes, you are right. I am stupid, and sorry, and ashamed. When are they coming?'

Autumn began with storms: winds howled; sleeting, sheeting rains fell. The ground became sodden and water lay in blustery grey reflected sheets in dips and hollows. The small stream where the rowans and silver birch grew burst its banks and rushed, mud-thickened, depositing fallen branches in untidy collections against the trunks of the trees. Days it rained – sometimes heavy, sometimes not, but it did not stop. Biblical rain.

Violet was busy making preparations for Christmas even though it was only the end of October. For so many years Christmas had passed them by. Those few years before the accident, before the boys . . . died – those years held happy memories: the tree, the decorations, the tinsel; paper chains licked and glued by the boys: orange–blue–red–orange–blue–red. Long strips of crêpe paper twisted and twisted into spirals of colour had hung from corner to corner sagging slowly in the heat of log fires. Then there were the years – far too many years – of nothing but a few colourful cards on the mantelpiece; no mistletoe from the orchard – not anything from the orchard. The fruits that had for generations been carefully wrapped in paper, stored on the slatted shelves in the outbuilding next to the byre, the body heat of the animals just enough to keep the frost at bay, waiting to be brought out at Christmas, polished and displayed in big china bowls on the sideboard – they had rotted on the ground. Blackbirds and wasps in abundance could never consume the quantity of fruit that fell or hung wrinkled and pecked from winter branches. This year, Violet wanted apples – apples from Henge orchard.

'Wyllie, will you telephone young Michael McCleish and ask him about gathering some of those apples?' Violet called from the kitchen where she was stirring an enormous bowlful of Christmas pudding mix.

'Stop your mithering, woman. We've not got the whole village coming to stay; just that young Maisie and her weird Aunt Avian.'

'Don't you speak about her like that – I know you don't mean it. There's nothing weird about having the Gift.'

Wyllie knew he did not mean it, but – the woman made him feel uncomfortable, uneasy, as if she could see into his soul: there was a dark place lurking in there – a place he guarded; only Callum McCleish had known of this secret, and he was long gone now.

'Phone him yourself – I'm out with the dogs.' Wyllie snapped, regretting it immediately. He walked – ashamed – back into the kitchen.

'Sorry. I'm away up to Henge later anyway to see him about some old bit of machinery he's found in the back of a shed. I'll ask him then.'

Violet smiled and returned to stirring and making wishes.

CHAPTER THIRTY-FOUR

They thought me fool enough to have hidden the cup here. They think we are children, and they, wise parents, who pat us on our heads and send us on our way. But I was a fool. If I had had the stones to throw, perhaps . . . ? Or perhaps not. I was betrayed; by whom does not matter: one of my own, one who had taken the Roman coin. They came before I reached the stag-headed oak. The rest you know.

The new minister had been appointed. This Sunday was his first service at Duddo Church. He stood nervously in the vestry, rearranging his robes. Timothy Eastman had been born into a family of clergy – his father, uncle and grandfather had all been ministers. It had been assumed since childhood that Timothy would follow. Consequently, in his early teens, Timothy had rebelled – and rebelled in style: drink, drugs, girls, motorbikes, tattoos; by the time he was eighteen his family had washed their hands of him. At twenty, fuelled by a combination of excess and the constant nagging desire in his head to keep on the move, the accident happened. When eventually he emerged bit by bit from the coma, he brought back with him a new sense of the spiritual parallel world he had inhabited for over six months. His family all converged on the hospital when the news came that he was regaining consciousness. The overwhelming sense of forgiveness and love all round was the first level of conscious awareness he had experienced on his journey.

He had been ordained six years later.

Timothy stood in the pulpit. A small congregation looked back at him; they stood, prayed, sang on cue. Some smiled as he caught their eye during the sermon; others did not. He ploughed through the traditional service until he found himself standing by the church door shaking the hands of his few, new parishioners.

'Thank you, minister – see you in a month.'

'Thank you, minister – the Women's Rural meeting . . .'

'Lovely service, minister; welcome to Northumberland . . .'

When they had all gone their ways, Tim went back into the church and sat himself down on a shining, lavender-scented pew.

'God – what am I doing here? Four churches, a few regulars – I mean, I wasn't expecting dancing, singing, happy-clappy religion, but . . . nothing here has changed for years, has it?' Tim sat quietly for a moment, hands in his lap. 'Oh, I get it. Thanks a bunch.'

The phone in Michael's office was ringing; Michael was just washing his hands in the bathroom next door and ran, hands dripping, to answer it.

'Hello, Henge Farm Woodland Burial Gardens – can I help?'

'Hi Dad, it's me.'

Michael sat himself down, wiping his hands down the thighs of his trousers alternating the hand holding the receiver.

'Hiya Dex. How are you?'

'Fine, Dad, fine. You and Mum OK?'

'Yep.' Michael smiled down the phone. 'Plenty of corpses around now the weather's getting colder.'

'Undertaker humour. I s'pose you get that from Solomon. Look Dad, there's something I wanted to ask you and Mum. It's about Christmas – I was wondering if Marcus could come and stay. I mean, he's got no family now 'cept his mum and she'll just be pissed the whole time.'

'Can't see why not. I'll have to check with your mum of course – she's in London today and tomorrow. Do you need to know now? You could phone her on her mobile.'

'No – no rush. You ask her when she gets back, will you?'

'Will do. Get off the phone now – I still haven't brushed my teeth,' Michael joked. 'Some of us have work to do, son –

not like you students.'

'Bye Dad, speak to you soon.'

In her kitchen, Alice was making mince pie filling. The room smelt of grated apple, cinnamon, nutmeg, brown sugar, dried fruits and brandy. She was waiting for the postman. He used to arrive just before nine, like clockwork. Most often, Alice would have met him at the gate as she came back from Nipper's morning stroll. Now it could be gone eleven before he got here. Alice was expecting a reply from Margaret: she had written several days before, inviting Margaret to spend Christmas and New Year at Orby. Nipper, dozing in his basket, raised his head and grumbled.

'Shh boy – it won't be the postie just yet,' Alice soothed.

The dog stood up and ran to the front door, barking loudly.

'Who can that be, then?' Alice said aloud, putting down the wooden spoon she had been using to mix the mincemeat. She walked to the front door and pulled back the bolt. A youngish man stood in the porch. He wore jeans, trainers and a T-shirt; there were tattoos on his arms.

'Hello, Mrs McCleish. My name is Tim, Tim Eastman.'

As he held out his hand to her, the name rang a bell.

'The new minister – we met at church last Sunday.'

'Oh, minister – come in, come in. Stop that, Nipper! I'm afraid the place is . . .' Alice flustered her way back into the kitchen, ushering the minister before her. She sat Tim down at the kitchen table and put the kettle on.

'You will have a cup of tea, now, won't you?'

The two of them were on their second cup of tea with a slice of fruit cake when the post rattled through the letter box.

'Look at the time, Alice: I've kept you from your work far too long. I only meant to pop round and introduce myself,' Tim apologised.

'Not at all, minis . . . sorry – Tim. I'm afraid it might take me some time to get used to calling you that: old habits die hard.'

'Indeed they do; but always remember – it's never too late to change.'

Alice saw Tim out and waved to him as he set off up the drive to Henge Farm.

'Well I never, Nipper.' I wonder what the Ollerenshaw woman will make of him, she chuckled to herself, stirring the grated fresh suet into the brandied fruit and sugar mix.

Dexter was home for the weekend. He had been studying top fruit production methods and had become mildly interested in the subject. The commercial sector bored him stupid: such a limited variety being grown. His tutor had been more forthcoming when discussing local varieties – old varieties that had been re-invigorated by the use of modern techniques using dwarfing or semi-dwarfing rootstocks. For a change, his father had nothing particular in mind for him to do. The paths had been cut for the last time that year; leaves would be the next problem; but this Sunday afternoon – what there was left of it before the sun sank early – was his – to do with as he pleased. Michael and Penny were snuggled up on the big sofa watching some old movie and eating chocolates. He could have gone to see Granny, but she would only have found him something to do: stir this; peel that. Granny McCleish had gone into a preserving frenzy. It was a glut year: plum trees, so often sparse bearers, snapped branches with the weight of fruit – damsons too. Apples clothed their trees, bending branches to the ground, the fruits still swelling in the ripening autumn. Dexter could have just crashed out in his room – listened to music – phoned Marcus. The thought of Marcus snapped Dexter back from his contemplation of what to do with his afternoon. He did not want to think about Marcus at all – not at this moment. Dexter pulled on his thick socks and wellies, shoved himself into a sagging old fleece of his father's and shouted through to his parents.

'I'm going out. See you later.'

The utility room door banged shut.

Dexter stood out on the drying green and looked out over the fields. He could just see the tree nursery – his baby, really. Brian had started him off; now very many of the trees planted in the burial gardens had been raised by Dexter himself. This provided a small income, boosting the income from his trust fund to a most comfortable level. He knew how lucky he was. He began to walk to nowhere in particular – just to mooch around aimlessly, looking at stuff here and there. As he looked, he could see everywhere the relevance of the course he was studying. He could see the trees growing, but now he understood something of how this happened. The boring biology he had endured at school was there – happening in front of him. With his hands he could touch the soil and know about how it worked, what it actually was, where it came from, how the moisture clung to each particle. He rolled a small ball of the soil in his hands – clayey loam, dark, sticky. He knew about that, understood it, it made sense. He wished he could make sense of Marcus in the same way. How could you learn about a childhood like that? Yes, Dexter McCleish knew very well just how lucky he was.

Dismissing thoughts of Marcus yet again, Dexter found himself at the small door into the walled orchard. So far, this area had been left untouched: there was some clause in the deeds or something – Dexter was not sure; anyway, that did not mean he could not go in there. The latch creaked as Dexter lifted it and pushed open the ancient wormhole-ridden door. Inside, the grasses and wild flowers of summer were dry and straw coloured, still waist high. Above this sea of blond, the trunks and crowns of the fruit trees, dripping with lichen and ripening fruit, rose. Their branches, untended for so long, had grown entangled in each other, supporting each other. Convolvulus twined its heart-leafed way up and around anything that grew, binding its way upwards in search of the sun, the celebratory white trumpets of its flowers pronouncing themselves in profusion. Dexter pushed his way around the orchard, trampling down undergrowth of spiteful nettle and seeded rusty dock. He absentmindedly picked an apple from a tree that looked as if it should never have been able to produce one – let alone the crop it bore. Its trunk, what remained of it, was gnarled and twisted, its centre sapwood almost nonexistent; thick bark, cracked and fissured, covered with grey-green lichen, made a hollow tube from the ground to which three branches clung, pulling the tree over in a drunken lurch. Dexter took a bite. The flesh was very firm and very sweet; juices ran into his mouth. He looked at the apple: it was a biggish thing – filled the palm of his hand; the skin was yellow with red stripes, deeply ribbed – not at all like the evenly-shaped, evenly-coloured apples Penny bought at the supermarket.

Dexter ate the rest of the fruit and threw the core into the undergrowth. He shoved more apples into his pockets to give to Penny and Michael. When he found the fallen cherry, Dexter stomped the weeds down around part of it and sat down in a patch of late afternoon sun. He looked around, leant back on a well-placed branch and enjoyed the solitude.

'These must be the apples Wyllie was on about the other day. Bloody lovely, these – better than your Golden Delicious from Tesco,' Michael said, later that evening. He cut a slice for Penny to try; she was dubious. 'Go on, taste it – scrummy.'

Penny reluctantly opened her mouth and Michael popped the slice of apple on her tongue.

'Give us a bit more – I can't decide if I like it or not,' Penny said.

'Liar! You know it's scrummy – go and get your own: Dex has left some in the fruit bowl.'

'Does Violet want some of the apples, then? Surely they know they don't need to ask. Shall I phone her? or do you think it's a bit late? They might have gone to bed.'

'Go on, give her a ring – it's only just after nine.'

Violet explained about the apple store at the farm and how to wrap the apples in tissue – only the good ones. Penny listened politely, and they arranged that Wyllie and Violet should come for as many apples as they wanted, whenever they wanted.

Next day, Penny noticed their Land Rover parked near the orchard wall. Knowing what she knew, she wondered how they could ever set foot in there. She certainly had no desire to go in there – where those two little boys had died.

Alice flicked the dust from her duster. The rainbow of light from the church window lit the motes, sparkling like fireflies, disappearing when they floated away from the sunlit beam. Alice looked up at the window. The manger and the cross: birth and death. Something was missing: where was life? She hummed quietly under her breath as she buffed up the pulpit.

Tim Eastman found himself drawn to Duddo Church. Of his four responsibilities, this small place of worship was his favourite. He stood on the path looking up at the plain exterior. The hanging baskets of summer now rocked, bedraggled and dying, in a gusty wind. At least the rain had stopped. The door was open; he wiped his feet on an old threadbare doormat that lay inside on the flagstoned floor. Alice heard his footsteps and looked up from her dusting.

'Alice, you have been busy. This church always smells of lavender and beeswax.'

'Morning minister – sorry – Tim,' Alice said. 'I'll be out of your way soon; nearly done.'

'No hurry, Alice – it's nice to have a bit of company – as well as that of you-know-who.' Tim raised his eyes heavenward.

Alice was not sure a minister should make those sorts of jokes, but she smiled anyway. The young man's intense eyes sparkled back at her.

'I love this building, Alice. It's so simple. The windows are very fine . . . what happened to the round one?'

'As far as I know it's always been like that – just plain glass. Shame, isn't it?' Alice looked up at the windows.

Tim joined her, standing by her side, looking up too. 'Maybe we should run a competition to design a panel – might be fun! What do you think?' Tim did not give Alice time to reply. 'By the way, you never told me that it was your son up at Henge Farm, running the Burial Gardens: wonderful place – first time I've ever visited somewhere like that. He said he was still waiting to hear from the bishop about consecrating one of the areas for Christian burial – which reminds me, I promised him I would chase that up.' He pulled a mobile phone from his jeans pocket. 'In fact, I'll do it now – no time like the present. I'll mention the window too – that'll keep the old boy on his toes.'

Tim pressed keys, then lifted the phone to his ear. 'Tim Eastman here; can you put me through to the bishop please?'

Tim took the phone outside and Alice returned to her dusting.

Tim Eastman stood at the pulpit in front of an almost-full church. He had been very busy, since his arrival, knocking on doors. His ordinariness, his lack of proselytising zeal, his ability to sit down with a family for a cup of tea discussing football, say, or motorbikes, if he got the chance, had encouraged some new faces to turn up for his services.

'Christmas is indeed the most important time in the Christian calendar. Of course, no one really knows on what day or what month the child Jesus was born. Equally, December twenty-fifth is not a random date picked out of the air by some early Christian. Our earliest celebration of the birth of Christ – whenever that may have been – has been superimposed over the period of winter solstice, Yuletide, or Mothers'-night. This time of the year was important for thousands of years before Augustine brought Christianity to this country. So on this, the second Sunday in Advent, I would ask you all to think of how the pagan festival, anticipating the lengthening of the days, symbolic of the triumph of life over death, bears close comparison with our Christian belief in the birth of a child who would die and rise again to save us all.'

Some of the elders sat open-mouthed by the end of this sermon. Tim had anticipated that response, and immediately he had finished, the pianist struck up the introduction to 'Jerusalem'. Nice rousing number, Tim thought: ought to bring them back on side. Tim Eastman was treading a fine line – and he knew it. As the congregation filed out of the church Tim had a smile and a word for each of them in turn.

The parish newsletter dropped through the letter box at Orby Cottage. There was to be a Christingle service at Duddo for the primary school children, at which they would perform the school nativity, on the twenty-second, at two-thirty. Anyone in need of transport to and from the church was invited to contact Mrs C Ollerenshaw of the local volunteer group on the given phone number. Coffee and cakes would be provided in the village hall afterwards, by the Rural. The newsletter also included details of a special competition, open to anyone, of any age, to design a new stained glass panel for the round church window. The winning design would be made and installed by a new resident, Mary Anne Keenan – a glass artist who had recently bought the old stable block at Todrig and renovated it into a home and studio. Mary Anne, Tim Eastman and the bishop were to be the judges. Entries were to be in by January tenth.

As the nights drew in, households throughout the village prepared for the Christmas holidays. Twinkling trees – some of which had been twinkling since the beginning of the month – appeared at windows. One or two inflated, illuminated Santas appeared in small front gardens, firmly anchored against the winter gusts. Shopping, and then more shopping, was heaved from car boots into the houses, freezers filled, presents hidden from inquisitive children.

Violet and Wyllie had no idea on what date Maisie was likely to arrive. 'Just before Christmas' was what she had written. Avian was due to arrive on the twentieth; she was staying until Boxing Day. The invitation to spend Christmas with the Turnbulls had come as a surprise. Avian had known that Maisie was planning to visit them then, and had imagined that Maisie would drift down to Railway Cottage as and when she felt like it. Avian had ummed and ahhed before accepting, but the opportunity to celebrate the winter solstice at Duddo stones was very enticing indeed – and she could perhaps visit Alice and Sarah. In the end she had written a letter accepting their kind hospitality.

Wyllie was sent to the station to collect Avian.

'Don't you pick her up in that filthy Land Rover either, you hear?' Violet insisted. Wyllie hung that set of keys back up and took down the keys to the clean car.

'Are you sure you won't come with me? What will I talk to her about?' Wyllie hesitated at the door, his hand on the handle.

'No, I will not – I've too much to be doing. Talk about sheep, or the weather – that's what you usually do.'

Wyllie backed the shiny black Range Rover out onto the road. He looked back at his beloved Land Rover, caked in mud. He would have felt much more himself in that: he felt wrong in the shiny vehicle – vulnerable – especially to this particular woman. Wyllie parked in the station car park at Berwick and looked up at the clock outside, checking it against the clock in the car. Twenty minutes, he thought. He popped into the Castle for a half of Guinness.

He wiped the white creamy froth from his top lip with the back of his hand and strode off down the slope to the station. Violet had insisted he go over onto the platform and wait, not just sit outside in the car. He fidgeted about on the platform, waiting for the delayed train.

He could not have mistaken her. Even if he had been blind the clip-clop of the wooden-soled clogs would have given her away. Avian was looking around – looking for him. Wyllie girded himself, straightened his back and walked towards her.

'Miss Tyler, shall I take your bag?' Wyllie mumbled.

'Mr Turnbull – how very kind,' she said, making a gentle joke of his formality. She followed him over the bridge and out of the station to the car. He was very uncomfortable – you did not need any sort of gift to see that. Avian said nothing: she did not want to discomfit the poor man further. It was strange, though – more than just a little embarrassment or shyness. Avian sensed he was shielding himself from her.

The journey from the station back to Duddo was quiet. Wyllie had no idea what to say to Avian. She sat calmly, her hands in her lap, looking out of the window and enjoying the scenery. When they arrived at the cottage Wyllie beeped the horn of the car and Violet came rushing out of the front door to greet Avian. Wyllie removed Avian's bag from the back of the car and left the two women hugging each other. It felt strange to see his wife so close to the woman; still, if Violet was happy, Wyllie was happy. He placed the bag in the hall and called to the women.

'I'll leave you two to catch up on your news. I'm away out with the dogs.'

Avian settled herself into the room Violet had prepared for her. Maisie was to have the room opposite, when she finally arrived.

Wyllie returned with the dogs, fed them and put them into their kennels for the night. He had wondered, when they moved, whether the dogs might like to live indoors now they were retired. The first night they tried it the three collies whimpered and howled; they peed up the cupboard fronts or on the floor – and one left an unpleasant surprise just inside the kitchen door. The kennels were quickly decamped from the farm on a flatbed trailer and installed in the garden with a temporary rabbit-wire run. Nights returned to peaceful cleanliness.

Over supper, Wyllie relaxed. Violet was on good form

keeping the conversation going and wheedling snippets of information about Maisie from Avian. Violet had become very attached to her memories of Maisie and their chats in the kitchen up at Henge. Violet had kept the girdle, and a large copper jam-making pot – which she had unearthed especially during the move, to give to the girl: they were wrapped for her present and waiting under the tree.

Violet and Avian cleared the table and washed up together. Wyllie took himself off into the sitting room and turned on the television. Avian and Violet came through with a pot of tea and some mugs. They sat together on the new sofa and chatted softly.

Wyllie changed channels for the news on BBC 1.

. . . and the chances of a white Christmas are high for those of you in the north-east of England and all of eastern Scotland, where there will be strong winds gusting to gale force due to the tightly packed isobars between the high pressure in the south and the low pressure sinking down from the north . . .

Avian had arranged to visit Alice the next day for lunch. She had intended to walk the couple of miles from the village, but Violet had insisted Wyllie drive her there as the wind was picking up and it had become very cold.

'Wouldn't be surprised to see a bit of snow later,' Wyllie said, as they got into the Land Rover. 'Look at that sky: very ominous.' Wyllie told of the winter long ago – 1963 – when the unexpected snow came heavily and persistently. He told of how he and Callum McCleish had to dig ewes in lamb out of six-foot drifts and get them back to the steading, and how birds lay dead and dying on the surface of the snow, covered quickly by more snowfall and more birds. 'We're about due another winter like that one – let's hope it's not this year,' Wyllie concluded as he stopped the Land Rover on the lane outside Orby Cottage.

'Thanks for the lift, Wyllie,' Avian called as she walked along the path and round to the back door. Leaning against the porch was a bicycle – knobbly tyred and brightly coloured – and coming from the kitchen Avian could hear voices. She was about to tap on the back door when a furious woofing began on the other side of it. The door opened and when Alice saw Avian standing outside she flung open the door and whisked her into the porch and out of the wind. Alice hung up Avian's coat and scarf in the porch and led her through into the kitchen.

Alice introduced her visitors. 'Avian, this is Tim – Tim Eastman; Tim, this is Avian Tyler. She was a great help to Violet Turnbull – cured her of her agoraphobia.'

'Oh – I didn't do much,' Avian flustered, 'just shared my own experience. It's amazing how much difference it makes to discover you are not the only one with a problem and that other people have overcome theirs.' To deflect attention from herself, Avian bent down to make a fuss of the wriggling, excited Nipper. 'Hello, old friend – and how are you?' she said, scratching behind the dog's ears.

'I should be going.' Tim stood up. 'Thanks for the tea and

advice, Alice – much appreciated.'

'Please don't go because of me,' Avian insisted, looking directly into the earnest eyes of Tim Eastman for the first time. She felt a shudder of recognition – not of him personally, but of another mystical being.

'No, I must go – so much to do; so little time to do it in. Christmas is a busy time of year in my job. Maybe we'll meet again sometime,' Tim said to Avian.

Alice showed Tim out, and wrapped by Alice in one of Callum's old scarves, he cycled off back towards the village. Alice came back inside rubbing her hands to warm them.

'That was our new minister,' Alice informed Avian. 'I'll get the kettle on – thaw you out a bit.'

Avian was surprised: of all the things that man might have been, the last thing she would have imagined was a vicar. They chatted over lunch – about Violet and Wyllie; about the burial gardens. Avian was very interested in that.

'You'll have to speak to my son Michael about that – I'm sure you'll meet him sometime over Christmas. Violet and Wyllie have booked a plot; so has my friend Margaret – have you met her?'

The wind strengthened as they chatted: it threw itself at the cottage making the windows rattle and draughts whistle under doors. Alice put more coal on the range and turned the central heating thermostat up. By two-thirty it was already getting dark.

'You had better think about going soon,' Alice said.

'Perhaps I should phone Wyllie to collect me,' Avian replied, surprised that Alice should expect her to leave so soon.

'No – not back to the village: you forget, Avian – I know about the twenty-first – the midwinter solstice. Callum always went up to the stones then – the longest night. In fact, Tim and I were discussing it before you arrived.' Alice smiled. 'I might even come with you – if you don't mind.'

The two women wrapped themselves up in big coats, scarves and hats from the porch.

'You can't walk up in those shoes, Avian; wear these old wellies again,' Alice insisted as she pulled on new, short, fleece-lined boots of her own. They bent their bodies into the wind and crossed the lane to the gate, Nipper excitedly rushing around their feet, menacing the whirling leaves. It was too windy to talk, but when they caught each other's watering eyes they smiled companionably. They wound their way up the spiral path towards the stones.

Avian turned her back to the wind and shouted to Alice.

'You go first! Someone is waiting!'

Alice said nothing. She looked deep into Avian's eyes and saw the same simple-heartedness that she saw in Tim Eastman. She thought what a nice couple they would make – well suited. Tim Eastman was a revelation to Alice: so different from the old minister. He was very interested to hear about Callum – his country law, his old superstitions. He did not dismiss those old ways as sinful – he found great similarities between the old religion and Christianity.

Nipper had already rushed past the last of the benches, stopping to pee up it on his way. He ran up to the centre of the stone circle and sat down, his tail wagging. Alice stood outside the ring. The wind whipped her scarf across her face; cold air stung her skin; her eyes watered. She wiped her cheeks with the back of her glove and stepped into the circle. It was calm – strangely and unexpectedly quiet: the buffeting wind stopped within the henge. Alice said nothing. She stood next to Nipper and waited. She felt an embrace of love and understanding coil around her, slipping intimately next to her skin: the touch of a lover. She thought she would cry, but then a chuckle began. It shook her shoulders, juddered its way up her neck, then tingled along her jaws, which opened to allow first the chuckle, then the laugh, to escape. The laugh became loud and joyous. Avian approached the circle and Alice turned to welcome her in just as the cloud on the western horizon broke, allowing a last, long beam of golden light to flood across the darkening landscape. The two women watched the beam undulate over the folded earth towards them. Momentarily the stones threw long sharp shadows, and then the clouds closed up, leaving the earth in grey darkness.

Avian had been subdued since their return. The kettle was on, Nipper had been fed and Alice had put several crumpets under the grill. Butter and home-made jam were laid on the table.

'I won't be a minute, Alice – I just need to use the bathroom.' Avian sat on the toilet; she felt faint, she felt afraid, and she felt elated. The spirit voice had spoken: Callum had spoken. Avian splashed her face with cold water, pulled herself together and went back into the kitchen. She drank the tea and ate the crumpets; and she listened to Alice say more about the new minister.

CHAPTER THIRTY-FIVE

How long my curse blighted this land: storm, drought, snows, a plague of tiny insects; a strange disease of sheep and cattle followed, which turned tongues blue, and broke and festered the skin. Abortion, miscarriage, deformity and pestilence: all the curses I drew down penetrated the land and those who lived upon it. For a long, long time the land around the stones was taboo: none tried to scratch a living, nothing thrived, people moved away – away from the old ways; and as they forgot, so my powers dwindled – none remembered me.

Then he came – the strong one – and the dregs of my curses were weakened with willow and rowan and mistletoe. But he was too late to save the twin children. I had kept her barren, the woman from the Isles, as well as the strong one's wife, for as long as I had been able, but his charms won over my enfeebled efforts and they both, in time, bore healthy infants. Eventually, the strong one became at one with the land and I became powerless; but for one lapse on his part – his underestimation of my malice –

with one last claw out from time and obscurity I stole those twin souls.

The telephone rang at Orby Cottage. Alice got up sleepily from the armchair in front of the fire where she had nodded off after Avian left.

'No, Violet, she left about four-thirty'. . . 'Well, she in-sisted on walking – I offered her a lift but she wouldn't let me. She said the wind had dropped and she really wanted the fresh air.' . . . 'She should have been back with you by now. She could have popped in to see Sarah Rigden – yes – phone Sarah – I bet that's where she is.' . . . 'Her niece has arrived? How lovely.' . . . 'Don't worry, Violet – she'll be at Sarah's, I expect. Bye for now, Violet.' Alice hung up and settled back in her armchair.

At six-thirty Brian Rigden answered his telephone.

'Hello, Mrs Turnbull – what can I do for you?' . . . 'No, not since I got home; hang on – I'll ask Sarah.' He left the phone and found Sarah with two fat children encompassed by her arms.

'No – Sarah hasn't seen Avian. What time did she leave Alice?'

Avian Tyler's body was found at eight-thirty that night, crushed beneath a fallen beech bough, partially blanketed by the soft, gentle snow that had begun to fall at seven, just as the search party was setting out.

Wyllie drove Maisie and Violet through the deepening snow to identify the body. Clearly an accident, the police saw no need to investigate and the coroner saw no need for a hearing. The body was taken to Solomon Arkwright and Son. Maisie, Violet and Alice arrived the next afternoon. Solomon Arkwright led them through to where Avian lay wrapped in a linen shroud in an open basketwork casket. Solomon left the women alone.

Through tears, the women said their goodbyes. Maisie delved into a bag she had brought with her and drew out two flattish stoneware bowls she had found in Violet's kitchen. Into one, she emptied a small bag of soil, into the other, salt. She laid these on her aunt's swathed body – one on her stomach, one on her chest. She lit little cones of incense and stood them around the casket on the draped table. Violet lit candles at Avian's head and feet. The women sat on the straight-backed chairs that stood against the wall, pulling them closer to Avian's body. Violet held Maisie's hand tightly.

They sat silently and still for some time; the cones of incense burned away, their rich, pungent scent filling the room. Coils of smoke rose gently, leaving little conical piles of ash. The candles flickered and guttered. Maisie released her hand from Violet's grip, and she stood slowly.

Avian Tyler was buried on Christmas Eve in the Vernal

Field of the Burial Gardens. Snow covered the ground and the digger had a hard task excavating the hole. No tree was planted that day.

Christmas Day at the Turnbull cottage could have been mournful. Wyllie rose early to avoid facing the grieving women, making himself tea in the gloom of the kitchen. He poured hot water onto the dehydrated dog food, which swelled and cooled as he gulped his tea. The sun was still below the horizon when he left the house. The world was clothed in a grey–violet blanket of soft, deep, luminous snow. The collies did not show their usual enthusiasm for exercise, emerging sleepily from their kennel as Wyllie opened the gate into their run. Wyllie set down their bowls of food and broke the ice on their water bowl, lifting the floes out and throwing them onto the snow. Warm food and fresh water enlivened the dogs, and they squirmed around Wyllie's feet, looking up anxiously to his face, waiting for instructions.

They headed off down through the silent village. Wyllie thought he must be the only person awake as the sky lightened shade by shade, the grey lifting, the violet taking over. There was not a breath of wind. He saw lights on upstairs at the Rigden's house, heard children's laughter, adult voices, the cry of a baby. Instantly he was taken back to those Christmases before the accident. He pulled off a glove and wiped his eyes with the back of his hand. This chill air, the growing light and memories had made his old eyes water. He walked on, the dogs clinging to his calves, constantly raising their eyes to make sure they were doing what their master wanted of them. At the white gate of the graveyard Wyllie stopped. He stood, looking over the gate at the enveloped ground. Lichen-encrusted lettered stones stood at attention, or at an angle, depending on their age, their caps of snow coral-tinged as the first rays of sunlight brushed them.

'Down,' he commanded the dogs, which slunk down onto the snow by the stone wall. Wyllie opened the gate; it creaked with a sound unexpectedly loud in the still air. He stood, one hand on the top of the gatepost, hesitant. Twice, during the years Violet had been incarcerated in the farmhouse, Wyllie had almost visited the twins' shared grave. Each time, he had arrived at an hour when the rest of the world was asleep: once, late at night, coming back from market with a few drinks too many in him, and once very early, like today – and this was as far as he had ever got: gate open, hand on gatepost, no one around . . . both times he had lost his nerve. He looked to his left across the headstones of families well known to him and his ancestors. The twins were over there, just behind the Celtic cross which marked their grandfather and grand-mother's shared resting place. Wyllie looked around – he felt someone was watching, but the world was an empty place that morning except for him, his dogs and the crows just begin-ning to stir and rattle in the stand of trees behind the grave-yard.

'Old fool – bloody old fool,' Wyllie muttered to himself,

his words coming out mingled with steaming breath. One of the dogs looked up.

'Get down, Bess; good dog.'

He bent down to rub the animal's head. As he stood up he felt dizzy; his vision blurred. He felt the ghost of an arm around his shoulder, felt himself being moved into the grave-yard, manoeuvered towards his children's grave. Then the arm was gone. Wyllie shook his head to clear his thinking and looked around. He was alone; there was a slight smell of burn-ing vegetation, yet there was no bonfire alight for miles. A silent barn owl swooped low over his head. Wyllie kept very still and watched it as it hung in the air listening for move-ment under the snow beneath, dropped, talons aimed into the snow, and rose gripping a shrew, mantling over its prey with mottled wings as the rodent was lifted in one claw to the rip-ping, hungry beak of the owl. Wyllie looked down to the slight rise in the covering of snow lying at the foot of a stone carved with two cherubs. The boys' names, the date of their birth and the date of their death were still clear despite moss and lichen; he had to brush snow aside to read the inscription.

Guilt slid heavily over Wyllie Turnbull as he stood there in the gathering light. The words of the story came back to him, as they had so often over the years. Here, standing beside the small mound, they rang through the air as clear as the church bell.

Wyllie could see the blue of their pyjamas, the maroon and beige of their woollen dressing gowns. He could smell the soapy cleanliness of their warm bodies, the smell of their hair still slightly damp from their bath.

'Finish the story, Daddy; finish it tonight, please,' two voices in unison echoed from the past.

Tears rolled down Wyllie Turnbull's fissured face. That was the night before – before the accident, before the twins tied lengths of rope around the boughs of the apple tree, before they argued about who would be William Wallace. One of them must have had first go, or perhaps they both . . . A deep sob shuddered through Wyllie's collapsing body; he placed his hand on the stone to steady himself. Once again he felt supported, as if dear friends had appeared on either side, taking his hands, taking his elbows; he smelt burning again . . . he thought he heard a familiar voice.

'Callum,' Wyllie whispered. He straightened himself. 'Callum – Callum McCleish!' he called into the awakening day.

The owl, disturbed by his cry, flew off without a sound towards the trees. Circling crows swooped down to mob it, wings angling. The owl evaded the noisy black crowd and flew serenely on. The dogs whined behind the wall, rose and slunk on their bellies towards their master, knowing they should not have moved.

'Get down,' Wyllie hissed.

The dogs obeyed, shivering with cold – or fear. Wyllie listened hard. He heard the owl call again in the distance, he heard snow fall from the branch of the yew, he heard the dogs panting, he heard the crunch of footsteps in the snow. He saw

Maisie and Violet, wrapped against the cold, come through the open gate. Violet draped a long woollen coat over her husband's shoulders.

'Where have you been, man? Look at the dogs – they're frozen.'

'Hush, woman – can you not hear? Listen, girl – listen, I know you can hear them. What do they say?'

Violet looked to Maisie, who replied in a matter-of-fact voice.

'It's Avian, and a man. They are both here because Wyllie needed them. Callum says to tell you that a trouble shared is a trouble halved and that you've to tell Violet. Avian says we are to have a wonderful Christmas and not to mope about: she will always be here – in the stream, in the valley, in the trees and in the sky above our heads.'

Violet pulled an ancient flask from a bag and poured three cups of steaming hot chocolate laced with whisky. The three stood by the grave, warming their hands and faces in the rising steam, shuffling their feet in the snow as if performing a strange dance.

Henge Farm kitchen came into its own that Christmas. It had been a very long time indeed since the house brimmed with people, with noise, with smells and with anticipation. Even Nipper had received special dispensation to visit for the day – as long as he did not go on the furniture. Alice felt a little wicked to be celebrating so unashamedly with poor

Avian just hours in her grave: she wondered if a minute's silence might be the proper thing to do, but all around her life carried on. Marsha had been sad – she remembered the lady with the long grey hair who had befriended her on the train – but her sadness had been momentary. Alice wished that Margaret had chosen to spend Christmas at Duddo, but even with Marcus being there, Margaret had declined the offer saying she preferred to spend Christmas alone.

'One can have too much of that family atmosphere,' she had said on the phone, emphasising the word 'family'.

Michael had driven down the snowy lane to collect Alice and Nipper for breakfast at eight-thirty on Christmas morning. Penny and Marsha had cooked piles of crispy bacon and a huge plateful of eggs, mushrooms and sausages, and as Alice arrived they were loading plates and placing them on the table. When they all sat down, Alice looked around at her family: Michael, her baby – her prodigal son; Penny, who had blossomed; Marsha, her eyes shining, sitting there next to Alex; Dexter next, then herself, and Marcus on her left. She wished Callum were here to see this . . . yet she knew, in some way she did not understand, that he was, and always would be.

When all the breakfast dishes had been loaded into the capacious dishwasher, they all trooped into the sitting room. An enormous bespangled tree filled a corner of the room; the log fire crackled and spat in the fireplace. The room was decorated as the sitting room at Orby Cottage had been decorated when Michael was a boy: ivy draped itself from the cornices, ruby-berried holly branches perched on picture frames. Dexter had made a beautiful Christmas wreath in the last week of term as part of a practical project, and he and Marcus had carefully laid it on top of their disorganised luggage in the back of the little red car and brought it to the farm. It should have hung on the front door, but Penny thought it so beautiful, with its golden cones and wired wax fruits, that it took pride of place over the mantlepiece.

Alice gasped.

'Do you like it, Granny?' Marsha asked. 'Dad says your house always looked like this at Christmas.'

Marcus led a tearful Alice to the chair beside the fire and handed her a sherry.

Piles of gifts lay beneath the tree and Michael was volunteered to do the handing out. The pile of wrapping paper and ribbon grew, as presents were unwrapped: for Alice, a beautiful cashmere cardigan chosen by Penny, in soft, muted green; sheepskin boot-shaped slippers from Marsha and Dexter, and a silver-framed black and white photograph of Alice, Callum, and Michael aged about six, from Michael. Alice had bought Michael and Penny a beautiful patchwork bedspread, made by one of the members of the Rural, from the craft sale the minister had held in the village hall before Christmas. Marsha and Dexter had money, socks, underwear, jumpers, and silly toys which made everyone laugh – a whoopee cushion for Dexter and a soft teddy for Marsha. Marcus, too, had plenty of gifts to unwrap; he had never imagined Christmas could be like this.

Close to tears, he remembered his gran – she would have loved all this. Alex also had presents. It was clear, as he unwrapped the rather formal tie that Penny and Michael had bought, that they had not met him before. Penny and Michael grinned and Alex laughed. Dexter set off the whoopee cushion and everyone collapsed into fits of giggles.

Margaret Allerton sat in her comfortable armchair, her feet raised on a footstool that Marcus had left for her to unwrap on Christmas morning. She had awoken to the sound of pealing bells, feeling rather Scrooge-like in her isolation. She had risen leisurely, bathed luxuriously in the foaming lather of a Stephanotis bath preparation – a gift she had indulged in for herself – and enjoyed a light breakfast. She wrapped herself up warmly and took a short walk along almost-deserted streets. A few of the faithful hurried home to baste the turkeys in their ovens, their greetings crystallising in the sharp air.

'Merry Christmas!' they called out; 'Merry Christmas!'

Humbug, Margaret thought, but she smiled a greeting in return. She hurried home through the slush of melting snow and ice, glad of her sturdy walking boots and stick. For her one-person Christmas lunch, Margaret had prepared breast of guinea fowl in a mango chutney and cream sauce with wild rice, followed by a mini extra-rich M&S traditional Christmas pudding with Devon clotted cream.

Margaret shifted her body a little – she was uncomfortably

full of rich, delicious food. She belched with a flourish and thought of Marcus. She knew he would be having a wonderful time with the McCleish family. She thought, without a hint of envy, of Alice surrounded by her kith and kin. Margaret had spent many – most – Christmases alone, generally out of choice, sometimes in remote and splendid solitude. This Christmas, she relaxed into her chair, rearranged the warm Black Watch tartan rug – a gift from Alice – across her knees and sat happily in silence until she fell into a deep, digestive sleep.

Violet Turnbull took Avian at her word: there would be no sadness around her table that year. On their return from the graveyard, once thawed out, Violet insisted on a word with Wyllie in the parlour, alone. Wyllie knew exactly what was on Violet's mind – he knew what she would say before she said it.

"'A trouble shared . . .' What trouble might that be, then?'

Wyllie poured himself a nip of whisky and offered Violet the same, which she accepted. They sat opposite each other in armchairs either side of the fire. Violet listened.

As Wyllie told his story she looked across at the stricken man. All those years . . . all those years and he had believed it was his fault – as she had believed it to be hers. His bent head, his hunched shoulders, his inability to look her in the face, his guilt – all screamed his anguish more eloquently than his stumbling words could. Violet pushed herself up out of her chair and took the three steps across to her husband. She bent creakily down and took his big calloused, scarred hands in her small gnarled ones.

They emerged from the parlour to find Maisie with preparations for the dinner well under way: a goose spat on its trivet in the oven, roast potatoes sizzling in the fat beneath; gooseberry sauce sat warming in a sauceboat on the warming rack above.

'Everything's under control, Violet – hope you don't mind?' Maisie smiled at the two of them, arm in arm at the kitchen door.

'Mind? I cannot remember the last time I had a dinner cooked for me, and never a Christmas one since I was a girl. You carry on lass, if you're happy to.'

After their dinner the three of them left the dishes where they stood, made a pot of tea, and took it into the parlour. Under the tree a small selection of presents sat waiting to be opened.

'Pass them around, Maisie lass,' Wyllie insisted. 'Save me bending all the way down there.'

Maisie handed the first beautifully wrapped small parcel to Violet: it was her present from Avian.

Tim Eastman was pleased with his first Christmas in the parish. The bishop was pleased with Tim Eastman's first Christmas in the parish, very pleased. Interaction between the Church and the community had been absent, apart from the efforts of Mrs Ollerenshaw and her Rural committee, for far too long. This new young minister had a way with him, drew people in – welcomed everyone. His enthusiasm and endless badgering had even been enough to persuade Church authorities to grant permission for the consecration of an acre or two of the new Burial Gardens near Duddo. The bishop was booked to officiate.

The window competition had been something of a headache for Tim – not that there were not plenty of entries – all fourteen children at the primary school had submitted designs, as had the playgroup. Most members of the Rural had entered, after an inspiring talk and demonstration before Christmas from Ms Keenan, the glass artist. (Mrs Ollerenshaw had made a concerted effort to persuade Ms Keenan to join the Rural, but had so far remained rebuffed.) Tim and Mary Anne had sifted the entries into possibles and impossibles and whittled it down to six – but the final choice was to be made by the bishop after the consecration ceremony. Tim and Mary Anne could see there was one outstanding design – simple, local – spiritual, possibly – but in fact, more than likely too controversial.

The bishop had been most impressed with Henge Farm Woodland Burial Gardens. He was a passionate gardener in his limited spare time and an amateur arboriculturist. He could see beyond the bare winter skeletons of the many deciduous trees, imagine the leaf break shock of spring green, imagine the dappled shade made by the thickening canopy in summer, the hues of autumn, warm and golden. A deeply spiritual, educated man, he had read of the discovery of the gold cup with great interest. He always felt that, had he not received the call, he might have been an archaeologist.

In the farm kitchen, after the ceremony, the few who had attended gathered for hot chocolate and large slices of Alice's famous coffee cake. The bishop extricated himself from the clutches of the Ollerenshaw woman and her clique and found sanctuary in conversation with Alice.

'I have to admit, Mrs McCleish, that I had my doubts when I first heard of this idea, but I have to say that what your son has achieved here in such a short space of time is quite remarkable.'

'Yes, I'm so proud – although I admit I wasn't sure myself, to begin with.'

Michael and Penny came over to join them.

'Bishop – thank you so very much,' Penny gushed.

Tim Eastman drove slowly down the drive from Henge Farmhouse. Through the stark tangle of boughs and branches the hillock, topped by its ancient stones, stood out against the steel-grey sky.

'Now, that is a view that links us with our ancestors,' Tim said to the bishop, drawing his attention to the scene. 'Since two and a half thousand years before the birth of Christ they've stood there, give or take a year or two – the oldest hint of the spiritual nature of humanity in this area.'

The bishop looked up. 'The Duddo Stones? Do you know, Tim, I was wondering why this place was called Henge Farm. I've heard of them of course, but I have never seen them before – do you think we have time to have a closer look?'

It would have been an unusual sight if anyone had been there to see it. Two robed clerics, their cassocks hitched up out of the wet grass, hurrying their way along the spiral path to the standing stones. They stood together at the top, the wind whipping their clothing.

They arrived wet, yet invigorated, back at the manse. The six designs that had been selected lay arranged on the scrubbed refectory table in the manse kitchen. Tim left the bishop to peruse the designs while he made coffee for them both.

'Well, bishop, what do you think?'

'I don't believe it, Tim – simply don't believe it!' Mary Anne Keenan trilled down the phone.

'You don't believe it? How do you think I feel?' Tim replied.

'How exciting! I'll get started on the preliminary full-size layout this week. What did we say the diameter was?'

Mary Anne finished her tisane and went out into her studio – a converted pigsty linked to the main house by a covered walkway festooned with the brittle tendrils of summer's long-dead climbing plants. She laid out a very large, square piece of art paper and found its centre point on the diagonals, she pinned a piece of string tied to a sharpened pencil at the centre and drew a circle the size of the round church window. Mary Anne taped the paper firmly to the drawing board and began to transfer and enlarge the charming drawing to its ultimate scale. All this was to be done in absolute secrecy. Only Mary Anne, the bishop, and Tim knew which was the winning entry. They had decided that the winner would be revealed in a dramatic flourish at the unveiling of the finished work.

Mary Anne had been very pleased to be approached by the local minister, a rather darkly handsome man: she would never have guessed he was a clergyman when he arrived at her door that morning. He had introduced himself, and she had invited him in for a cup of tea – after all, that is what you do with clergy, whatever their denomination. They talked over the tea about her work, she showed him around her studio, they had another cup of tea, and he told her of his idea for a new church window. Not once did he ask if she were a churchgoer; he never mentioned his services. By the time he left, Mary Anne had somehow agreed to make up the winning design at a horribly reduced rate and cost of materials only. Still, it would be worth it – a chance to begin to integrate with the community and a chance to show off her work locally.

An air of mystery and suspense was created by the arrival of scaffolding at Duddo Church, supplied free by the local builder, who also found himself installing the window for no more than two men's wages for the three days it took. Several people gathered to watch the old window be carefully removed and lowered down to the ground. More arrived next day in an attempt to catch a glimpse of the new window, but they were thwarted by the screen of tarpaulin curtaining off the view. The church doors were locked to keep the inquisitive away. A disappointed little crowd shuffled off, muttering, in groups. They turned and peeked up at the arrival of a flat back van with a large disc, carefully strapped and buffered, secured upon it. It was the new window, but wrapped to protect and shroud it.

The scaffolding and tarpaulin remained in place until after Sunday service. Inside the church, the window had been covered by an old velvet curtain that Tim had found under the stage in the village hall and had rigged up with the help of the builders. One builder, Murray Shepherd, had been volunteered to man the scaffolding on the Sunday. He waited up there until the congregation had entered the church, when he was to remove the outside tarpaulin. This he did, then scurried down to squeeze himself into a standing space at the back of the building.

The bishop was to unveil the new window in person – of this Tim Eastman was very glad indeed. Those who disapproved – and he knew there would be some – would not have far to go to make their complaints, and complaint would be awkward as the bishop had judged the competition and was himself unveiling the winner.

Tim had carefully worded his sermon, gently leading his flock towards the revelation. The bishop almost grinned when the sermon ended and the final hymn was sung.

'Amen,' exclaimed Reverend Eastman.

'Amen,' the congregation agreed.

'And now, the moment we have all been waiting for – and quite possibly the reason this little church is bursting at its seams today – I give you – the bishop.'

The bishop rose and took his place at the pulpit. He turned to face the congregation.

'It does my heart and soul good to see this place of worship so full that many of you have stood throughout the service. The Reverend Eastman has only been with us here in this parish for less than a year, and yet in that short time he has made his mark on our community. Today we have the opportunity to make a mark of our own, a mark that represents our time, our culture, our faith; and yet harks back to the days before either the resurrection or the birth of our Lord Jesus Christ. The birth of Jesus, as we see here in this beautiful glass panel, was humble; his death, the death of a criminal, horrific; yet we know his life and death were not in vain: he showed us the way to God, and by his resurrection gave us everlasting life. It took a long time for the word of God to reach this part of the world. What spiritual path did those ancestors of mine and yours who lived here before then follow? We do not really know, but we do know they were people just like us –

like you and me – who needed answers, who knew there was a greater power than themselves which governed their lives. They, too, needed a focal point to their communities, something that brought them together, a special place; and our new window – your new window – I think, illustrates just that point. And so, it gives me great pleasure indeed to unveil the new round window of Duddo Church, designed by Aaron Rigden of Year One, Duddo Village School.'

The bishop tugged at the rope holding the curtain in place over the window; for a second only dust showered down, then suddenly the curtain fell and the sun streamed in through a panel of shimmering glass depicting a low green hill dotted with flowers and a blue sky, and on the top of the hill, standing stones. Mary Anne had not altered the design at all – its perspective was wrong, the stones appeared too large, the hill too small, yet there was no doubt that these were the Duddo Stones – there was even the spiral path curling up to them.

An instant of silence, then voices murmured.

Aaron shouted, 'My drawing, Mummy! Look Mummy – my drawing!'

There were the expected sharp intakes of breath and shocked expressions, but not many – and who could complain? There was the minister; there was the bishop. Some people began to clap; others joined in. Dissenters were outnumbered. Celia Ollerenshaw's open mouth snapped shut; she was speechless.

Dexter McCleish stood in the cold mist with his fellow students watching Jon Weston, the new tutor, demonstrate the art of winter pruning apple trees.

'Here we have a perfect example of the branches having been summer pruned very skilfully. This makes our job of winter pruning much simpler. The majority of winter pruning involves the cutting back of leading shoots to maintain the shape of the tree – the technique is the same for standing or trained trees. Now, you – where would you prune this branch?'

Each student in the small practical group had to identify the correct pruning place several times before they were each given secateurs and a tree to prune. Jon Weston moved from one tree and from one student to another, guiding and helping. Jon Weston was passionate about top fruit, and apples in particular.

Dexter stood back from his tree, walked around it and decided to take out a branch that was crossing and rubbing against another, causing a wound. Jon Weston heard the sound of a pruning saw in action and turned quickly to see who it was and what they were hacking away at.

'What are you doing? This is supposed to be a winter pruning class, not bloody tree surgery,' Jon huffed.

'Sorry, but this branch was crossing and rubbing: it did have to go, didn't it?'

'Well, yes, I suppose – but I wasn't expecting anyone to show quite so much initiative and knowledge. Are you particularly interested in malus species?' Jon eternally hoped for a potential protégé.

'Not particularly, except at home we have an old walled orchard, with loads of huge old apple trees, and I was thinking of having a go at tidying it up. There's one ancient old thing, looks almost dead – hollow and stuff – but it still had loads of fruit on – really scrummy crisp, juicy apples. The old lady who used to live there told me about it – planted by her mother-in-law's great-grandmother or something. She came and picked some fruit to store for Christmas.'

'I don't suppose she knew the name of it?' Jon Weston's buried deepest desire stirred within him.

'Yeah, she did, but she must have been mistaken – she's very old. She called the apple the 'Painted Lady' – well, it was colourful – yellowish with red stripes.'

Jon Weston's gut knotted.

Dexter continued, 'I entered it into Google and it only came up with butterflies and portraits – no apples.'

Jon Weston stood speechless – sure he must have misheard, misunderstood. Here in front of him was a young man who, if he were right . . . it was unimaginable. A list of apple names spun through his whirlpooling mind: 'Quart Apple', 'Trumpeter', 'Scarlet Tiffing', 'Sugar and Brandy', 'Painted Lady' . . . 'Painted Lady' . . . Painted bloody Lady! Hastily he brought the lesson to an end and dismissed the surprised class who were pleased they would get an extra quarter of an hour on their lunch break.

Jon Weston rushed to the reference section of the college library. He needed no direction from the librarian; he knew where it was: here – 'The National Apple Register'. He turned to the index and ran his finger impatiently down the list at 'P'. Page 1674. He rifled through the pages, too excited even to move to a desk and sit down.

'Painted Lady . . . in existence 1883, described 1831 . . . last known example blown down in gale, twenty-third September 1944 at Bradley Hall . . . size: medium; shape: conic, convex, ribbed . . . skin: yellow striped red; hard yellow flesh, sweet . . . mid-to-late season.'

His yell of triumph, unsuitable in the hushed library, echoed down the corridor. The librarian raised her head to scold the noisy student only to see the new tutor skipping between the shelves in unrestrained celebration. She coughed loudly. Jon stopped, one foot still raised in the dance. He realised where he was and saw that the few denizens of the library were all looking at him. Respectfully he placed the Register back on its shelf and slunk off, his head bowed in an attempt to hide an expression of sheer glee.

Marsha McCleish, warm and damp from a long hot bath, wrapped in an enormous soft towel, lay sleepily on the sofa in front of the fire. Behind her, sitting at the huge table he used as a desk, she could hear Alex muttering to himself. At first she had found this habit of his unnerving – she would be in the kitchen and hear him, thinking he must be talking to her.

She would shout through and he would reply:

'Nothing, I was talking to myself – sorry.'

And he would laugh and come through to the kitchen and they would kiss. She had been surprised at how romantic and old-fashioned he had been. The phrase, 'charmed the pants off her' summed it up succinctly, she thought. His flat had been remarkably tidy and well organised. Initially she thought the tidiness had been for her benefit, but she learned that Alex was not quite what you might have imagined from first impressions.

'So, is that work or pleasure?' she asked; 'and is it more interesting than me?'

'Oh yes, far more exciting than the pleasures of the flesh,' he teased.

'What is it then? Tell me.' Marsha stood up and pulled the towel around her so it did not trail along the floor. 'That's Northumberland,' she said, looking down at the Land Ranger map spread out on the table. 'Where is Duddo on there?'

Alex pointed out Henge Farm, the standing stones, Granny McCleish's house.

'You're looking for ley lines, then?'

Alex was always hunting for possible ley lines. He nodded and pulled her by the waist onto his lap.

'Show me,' Marsha insisted. 'And you can stop that – ley lines are "far more exciting than the pleasures of the flesh"!'

Alex gently shoved her away in playful rebuke. He took the long transparent plastic ruler he used for the purpose and laid it on the map.

'Let's assume the stones are the pivot of the ley line.' And he set the centre of the ruler on the stones. 'Now look around for other clues – tumps, fords, moated mounds, sites or remains of old ponds, forts, beacons, relevant place names, farm names, marked stones, footpaths, bits of road . . . and we'll try and line a few up. Line up two or three and it could be just coincidence; line up more and it's worth investigating further.'

'So why the interest in Duddo again?' Marsha asked.

'Several reasons I suppose – mainly because the dig was inconclusive. We found no indication of why something as rare and valuable as the cup, then and now, should end up under the compost heap in your granny's garden.'

'Because of the stones?' Marsha guessed.

'OK – but to be honest, the site is not on the Stonehenge scale; it's the equivalent of a tiny parish church compared to a cathedral. There must be something we missed.'

'And you think if there's a ley line to follow that might help?'

'Could be . . . could be – but just at the moment I think there's something else I'm missing.' He grabbed at the towel and pulled it away from Marsha's body.

Later, entwined beneath the duvet, they chatted.

'Do you think your mum and dad could bear to have us visit for a week?' Alex joked.

'I'm sure they'd be thrilled, and it would be great to see Granny. Why do you want to go?' Marsha snuggled closer to

Alex's warm body. 'What's the catch?'

'No catch – except I'd like to investigate the area in more detail; the map looks promising, so you'd need your walking boots.'

'Why am I not surprised?' Marsha giggled, tickled Alex gently, kissed his chest and turned over to sleep.

Alex lay still, listening to Marsha's soft, rhythmic breathing. Moonlight streaming through the window starkly lit a portion of the room. Alex knew there was something to uncover, some mystery surrounding the cup – an object far too valuable just to have been discarded – and the set of carved stones, and the scoop. He drifted off into unsettled sleep.

Around the pine table in the kitchen at Henge Farm sat the McCleish clan: Michael, Penny, Marsha, Dexter and Alice. With them were Margaret, Marcus, Alex and Solomon Arkwright. Empty plates from Sunday lunch littered the table; conversation and wine flowed in equal measure.

'Well, Michael – that window at the church is a proper godsend. I could not have imagined a more appropriate link between the church and the burial gardens no matter how hard I might have tried.' Solomon Arkwright could see the marketing potential of the link and would exploit it mercilessly.

'You see, Professor – sorry – Margaret,' Alex corrected himself. 'It came to me as we drove into the farm on Monday. I remembered the site camp in the orchard, so after we got settled I took myself off to have a mooch about. Sitting there alone in the silence – except for the blackbirds and the wasps – I looked around . . . and it came to me! The circular orchard, the dip in the ground level on the inside and the way the wall sits on a slightly raised ridge: I think the orchard is the site of an earlier henge, much bigger than the stones. It all fits – gives a reason why the cup might have found its way here – explains the unusually large number of grave mounds. This site may have been a major early ritual site for the whole area. I believe the stones themselves to be a later addition – a marker and gateway along the main approach route of visiting pilgrims.'

Margaret nodded sagely. 'And how do you propose to find out if you are right?'

'I've written to Professor Mortimer,' Alex replied.

'Ah, George . . . yes, quite right.'

Penny, Marsha and Alice began to clear the table.

'Oi,' said Marcus. 'Leave that lot; me and Dexter'll clear up.'

'Oh, will we?' Dexter broke off his conversation with Michael. 'Not till I've told everyone my interesting news.'

Everyone turned and looked at Dexter, curious to know what this interesting news might be. He stood up importantly.

'Nice to be the centre of attention for once,' he joked. 'No, really, I have got some news. You know those apples we had at Christmas, the ones Mrs Turnbull was so keen on? Well, I was talking to my tutor who is an apple wizard, and he was really interested and desperate to see the fruit. Mrs Turnbull still had some stored away in her loft – we'd scoffed all ours – so I took some in to show him. You'd have thought I had given him a winning lottery ticket. Anyway, to cut to the chase, the apple tree in our orchard – that old falling down, rotten thing – could be just what Mrs T said. It's called the Painted Lady, and it's been lost since 1944. The very last one was blown down in a gale, and I suppose all the gardeners would have been away at the war or something because nobody saved scions for grafting – so everyone thought it was lost forever – extinct. He's sent it away to some place where they can make sure, but it does look like we have the last specimen. It'll be a while before we know – but if it is, we can bring it back into cultivation.'

'How exciting!' Margaret said to Alice. 'Lost archaeological sites, lost apples, lost and found gold cups . . .'

Everyone except Dexter and Marcus left the kitchen and headed, wine glasses in hand, to the sitting room, chattering and discussing. Marcus began to clear the plates.

'You bastard!' he hissed at Dexter. 'I thought you were going to tell them.'

'As if!' Dexter replied, with a smile. 'That's one bit of news I don't think they are quite ready for yet.'

Alone at last in the homely kitchen, the two young men drew each other into a close and loving embrace. At the same moment Margaret, who had returned alone to retrieve a forgotten glass of sherry, quietly opened the door.

Printed in Poland
by Amazon Fulfillment
Poland Sp. z o.o., Wrocław